FIGHTING *the* FOG

Andrea Hulshult

FIGHTING *the* FOG

TATE PUBLISHING
AND ENTERPRISES, LLC

Published by Tate Publishing & Enterprises, LLC
127 E. Trade Center Terrace | Mustang, Oklahoma 73064 USA
1.888.361.9473 | www.tatepublishing.com

Tate Publishing is committed to excellence in the publishing industry. The company reflects the philosophy established by the founders, based on Psalm 68:11,
"The Lord gave the word and great was the company of those who published it."

Published in the United States of America

ISBN: 978-1-62902-517-9
Fiction / Action & Adventure
13.12.03

DEDICATION

For the darling little girls who hold the key to my life, my heart and my soul. I love you all the way to the moon and back.

For my BFF—thank you for supporting this book and for being my creative consultant. And thank you for obeying the two-mile radius rule.

For my wonderful and amazing mother.

For Jama—you are a daily inspiration to me.

For Jet—my European anchor.

CONTENTS

But friendship is precious, not only in the shade, but in the sunshine of life, and thanks to a benevolent arrangement the greater part of life is sunshine.

—Thomas Jefferson

NOVEMBER

"Kai, your ink is showing. Cover it up. We don't need you to be remembered because of that big tat on your back."

I watched through my binoculars as Kai pulled the stylus out of her makeshift ponytail with a swift, one-handed motion, and her long, straight chestnut-brown hair fell halfway down her tan back, covering up the ink I was griping about. Kai placed the stylus back in her souped-up BlackBerry, a project Kai was quite proud of actually. She had done the rewiring and software programming herself to make her BlackBerry "off the grid." It ran on solar energy or a drop of water, like the alarm clock on her nightstand. Besides me, it was her best friend. And it probably had her number one best-friend spot because she could turn it off, throw it in the Potomac, or wipe the hard drive clean and reboot anytime she wanted. After four years of hysterics, hunger strikes, soul-wrenching devastation, and anger that runs as hot as the earth's core, I was surprised she hadn't thrown me into the Potomac. I had wanted to throw myself in the Potomac on a few occasions.

It was November and a picture-perfect, sun-drenched day in Jaco, Costa Rica. I could see the turquoise and teal waters of the Pacific Ocean from our hotel balcony, and the unmistakable smell of seawater invigorated my senses. I had always loved the smell of saltwater, especially waking up to it in the morning. The water was crowded today with surfers, but I suspected it was always crowded since Jaco is a popular surf town and home to some of the world's best surfers. It is also a mecca for a wild nightlife, apparently a desired combination for surfers. The wild nightlife was also an attraction for Kai. This is why she insisted we tack a vacation onto our visit to Jaco since our current case brought us here anyway. She said we needed a little fun. Well, she really directed that needed-a-little-fun comment at me. Apparently I hadn't been much fun lately or lately like in the past four years.

Normally in November, I am in Fiji; well, Kai and I are in Fiji. Kai was very persistent, almost threatening, that we would not be spending this November in Fiji. But I always spent November in Fiji since Ryan. I had spent half of the last three years secluded in our Fiji vacation house. It just felt like the right thing to do this time of year. My soul was still being consumed by a black fog, and my heart ached from all ventricles. My soul still burned with hate and anger, and none of me had begun to mend. I had discovered that Fiji was a bit disconnected from the world, and people left me alone there. No phone calls. No strange poor-Mel looks. No whispers behind my back, asking Kai how I was doing (a.k.a. "Has Mel cracked yet and started eating postage stamps?"). No e-mails. No clients. No visitors. Just Kai.

I could lose myself in reading, soaking up the rays on the beach, and not having to take off my sunglasses. Sunglasses were very important to my daily attire. They allowed me to let the tears flow whenever they came. And they still came often. Very black waterproof mascara, big sunglasses, and Rainbow flip-flops were the most important items in my daily Fiji wardrobe. When I returned home to Washington, DC. I wore the Rainbows a little less.

"Mel, are you daydreaming? I think I have a visual on our guy. North twenty-five degrees. He is sitting at an outdoor café table under a brown-and-green striped awning. He is wearing a plaid polo, light tan khaki Bermudas, sunglasses, and a white Panama hat. I wonder if the woman sitting next to him was the mysterious Pilar. The female has wavy, long, black hair; black sunglasses; and is wearing an ecru linen sundress."

"I see them, Kai. Do you really think she is with him? Like *with him* with him?" I asked in my slightly annoyed voice. Based on the level of Pilar's beauty and the level of AJ Ruggle's handsome prince score, something was going on with them two. It was the Costa Rican "Beauty and the Beast" rendition, and there wasn't a rose in sight. As soon as my brain thought *rose*, I had a flash of my last bouquet of roses from R——.

And there it was. I said the rest of his name under my breath so Kai wouldn't hear, but she could complete my sentences, so she knew what I was thinking, and the tears were welling up in my eyes. I didn't want Kai to see me cry. She has seen enough of that over the last four years. *Darn it, Mel. Get it together*, I told myself under my breath.

"Mel, you there? You went silent on me. I know that you are not in Fiji for November, but I couldn't stand to see you sulk and mourn one more November away. And we are working here, so let's hypothesize why a beautiful woman would be interested in a geeky little accountant who wears plaid polo shirts."

"I'm here. So what is our plan with Romeo?" I asked Kai, who was on the ground. I was in our hotel balcony. She got to call the shots since she was closer to our target.

"Well, let's see if Romeo or Juliet leave the table, and then we intercept him and see if he will talk to us. I'm really not in the mood for a chase today, so hopefully we can get to him while he is sitting and doesn't have the chance to flee. I'll keep eyes on him until you get down here, so get moving," Kai ordered.

"Oh, you're no fun. We haven't had a good chase in a while. I'm on my way," I said with some sass into my Bluetooth earpiece. I loved hands-free talking because it…well, kept my hands free. I was sure that I will die of brain cancer from having the headpiece attached to my ear, but it would be worth it.

I was on the eighth floor of our magnificent beachfront resort. I preferred to stay in five-star resorts whenever possible. Sometimes our work took us to remote spots and debunked, little towns where we were lucky to find a two-star hotel. But hotels were one of my indulgences, and I indulged whenever I could. There is just something comforting about excellent hotel service at your fingertips. I loved getting anything I wanted delivered any time of the day or night. I loved the plush bedding that resorts are famous for, and no matter how hard I looked, I couldn't ever find bed linens that were equivalent to hotel sheets so I could sleep luxuriously at home. Why was that? I also took full advantage of on-site spa services. Massages, pedicures, manicures, and eyebrow and eyelash tinting were my favorites. I had dark-blond hair and light-ivory skin. It was a necessity to have my eyebrows tinted a copper brown and my eyelashes tinted black so I looked a little alive. Even though I wore very black mascara almost eighteen hours a day, I still had to have my eyelashes tinted. I refused to show my face in public without some color. It was really therapy for me. Looking in the mirror and seeing bronzed, sparkling eyebrows and black eyelashes without mascara just did something for my soul. It made me feel a little prettier than I was. And whatever gets this girl through a day is what I do.

I hadn't had the opportunity to visit the hotel spa yet, but if all went well with AJ Ruggle today, I would be soaking up the spa services later. Kai and I can never tell which clients are going to cooperate and which ones are going to give us a hard way to go. AJ Ruggle seemed like a reasonable guy based on what we heard when we met with his family. But reasonable guys just don't disappear off the face of the earth for no good reason. Usually the people we search for are hiding or running from something or someone. We have yet to search for a missing person who just decided to take an extended vacation somewhere and not let anyone know. AJ Ruggle's story was a little different though. He was a successful systems software engineer from DC. When he didn't show up for his niece's wedding in August, his parents just knew something had happened to him. They never saw or heard a word from him after that. According to his parents and brothers who hired Kai and me, AJ never missed a family event and called his parents once a day. AJ wasn't married and wasn't in a relationship that any of his family members were aware of. He simply vanished. His family filed a missing-person's report with police and went through all the channels of seeing if he had been harmed, kidnapped, or even killed. The police's investigation turned up no foul play or clues of any kind. AJ hadn't used his cell phone or any of his credit cards since he vanished. His employer said he had taken a leave of absence, but that was all information they would provide, so the police closed the missing-case report, since he wasn't missing after all. Sometimes people leave and didn't want to be found. Kai and I believed this was the case with AJ Ruggle, but it was our job to find missing people—involuntary or voluntary missing ones.

Even though AJ voluntarily took a leave of absence from work, his family was desperate for answers. Desperate to end the unknown feelings of despair in the pit of their stomachs. And I know this feeling. A despair so deep that it sucks the living life right out of your lips and replaces it with this black fog. Your soul becomes lost in it, and it consumes your body. You lose all hope and faith in the world because you can no longer see it. When you open your eyes, you can only see this black fog in front of you. Your entire life no longer makes sense, and you can't go on until you find out the answers to the questions that your soul and heart keep repeating in your ear. This is another benefit to wearing sunglasses all the time. The darkness keeps me company.

This is why I quit the agency and went solo. I took a year off work after Ryan's death to mourn. When the despair never went away and I couldn't find the old me to return to my old job, I quit. One's mind has to be sharp and one's senses clear for agency work. And I was nowhere near clarity. Kai, being the closest thing

I will ever have to a sister and being my best friend, decided to come with me. I told her that quitting the agency was a crazy idea because she had a promising career. But she insisted that tracking down people who did and did not want to be found was worth the corporate sacrifice. She wanted to be her own boss and have glamorous, worldly adventures with her best friend. I wouldn't call our business glamorous, but we seemed to enjoy what we do. I am still not sure why she considers me her best friend, but after sixteen years of what the two of us have been through, we are just an automatic part of each other's lives. We have no other immediate family that we speak to—for various reasons. Kai is my family. So we help reunite families who want to be reunited. Sometimes it is a happy ending, and sometimes it isn't. Families are a complicated entity, and usually there are underlying reasons and circumstances that lead families to hire me and Kai. They just may not always be aware of them.

I have yet to see any man in any country of the world deny Kai Silva the opportunity to speak to him.

I jumped when I heard the ring tone and felt my phone vibrate in my front pocket. I felt doom come over me, and each time I heard this ring tone, I lost seconds, minutes off my life. My mood immediately went from being high on adrenaline to high on rage. As the voice mail ring tone beeped, I wondered what the devil herself would have to say today.

I finally was at Kai's side and had a full visual on AJ and his acquaintance. I could feel my eyes go into the people-watching stare, but I couldn't help it. AJ's female acquaintance was simply stunning. Based on the pictures and information we had gathered from his family, we pegged AJ as the standard, run-of-the-mill computer geek. He had round-rimmed glasses that were a bit out of style in all the pictures, but he had sunglasses on today.

"Guess who's escaped from crazy town and left me a voice mail?" I sarcastically and rhetorically asked Kai.

"Are you kidding? She has impeccable timing. I swear she implanted a bug in you while you slept at some point. Did you listen to it?"

"No, I'm already mad and aggravated and don't want to lose our guy," I said.

"Well, AJ Ruggle and his acquaintance aren't on the move, so let's enjoy a little Lilith entertainment," Kai egged me on.

We were across the street pretending to be shopping at a local beach clothing store. I played the voice mail and put the phone up between our ears. As I heard her voice, the two competing emotions of hate and uneasiness swept over me.

"Melanie Alexander, Lilith Alexander here. I still find it unacceptable and bewildering why you are incapable of answering your phone. You don't have a job, so what exactly is it that you do all day? You know how difficult life has been for me and that it is the month of November, or are you too drunk to know what month it is? I expect a call back within the hour, Melanie Alexander."

I could see the laughter making its way up Kai's esophagus, and before I could tell her to refrain from laughing at my life so I could scream my head off, her elbow was in my ribs.

"They're on the move," Kai said.

I immediately turned around and got a visual on our subjects. They were standing up and then stepped out onto the sidewalk. Their food was still on their table, and they hadn't eaten much of it. Did they get spooked? But since they don't know who we are, there was no way they saw us or knew that they were being followed.

We stayed on our side of the street and casually followed them. They seemed to just be window-shopping and enjoying the afternoon sun. Being patient was the most important part of this job. And we were very good at it.

AJ's model of a girlfriend went into a bakery and tea store; well, that was what I assumed it was from this side of the street. It was called Steep My Crepe.

"I'm intercepting," Kai said as she started crossing the street. I grabbed her arm.

"Let me go," I said in my I-need-to-beat-something-down voice.

Kai immediately stopped dead in her tracks and said, "No way. I don't need AJ Ruggle with black eyes and bloodied up." Kai swiftly and gracefully crossed the street. Keeping my eye on them both, I made my way down the sidewalk in case he ran. Most of the time runners run in the opposite direction of the person they are running from, so I would be conveniently down the street waiting for AJ to come my way. A few pairs of wandering eyes were following Kai's legs cross the street. She was five foot ten without heels and had on red-bottom Christian Louboutin espadrille wedges. Kai had impeccable taste in shoes. I have seen her chase down armed suspects in heels and catch them. We rarely chased anybody down nowadays, but Kai used her heels for the stunning effect—to make her long, lean, perfectly sculpted legs look even longer. She was an avid runner and swore by yoga. She was a perfect fit for this line of work. The world loves beauty. And so do most men.

"Mr. AJ Ruggle, Kai Silva, Can I—" I heard Kai say through my cancer piece.

AJ took one look at Kai, and he ran. Apparently AJ wasn't very smart because he was running down a crowded sidewalk filled with people, café tables and chairs, and racks and stands from stores. There was hardly room to walk. What was he thinking? It pissed me off to put the Ds to work.

"But at least I get to hit someone. Too bad it's not with my fists," I said under my breath.

I could hear Kai's wedges coming down the sidewalk, and I did a 180-degree turn and *bam!* I chest-bumped AJ with my Ds. He stumbled backward into the arms of the irresistible Kai Silva.

Kai grabbed his elbow and said, "Now, AJ Ruggle. Let's try this again. I'm Kai Silva, and this is my partner, Melanie Alexander.

We are private investigators. Your parents and brothers hired us to find you. Would you like to talk to us in private or right out here in public? It's your choice."

I could see by the wrinkling skin in between his eyes that his mind was working at triple speed trying to determine how exactly we were able to locate him. And exactly what he was going to do about it. People have yet to figure out that they can run, but they can't hide in this world of technology. There are people, electronic foot printing, mobile phones, and cameras everywhere. There are no hiding spots left on earth.

Kai still had him in an elbow lock as she was impatiently waiting for his response. If you ran from Kai, it triggered her bitch switch.

Just then the model came speed walking to AJ's rescue. Speed walking was the sure way to rescue a guy. She sure did look like a piece of work as she approached.

She then looked at AJ and then turned her head to Kai and said with an English accent, "What in the bloody hell is going on here? Have you gone barmy?"

I had an abundance of repressed anger that could be channeled at a moment's notice.

"AJ, you have exactly three minutes to explain yourself or I tell the lady about how you like your goolies rubbed during play time," I said.

Kai shot me a look out of the corner of her eye. She was laughing hysterically inside right now. It was time to play dirty. This was my warning message—my you-don't-want-to-miss-with-me-or-I-can-make-your-life-superuncomfortable message.

"Can we please move this to a more private area to talk?" AJ asked as he nonchalantly wiggled out of Kai's elbow lock. He must be pretty embarrassed right about now to be in an elbow lock by a beautiful woman who just chased him down the street.

"Pilar, these are private detectives that my family hired to find me. Let's talk," AJ said as we began walking. We walked a block south and sat down on a concrete bench.

It was graffitied, and the afternoon sun made it a nice bum warmer. Kai, AJ, and the arm candy also known as Pilar sat on the bench, and I stood in front of them as the bodyguard.

"I know my mother hired you. Look, here's the story. I studied at the University of San Jose for a semester my senior year in college as part of a bilingual engineering program. One weekend, we went to Jaco to surf, and I met Pilar. Back in July, I received a message on Facebook from Pilar, and she told me that we had a daughter, Maria. I agreed to come to Jaco and take a paternity test. I am Maria's father."

Gotta love Facebook, I thought to myself. Every Facebook user had a permanent digital record of their lives, one that could never be forever erased or forever forgotten. Apparently the matriarch of the Ruggle family a.k.a. Mrs. Jane Ruggle was the real reason AJ had not informed his family of his new life. There is always a reason in our line of work. Always. There is always a reason why someone runs or leaves. Over the past few years, Kai and I have located some interesting people—some who wanted to be found and some who did not. But people don't run or hide for fun. They run for a reason.

The crease in between his eyes was the mark of man whose life had been changed in an instant. Even when he relaxed his face, the crease was still there. Maybe he should think about some Botox.

"You know your family filed a missing-persons report, right?" Kai started in. "Your family is worried about you. Are you going back to DC?" Kai asked in a very professional manner. I am sure she was trying to preserve our professional image after my "goolies" comment. I was trying to not laugh at the thoughts in my head. Okay, so maybe I was mental after all.

"I have no plans to return to DC. Just tell my family I am fine," AJ said, starting to be irritated.

"Can we at least have an address, phone number, or e-mail address where we or your family can contact you at? I know it would put your family at peace if they had some contact information or knew they could get the information from us." Kai pressured again.

"Tell my mother I am fine, healthy, and I will call when I… well, call her," AJ said. His tone was getting increasingly more annoyed as the conversation focused on his mother. "Take a picture of us and send it to Jane for proof of life," AJ said.

Kai snapped a picture with her BlackBerry, and AJ was holding up three fingers over his lower stomach like he was flashing a gang sign. He sure did have some mother issues. I assumed the three fingers meant the darling Maria and would drive his mother crazy as she analyzed the picture for hours—probably days. Before either of us could ask further questions, AJ and Pilar got up. I let them pass. It was obvious he wasn't in the mood to chitchat. I hoped this picture would be good enough for Mrs. Ruggle. I knew it wouldn't be, but after all, we were PIs, not bounty hunters.

THERAPY

"That was exciting," Kai said sarcastically. "I haven't chased any-one in a while. But seriously—who tries to escape from a busy city street? Your classic Mel chest-bump move was awesome. Your tatas of steel can stop a moving body," Kai said with a laugh.

"At least the Ds are good for something," I said. "And at least I got to hit someone. Thanks for not letting me go after him. I probably would have giving him the beating Lilith deserves."

"Don't let that crazy, old bag get the best of you. You should be numb by now. She is mentally unstable. She is the reason you need to run with me. The streets of DC can take the beating you need to give."

I was not in the right state of mind to discuss my feelings for Lilith. So I purposely changed the subject. "Should we tell the Ruggle family about Pilar and Maria? AJ didn't exactly provide us instructions not to," I said with raised eyebrows. I was in the mood to cause some trouble. "And what was the gang sign about?"

"Gang sign?" Kai asked.

"Yeah, when you took their picture, he flashed a three-finger gang sign. Look at it," I instructed.

"What a creepy dude," Kai said as she studied the picture on her phone.

"When we get back to our hotel, I will e-mail the Ruggle family and send them the picture. I will tell them he is fine and well and that the girl in the picture is his girlfriend and that she has a grandchild," I said.

"She is going to flip out," Kai said.

"I know, but since AJ asked you to take a picture, I have to explain who it is. And then I'll have to explain that Pilar is the mother of her granddaughter and that AJ will call when he calls. There are some definite family issues going on under the Ruggle roof," I said. "See, I'm not the only one with mother-in-law issues. Pilar's got herself a Lilith spawn."

"Now you have one more reason to thank yourself for making this trip an extended vacation. We will be out of the office after we break the news to Jane, and Lilith has no idea where you are," Kai said with a self-fulfilled look on her face.

I hip-bumped her. She should be thankful I didn't bump her face with my fist.

◆━━━◆◈◆━━━◆

Finding AJ had been one of our easier cases. His family had provided pages of information about AJ's life. We pretty much had AJ's life story. After we spoke to his employer and discovered that he was telecommuting from Costa Rica, a flag went up because we remembered from reading his life story that he spent part of his senior in San Jose. We interviewed a few of his college buddies, researched his Facebook friends, and that led us to Pilar. Technology made our jobs so much easier these days.

"All this talking of family issues reminded me that I forgot to tell you that I got an e-mail from my brother. He wants to know how I am, where I am, and if we can talk on the phone."

"Holy crap. You haven't heard from him in like eight years. I wonder what he wants," I said.

"Who knows? I don't plan on responding. I still don't believe that I am related to any of them," Kai said. I could hear that she was becoming annoyed with the topic, so I didn't push it any further. Kai's family was an interesting bunch. Kai left home when she was eighteen for Stanford and has never been back. Not for one holiday, birthday, anniversary—nothing. She hasn't spoken to her parents in years. They used to call me in order to talk to Kai, but they don't even call me anymore. Kai's parents are very disproving of Kai's choice of careers. For a while they thought that we were "life partners" because they just couldn't understand our friendship. Our friendship runs deeper than most royal bloodlines. We will take each other's secrets to the grave and would give each other's life for the other. After I married Ryan, Kai's parents backed off the lesbian theory.

I was enjoying soaking up the rays of golden sun on my skin as we enjoyed our lunch. It felt so good to be outside and looking out at the ocean. There is just something tranquil about watching the waves lap the shoreline in such harmony. The water was this amazing turquoise color, and I was so at peace sitting here. Every muscle in my body was relaxed for the first time in a long time. The sun was doing my soul some good. I was surprised that I felt so light at this moment—like my body was floating above the chair I was sitting in. I can't recall the last time I felt this way. Kai was right; Costa Rica would be nice in November.

We finished our lunch, paid, and began the walk back to the hotel. We decided to take the beach route back, which seemed like the perfect thing to do. Kai slipped off her heels and carried them by the strap. I took off my Rainbows too so the soles of my feet could enjoy the warm, soft sand. We walked along the tide line so we could enjoy the warm water as it massaged our legs and feet.

"Mel, I say we go out tonight and celebrate. It is time for you to join the world of the living."

And the therapy session had begun.

"Do we really have to have this conversation right now?" I snapped back.

"Yes, we do. It has been four years, Mel. I have allowed you to grieve for four years. I let you drag me halfway around the world to Fiji. I moved into your DC brownstone. I slept in your bed with you for months."

It seemed like we had this conversation a lot lately. I knew Kai was only trying to help. Heck, she had seen me at my absolute worse. I think my absolute worse lasted about a year. From the moment I collapsed at Dulles when they flew Ryan's body back to physically dressing me for the funeral, she was there. I remember her forcing me to eat for weeks after Ryan's death. She literally had to feed me. She put her life on hold to save mine. I could never repay her, but she knew I would do the same for her. I guess that was my repayment plan. If Kai ever needed me like I needed her, I would put my life on hold to be at her side, no matter how long it was for. It had been four years for Kai. I guess she was ready to move forward and assumed I was too. Four years? Had it really been four years? It had. Almost four years to the day.

"I know you're right. But my heart is still in pieces, and I am not sure if the pieces even fit together right anymore."

"Maybe you need some new pieces," Kai said.

"I am sorry that I have been a pain in your arse for the past four years, Kai."

"Girl, you have been a pain in my arse for the past sixteen," Kai said smugly.

I bumped into her on purpose with my hip, and she stumbled a few steps in the sand.

"Don't make me kick your butt in front of all these surfers, Mel. You would be embarrassed."

I chuckled at her, something else that I hadn't done much of lately.

We finally reached our hotel, and we took the elevator up to our room.

I opened the French doors to the balcony and sat down in one of the lounge chairs. The salt in the ocean air burned my nose a little as I inhaled, but the smell of saltwater was well worth the burn. I opened up my MacBook and started an e-mail to the Ruggle family:

Mr. and Mrs. Ruggle,

Good day. I have wonderful news to report. We have
located AJ and were able to speak with him today. He is
in Jaco, Costa Rica. He is working for his company from
here. He has asked that we let you know that he is well,
healthy, and doing fine. He said that he would contact you
when he was ready to talk. He just needs some time to figure a few things out. Please be assured that he looks great
and came to Jaco willingly. We spent about an hour talking
with him today at a café. He has some news to share but
asked us that we not share it with you because he wants
to deliver the news himself. We would like to respect AJ's
wishes and hope that you will as well. He did give us his
business card with his e-mail and international cell phone
number in case you want to get a hold of him. You will find
a copy of his business card attached. But he assured us he
will be contacting you. I know you wanted more information, but we prefer not to meddle in family business. We
will be back in DC on Tuesday if you would like to meet
with us. We hope this news puts your mind at ease.

Sincerely,
Melanie Alexander and Kai Silva

Since the door was opened, I yelled, "Business is taken care of.
What should we do this afternoon? I feel like going to the spa.
Let's get pretty for our celebratory evening."

Kai grabbed my hand before I could change my mind and
pulled me out the door.

"Finally my Mel's back," Kai said.

BEAUTIFICATION

We made our way down to the spa, which was on the main floor of the resort. The entrance was flanked with white Roman columns on either side of a seamless glass entrance. The floors were Italian marble, and I felt like I should be in Europe. The young girl at the impressive leather desk ever so politely asked how she could assist us today. She spoke English to us, so she must have assumed we were Americans. Kai looked at me and turned her lips up just slightly, which meant that she wanted everything the spa menu had to offer.

"We would like stone massages, facials, body wraps, manicures, pedicures, and Mel needs a haircut," Kai said as she titled her head toward me, indicating I was the Mel who needed a haircut. What was wrong with my hair?

The young girl said, "Right this way." And she led us to a changing area. We slipped out from our clothes and put on plush, white spa robes and white rubber flip-flops—the kind that you can really only wear once. Our first stop was the masseuse.

We had two female masseuses, which I know disappointed Kai a little. But it was a hot-stone massage, and it was sensational. As I lay face down on the table, I could feel my muscles relaxing, and the stress and tension of the past few years escape my body. If Kai hadn't been within arm's reach of me, I probably would have started to cry. I knew Kai was sick of seeing me cry, but the tears still came so easily. Sometimes they came out of nowhere, and I could not hold them back. But I focused my mind on happy thoughts. Whenever I was in a peaceful, silent place, my mind began to race and flash back on memories. But today I tried to channel those memories to the future—to my future and what it held. At this moment, my mind was flashing our days in the academy, my college years at Stanford, my mother and father's wedding picture, and my first trip to Paris. I was currently standing at the top of the Eiffel Tower taking in all of Paris. I was naming off the landmarks. For once my thoughts hadn't jumped right to Ryan, but I knew he wasn't far behind. He would make an appearance soon. He always did.

I never imagined that my life would turn out quite like this— that I would be a widow before age forty. I never thought I would marry—that was until I met Ryan—the only man worth marrying. We had been married three blissful years. We eloped to Vegas one weekend after dating only six months. Kai came with us along with Ryan's best friend, Jake. This was totally out of character for my conservative self, but Kai said if it felt right, I should follow my heart. So I did. I wore a simple, white, strapless gown that was knee length and ballooned out at the bottom. Ryan wore his military dress blues.

"Mel, are you asleep?" Kai asked as she tapped me on the shoulder.

It took me a minute to come back to the present, and I opened my eyes. I must have detached myself from reality for a few minutes.

"Yes," I replied, not truly convinced yet. "What's next?"

"Facials are next. Right this way, please," said our spa hostess. We lay down on the estheticians' tables and were side by side once again.

My body felt warm and relaxed, and I almost forgot where I was.

"Why do you think I need my haircut?" I asked Kai. She could hear the sass in my voice.

"Your hair hasn't been cut in probably four years. You need a trim and a new style. You know that I only want what is best for you, but that hair is a mess."

"Does it really look that bad?" I asked, a little worried that my hair really did look that bad. I really haven't given my hair style or lack of style any thought in years.

"Mel, it just needs a nice cut. You never wear it down. It is always pulled back. You got to live a little, girl."

"So what do you suggest I do with it?" I asked.

"I think you should start by getting about five inches cut off and adding some layers. A few highlights might be nice too."

Five inches would leave my hair right at my shoulders. Maybe I could handle that. Maybe I could handle some highlights too.

Just then the estheticians came in. Within a few minutes, we had tea bags on our eyes to help get rid of the undereye circles—again, do I really look that bad? At least Kai had teabags on her eyes too. Kai had a strict regimen of health and exercise. She had for years. She ran three miles every morning at 6 a.m.—rain, shine, sleet, snow, or heat. Then she did an hour of yoga three days a week alternating with Pilates. She also sparred at our local gym a few days a week or when she needed some stress relief. She took one day off a week from the yoga and Pilates regiment, but she ran every day. She ate a strict diet of organic foods and rice milk. Kai thought it was unnatural for humans to drink another animal's milk. She did drink water religiously and drank organic coffee. As long as I had organic coffee in the coffeemaker every morning, she had some. I really admired her for her regimen; it was too strict for me. I ate what I wanted and exercised when I wanted or when I did not want to. I hadn't had a regular workout routine since I left the agency, and my flabby body showed it. I hadn't gained any weight, but my muscle tone had definitely left. Maybe I should start exercising again. Maybe I could tag along with Kai. Maybe I didn't want to sweat that much. I could try her organic diet though. It had to be healthier than mine. Kai always said she was going to outlive me. We promised each other that after we outlived our husbands, we would be roommates in a retirement home and cause all sorts of trouble. This seemed like a great way to live out the last years.

After the esthetician assured me that my skin was exfoliated, moisturized, and glowing, Kai and I had body wraps. There is something about being wrapped from head to toe in saran wrap butt naked that makes you question your sanity. Now I knew how my leftovers felt in the fridge. I had had seaweed wraps and mud wraps before, but never had I been wrapped up like leftovers.

"Have you checked our work voice mail since we have been down here?" I asked Kai.

"No," she responded. "I'm on vacation."

"This is a working vacation. I'll check it when we get back to our room to see if we have any potential clients waiting for us when we return to DC," I replied. "We need a new case or two."

"I think we should be more selective about our cases from now on and only take ones that have the potential for international travel. I could get used to this. I think I am past our early days of tracking through the back country of Alabama," Kai said. "What a way to remember our first out-of-state PI trip post-Ryan."

"I know. But the scar from the twenty-four stitches in my left arm from that hunter's bullet will be a lifelong reminder for me," I said as I was having a hard time keeping a straight face.

Kai and I busted out laughing at the same time.

"I hope our PI business never gets that desperate again," I replied.

"Me too, but we do need every case that meets our standards," Kai replied.

Kai and I mainly advertised in legal publications. Since most of these publications were read by attorneys, the calls we got were either from attorneys or from clients that attorneys had referred to us. Most of the time these cases were a little more qualified than Joe Shmoe off the street looking to find his ex-girlfriend so he could get back the money she had taken from him. Yes, this really happened. We had a guy call us asking us to help him find his ex-girlfriend because she owed him money. But he just wanted us to get her address so he could go ask for the money. Do we look like we are idiots? And yeah, like we are going to believe he is going to ask for the money nicely. You can bet he was denied our services. We know those types, and those are cases we do not take.

We also get referrals from our former colleagues at the agency and by word of mouth. We took on about eight to ten cases a year. We are quite selective about our cases. We didn't chase after just anyone. We refuse to take on cases where people are looking for exes, money, or minor children. We also don't serve clients who are felons or convicted criminals. If you come into our office and seem creepy or your story seems creepy, you are denied our assistance. We have standards and a low tolerance for creepiness. We also have a low tolerance for idiots. We have learned to read between the lines too. Once a woman came into our office asking if we could help her locate her long-lost grandmother. After we gathered some preliminary information from her, we did our own client research. We found out that the woman had been convicted of stealing a car and $1,000. Guess whose car and money she stole? Her grandmother's. We didn't take that case either.

After we were unwrapped, it was on to manicures and pedicures. These were uneventful, but it felt great to have pretty nails and toes. Nothing like a burst of color on the nails and toes to bring a boost of happiness. I selected a dark red for both my nails and toes because they had to match. My self-diagnosed obsessive compulsive disorder couldn't have unmatched nails and toes. Kai did a French manicure and pedicure, which is classy Kai style. I don't think I remember the last time Kai actually had color on her nails and toes. The French manicure was her signature.

Now that our hands and toes were buffed and polished, it was time for my new hairstyle that Kai insisted I needed. The stylist washed my hair, and then I sat down in the chair and sighed. I felt apprehensive about getting my hair cut. I could never replicate the style when left to my own accord at home. I wanted something low maintenance that I could actually fix myself. I owned a hair dryer and hair iron, so I knew how to operate those two things. My semiwavy hair didn't require too much effort to be straight, and that was how I liked to wear it when it wasn't in a ponytail.

"What would you like to do with your hair today?" she asked.

"*She* would like shoulder-length hair with long layers and some blond-and-gold highlights," Kai said before I could open my mouth to respond.

"Oh, I would? Yeah, I guess I would."

I closed my eyes and let the woman work her magic.

"Okay, you may open your eyes, ma'am," the stylist said.

I told myself that I would love it no matter how hideous it looked. I couldn't change it, so I might as well accept it. I counted to myself, *One, two, three.* Then I opened my eyes.

"Wow. It is actually really cute. I looked a little younger and a lot refreshed." My hair fell just right on top of my shoulders and framed my face. It had my natural wave, and the highlights really brightened up the dark blond. It was sexy without looking like I fussed over it. A great haircut can do a girl a lot of good. It is cheaper than therapy.

It would become expensive to travel to Costa Rica to get my hair cut, but it just might be worth it.

MECCA

By the time we got back to our room, it was dinnertime. We ordered room service and enjoyed our dinner outside on the balcony, soaking up the warm evening sun. There was a light, refreshing ocean breeze that provided natural air-conditioning without blowing our napkins away.

While we waited for room service to arrive, I checked our office voice mail. We had two messages. I was quickly writing down the details as I listened.

"Kai, we have two messages. The first message is from a Mrs. Brown, and she is searching for her sister, or at least that is what I think she said. She had a heavy accent that I can't place. I am thinking maybe Romanian—at least it sounded like a romance language. The second message was from a John Danville who needed help locating his estranged daughter by his second wife. I guess we will call them back and qualify them when we return to DC."

"Enough work talk. We are on vacation. You wanna know what I am thinking?" Kai mischievously asked. She cocked her perfectly arched left eyebrow at me when she said it. I knew she was up to something.

"I am sure I do not want to know," I replied.

"I say we go out tonight and dance. We haven't been out dancing in years. I bet your salsa could use a little practice."

"I don't know if I remember how to salsa," I said.

"It is just like riding a bike, Mel. And when did you forget something? You remember every detail of every case we have ever worked. No excuses, Mel. And you are in luck, I just happened to pack your strappy silver Jimmy Choo heels, which just happened to be perfect for dancing. You are welcome."

"Humph," I said as I exhaled a large breath of salty air.

And with that I knew that I was going out dancing tonight. Kai and I took dance lessons back in college; and we could salsa, waltz, samba, and fox-trot. Kai used to date a dance instructor, and she was an amazing dancer. I knew the steps and could move fluidly, but Kai was a piece of human art when she danced. I actually enjoyed dancing and was unexpectedly looking forward to an evening out.

Kai never got into trouble or anything like that, but she liked to dance and have a few cocktails. Being former agents, we never lost our composure or let our guard down, but Kai certainly did let her hair down. If Costa Rica men were like men in any other part of the world, Kai wouldn't pay for a drink the entire evening. She never did. But Kai was particular about the men she dated. She had high standards, and they were rarely met. She had lots of dates, but few serious boyfriends. With our line of work, it was hard to have a serious relationship since we traveled and never quite knew where we would end up. Kai's last serious boyfriend was about a year ago. He was a DC police officer. A very handsome DC police officer. He was tall, like six feet five inches and had a body of an Olympic athlete. His arms were huge limbs of steel with perfectly cut biceps—they reminded me of Ryan's. Ryan's arms were one of my favorite features. They were so sculpted and so hard that they sucked you into his body in the most tender way. When I hugged him, I felt like nothing in the world could come between us. They were my comfort and my protection. They were my safe spot when the world got rough. I wonder if Kai felt the same way in Carlos's arms. I'd have to ask her. I would have dated Carlos myself just to stare at him, but Kai and I had a rule: we never dated each other's leftovers. We never had, and we never would.

When we were in DC, Carlos still stopped by every now and then to take Kai to lunch or coffee. Kai told me that she thought Carlos might be the "one," but she wasn't ready for that or couldn't bring herself to accept that maybe she had arrived at that stage in life. She told Carlos the truth, and he gracefully accepted it like any gentleman should. Maybe he thought Kai would come around; maybe she would. Kai and I preferred to date gentlemen. The kind who open doors, pull out chairs, offer their hand, place their hand in the small of our backs, and the kind who respected us for the women that we were. They were a hard breed to find these days, but we managed to locate a few every now and then. Well, I had found one, and Kai had found a few more in her life. But not many.

After dinner, Kai was ready to get dressed and go out and check out the mecca of nightlife Jaco was known for.

"I wonder if the surfers are gentleman by night," I asked Kai jokingly.

"Maybe we should find out," she replied. I could tell by the you-are-going-out-with-me-tonight-no-matter-what look she gave me that she was serious about finding out. And I have seen Kai arrest men twice her size, so I really wasn't in the mood to mess with her this evening. Kai and I used to spar and work out together, so I knew her strength. In my lack-of-exercise-for-four-years state, she could totally kick my butt. I felt a little embarrassed by that. My subconscious was telling me that Kai was a better agent, and I don't know if that sat all that well with my competitive personality. I began to wonder why I just cared about this now. But I did. I realized that I felt different today. Was the old me starting to break through my solid iron-nickel core? I knew and accepted that the old me died with Ryan that cold, rainy November day, but maybe—just maybe—parts of the old me were going to be resurrected. I hadn't come to the realization that I was ready to find out who I might be as Ryan's widow, but I felt like maybe I wanted to find out today. It had almost been four years to the day that changed my adult life—which changed my definition of life permanently. I could never see the other side of my life through the black fog that had surrounded me for the past four years, but I thought I saw a hole in the fog today. Could it be? Had I mourned enough to cause the fog of death and despair to dissipate? I felt a twinge of guilt shiver down my spine; its remnants left goose bumps on my arms and legs. Was I ready for life without Ryan in the world of the living? Would he want me to be dressed in something that would make me hear one of his favorite "Ryanisms"? Ryan had a library of Ryanisms. On the occasions that I wore a dress that Kai had most likely purchased for me, he would take my fingertips in his massive hands and say, "Every ounce of you is beyond the beauty of the Seven Wonders of the World." He would then step in closer to me, tenderly take my face into his hands, and kiss me with all the passion of our very first kiss. The kind of passion that makes your body shudder, and all the cares of the world disappear. I can hear his voice in my head when I remember all the moments he said this to me. There is something about knowing that you are the most beautiful, sexy woman on the planet to someone. I actually believed that when I was with Ryan, his world stopped. Damn, did I miss that.

"Mel, are you daydreaming? Let's get a move on it before you turn into a pumpkin."

I snapped out of my moment and focused on the dress Kai had laid out for me on the bed. Of course Kai had packed a dress for me. She probably had been silently scheming to make me go out for months. It was a black faux wrap dress that hit about an inch right above the knee and tied on the left side. It wasn't low enough to show off the tatas, but it came close. It had pockets, which I loved. It looked really fantastic with my silver Jimmy heels, which weren't too high. After all, we were in a beach town. As I ogled over myself in the full-length mirror, I was surprised with how amazing I really did look. Sure I was flabby in places, but not bad for what I had been through. I would take it. Were more holes invading the fog?

Kai decided to wear a charcoal-gray empire-waist dress that hit her a few inches above the knee. It had cap sleeves and beautifully hugged her silhouette without being too revealing. She paired it with her aqua three-inch heels. She looked stunning. I thought we were overdressed for Jaco nightlife, but we were dressed. Well, I was dressed for once.

As we walked out of our room, I glanced at the clock, and it which said 9:00 p.m. It was almost my bedtime.

We walked to a popular night spot that our resort concierge had suggested. It was called "Driftwood." It was a brief walk—only a few blocks. As we walked, we saw lots of people heading to the city center for an evening out. The crowd wasn't shoulder to shoulder yet, but there were people on all four sides of us. Everyone was friendly, and we even got a few "looks." I called these "eye scans." Like I can't see someone scanning me from head to toe with their eyes; I hated these types of men. If they thought their eye scan was too inconspicuous for me, they were too dumb for me to date. The night air was warm, but the ocean breeze was starting to cool things off slightly. I wasn't too hot that I was sweating, but I didn't need a sweater yet and wasn't sure if I would. This was perfect November weather compared to the cold and nippy DC Novembers.

Kai and I were both people-watching while we walked. I knew exactly what she was doing because I was doing the exact same thing. We were scanning the crowd, getting our bearings, and noticing our surroundings. It was the old agents in us, but you never knew when you would need an escape route. I also knew Kai knew I was daydreaming of Ryan back at the room. She had that Mel-do-you-want-to-talk-about-it? look on her face, but I had yelled at her so many times in the early years for asking that question; she knew I would talk if I wanted to. And I didn't at this moment.

The Driftwood sat on the beach, and we could hear the live music from the sidewalk as we neared the entrance. We walked in, and it was crowded already. I scanned the place and saw a few seats at the far end of the bar. The rear patio was open to the beach, but it was gated off by a little black wrought-iron fence to keep the non-Driftwood patrons from entering beach side. The back wall of the place was one huge glass window. The view of the ocean and the mountains were breathtaking. There was a small crowd of people on the dance floor, and it looked like they were salsa dancing. To my pleasant surprise, we were not as over-dressed as I imagined. There were other women similarly dressed, and then there were some in short denim skirts and flip flops, but all were dressed tastefully. The Driftwood seemed to be a classier joint than I expected for what the surf and nightlife mecca Jaco is known for.

I always let Kai lead in these types of situations. She was much more social than me and had the grace of the queen of England. Kai instinctively knew how to act in any situation. I followed Kai over to the two empty seats at the far corner of the bar. I noticed that the bar was like a piece of art. It was a massive piece of teak that I assumed to be native to Costa Rica. It was a beautiful honey color, and I appreciated the craftsmanship as I bellied up to it. I hadn't bellied up to a bar in ages.

"So, girl, what are you drinking tonight," Kai asked.

"My usual—dirty martini."

Kai sighed. "Well, at least you are drinking those in public now." Before I could respond, Kai quickly added, "I'm kidding; I'm kidding." So what if I used to drink martinis a few times a day, at all hours of the day, during the first few months after Ryan?

"Funny. I know you think I should have gone to AA during those first few months."

"I was just glad you were eating—so what if it was gin and green olives," Kai replied.

Since no man could resist the beautifully stunning Kai, the bartender was already standing in front of us.

Kai ordered my martini and a greyhound for herself. A greyhound was Kai's signature drink. It was gin and grapefruit juice and was a shade of cotton-candy pink when it was mixed. Kai liked to start with these and then she would move to gin and tonic. We were gin girls and proud of it.

"Kai, I have a confession to make. I am actually glad that you dragged me out tonight. I am feeling a little better this week than I have in past Novembers. I just want to thank you for the millionth time for still being my BFF after the hell I have put you through."

"Really? And you don't have to thank me. You know I would take a bullet for you," Kai said with this look of awe and shock on her face. Her eyebrows were squished together, and her lips were apart.

"Really. For the first time in a long time, I don't feel like I want to die. Do you think this is a sign that I might be starting to recover? I'll never be over Ryan, and my heart will always hold a spot for him, but my soul feels a little less dreary. I know this is some heavy crap for a bar, but I just have felt differently the past few days. It is almost as some of the black fog is starting to clear."

"Mel, I could cry. Seriously. It has been a long four years, but the grieving process is different for everyone. I am so relieved to be having this conversation with you. Maybe you are starting to open the next chapter. It is encouraging that you *are* out and seem to be happy to be out," Kai replied.

"Maybe..." I stopped midsentence. I could see two guys approaching us out of my peripheral vision. I used my eyes to tell Kai the direction they were coming from. She slyly smiled and cocked her eyebrows at me. Couldn't I just have a conversation with Kai before the bar flies started to swarm?

"Can we buy the two most beautiful women here a drink?" the one closest to Kai said.

"It looks like you two have good timing; our drinks are looking a little low," Kai responded in her sweetest voice ever. No male on the planet could resist Kai Silva.

"I'll take care of it," he replied. "A dirty martini for you and a greyhound for you?" he asking quizzically.

"Well done. The martini is easy, but nailing the greyhound is impressive," Kai said. And with that confirmation, the guy closest to Kai called the bartender over, and we had our drinks within a minute.

The guy who had been doing the talking said, "I'm Will."

The other guy said, "I'm JR."

"I'm Kai."

"I'm Mel."

"Well, Kai and Mel, it is nice to meet you both," Will said.

"So, what are you ladies doing in Jaco?" JR asked.

"We are mixing work and pleasure," Kai said. "What brings you guys to Jaco?"

"We are here for the waves," JR responded.

I was taken aback by the soothing sound of JR's voice. It was soothing to my soul even though he had only spoken a few words. His voice was smooth and controlled, and it lured me in. I didn't like it one bit. I wasn't falling for his bar pickup persona. I was trying to hear an accent to figure out where he was from, but I couldn't pick up on anything. He must be American. As I was taking in their faces, I realized just how handsome both of these men were. They were tall; I was estimating six foot two- or six foot three-ish. They were both muscular. Will has a more olive complexion with dark-brown hair with some highlights. I was hoping the blond streaks were from the surf and sun. I had an issue with guys who purposely highlighted their hair—way too high maintenance for me. JR had light-brown hair and more fair skin, but he was tan. Both of their hair was cut short with the top being a little longer. They were wearing jeans and polos; they looked like high-end brands as I scanned their clothes for some tags or hints for what the designer was. I decided I should stop staring before they thought I was a freak. But they did fill the shirts out nicely. A million different thoughts were running through my head. I felt guilty for being instantly attracted to JR. I felt like I was betraying Ryan and myself. I tried to focus on the conversation before I hyperventilated with all my thoughts.

"So what kind of work do you two do that brings you to Jaco?" JR asked.

"We're private investigators," Kai replied.

This always brought on follow-on questions. Like, two women couldn't be PIs.

"You two on a case down here?" JR asked.

"We are, but the case is closed, so now we are vacationing," Kai said.

"What do you guys do?" Kai asked.

"We are in the United States Navy. We are based out of Annapolis, Maryland," JR responded.

Kai shot a look at me as I froze. Kai could see the huge lump in my throat forming and the tears that were about to flow. My entire body tensed up, and Kai knew there were only seconds before I had a Ryan moment.

"So, do you navy men know how to salsa?" Kai quickly asked.

"We do. Would you ladies like to dance?" Will asked.

Kai and I said sure at the same time as I fought back tears. It was either dance or sit at the bar and cry. I hope they couldn't hear the bubbling up of tears in my voice when I answered, but I wasn't going to melt down at the bar just yet.

JR reached out for my hand to help me off the bar stool, and he led me to the dance floor by placing his hand gently in the small of my back. Will offered his hand to Kai as well and led her to a spot next to us on the dance floor. It was starting to get crowded, so we were almost shoulder to shoulder with other couples dancing. JR took my hands, and we waited for the next beat to step. Kai was right; she was always right. The steps did come right back to me just like riding a bike. I was impressed by how fluid my movements were. JR was leading and was a good dancer. During the holds and turns, his hands never lingered and never accidentally brushed anywhere they shouldn't have. The salsa can be a sexy dance even for two complete strangers, and I was focusing hard not to give off the wrong signals. A part of me felt like I was cheating on Ryan, but I was really enjoying myself. I felt a sense of freedom while we danced. JR seemed to be enjoying himself. As we danced, he began to focus more on me and gazed intently at me. I could tell he was watching me. I looked over at Kai and Will, and they were also enjoying themselves. Kai is an excellent dancer, and she was drawing a small crowd of people to watch her. We danced three more songs, and then the DJ slowed down the music. I felt a sense of awkwardness as the music slowed. What to do? What to do?

"You want to dance?" JR asked in a very gentlemanly voice.

I gave a quick glance over at Kai and Will, and they were dancing, so I guess I would too.

"Sure," I said.

Sure. That was the best reply I could think of? Really? I was not up for this. I couldn't do this.

JR gently placed his right hand on my lower back and drew me close to him without any effort. I put my left hand on his massive bicep, and he took my other hand into his, and we danced. As my hand gripped his bicep, I was beginning to think I had a bicep fetish. I told myself, *Focus, Mel, focus!*

"So, where do you live?" JR asked as he moved me even closer to him.

"DC. Kai and I are roommates."

"How long have you been stationed in Annapolis?" I quickly asked. I wasn't ready to be asked my life story.

"Two years."

"Do you enjoy the East Coast?" I asked. I was finding it difficult to have a conversation with a stranger. Kai was right. I had been away from society too long.

"Yeah, I like the East Coast. I grew up in Denver, so being near the Atlantic is good for my line of work."

"So how did you and Kai become PIs?" he asked.

"I'm not really sure. My father is a police officer, so I guess it just runs in my blood. We were both criminal justice majors in college, and one day we just filled out the application, paid the fee, got fingerprinted, and waited ninety days."

I wasn't going to tell a stranger that Kai and I were retired special agents. We rarely told people that we were agents. Some of our friends and family members thought we worked for the government. Some of them still thought we did.

"So what do you do in the navy?"

"I work in financial operations at the base."

Immediately my head went into agent mode. This guy was lying to my face, and I didn't appreciate it. Maybe I was just making myself refuse to be open to anything or anyone. But what the heck did *financial operations* mean anyway? It sounds like a line of BS I analyzed as my arm was currently glued to his huge bicep. Yeah, he had too many muscles for accounting or financial operations or payroll or the million other jobs in financial operations. This wasn't going to work out. It was time to bail. Good thing Kai and I had a code word for bailout. We had a code word for everything.

Just then the music returned into dance tune, and before we had time to figure out what our bodies were going to do, Kai and Will came over.

"Want to get a drink and sit outside?" Will asked.

Kai and I looked at each other, and Kai said, "That would be nice."

Kai and I headed toward the beach patio. We instinctively slipped off our heels so we could walk in the sand without looking like drunks. The guys were getting drinks. Kai and I found a high-top table with no stools, so I was thankful for taking off my heels. The evening air was crisp, but not chilly. The sky was clear and dark and sparkled with stars. I could see the reflection of the stars off the water. What a peaceful view for being outside a bar.

"Are you enjoying yourself?" Kai asked. "You looked great out there, girl."

"Dragon," I whispered.

"Are you kidding me?" Kai said through clenched teeth. "You need to relax. I'm not letting you bail. So, are you enjoying yourself? You looked great out there."

"Glad to hear I didn't look like a fool. I actually enjoyed dancing. I think JR is full of crap, and I still feel like I am cheating on Ryan for just being out," I answered. "Dragon," I said again.

"I'm ignoring you on purpose. Ryan would be thrilled to see a smile on your face again. He always wanted what made you happy—you know that."

"I know. But *he* made me happy."

"How's Will?" I quickly changed the subject since Kai was ignoring the code word. What good is a code word when it is ignored?

"Hot," Kai said with a smirk on her face. "He could actually keep up with me on the dance floor. He seems to be a gentleman. We have this chemistry too. I'm interested."

"How much have you had to drink? You never like anyone, especially some strange navy man. What has gotten into you?"

"I know. I don't know what has gotten into me, but I like how he makes me feel."

"Oh, he asked how we became PIs, and I gave him our usual story; just in case Will asks, you can give him the same lines."

"Okay, cool. Thanks."

Just then the guys returned with our drinks. Kai had switched from greyhounds to gin and tonic. I was still drinking my signature martini. The guys both had bottled lagers.

"So where did you ladies learn to salsa like that?" Will asked.

"Stanford," Kai replied.

"You guys are Stanford alum?" Will said quizzically. I didn't like his tone—like we weren't capable of graduating from Stanford? He better watch himself.

"Yes, we are. I have a double major in political science and criminal justice, and Mel has a double major in criminal justice and history," Kai answered.

"Brains and beauty," Will replied. He was digging himself a hole. Of course we had brains and beauty.

He better watch himself, I said in my head again. Since Kai wasn't obeying the code word, I was going to play hard ball. These two had no idea what they were up against. I had enough grief and angst to be my own power supply.

"So, Mel, do you have a preferred era of history?" JR asked.

"Early American history, hence why I live in DC," I said with a little bit of attitude. I was still agitated from the Stanford comment.

"So, where did you guys graduate from?" I asked.

"The Naval Academy, hence why we are in Annapolis," JR replied with a smirk.

Okay, I might have deserved that one. *Mel, knock it off*, I told myself. I was beginning to think I was developing multiple personalities. Why couldn't I just relax and enjoy the evening? I decided to focus on the conversation instead of the voices conversing in my head.

"How long have you guys been in?" Kai asked.

"Ten years," Will answered.

"So where in DC do you girls live?" Will continued.

"We have a brownstone in Capitol Hill," Kai replied.

"That is prime real estate, especially for an American history buff," JR said.

Were they realtors now? Why couldn't Kai and I have had just a girls' night out? Guys always had to complicate the situation. Why couldn't they just leave two girls alone? Well, the answer to that was easy—testosterone and the little part that controlled it. I was drawn out of my all-guys-want-is-a-booty-call mental commentary by Will's voice.

"How long you girls in Jaco?" Will asked.

"We fly home Monday," Kai said.

"How about you guys?" she asked back.

"Tuesday," Will said.

I was beginning to feel the martinis. I looked down at my martini glass, and this one was already half gone. My face was flushed, and my cheeks were warm.

JR glanced down and saw that my shoes were off. "Do you ladies want to put those barefoot feet in the water?"

Kai and I looked at each other, and we didn't even have to nod our heads or speak, but I knew what Kai was thinking. She would be up for it. Dang it.

"Why not?" Kai answered.

We made our way to the beach, which was still sprinkled with people out for a moonlight walk. There were a few people in the waves enjoying an evening swim.

We were all walking side by side, and the water was still warm on my feet and ankles. I walked on the inside of JR in the surf; Kai was on my left. I had my shoes in my right hand, in case JR got any wild ideas. I still wasn't sure what his game was or what his intentions were, so I had my guard up. I could hear Kai and Will chatting about running and working out.

"So what do you do for fun besides salsa?" JR asked.

Fun? I had no idea what I did for fun except cry, but I would have to make something up on the fly.

"We've been busy working lately, but I like to box at the gym when I can. There's a gym within walking distance of our place, so it makes it easy to get there. How about you?"

"I'll make sure I don't try anything funny," he replied with a smirk. So do you straight up box or do tae kwon do, Brazilian jiu-jitsu?"

"Actually I prefer Jeet Kune Do," I said. *Let's see if he knows what that is.*

"A Bruce Lee follower," he said.

"You're good. Kai and I are sparring partners," I added. So what if I hadn't been to the gym since Ryan? But I used to go. He still hadn't answered my question about what he did for fun, and I wasn't forgetting either. I was already tired of talking about me.

"You seem to know a bit about martial arts. Do you spar?" I asked.

"I'm more of a runner. I'm just an Ultimate Fighting fan," he replied.

I was taking mental notes so I could tell Kai later. He was more than just a runner, and his biceps made him a liar.

"So do you run marathons?" I asked.

"Yea. I've ran two, but lately I've been running half marathons or relays," JR replied.

"I don't have the dedication or desire to run that long at one time," I said lightly. I was trying to come down from the attitude problem I was having this evening, and the martinis were starting to kick in. I was loosening up, much against my desire.

"So, are you and Kai going home to boyfriends?" JR asked so casually that it caught me off guard.

"Well, actually, I'm a widow," I answered, which was all I was able to get out. I never heard myself say that before. I was fighting back tears, but I was trying to remain strong. I tapped into my former agent self. It was easier to hold back the tears if I was pretending to be someone else.

"Mel, man. I'm sorry," JR said, looking for the right words.

I took a deep breath and decided to break the silence. "My husband was killed in action in Afghanistan. He was a special forces officer for the army. He was conducting a special reconnaissance mission in the Kabul region. His team came under fire, and he took a bullet for one of his teammates who had just found out he was expecting a baby. Of course all the information is classified, but the officer who my husband saved told me that Ryan, my husband, pushed him out of the way and said, 'A child needs a father. If anything happens, tell Mel I love her.' My husband's teammate and his wife had a baby girl, and they named her Melanie Ryan."

JR stopped walking and had a very intense look on his face. He turned toward me. I stopped as well.

He saluted me and said, "I am honored to be standing beside the wife of such a noble and honorable soldier who gave up his life for his country and his friend."

Tears streamed down my face. This is why I wore waterproof mascara.

We walked in silence for a few minutes, I assumed, so I could gain my composure. I was a train wreck. I should really go home. I was able to stop the tears and prevent the heaving sobs from coming. *But this is who I am now. Take it or leave it.* And darn it—pretending to be my former agent self failed miserably for fighting back the tears. I needed a new persona. Where was the old, made-of-steel Mel? I missed her.

"Do you want to talk about it?" JR eventually said after what seemed like minutes.

"No, not really. I've done enough talking and thinking about. I secluded myself on an island for a few years. It is great therapy."

"What island?" JR asked with a quizzical tone in his voice.

"Fiji. Kai and I have a beach house in Nadi. We spend quite a bit of time there."

"So, do you girls surf?" JR asked, intrigued.

"No, we sunbathe," I replied, smiling.

JR chuckled.

"How about a surfing lesson? Fiji has some of the finest surfing on the globe. You should really take advantage of it." I was thankful for the change of subject.

"Yeah, that might be fun." Fun? Did I just agree to a surfing lesson? And I just realized that I didn't cry talking about being a widow. The made-of-steel agent Mel was still alive and well. God bless her.

"How about breakfast tomorrow morning at 7:00 a.m., and then we can hit the waves?" JR asked.

"At 7:00 *a.m.*? You know we're on vacation right?" I said with a smile. The tears were retreating.

"Yep, 7:00 a.m. We'll meet you at the hotel restaurant. It'll be a good time."

"All right, sounds good. I'll tell Kai."

I turned around to see where Kai was, and they were—about twenty feet—behind us. From what I could see in the darkness, Kai and Will were holding hands. I was surprised because Kai really isn't the holding-hands types in the first hours or days of a new relationship. She took awhile to warm up, if she warmed up.

"Where are you staying?" JR asked.

I turned around again and pointed to our resort, which you could prominently see in the distance due to the million lights that lit up the outside of the resort grounds. "The Jaco Beachfront Resort."

"You girls travel in style."

"Would you expect anything else?" I said with a little bit of attitude.

We walked in silence for a while, and JR didn't try to hold my hand again. But he did take my shoes and hold them with his in his right hand. The night air was salty and sweet. I was trying to pinpoint the source of the sweetness and decided that it was from the flowers in the many flower boxes that decorated the beachfront cafes and shops.

JR started to chitchat again about surfing and Kai.

"How long have you known Kai?" he asked.

"We met at Stanford," I said with a smile and raised eyebrows. This would give him a clue to my age. I had been trying to calculate his age all night, and I was thinking I was older than him.

"So are you from California?" he asked.

"No. I'm actually from Montana."

"Really? What city?"

"A small one—Whitehall. I prefer the city." I was hoping he would get the hint to not ask me any more questions. I really wasn't in the mood.

I stopped to wait for Kai to catch up since we had been walking for a while, and now our resort was out of sight.

"Shall we turn around?" I asked.

We turned around and started walking toward Kai and Will, who were hand in hand. I would have to get the scoop on Will before the night was over. This was not Kai's typical behavior.

When we were within a foot or so of Kai and Will, JR said, "Will, you want to teach these girls how to surf tomorrow after we treat them to breakfast?"

"Sounds like a plan. So you guys want to learn to surf?" Will asked.

"Well, they have a beach house in Fiji, and they don't surf," JR replied before we could.

"I'm in," Will said.

We all turned around and began the long walk back to the resort. I was enjoying the waves lapping my feet and legs. The rhythm of the water was therapeutic.

I tripped on a rock or something in the sand and instinctively and subconsciously grabbed onto JR's arm for support so I wouldn't fall and get all wet and sandy.

"Thanks," I said, smiling.

"Anytime."

When we reached the hotel, we all walked into the lobby together. JR bent down and put on my heels as I balanced my hand on his shoulder. Will did the same thing for Kai.

"We'll see you girls at 7:00 a.m.," JR said.

"Sounds good. Thanks for the evening," I said.

Will pecked Kai on the cheek, and JR kissed my hand as he held it a little too long. He knew I was emotionally damaged.

Hopefully he would stand me up for breakfast, and I would easily be rid of him.

"Spill it," Kai said as soon as the elevator doors closed.

"Can't we talk about this tomorrow?" I pleaded.

"Absolutely not. Are you back? Is my Mel back?"

"I don't know. It felt good to be out, but then the voices in my head were having sarcastic conversations. I think JR is younger than me, and that doesn't sit real well. I think he is lying about being in financial ops. I told him I was a widow, hoping it would scare him off, but instead I got myself a surfing date. I don't know what I am feeling right now. I thought about Ryan all night, Kai. I can't comprehend it all right now. I didn't plan for this, and my mind is going in a thousand different directions. I feel guilty, nervous, anxious, and excited all at the same time. Can we please talk about you and Will? I saw the way you were dancing with him and holding his hand on the beach. And the peck on the cheek. This is not typical, Kai."

"All right, so I will let you off the hook and tell you about Will. So, you are right—totally not my thing to be so into a guy so soon. You know that I like to play a little hard to get, but I really like Will. And I really never like anyone. We really hit it off, and the chemistry between us is electrifying. He sends chills up my spine. I am little weirded out myself. So not my thing."

"Do you think they are younger?" I asked Kai.

"I don't know. But I would think maybe a few years? Does that make us cougars or pumas?" Kai said with a laugh.

"Shut up. I can't think about that. I feel old. And why do I attract military men? This is just what I need. I can't go through this again."

"Maybe military men are your type, Mel. They work in finance. How dangerous can that be?"

"But do you really think they work in finance?" I said. "Did you see the size of JR's biceps? Come on, girl. We are smarter than that."

"And Will has a six-pack of abs too. They may just be lead-ing us on, but I want to find out," Kai said. "We can take care of ourselves."

"See, this is why I should be in Fiji. Life is simple there. And how did you see Will's six pack?"

"First of all, life is lonely there, Mel. And I felt Will's rock-hard six pack rubbing up against me during the salsaing," Kai replied. Before I could respond, she said, "Do tell me one thing: Do you like JR?"

"No," I answered.

"Good. I hope you have a horrible time surfing tomorrow then," Kai said with a smirk.

"Oh, wait a second. You didn't obey the BFF bailout code," I said.

"Seriously, Mel? You can't use the bailout code when I am right there, and there is no reason to bail."

"There was plenty of reason to bail. He was lying to my face," I said. "And because you didn't obey the code, he tried to hold my hand, and I denied him."

"What! Why?" Kai asked with a puzzled look on her face.

"I told him I was a widow hoping he would bail, but he stayed.

"Wow. You told him about Ryan? That is huge for you," Kai said.

"Yes, I told him how he died. It just sort of came out. But my widow planned backfired though. Now we are having breakfast. I am hoping he stands me up," I said.

"Will you stop it? You are not damaged goods. You didn't bring this on yourself. You have a broken heart and soul, but they are on the mend. I am glad JR didn't buy your story. And your butt is going to breakfast," Kai ordered.

We arrived at our room and went to our separate bathrooms and got ready for bed. It was almost 2:00 a.m. according to the hotel clock, and that was the last thing I remember.

DISGUISES

I suddenly sat straight up and looked at the clock—5:45 a.m. As my half-asleep fog-filled brain tried to process what time it was and why I woke myself up, I realized that the date was November 11 and my brain was officially telling me it had been four years since Ryan passed. I wasn't sure if everyone's brain had a built in calendar, but mine sure did. Before I could decide what to do, I heard my BlackBerry vibrate. I fumbled for my BlackBerry on the nightstand before I could even wrap my head around the date. I had a new voice mail. Who was calling me at this hour?

> Melanie, this is Lilith, Ryan's mother. I don't know if you know this, but today is November 11. It has been 1,460 days since Ryan passed, almost to the hour. I was calling to remind you to think of him today. I miss him terribly. Call me if you want to talk. I haven't heard from you in forever.

"*What a*—!" I screamed. I was so furious I couldn't even complete the expletive.

"Mel, everything okay? What's going on?" Kai whispered in her sleepy voice.

"Sorry to wake you, but I just listened to a voice mail from Lilith," I said with an exasperated sigh.

"Mel, you know she is crazy. Don't let her get to you. Let me listen to her message."

I passed my phone over to Kai so she could listen to Lilith's nonsense for herself.

I heard Kai chuckle as she listened. "She gets crazier by the minute," Kai said. "Okay, let it out," Kai said. As my best friend, she knew what was coming.

"Of course I know what day it is! And I know that she is Ryan's mother! How stupid does she think I am? And why can't she calculate time in years like every other human being on the planet? I need some coffee. I need some coffee with gin. Where is the gin?"

I made some coffee and found the gin in the fridge bar while it brewed. I did not care how much the gin cost. I poured some into my coffee and went out on the balcony to get some fresh air. I didn't care that it was 6:00 a.m., and I was having gin with my coffee. The salty ocean air helped me to focus and clear my head. I was still silently screaming obscenities at my former mother-in-law in my head. This was the woman who asked her ninety-five-year-old mother for gas money every time she came to visit her. If I was Lilith's mother, I would refuse to pay her gas money so she wouldn't visit. But who asks their own elderly mother for gas money for coming to visit? Lilith. That is who. And Lilith was not hurting for money. She was just awful. Ryan never saw the side of her that I did, but that woman was mean and ruthless to me. At Ryan's funeral, she said these words that I will never be able to erase out of my brain: "Melanie, you look awful. Maybe you should look into taking some vitamins."

I thought Kai was going to punch her. If we hadn't been at Ryan's funeral, she probably would have decked her. I could hardly stand by myself and my husband had just died, and she has the nerve to tell me I looked awful and needed vitamins! Of course I looked like hell! I have looked like hell for four years! Ryan thought she was sweeter than the "blue-ribbon-winning apple pie at the county fair," but she truly is the devil in disguise.

Every time I heard one of her messages, I lost a few seconds off my life.

So in less than an hour, I would be having breakfast with another man. I knew that this day would come, but I didn't want to accept that it had come. But Kai was right. Ryan would want me to be happy, but I felt so guilty. Would the guilt ever go away?

I think we needed a new case or two so I would have a distraction and something else to focus on. Hopefully the voice mails on our office phone would turn into cases. Having all this free time on my hands was starting to get to my conscience. I had too much time to think. Too much time to relive the last seven years—three with Ryan and four without.

Kai came out and joined me on the balcony.

"Tell me what is going in that head of yours, girl," Kai said. "Talk to me."

"I don't know. We are supposed to have breakfast with JR and Will this morning at seven and then go surf," I said. "I should be in Fiji. I can't have breakfast with someone else on November 11."

"Mel, stop it. You don't need to be in Fiji. You have been amazingly strong all week. You are going to get dressed today, and you are going to breakfast with me. You are seeing JR, and you are surfing. Period. Now let's get dressed."

I finished my coffee and felt a little too relaxed for six thirty in the morning, so I knew the gin was kicking in. I hope JR wouldn't smell it on my breath and think I had a problem. I didn't need to answer any more questions this morning. I went inside and began to rummage through my suitcase for my bikini. When I found it, I laughed aloud because the bikini in my suitcase was Kai's doing. She had replaced my conservative bikini for a skimpy one. One that would make me explain the ink on my body during my surfing lesson.

"Ouch! What the heck is your problem?" Kai yelled as I snapped my bikini—her bikini—at her back.

"What is this? You swapped out my bikini for this!"

"I just thought you needed to get a little more sun than your suit with the shorts. You have a sexy, hot body, and you need to show it off a little more than you do. I know what you need," Kai responded.

"Now I am going to have to explain all my ink to JR."

"He is going to think it is hot," Kai sneered.

"Will you stop with the *hot*? Is that your word of the week or something? I don't need for him to think it is hot. I don't need any more complications," I argued back.

"Shut up. You need complications. You need to feel again. You need this," Kai said sternly. "Now get dressed."

This is how Kai and I worked. We were each other's conscience and each other's strength when the other one needed it. She had just been carrying me for the past four years, so I at least I owed today to her. I put on Kai's bikini, and I admired myself in the mirror. Not bad for being where I had been in the past four years. I threw on khaki shorts that had a cuff and hit me about midthigh. I found a turquoise baby-doll organic cotton T-shirt and slipped on my white Rainbow flip-flops. I threw my hair in a ponytail and put my sunglasses on my head as a temporary holding place. I rubbed on some sunscreen—no new wrinkles were welcomed. I put on mascara and some lip gloss. I threw some water, sunscreen, hotel beach towels, extra clothes, and my BlackBerry into my beach bag. I noticed the e-mail icon on my screen and was hoping it was work related. I would check it later.

"I love you, Ryan," I said in a whisper. "I miss you every second of every day."

I went to see if Kai was ready.

She was just packing up her bag, and then we stepped out the door.

JR and Will were already at the restaurant sitting at a round table for four. As we approached, they stood up and pulled out our chairs.

"Good morning, ladies," JR said.

"Morning," we replied in unison. We chuckled since we said the same thing in unison—we shared a brain.

I looked over the menu and was suddenly feeling thankful that at least JR showed up. Apparently I didn't appear to be the hot mess I really was inside. I ordered a caffe Americano, veggie omelet, and toast. I never ate meat in foreign countries. It was one of my OCD rules.

I knew what Kai would order even before she ordered it. Her veganism made it easy. She ordered a fruit plate, oatmeal made with bottled water, and espresso.

My BlackBerry beeped, and I dug it out of my bag. It was just another e-mail. I tapped the icon, and it was from Mrs. Ruggle. I wondered how she was taking the news. I would have to read it later. I couldn't wait to get back home and get back to work. I couldn't handle an extended vacation with endless hours to think. My brain needed focus—it needed a purpose.

I heard the guys and Kai talking about surfing and Fiji, and I was off in my own world. My mind was racing. Today was the day that changed my life four years ago. I felt like I was starting a new chapter today. It was all bittersweet.

"Mel, how's your breakfast?" JR asked.

"Oh, fine. Thanks. Yours?"

"It's good."

I hadn't even noticed what everyone else was eating and that they were actually eating while my brain was going one hundred miles per hour.

"You girls vegetarians? I don't see any meat on those plates," JR asked.

"Umm, no, not me. I eat whatever I want, but I don't eat a ton of meat. Actually, now that I think about it, I haven't had any meat in a few months. I guess when you spend six months a year eating fresh fruits and veggies and nuts in Fiji, you don't really miss the meat. Kai is a vegan though."

"A vegan—no animal products, right?" Will asked.

"Right—food or productwise. I don't eat or use animals," Kai said.

I was not surprised when Kai became vegan right after we became agents. It fit her strict exercise routine and her self-discipline.

"How did you end up buying a beach house halfway around the world? Doesn't it take at least two days to get there?" Will asked.

"We just wanted a place where we could unplug from the world. And yeah, it takes a few days to get there if nothing goes wrong," Kai answered.

Again, I was thankful Kai answered with such grace, never hinting that I bought the house and was there within two weeks because I was so mentally unstable that I might need inpatient treatment.

The server was clearing our table, and the guys paid the bill. We headed out to the beach. The guys said they were going to drive their Jeep down to a different parking lot, and they pointed to where they were going. I saw two large surfboards strapped to the top of the Jeep.

Kai and I walked the beach to where the parking lot was. It wasn't a far walk at all. We could see the guys unloading the surfboards.

"Kai, I am glad to see that the guys are wearing long board shorts and not banana hammock Speedos."

Kai burst out laughing and said, "I wish I knew what went through your head when you were silent. I would probably pee my pants laughing all day."

"Well, I just hate guys in Speedos. If they wore banana hammocks, I would have to leave."

"No more gin in your coffee," Kai said still laughing.

"So you ladies ready to surf?" JR asked.

They laid down two huge surfboards on the sand. They were probably eight feet in length.

"First, we need to lay down some rules," JR said.

"Always look for the life guard stands and life savers so you know where they are." He pointed to some a little ways down the beach.

"Do you see those flags?" he asked as he pointed out in the water. "Usually surfing is not allowed between the flags where people are swimming. And try to stay out of the way of other surfers. It really pisses us off." JR winked at us as he said this. "Questions?"

We shook our heads no.

"Second, let's practice," he continued. "We are going to practice standing up on the board. You will lie on your stomach and snap to your feet. I'll demonstrate."

JR got on one of the boards and lay down on his six-pack stomach. This was one of the first things I noticed when he took his shirt off at the beach. He quickly was on his feet in a crouching stance. I had no idea how he did it—it happened so fast.

"Here it is in slow motion." He lay back down on his stomach. He said, "After you paddle, you will put your hands on the side of the board, called the rails. Push up and snap up into a crouching position. You never want to just stand straight up. You always want to keep your knees bent."

He demonstrated this for us a few more times.

"You girls ready to try?" he asked.

Kai and I walked over to a board and stood on it. It felt like it was made of foam. Kai and I would try anything once. So here went nothing. We both lay down on our stomachs and tried to snap up. Our first attempt wasn't too bad from my opinion. We moved a bit slowly, but I knew we would be quicker on our next attempt. Kai and I liked physical challenges and could be quite competitive. I knew she was thinking like I was—we wanted to show these guys who we were. My competitive side kicked in, and I was focused and determined. Kai and I tried a few more times, and each time we were quicker and more graceful.

"You guys are doing great. Practicing like this will help your muscles remember what to do when you get out there," JR said.

"All right. I think you girls got this. So let's paddle out to the whitewash and see if you can stand up. We will go with you both and instruct from the water," JR continued.

Kai and I walked over to our bags and took off our clothes. I felt a little risqué for undressing in front of them. Our backs were to the guys so we wouldn't create too much of a show.

I was waiting for the question about our ink—tattoos. Kai had a huge mural of dahlias on her back—her favorite flower. It took up the top half of her back and reached from side to side. It was a piece of art. I had a lei of plumerias high on my right thigh that went all the way around. The petals were white with yellow radiating from the stigma. It looked like a yellow teardrop on a white flower petal. Ryan's name was written up the side of one of the flower petals. The Green Beret motto *De oppresso liber* was written up the side of another flower. In Latin this phrase meant "to free the oppressed," which is what Ryan died doing. I got this after he died. We had honeymooned in Hawaii, and this tattoo always brought happy memories of us to my mind. Kai and I also had one more tattoo—a token of our Stanford days and possibly the only regret we both had. Our senior year we got the kanji symbols for courage and bravery, the Yuuki, on our, well, very private areas. The Yuuki symbols mean brave, courageous energy. You could see one of the ends of the symbols on my bikini line, and I was praying that JR wouldn't see it. Kai and I had thought about having these removed, but we never got around to it. To me, tattoos were a very private and personal thing, which is why mine were in places where only certain people got to see them. My non-Kai–approved bikini had boy shorts, which covered up my ink just fine. I would get her back for the bikini switch.

As soon as I turned around, JR's eyes immediately went to my thigh, which I expected. He came over to me.

"Beautiful ink. What is it?" he asked.

"It is a lei of plumerias."

He put his hand on my thigh and rubbed his thumb over the flowers. A shudder went up my spine as I tried not to react or move.

"I didn't peg you girls for tattoo girls. Kai's is like a piece of art."

You couldn't miss Kai's tattoo, so I knew they both saw it when she took off her shirt.

Whew. At least he didn't see the other one. I prayed that my tatas wouldn't fall out of my bikini top while I was attempting to surf. Again, I thought of how I would get Kai back.

The water was warm, and there was the slightest breeze in the air. The sun's rays warmed my skin without scorching it, and I felt a sense of peace come over me. I was relaxed and ready to become one with the waves—or drown in them.

Will and JR showed us how to paddle, and they held on to our boards the first few attempts. Paddling required much more arm strength than I apparently had, and my arms were already tired. I bet JR's huge, sculpted biceps didn't get tired from paddling.

Dang, Mel, enough with the biceps, I silently scolded myself. I should tell Lilith about my bicep fetish to see if she could find me an alcohol and bicep rehab facility.

Kai and I both stood up on each attempt, but we didn't stay up for long. A few times JR caught me before I hit the water. On the fifth attempt, he let me go by myself and stood in knee-deep water and watched. I was able to stand up and ride a wave for a few seconds. I admitted to myself that I was having fun, and surfing was freeing. I liked the wind blowing my hair and being separated by the water by just a piece of foam. It was empowering. Kai and I had lived through Hurricane Isabella, and we knew firsthand the power of water, and here I was standing on top of it.

RUSH

We surfed for a few hours, and we were getting the hang of it. We were able to stay up longer, and our balance was improving. We were still in the whitewash, but I wasn't ready for the rush of the big waves yet. It was like skiing on the bunny slope. Kai and Will were down a few hundred yards from us, so I really couldn't hear them, but they seemed to be having a good time. JR and I were laughing at my tumbles and falls; some of them were graceful, and some of them were downright ugly.

After one particular fall, I got back on the board and sat there straddling it letting my legs dangle in the warm water. I was just taking in the postcard view of the coast line: green-covered mountains, turquoise waters, white and soft sand, and a lapis-blue sky.

JR came over, and he just cut through the water like it was air.

"Is this a battle scar?" JR asked as he rubbed his fingers over the three-inch scar on my left bicep.

"Yeah. I was grazed by a bullet by some hunters while we were tracking a missing person in the backwoods of Alabama. It took twenty-four stitches to close it."

"You could have been killed if you were standing a few inches more in the wrong direction. Your arm could've been blown off," JR said.

"Occupational hazard."

Our eyes lingered a little too long, and I could feel the butterflies stirring in my stomach. He swung my right leg over the side of the board so I was sitting facing him. He put his hand on my waist and pulled me closer to him. His cradled my face in his huge hands, and he ever so slowly leaned into my lips. I felt this feeling of panic and resistance come over me, but once his lips started to kiss mine ever so carefully, I couldn't fight it. I didn't want to fight it. So I kissed him back. His lips were a perfect fit over mine. Each kiss was purposely planted like he had studied a map of my face. For those sixty seconds, the butterflies in my stomach had spread to the rest of my body.

"You ready for a break?" JR asked, smiling.

I nodded. I was breathless, speechless. What do you say after your first kiss in four years?

He smiled, kissed my forehead, and helped me off the board so he could tow it into shore. I saw him smile out of the corner of my eye. He knew the kiss was why I needed a break.

I dried off a little with my beach towel and then wrapped it around my waist.

"You did great out there. Quite a natural," JR complimented me.

"Thanks. I had a great instructor."

We watched Kai for a few minutes, and she was looking like a natural out there too. Will was watching her from a farther distance than JR had watched me, but they looked like they were having fun. Will would help Kai when she fell, and I even saw Will sneak kisses on Kai's cheek in the few minutes that I was watching her. I was so glad to see her enjoying herself. She had put her life on hold for me for so long, I felt guilty that Kai was missing out on love and life. She continually reassured me her life could wait. I knew of no one else who would put their life on hold for four years, quit a job they loved, spend six months of the year halfway around the world on an island to ensure that their best friend didn't end up in a psychiatric ward. I at least owed her the opportunity to explore how she felt about Will. Kai always had dates, but she was hard to impress—she rarely kept anyone around for long. Carlos was the last guy she dated seriously. Kai was just a free spirit who didn't mind being alone, which is why we were best friends. We really only liked each other.

"Do you guys have any more cases you are working on?" JR asked.

"We have a few voice mails and e-mails to return when we get back to the office. Hopefully some of those will pan out for us. I feel like I have been away from the office too long. I like working."

"Where is your office?"

"In our house. We don't really like to have clients to the house so we meet them on their turf," I answered.

"Do you shoot or own a gun?" JR asked.

"I do. It is one of my outlets. My other outlet is sparring with Kai. Kai spars a few times a week and is an amazing fighter. We have to be able to defend ourselves if the situation arises."

"Has it ever arisen? JR asked.

"A few times. We had to chase down a couple of people we were searching for and then they struggled with us for a few minutes. For some reason, people underestimate us."

"Most beautiful women aren't trained fighters and marksmen," JR said.

"So you could really kick my butt then right?" JR chuckled.

He had an amazing smile and the perfect teeth. They were the perfect shade—a brilliant pearly white. I bet he had braces to obtain that smile. His smile warmed me from head to toe. I think I was beginning to like him, but I didn't want to. There were a few moments while I was surfing—or trying to surf—that Ryan's face flashed in my mind. Moments when I wished Ryan was in the water instead of JR.

"Maybe. You want to find out?" I asked jokingly.

He put his fists up and stepped into the orthodox boxing stance.

"You are on," I said.

JR flashed his melting smile.

Kai and I boxed and kick boxed each other every now and then—well, before Ryan. Kai went to the gym a few times a week to spar and workout, but not me. I didn't have the motivation. But the skills I learned as an agent are forever engrained in my brain. I was ready to show JR what I was made of. Now, how could I box in a skimpy bikini? JR just might get two shows at once if my suit malfunctioned.

We began to spar, and my reflexes were quite good. We were trash talking each other a little and joking around. We began to throw a few kicks and were having a good workout. I was starting to sweat. My tatas were bouncing around a little too much in this bikini top. I am sure JR was enjoying the view.

"This isn't the best sparring outfit," I joked.

"It is the perfect outfit. You're very motivational."

"I'm putting on my shirt. I can't really take fighting seriously in a bikini."

We stood there on the beach looking at each other. Should I move to get my shirt out of my bag? I wondered what he was thinking. It was like time had stopped, and I had to restart it by moving. But he moved first. His hands returned the ink on my thigh, and he was tracing the flowers again. I saw the expression on his face, and I knew then that he saw it.

"Do you have another tattoo?" he asked as he looked at my bikini line.

Apparently all the sparring had shifted my suit a millimeter off my bikini line, and he could see the tail end of my tat. At least I had had a Brazilian bikini wax a few weeks ago at Kai's insistence for preparation for this trip, and that was all he saw. I would have to thank Kai later for making me get a Brazilian. This could have been an embarrassing situation for an entirely other reason.

"I do. Kai and have the same tattoo in the same spot." Hopefully he would take the hint and not ask to see it.

"What is it of, and how big is it?" he inquired. He had a very quizzical look on his face like he was calculating the exact size and location of my Yuuki.

"It is the Yuuki. The kanji symbols for courage and bravery."

"Hard-core," JR said, which apparently was the only response he could muster.

I so had to get this stupid tat removed. I wondered if he was thinking of this tattoo as a tramp stamp. I felt uncomfortable for the first time all day. The stupid things college girls do.

I started to get dressed as my suit was almost dry. Just then Kai and Will were approaching, and I was thankful.

"Hey, girl," Kai said.

"Hey. Did you have fun out there?"

"Yeah, surfing's a good workout. Maybe we can buy some boards in Fiji. How about you?" she asked.

"I definitely think we need to surf in Fiji. It was fun."

"You both look like naturals out there," Will said.

"We saw you two sparring. Who won?" Kai said jokingly.

"We were just messing around. I can't kick someone's butt wearing a bikini unless my life was at stake. But I think I could take JR," I said.

Everyone chuckled.

"I want a rematch to protect my reputation," JR said.

"Thanks for the lessons, guys. It was a lot of fun," Kai said.

"Yeah, it was. Thanks again," I added.

"Sure, ladies. Do you two have dinner plans?" Will asked.

"I don't think so," Kai responded.

"Great. We will pick you two up at 7:00 p.m.," JR ordered.

I am not sure who he thought he was ordering us to dinner, but it bothered me.

We all started to walk toward their Jeep so they could load the boards. JR put his hand on the back of my neck and kissed the side of my face—right above my ear.

"See you later," he said.

"Bye," I said smilingly.

Kai and I started the walk back to our resort.

"I saw Will kissing your face out there," I said to Kai.

Kai smiled. "I really like surfing."

"And you really like Will."

"I do. We just have fun, and he doesn't annoy me—well, not yet anyway. I'll see where it goes. I'm enjoying the moment. But at least I can tolerate being around him. You know how I am—I get bored with most guys, and when they begin to annoy me, they have to go."

"Oh, I know how you are. I am glad Will can keep your attention for now," I said.

"Now your turn. Give me the scoop on JR. And I saw the kiss. So spill it," Kai pressed.

"I was hoping you didn't see it so I wouldn't have to explain it," I said jokingly. Kai knew that I told her everything anyway.

"It just sort of happened. It was just one of those moments where our eyes lingered for just a little too long, and the chemistry kicked in. It was a really nice kiss, Kai. My head is so confused right now. I can't even think straight. It should be Ryan. But I enjoyed the kiss. Time stopped for the moment. I felt alive again, but now I feel guilty and confused. I just want to go back home and get back to work."

"Listen to me. You need this. Your soul and your heart need to feel again," Kai instructed.

"I don't know what I need to feel. But I could really use some lunch." I was so tired of talking about my feelings.

Kai took the hint, and we walked for a while in silence.

"I have been analyzing mine and JR's beach sparring match, and he has some moves that are more advanced than standard navy training. And I am beginning to think that I gave myself away too out there—how does a PI learn to spar like that?"

"I don't think you gave yourself away, but I did see a few nice moves from him though.

He probably spent the majority of the fight looking at your bikini top," Kai said.

"We have to do some PI work on them when we get back," I replied.

Kai and I ordered room service and ate lunch on our balcony. I decided to check our work e-mail account and read Mrs. Ruggle's e-mail. It said,

> Dear Kai and Mel,
>
> On behalf of the Ruggle family, we are sincerely appreciative of your update and your investigative work to locate AJ. We are comforted to know that he is safe and well. Thank you for his phone number. We have called him and left a voice mail and am hopeful that he calls. Is there any other information you can tell us about why he left and why he hasn't contacted us? Can you please call us upon your return so we can further discuss? Again, thank you for all your hard work and your concern for our family.
>
> Sincerely,
> Jane

"Kai, Jane Ruggle sent us an e-mail, and she wants us to call her when we get back to the office."

"All right. Any other e-mails?"

"Nothing of value. We just have those two voice mails to return when we get back," I replied.

"I wonder where the guys are taking us for dinner," Kai said.

"I know. It will be interesting to see what they have up their sleeve. I don't know about you, but I need a nap."

I lay down and closed my eyes, hoping it would clear my head. When I awoke, it was 6:00 p.m. I had to get ready for dinner.

"Kai, do you have anything for me to wear tonight?"

"Now what do you think the answer is to that question?" she replied. I could hear the sarcasm in her voice.

"Awesome. Show me what you got in my size." Luckily Kai and I were the same size.

I selected a chocolate-brown strapless silk dress with appliqué roses on the bodice. It had a ruched sash at the waist. I put on a pair of nude, strappy, three-inch stiletto sandals. Kai made me buy these shoes a few months ago. Actually, Kai ordered them online and told me I would love them, and I did. I had worn them around the house since I never went out, but I loved them nonetheless.

Kai wore a gold-colored chiffon sleeveless sheath dress with a ruffle trim lining the V-neck. It looked fantastic with her golden beach tan and dark hair. She was wearing what she called her I-own-the-room shoes—four-inch Manolo Blahnik T-strap sandals. The strap was adorned with a variety of colored gemstones. They were magnificent, and Kai looked like a supermodel in them. And for $895, they should make you look like anything you want them to. I didn't charge Kai rent, so she spent her rent money on shoes, and they were worth every penny.

DRIVEN

We met JR and Will in the lobby promptly at seven. Every pair of eyes was on us as we stepped off the elevator. It was like a vortex that forced everyone's eyeballs on us. I assumed they were looking at Kai. A pair of $895 heels sure did a lot for a girl. Maybe I needed a pair.

Will and JR kissed our cheeks simultaneously.

JR whispered in my ear, "You are stunning." I felt my face blush.

He offered me his arm, and we walked out of the lobby. The Jeep was parked right outside, and the guys opened the doors for us. JR and I sat in the backseat.

"We have reservations in San Jose at nine," Will said.

"San Jose?" Kai and I said in unison.

Kai and I could take care of ourselves, so I wasn't really worried about the fact that we were going to San Jose with two navy guys we met yesterday. I just wasn't in the mood to plan our escape. Kai and I had been friends and partners long enough to know exactly what the other was thinking. I knew she was calculating an exit plan, and I was too. Better to be safe than sorry. Between the two of us, we had enough "supplies" in our handbags to handle almost any situation. Our handbag inventory included Super Glue, mace, pepper spray, a lighter, metal nail file, sleeping pills, GPS, extra cell phone battery, small roll of electrical tape, and a knife; Kai carried her sheath in her bag when it wasn't strapped to her thigh. There was no way Kai had a knife strapped to her leg in that dress. We had bought the knife during our first trip to Nadi from a local place, and it was one of Kai's favorites.

Every so often JR would rub my knee for a brief second. He was a glutton for punishment if he wanted to get mixed up with me and my baggage. Heck, I didn't want to get mixed up with me and my baggage.

JR placed his hand on my knee and kept it there. He paused, waiting for my reaction. There was none. My body didn't jerk or wince. Then it happened. Whatever part of my brain, maybe the deep limbic system, started to awake from its four-year state of slumber, and I began to feel again. I wanted to jump on his lap, but I was able to refrain. As I looked at JR, who was still staring at me, I felt this sense of desire in the pit of my stomach. My body knew what I wanted, but my brain wasn't willing to accept it yet. It was almost like I was under a spell in JR's presence; I was drawn to him by an unknown force that I wasn't strong enough to fight. My brain had adjusted to living in the fog. The fog had become my comfort, my mask. I wasn't sure if I knew who I was without it. Maybe the fog was starting to dissipate altogether. Maybe it was time to take off the mask.

"Are you sore yet from surfing?" JR asked.

"Not yet, but are you predicting that I'm going be?" I asked.

"You may be in the morning. I thought you may be feeling it by now. You worked hard out there today."

"I'm sure I'll be fine. I didn't even break a sweat out there today," I said with a smirk. So what if I hadn't worked out in years, I was never going to let JR know that. Great, I wouldn't be able to walk in the morning. Kai would have a lot of fun with that. I would never hear the end of her you-have-to-go-to-the-gym-with-me speech now.

"Too bad I won't get to practice surfing in DC. Our brownstone isn't on the beach."

JR laughed. "So do you hate surfing, or was the instruction bad?"

"I guess I just prefer activity where I get to kick some butt," I said with a smile.

"So, how do I contact you in case I need some Jeet Kune Do lessons?" he said with a smirk.

I pulled out my business card without flashing the contents of my purse and handed it to him. He immediately programmed my number into his phone.

"Your turn," I said as I handed him my BlackBerry.

"Damn, you're pushy," JR replied with a smirk and a wink.

"As long as you know it," I responded as I winked at him.

"Noted," he said.

I gazed out the window and could tell San Jose was approaching as the skyline was becoming more populated and crowded. I focused on the view and tried to gather my thoughts before we arrived at our destination. I hoped I wouldn't call JR "Ryan."

After a few minutes, we were in the city, and Will was expertly navigating the busy downtown streets. People were out walking, eating, and sitting under the San Jose night sky. We pulled in the front of the Lapis Helados restaurant. I knew I had seen the name somewhere before. My mind was searching its archives to pull the information. Got it—*People* magazine. Celebrities dine here. Wow. These guys had class. At least Kai and I were dressed right for the place. I wonder what JR and Will would have done if we would have stepped out of the elevator in jean skirts and tank tops.

Will and JR got out of the car, opened our doors, helped us out, and handed the keys to the valet.

As soon as the restaurant doors opened, I felt like a celebrity. All eyes were on us, and I even saw a few heads turn. Maybe people just expected to see celebrities walk through the door, and looking was an innate reaction. Again, maybe it was Kai's Manolo Blahniks.

We had a reserved table toward the back. Above our table hung this dazzling glass chandelier. It was made up of glass-blown teardrops that were lapis blue, clear, gold, and black strung on clear strands. When the light reflected off the chandelier, it sparkled like stained glass. It was stunning. The restaurant had the ambience of glamour and sophistication. You could feel it in the air. The walls were painted a creamy gold. The tables were all clear, and the seating was either white tufted leather or brown velvet.

There were white candles in tall clear vases placed perfectly on gold console tables with warm underlighting. It was easy to see why it was popular among the rich and the famous.

The guys ordered a bottle of red wine. After we ordered from the Italian-influenced menu, Will proposed a toast.

"Here's to a great evening graced by beauty," Will said.

"Cheers," we all said in unison as we clinked our glasses.

Damn, that was impressive for a navy accountant. Perhaps it was part of his get-Kai-in-bed plan. I bet he used this line all the time.

"What made you guys choose this place? It's lovely," I asked. I was curious about how they found it and why they had brought us here.

"This place is a known popular hot spot. Some of the professional Jaco surfers come here," Will answered.

"But what if we would have come down dressed in tank tops and shorts?" I asked.

"I guess we would have gone to plan B. But we figured you two for classy girls," Will said.

"So where are you girls from?" Will asked.

"I grew up in Whitehall, Montana, which is a very small town," I answered.

"I grew up in Honolulu, Hawaii," Kai said.

"Kai, if you are from Honolulu, then why don't you surf?" Will asked.

Now it was my turn to deflect the conversation so Kai wouldn't have to talk about her least favorite topic—her family. I would let her respond and see if she gave Will the truth or if she told Will the fake response she usually used.

"My family just wasn't really into surfing. I just never got into it I guess. I played beach volleyball instead," Kai responded.

She gave the fake answer. So this should hopefully satisfy Will's inquiry.

"Tell us about Whitehall, Montana," JR said.

"There isn't much to tell. It has a population of about one thousand people, and everyone knows everyone's business. When you think of a small town, Whitehall is it. Close your eyes and imagine a Main street with brick sidewalks, movie theater, drugstore, hardware store, and feed store. That was downtown Whitehall. I haven't been back in years."

Just then, our dinner arrived, and I was thankful for the interruption. I really did not want to talk about my experience growing up in a small town. I had never felt like I belonged there and hadn't been back in fourteen years. I was the black sheep of the family—people always told me that I was too big for Whitehall. And they were right. I spent my entire teenage years feeling suffocated and stifled. I just felt like I didn't fit in—that there was something else out there that was gravitationally pulling me out of Whitehead. And that was Stanford.

"So what do you ladies do when you're in DC?" JR asked us.

I looked at Kai, and I could tell that she was going to answer first.

"Well, I run, do yoga, and Pilates. We like MLS soccer, so we have season tickets to DC United. We like DC culture, Museum Row. Mel's into art."

"What kind of art?" JR asked.

"French Impressionism and post-Impression are my favorite periods, but I have an appreciation for all art," I responded. "I once dragged Kai around the world over a two-year period so I could see every Vincent van Gogh painting."

"I learned a lot about art those years and that Mel was a little crazy over it," Kai added slyly.

"You've seen every Van Gogh painting in the world?" JR asked.

"All the public ones. He's my favorite painter."

"So how did you guys learn to surf?" I asked.

"Being in the navy makes you like water, so we boat, ski, surf," JR responded.

"Can you surf in the Atlantic?" I asked.

"You can, but it isn't great. That is why we like to surf when we are traveling," JR continued.

"So what do you guys do for fun in Annapolis?" Kai jumped in.

"We work a lot, but we are football fans; we run, bike, boat," Will said. We had talked throughout dinner, and mine was absolutely divine. After dinner we ordered another round of drinks. I had my standard dirty martini, and Kai was drinking gin and tonic. The guys both had beers. I didn't have my watch on, but I knew we had been here for a good two hours. The guys paid the bill, and we all decided it was time to leave.

"Thank you for dinner. It was wonderful," I said.

"It's our pleasure, ladies," JR answered.

Once again they opened our doors and helped us into the Jeep. I was looking forward to the drive back to Jaco. My eyelids were beginning to feel heavy, and I was hoping I could stay awake. I would hate to drool on JR.

When JR got into the Jeep, he kissed me on the cheek, and when he unexpectedly moved down to my neck, I gasped. The butterflies were back, and my heart was racing. He made his way back up and kissed my lips to close the deal. I don't know if I could take much more. He wrapped his huge sculpted arm around me and pulled me into his side. I laid my head on his shoulder and closed my eyes just to regroup.

I heard a voice say, "Mel. We're back." It took me a minute to process the voice and come to, but then I realized I had fallen asleep. I opened my eyes, and I was still in JR's arm. He kissed me on the side of the head.

"I'm sorry I wasn't much company," I said apologetically.

"Having a beautiful woman asleep in my arms is perfect company," JR replied with a smile.

Kai and Will were already out of the Jeep and saying their good-byes outside the resort lobby. JR came over and opened my door and helped me out of the Jeep, which I was thankful for. A few martinis—okay, quite a few—and three-inch heels that I had been wearing for six hours didn't help my coordination.

"Mel, would you like to have dinner with me when we all get back to the East Coast?" JR asked.

I nodded and softly replied, "Yes."

He picked me up off the ground and tenderly kissed my lips. He lingered this time, but it was still polite. He put me back down and said, "Good night, Mel."

"Good night," I said.

Kai was already walking inside, and I said good night to Will as he passed me.

Mel and I waited for the elevator in silence. As soon as we stepped and the doors closed, we both let out a huge exhale. We laughed at each other.

"I don't think JR and Will are financial ops or accountants or whatever they are," Kai said with a laugh. "Can accountants be so sexy and well-mannered?"

"I know. I get the same feeling. I know I have been out of the game awhile, but I feel dreamy. It feels like we have known them longer than a few days. It almost seems like a setup," I replied.

"Mel, seriously? Who would investigate us? How strong were those martinis? And you go, girl, for having like three at like $15 a pop. But I'm game to figure out what they are up to. Maybe they are the real deal, but I am going to find out as soon as we get back to DC," Kai said.

"I was already planning on doing that," I said.

Kai and I got ready for bed, and I was too tired to even talk.

DELIVERY

When I awoke to the sound of a knock at the door, I remembered that I had dreamed about Ryan. I had dreamed about our wedding and our honeymoon in Hawaii. And I had also dreamed of the day I buried him in Arlington. I was at his grave site, supported by Kai. The knock kept coming, and I got up and put on the complimentary hotel robe. I peeped out the peephole, and it was room service. I opened the door, and there were two huge vases of flowers. The bellhop brought them in and put them on the table in the living room. I gasped when I saw him bring in the flowers. There was a huge vase of plumerias, which I assumed were for me, and a vase of dahlias, which I assumed were for Kai. I opened the card addressed to me:

> As we advance in life it becomes more and more difficult,
> but in fighting the difficulties, the inmost strength of the
> heart is developed.

I stood there in silence trying to catch my breath. The card was barely staying in my fingertips as I read it over and over. I knew this quote. It was from Vincent van Gogh. I had read his biography three times. I was sure of it.

"What's going on, Mel?" I heard Kai say from the bedroom.

"We got a delivery."

Kai came out, and she stopped midstep as soon as she saw the vases of flowers.

"Are you kidding me? They really sent us dahlias and plumerias?" Kai said.

"Mel, are you all right? You are looking a little green in the face. What does that card say?"

Kai took the card from my hand and read it.

"What century is JR from? What the heck is this supposed to mean?" she asked me.

"It is a quote from Vincent van Gogh." I annunciated each part of his name and puckered my lips on the last syllable. Kai could tell I was processing this entire situation.

I saw Kai opening her card and was wondering what hers said. She read it aloud:

"A *hui hou*," she said.

I knew it was Hawaiian, but I had no idea what it meant.

"It means 'until we meet again.'"

It takes a colossal event to shake Kai. But at this moment, I could tell she was shaken, almost in shock. Her body was perfectly still, and she was holding her breath. It was like her brain couldn't make her heart beat and her lungs breathe as it was processing the information on the card. I had only seen Kai like this a few times in sixteen years. The first time was when she read her acceptance letter into the academy. The second was when we had located our first body. The last time was when I told her Ryan died.

"That's really sweet," I said trying to break Kai's silence.

"Are these guys the real deal?" Kai asked with a hint of skepticism. You know I hate being crazy over a guy."

"Hopefully our investigative work on them turns up some answers," I offered.

"Are we being too ridiculous here? We can't even be grateful for the beautiful and thoughtful flowers. We just assume they are up to no good. Has the world really come to this?" Kai asked.

She continued. "Or have we lost faith in humanity? The crazy people of the world have tainted the rest of us, so we are constantly skeptical and looking over our shoulder. Maybe these guys are the real deal and just have some old-fashioned manners we aren't accustomed to."

"I feel the same way; I don't know what to think or believe either. But I don't need some psycho stalking me. My nerves can't take any more heartache and drama," I said.

"Even if they turn out to be psychos, I want you to know that I am proud of you for taking a chance with JR—or at least being open to taking a chance with him. You are too young to be alone."

"Why do I feel so guilty?" I asked Kai.

"A part of you will always love Ryan. You didn't ask to be a widow. But the rest of you deserves to love someone else too. Not that I am saying that JR is the one, but at least see what it goes and see how you feel."

"Maybe I should see my shrink when I get back to DC. I am having a difficult time sorting all these feelings out. I don't know how to process the new feelings without losing the old ones," I replied.

"Well, as your surrogate shrink for the past four years, I say we spend our last few hours in Jaco at the beach soaking up some vitamin D. Sun, fruity drinks from the cabana, and people watching are exactly what you need right now."

"Sounds perfect," I replied.

We both laughed and went to get dressed.

We rented some beach chairs from the resort cabana and ordered two fuzzy navels; it was too early for martinis and greyhounds. Orange juice counted as breakfast food, right?

Kai and I had been friends long enough that we didn't mind silence. We spent the time on the beach in our own worlds. I checked the news and my e-mail and started doing a crossword puzzle. Kai was just soaking up the rays listening to her playlist.

"Kai, I am going to grab some lunch so I don't have to eat airport food. What some?"

"Sure. Thanks, Mel."

I ordered two veggie sandwiches without cheese or mayo and side salads from the cabana. I replaced our fuzzy navels with Cokes. We had to leave for the airport in an hour, so we ate lunch beachside soaking up every possible minute of sand, surf, and sun.

We took a private taxi to the airport. We had a direct flight to Reagan, which was very convenient. We could take the Metro to our house and just have to walk a couple of blocks. It was heavenly. We walked whenever we could instead of driving. DC traffic was not for the faint hearted, and parking was a nightmare all its own. We could usually walk or take the Metro faster than we could drive. Even though we preferred to walk, we each had a car. I drove our "work" vehicle, which was a Ford Escape Hybrid. It was black and inconspicuous. If you are doing surveillance on someone, you can't roll up in a flashy luxury car. It just isn't good for business. It also handled well in the snow that was dumped on DC a few times a winter. Kai drove the flashy car. Kai loved cars almost as much as she loved shoes. She drove a 1999 Chevrolet Corvette hardtop. It was Nassau-blue metallic and was parked in the garage of our brownstone. Kai didn't drive it as much as she used to or wanted to. But she loved that car. She said it was cheaper than having a shrink—when you are an agent, sometimes you need psychological intervention for the things that your eyes see. The world is full of horrible sights, and the brain is unforgiving. For Kai driving a fast car that had the potential of going at almost two hundred miles per hour was more effective than therapy.

We didn't talk much on the ride to the airport because we didn't like strangers hearing our conversations. We texted back and forth on our BlackBerrys a bit so we could converse silently. We hated eavesdroppers. We were wondering about JR and Will. We couldn't take the beautiful vases of flowers with us, so we each took a few flowers and were hoping they would survive the trip home. So what were JR and Will's stories? Kai and I were formulating a plan to find out as soon as we had all PCs and databases at our fingertips.

The flight home was uneventful. Kai and I were in first-class because we had a low tolerance for coach. We preferred the space and quietness of the first-class cabin. My self-diagnosed OCD couldn't stand to be coughed and sneezed on, and it absolutely couldn't stand to be touched by a stranger's knee or elbow. Paying for a first-class ticket was cheaper than posting bail and legal fees for beating the daylights out of some stranger who violated my OCD bubble.

Kai and I had gin and tonics on the flight home and mostly kept to ourselves. Kai had her music on, and I was trying to rest. I had my eyes closed, but I rarely slept on planes, but if people thought you were asleep, they were less likely to bother you. I was letting my mind wander to places where I know it shouldn't. I was thinking of Ryan and JR. My mind was trying to decipher why I attracted military men. Seriously. Why did I attract guys who had one of the most dangerous jobs in the world? Was I self-mutilating? Did I enjoy the pain? Or was it my job? Did my job attract men with the same background and skill set? All these questions raced through my mind as I tried to make sense of it all. Ever since Ryan, flights had been the worst torture for me since I was alone with my thoughts for hours. There was no way to control your mind on an airplane. There was no place to go and nothing to do except talk to your seat neighbor or talk to yourself in your head. So I did the latter. This flight had the added complication of JR. I was trying to figure him out. Was he really just a wonderful guy whose mother I needed to thank for raising him so chivalrously? Or was he too good to be a coincidence? My brain couldn't deny or accept the chain of events. Two handsome American guys with backgrounds somewhat similar to ours just happened to be in the same beach town in Costa Rica at the same bar as us. Could this really be a coincidence? Or was this a setup? Our agent backgrounds made us analyze every situation from all angles and consider all possibilities. We never let our guard down. I needed to figure this JR-Will thing out before my brain would rest. I hoped our next cases kept us close to home. I needed a break from having uninterrupted time in the air to think.

We finally landed at Reagan, and I was relieved to be on American soil and only minutes from home. I had spent enough time thinking and talking about my feelings and emotions over the past few days. I was mentally exhausted and needed a new case for a distraction.

It took a few hours to collect our bags and make our way through customs. We then headed to the Metro station. It was a short ride to the stop near our house, and I was thrilled to be in DC. The air was much colder, and I could tell that winter wasn't far off. I enjoyed seeing all the things that I found comfort in— all the things that represented democracy and freedom. All the things that Kai and I used to risk our lives for. My favorite DC landmark was the Lincoln Memorial, and my heart warmed as we went past it. There was something about Abraham Lincoln that brought peace to me. He had visions and thinking beyond anyone in his era. I always wondered how some people have the power to change a nation and its people.

I could see our stop, and it felt good to be home.

"You want to stop for Chinese on the way home?" Kai asked.

"Sure."

Even though we had been gone less than a week, I missed my Chinese food. Kai and I ate Chinese from the same place at least twice a week. We weren't big on cooking. And when you could walk a block to get the most delicious Chinese food that you didn't have to cook or clean up, why stay at home at cook? Kai and I frequented the same restaurants and enjoyed carry-out. Our weekly menu included a vegan place, Chinese, Italian, Indian, Thai, and pizza. We usually had fruit and juice in the fridge. We also loved coffee. Our coffeepot started brewing our favorite organic blend at exactly the same time every morning.

Kai liked hers organic and black, but I only drank mine after it tasted like liquid candy.

We got off at our stop and walked to the Chinese place. The couple who owned it knew us by name and were very friendly. We placed our orders and waited inside since the night air was chilling. I usually didn't mind the snow and cold, but after being in Jaco, I was freezing. Our food was ready in less than fifteen minutes, and we walked home. It was only a five-minute walk, and we were enjoying seeing the neighborhood. No one was out on their porches or walking, and this was always a tell-tale sign that winter was coming. We arrived at our brownstone, and Kai grabbed a huge stack of mail from our mailbox, and we opened the door. Home sweet home.

Kai and I looked through the mail while we ate our dinner at the kitchen table. As usual, there were a few bills and lots of garbage and magazines. I didn't feel like unpacking my suitcase, so I just left it in the entry. I would get to it tomorrow.

After dinner I decided that a long soak in the bath was exactly what I needed.

KNIGHTS

When I awoke to the smell of coffee instead of saltwater, it took my mind a few seconds to reorient itself, and I realized that I was home. And it was a workday.

I got up, showered, dressed, and headed downstairs for my beloved cup of coffee. Kai was already up and out for her morning run.

I sat down at my desk and turned on my Mac. I decided that I would do some research on JR and Will first. I pulled up JR in my BlackBerry contacts and typed his full name, Jenner Romero, into my search engine. So that is where the *JR* must come from. I assumed that with a name like *Jenner,* he preferred to go by something else. As I scrolled through the results, there was nothing useful. I entered his name into the social media sites, and nothing relative was returned. I knew he had graduated from the Naval Academy, so I went to their website to see if I could find his graduation or alumni record. I did find a Jenner Romero listed in the alumni directory, but there was no address, phone number, or e-mail. At this point I was disappointed, but not concerned. If I typed my name into search engines and social media websites, you wouldn't find me either, but I had done that on purpose. I didn't want a virtual record of me.

I decided to try my luck with Will. Kai told me that Will's last name was *Greensburg,* so I typed his name into the same websites, and nothing. Kai said she thinks *Will* is just *Will,* and not *William,* but I would search on both just in case. Unless these guys were trying to hide something or didn't want anyone to find them, why would they purposely leave no trail? After I returned all the phone calls, I would try searching for them in some online databases that we used to find missing persons.

I decided to call Mr. Danville first. I spoke with Mr. Danville on the phone and gathered as much information as I could. I explained our rates and how we worked. He wanted us to take the case, and I told him that I would have to review his information and let him know. His name was John Danville, and he was fifty years old. He had a daughter by his second wife who he hadn't seen since she was two years old. Her name was Amelia Marlowe. His second wife's name was Lynette Marlowe. John told me a bit about Lynette and that she was a nurse. He told me where she worked when they were married. He hadn't talked to her in seventeen years, so his information probably was a bit outdated, but it could help. He had Amelia's date of birth, but that was it. He thought that Lynne's husband, Buck Marlowe, had adopted Amelia, but he wasn't certain of it even though Amelia had Buck's last name. If John had Amelia's birthday right, then she would be nineteen. John hadn't heard from Amelia or Lynne in over seventeen years, so his memory may have been a little foggy, but at least he had a name and a date of birth. He also said that when he saw them last, they lived in Baltimore, Maryland, but he wasn't sure if they were still in the area. But what he told me next was heart wrenching, as most missing persons cases are. He said that he was recently diagnosed with Huntington's disease and wanted to let Amelia know so she could be tested and consult with a doctor for possible prevention if the test was positive. I thought this was noble of Mr. Danville. He didn't seem bitter on the phone about not seeing his only daughter in almost two decades. He just wanted to find her so she could be tested and possibly avoid the same fate as him.

I was fairly sure we would take this case as it seemed like we had enough information go on and that John was a legitimate client. I would discuss it with Kai when she can back from her run.

I dialed the phone number for Mrs. Brown, who apparently was searching for her sister. The message on the voice mail said, "Brown's Blossoms," so I guessed Mrs. Brown owned a flower shop. I left her a message to return my call.

I looked up Mrs. Ruggle's phone number and dialed. She answered the phone even before it had time to ring.

"Hello," a sweet voice answered.

"Hi, Mrs. Ruggle, this is Melanie Alexander. How are you?"

"I was hoping that it would be you or Kai. I can't begin to thank the two of you. I actually spoke with AJ and he told me about Pilar and Maria. Did you get to meet them too?" Mrs. Ruggle asked. I could hear her voice begin to waver. I wasn't sure if it was from anger, anxiety, or sadness, but she was having a difficult time holding it together. I sensed that maybe she was a bit upset for being deceived, but I couldn't be sure of it. I could only imagine what she was feeling. I guess was relieved that her son was alive, safe, and healthy. But now he was engaged to a woman she had never met and was a grandmother.

"We did get to meet Pilar. She is very beautiful and she and AJ seemed to be very happy. I believe she is English based on her accent. Maria was at school, so we didn't get to meet her," I answered in my most sincere and reassuring voice.

There was a long pause on the line and I patiently waited for her to respond. I didn't want to intrude on her thoughts because apparently she was thinking.

"Can I ask your personal opinion?" Mrs. Ruggle quizzically asked me.

"Of course. I will do my best to respond," I said understanding exactly how she felt—I knew what it was like to have your world changed in an instant.

"Do you think he'll ever come home?" she asked with tears in her voice.

"I have no idea what his intention is. But I will say that everyone realizes how important family is and I think that is what AJ's doing now. I don't believe he's forgotten his family back home. Mrs. Ruggle, did you ask AJ about visiting him in Costa Rica?" I asked.

"No, but I think that's going to be my next question to him. Perhaps it's time for me to bring a piece of his family to him and his new family," Mrs. Ruggle said. Her voice was a little stronger.

"Thank you again. The entire Ruggle family is grateful for your services."

"You are very welcome. Please let us know if you need anything else," I replied.

"I will. Thank you. Good bye," Mrs. Ruggle said.

"Good bye, Mrs. Ruggle," I said.

According to the PI business, the Ruggle case could be considered a success and labeled solved. The missing person had been safely located. In the grand scheme of things, our job was easy. We had no emotional connections to our cases, which made it easy for us to close them and move on to the next one. But as a human, I couldn't help consider the lasting consequences for the Ruggle family. This would be something that would forever change their family dynamics and history. I hoped that the Ruggle family appreciated the fragility of life and would welcome Pilar and Maria with open arms into their family. Only time would heal the growing pains that the Ruggle family was experiencing.

In our line of work, we never received update calls years later to see how the family is coping. Who wanted to talk to the messengers whose detective work brought permanent change—sometimes welcomed and sometimes not? I was really hoping for the best for the Ruggle family.

I heard Kai open the front door.

"Hey, Mel."

"Hey, girl. I am in the office working. How was your run?"

"Refreshing. The fall air smells of dried leaves and puts me in the mood for Thanksgiving."

Kai came into the office and sat down, drinking her water.

"So, have you snooped on JR and Will yet?" she asked.

"A little, but I didn't turn up much. All my searches were nil so far. No social media or search engine hits. I did hit on the Naval Academy alumni record, but that was it."

"Interesting. I'll help you after I shower and eat some breakfast."

"Okay. I think we have a new client—a Mr. John Danville. He wants us to help locate his estranged daughter because he was recently diagnosed with Huntington's and wants her to know. Huntington's can be hereditary."

"Did he have valid information?" Kai asked.

"Yeah. I have names and a DOB on the daughter. I'll start the preliminary research, but I am confident this is a legitimate case."

"Sounds good, Mel. I'll be back in less than twenty."

"I'll let Mr. Danville know we are taking his case if my preliminary research is solid."

I called Mr. Danville and let him know that we would take his case and be in touch after our preliminary research. I could never promise when I would have a lead or some information because you never knew how long the research would take—especially if the client's information was false. After doing some preliminary research, we would meet with Mr. Danville in person to gather any additional information and ask questions based on the information we did find.

My mind was enjoying being back at work. Keeping busy was the key to my survival and sanity. My mind couldn't be left unattended for too long, or it started to think crazy thoughts. I had thought too much in Jaco, and now with the complication of JR, my mind was in overdrive. If I took a chance with JR, would I lose what I had left of Ryan? Should I continue to honor Ryan's memory and our love by being alone? The despair and turmoil I felt these last few days was more than my fragile heart could bear. I was screaming on the inside for answers—for guidance. I was waiting to hear Ryan's voice—to hear what he would want me to do. I was afraid that JR would drown out Ryan's voice, and I would forever be without him.

I used to write down my feelings in journals so I could express in words what my mind, heart, soul, and body felt, but after filling up thirty journals, I quit. Apparently I had no problem finding the right words, so why waste more paper on words that would never bring back Ryan?

I heard Kai coming into the office, and I snapped out of the mental vacation I was taking.

"So, you want to work the guys or the Danville case?" Kai asked.

"I'll take Danville. Let me know what you turn up on our knights in shining armor."

I ran Amelia Marlowe's name and DOB through our standard search protocol. I copied and pasted the hits of information I found into a dossier so we could analyze it later. We used the LexisNexis database, the Department of Corrections, standard search engines, social media networks, newspaper archives, death notices, family genealogy websites, and public phone and address directories.

I was trying to locate an address, phone number, marriage, or death notice. I also searched by "Amelia Danville" in case she used that name. I also searched on Amelia's parents' names as well. I had located the high school she graduated from, which was a local Baltimore City school, so hopefully she was still in the area. However, I never found an address for Lynette and Buck Marlowe, which didn't make sense since Amelia graduated from a Baltimore high school.

I would have to call the high school to see if they would give me any additional information. Due to all the privacy acts and laws these days, I doubt they would, but sometimes you could tell people a sob story, and they would help you.

I didn't find a marriage or death notice, so hopefully she was still "Amelia Marlowe" and still alive. When women married and changed their names, it always complicated the records and the process of finding them. I was puzzled that I couldn't find any information on the Marlowes.

"Finding anything?" Kai asked.

"A little. We got stuff to work with," I replied. "How about you? Do our knights exist?"

"Not yet. All I can find is their Naval Academy alumni entries, but there is no picture, so who knows if it is really them. But I will find them. Nothing stops me when I am on a mission."

ERUPTION

For the past two days, Kai and I had been working on the Danville case and snooping on our navy accountants. We had settled back in to being home, and it felt good to be productive.

My prediction was correct that Amelia's high school would not provide me with any information. However, we did unearth a few interesting facts. Our search for "Buck Marlowe" turned up a death notice in Baltimore County, and the newspaper obituary mentioned a Lynette and Amelia, so it must be the right Buck. He passed away last year. Since Amelia wasn't a minor when he passed, there was no record of her in the Social Security Death Master File, which would have been helpful. Another interesting fact we turned up was that Lynette Marlowe had more recent hits as "Lynette Danville." So she either changed her name back after Buck died, or she was using her ex-husband's name as an alias. People sometimes did this if they had a felony record or had filed bankruptcy. We couldn't locate any felony or bankruptcy records for a Lynette Marlowe or Lynette Danville. Kai and I wondered what Lynette was trying to hide.

Kai's research on our accountants had turned up nothing more than our original searches. We were tempted to call the US Navy to see if they were on active duty, but we thought that would be a little stalker-ish, so we decided against it. With our luck, the person who manned the navy phone would be good friends with JR and Will, and then they would know we were checking up on them. But they do know we are PIs—so they have to expect that we would do a little background checking.

We had yet to hear anything from JR and Will since we returned to DC. If we didn't hear anything from them, then problem solved. If it could only be so simple.

And as soon as my brain thought the word *simple*, I heard my voice mail ring tone. And immediately I knew it was Lilith because I had set her number to go straight to voice mail.

Of course, it was Lilith. She apparently was eavesdropping on my brain from the dark sewer drain she festered in because she had to dial my number just when I was thinking of my life being "simple." I was beginning to think she had my house bugged. Kai and I did do a bug check of our house years ago because Lilith was really that crazy. I often thought of changing my phone number so I would never have to hear from Lilith again, but I don't think that would have stopped her. She would still find me. And in some strange way she was my last connection to Ryan—good or bad.

When Ryan was alive, I always made him talk to his mother. I rarely spoke to the woman unless we were in the same state. Even then I tried to keep my distance. I always tried to have a "work emergency" when we were planning on visiting her, and Ryan would go by himself. I was afraid that when he wasn't looking, Lilith would bite me and turn me into a vampire or cast some horrible spell on me. I once asked Ryan why she hated me, and he was in total denial. Apparently she thought I was an angel sent from heaven when she was talking to Ryan, and then I was Satan's first mate when he wasn't around. Lovely woman, I tell you. She has said the most awful things to me over the years. Ryan always thought I was exaggerating or misinterpreting her comments, but I was not. She was awful. And she still was.

Kai and I needed some entertainment today, so I called her into the office.

"Lilith just left a voice mail. Wanna hear it?"

"Absolutely. Let's see what the devil herself has to say today."

> Melanie, this is Lilith, Ryan's mother. Did you get a new phone number? I called you on the 1460th day since Ryan passed, but you haven't called me back. Did you get remarried, and you are avoiding my calls? I will always be a part of your life. If you are having trouble remembering who called, maybe you should stop drinking and take some *Ginkgo biloba*. If you need an AA sponsor, I would be honored to sponsor you. Call me back so I know you are all right. I would hate to have to file a missing person's report on you.

"*What a flipping nut job!*" I shouted at the top of my lungs as I slammed my fist down on my desk.

"Mel, she never ceases to amaze me with her crap. Seriously. She is psychotic. I think you shouldn't even listen to her voice mails anymore."

Kai could see the steam coming out of my ears and that I was about to explode. And then Mt. Melanie erupted.

"*AA! Sponsor me! Remarried! Gingko biloba! Missing person!*" I shouted at the top of my lungs at Kai.

"She is going to be a missing person real soon!"

"Now, Mel. Calm down. You know she is crazy."

"*You want me to calm down?*" I was still shouting, and my body was starting to shake.

"Okay, we are going to the gym to box. You need to let off some steam. I'll get your shoes."

I could see Kai throwing my stuff into her gym bag, but I couldn't move. I was frozen, shaking from severe anger. My feet wouldn't move. My mind was thinking about slashing her tires, strangling her with the stupid silk scarf she always wore, poisoning her afternoon tea, and beating her head in. I thought that beating her head in would be the best way to go. I started to take some deep breaths so I could clear my head and disperse my anger. Maybe the time had come to change my phone number.

Just maybe I had become strong enough to cut that final connection to Ryan.

Kai pulled my arm and dragged me out the front door.

The gym was an eight-minute walk, and the brisk, fall air was helping to cool down my temperature. I couldn't even talk in complete sentences to Kai. I was just dumbstruck by the nonsense that was Lilith.

The gym Kai went to, and I used to go to, was owned by a friend of ours, Seth. He was an old friend of Ryan's father and retired DC SWAT. He had frequently checked in on me after Ryan's death. Kai preferred Seth's gym because he worked her hard and pushed her to her limits. And he was one of the few guys who could actually whoop Kai's butt.

"Melanie Alexander in the living flesh and on American soil?" Seth greeted me with a smile on his face.

He came over and gave me a massive bear hug that almost broke my ribs.

"What occasion finds you in my gym?" he went on.

"Kai thinks I could use a little boxing today. "

"So your temper's back, I see? You look really good, Mel."

And Seth was right. I hadn't been this mad since the forty-eight-hour rage I had when I was told that Ryan was killed. It was coming back to me now. I had screamed and punched and cursed for forty-eight hours, and then I went numb for four years. I really hadn't been this fired up in years. Wow, maybe the fog was starting to lift, and my soul was awakening from its coma. Maybe I wasn't numb anymore. I had felt things with JR in Jaco and now this.

"Thanks, Seth. So do you. It feels good to be here. Do you still have the skills to get this body back in shape?" I said with a smile.

"Heck yeah. You and Kai, get in the ring."

As I stepped into the ring, I felt like I had gone back in time to the days where Kai, Ryan, and me boxed and worked out. I hadn't been in this place since the day Ryan passed. I took a deep breath and tried to focus so I wouldn't make a total fool out of myself. Kai had always been the better fighter, but I was the better marksman.

My muscles moved into the starting stance, and I was beginning to remember how to move my body. As we started to spar, I was a little slow to respond, and my muscles were stiff, but I was moving. It was obvious that Kai was taking it easy on me, and I was grateful. I heard a few joints pop and crack, but I kept fighting. After a few minutes, I had found my center, my focus. I was in the zone, and my moves were more precise and faster. I could already tell that I wouldn't be able to get out of bed or walk tomorrow, but it felt good to fight. My body hadn't had an adrenaline rush in such a long time that I was almost high.

Kai and I sparred for forty-five minutes. Every inch of my body was either soaked or dripping in sweat. My muscles ached from head to toe, but I felt really good. I was proud of myself for still having the skills I used to live for. And it felt good to be back in the gym with Kai.

"Not bad for a retiree," Seth said.

"Kai, you took it way too easy on her," he continued. I knew there was truth to that statement, but that's what best friends were for.

"How do you feel Mel?"

"Besides sweaty and sore, I feel fantastic. What an adrenaline rush. And I don't feel like I have to puke…yet."

"Fighting is therapy for the body, mind, and soul. You shouldn't have stayed away so long," Seth said.

"Thanks for bringing me here. It felt great to be in the ring with you," I told Kai.

"Just like old times. I am glad you let me drag you along. Will you come back?"

"Yeah, I think I will."

I wiped off some of the sweat and drank some water as Kai continued onto her strength training circuit. I could see Seth approaching out of my peripheral vision.

"Mel, I'm so glad to see you here. Are you doing okay?"

What he was really trying to ask me was, "Mel, have you been released from the psych ward yet, and are you able to function in society again?" I got the are-you-doing-okay question a lot. I knew the secret meaning of it.

"I'm doing fine. Thanks for asking. Kai and I just got back from a working vacation in Costa Rica. The sun and surf did me some good."

"You had me really worried for a while there. Kai kept reassuring me that she was taking care of you. I miss him too, Mel."

"Kai saved my life and saw me through the darkest hours. But I really am doing okay these days."

Wow. That came out of nowhere. And it all came out without tears. I didn't quite know what to think of these new emotions I was feeling. I was so comfortable with the gloomy and depressed ones I had had for years. I knew them. We were old friends, but they were starting to feel lighter. My world-darkening curtains had finally opened to let in life.

mInInG

The Danville case never let my brain rest, and I was determined to find the missing link. It was 7:00 a.m., and I was already in our office working. As usual, Kai was out running. We were going to the gym today, and I was looking forward to it. I was craving another adrenaline rush.

I was doing some more searching on the Danville case and got a hit on a LPN license for Lynette Marlowe. The Department of Consumer Affairs database lists the last address of the person, so at least we had an address for Amelia's mother. The address was in Anne Arundel County, Maryland. It looked like Kai and I would be taking a surveillance drive later today. I was beginning to think I was becoming an adrenaline junkie because I was again craving the excitement of finding Lynette. What would she be like? Would she help us, or would she pull a gun on us? Would Amelia be with her? I loved the thrill of the hunt.

I printed out the dossier of information we had mined for the Danville case. I found that sometimes if I studied the dossier, the data would speak to me.

Danville Dossier

MP: Amelia Marlowe (Danville)Age: 19

DOB: 3/4/1992

Education: Graduated from Northwestern High School in 2010

Client: John Danville (Father)

Mother: Lynette (Danville) Marlowe

LPN License Address: 5589 South Columbia Blvd Suite A5 Hanover, MD 21076

Spouse: Married to John Danville 8/16/1990–1/5/1993

Married Buck Marlowe in 1994. Buck Marlowe DOD 12/22/2010

I held the dossier in my hand and paced around the house thinking. I was staring at the data and walking, like I was on autopilot. I refilled my coffee, watered the two plants that were still miraculously alive, put the recycling in the bin—just mindless tasks to occupy my body while my mind was deep in thought. So why could we find more information on Lynette than on Amelia? Where was Amelia? What nineteen-year-old didn't have a Facebook account, or maybe she had her profile set to private? Did she change her name? Did Lynette go back to using Danville? Maybe Amelia had changed her name or married and the record wasn't public. Where does a nineteen-year-old hide? And what does she hide from?

I heard the text message ring go off on my phone, and I returned to the office to see who it was. Not many people called or texted me these days. Most of my friends had been very supportive the first couple of years after Ryan died, but when you don't return calls and buy a house in Fiji, people think you have fallen into a dark abyss. Some of my own family members didn't even know that Ryan had passed. Kai had called my parents since I wasn't even capable of speaking for the first few weeks, and they didn't even come to the funeral. I know that it is difficult to get a flight from Whitehall, Montana to DC, but they could have come afterward and stayed with me. They didn't even send me a sympathy card. They haven't even called in two years. I hadn't called them either, but I was their only daughter after all. I have one older brother, Mitch, and we were close growing up. I actually had a very memorable childhood. My father was a police officer and my mother was a secretary. My brother played football and baseball, and I played soccer, which was really the only sport for girls. During my junior year in high school, Mitch lost an arm in a car accident, and that is where things started to get weird in my family. I hadn't been severely impacted by his accident; he was still alive and had one arm. I thought he was very lucky and should be grateful that he wasn't paralyzed or—worse—dead. I was the only one in the family who thought this way, and they thought I was unsympathetic and "mental." It took Mitch many years to get past the loss of his arm, but he is now married and had two sons of his own, last time I heard. He could have more by now. My parents, especially my mother, never quite recovered from Mitch's accident, and they never forgave me for the way I felt. The rest of my high school years were difficult, and I spent my time on the soccer field or in my room studying. Since my family was still coping with Mitch's accident, they just left me alone. This is where I really became the black sheep—the youngest and only daughter who wasn't sad for her brother. My academic scholarship to Stanford was my one way ticket out of Montana, and I never expected to return—and I rarely did. So when Ryan died, I guess my family thought I got what I deserved.

Since I have had lots of time to reflect on my life in the past four years, I have come to the conclusion that Mitch's accident and my reaction to it is why I became an agent. It is also why I have always been drawn to search for missing people. My subconscious believes that if I can just find someone somebody loves, they should be able to look beyond the past and be grateful for the time they have left together. On the occasion that we located a body instead of a live missing person, I felt the same way. I felt that my discovery could put the family at peace, let them grieve, and make their future worth living for. They no longer had to be consumed with the unknown. Perhaps I should take my own advice and make amends with my family and revel in the time I had left with them.

When I realized that my mind had taken another mental vacation, I remembered why I came into the office—my BlackBerry. I checked the text message, and it was from JR: "Hi, Mel. Are you free Friday? I'm thinking of you."

Today was Thursday, and I was beginning to wonder where our mystery men were. Kai and I weren't able to turn up anything else on JR and Will, which made us suspicious. Usually we could find something. It was almost like they didn't want us to find them. Kai and I weren't even sure if we would hear from them, but at least we were wrong about JR. I had a feeling that when Kai returned from her run, she would have a text message too.

I texted back, "I'm free on Friday. Thanks for the plumerias; they were beautiful."

Before I had time to think about what all this meant, I heard another beep: "I'll pick you up at six. Can you text me your address? Dress down, no heels. You should probably wear running shoes. I'm glad you liked the flowers."

I texted him my address and then all of a sudden a wave of warmth came over me that made my cheeks blush. Where was Kai? I needed her analysis of these text messages. Why would I need to dress down and wear running shoes on a Friday night? Where was he taking me? It looked like I had another case to work. I was thankful that I only had a little more than twenty-four hours to analyze and predict where JR was taking me. If I had much more time than that, I would drive myself crazy over it. It would rule my every thought and occupy every second of my conscious thinking. I had always been this way, even when I was little. I would become obsessed with a certain toy or book, and it would be all I played with or read for weeks at a time. I was the same way when I was working a case. I lived, breathed, dreamed, and thought about it. It was almost as if I transported myself into the case and saw it through my eyes in 3-D. I would often close my eyes and imagine myself interacting with the people involved and walking the path to find the missing person. My visions were like I was living in a video game. It was often when I was in this video game mode that I found clues or figured out the missing piece. I thought of this skill, if you can call it that, as another sense. A sense that let me tap into the minds of the people I was searching for. Toward the end of my agency career, I was often put on high-profile or critical missing-person cases. My video game sense never failed me on any case. It always led to the right road and the right moment. We didn't always find our missing person alive, but we found them.

I hadn't yet tapped into my video game sense on the Danville case, but I was close. After we checked out the address we had for Lynette, my brain would be ready to engage in its ultra-reality sense.

How many miles was Kai running today? We had two cases to investigate—make that three. I needed to figure out where JR could possibly be taking me. So what do you wear with running shoes on a date? Was I really going on a date? *A date date?*

GENETICS

"Mel, where are you?"

Finally, Kai was back.

"In the office."

"Hey, girl. I got a text from Will. Did you get one from JR?"

"I did, and it has been driving me crazy! What took you so long?"

"Are you like some giddy high school girl? *I think you have a little crush on JR*," Kai said in this sassy sing-song voice.

"Stop it. I just want to know what it means. I am a little rusty on this stuff."

"He's into you, Mel. And you have no idea how thrilled and relieved I am to see you feeling this way. Your soul is no longer this black vapor that numbed you from head to toe. I want you to be a giddy high school girl. So what did he say?"

I showed Kai the text messages.

"Well, it seems that we will be going out separately," she said. She showed me her phone.

> Sorry it's been a few days. I've been tied up at work. Would you like to go out Friday night? Dinner? Dancing? How about I pick you up at seven? Miss you. And text me your address.

"Will is a little more informative than JR," I said.

"So, they have been busy at work. I wonder what keeps accountants so busy that they can't ask us for dates until Thursday.

You know the rule is Tuesday. And did I just accept a date over text message? That can't be proper etiquette!" I continued.

"You and your Emily Post etiquette. I seriously doubt any men of our generation know that they are supposed to ask out a girl by Tuesday for a Friday date," Kai replied.

"I just like to be treated like a lady. The loss of this value has been detrimental to our society. Life was so less complicated in our grandmothers' era."

I had still had my grandmother's Emily Post book of etiquette, and I had it memorized. I felt like it was my duty to keep what it meant to be a lady alive.

"Oh will you get off your etiquette soap box? Emily this and Emily that," Kai said in her best sassy voice.

"Fine, but someday you'll be thankful you have the book of etiquette memorized by default. So where do you think JR is taking me?" I couldn't help but think about it. It was the detective in me.

"Well, I say we focus on the shoe aspect of his message. You must be going to do something that requires being on your feet."

"So let's see—walking, biking, climbing, or shooting?" I was thinking aloud of the possibilities.

"Why don't you just be surprised?" Kai asked.

"Maybe a lot of walking or biking or climbing or shooting," I suggested again, hoping Kai would answer me.

"Do you really think he is going to take you shooting on a second date? And makes you think he shoots anyway? If you are in the mood to shoot something, we can go to the gym and work it out or we can go to the shooting range and see how rusty your skills are. I think the mystery date is kinda romantic," Kai said.

"Do you think I am really ready for romance? I feel so nervous and anxious."

"You are ready. You are in the States for November and we don't have any plans soon to return to Fiji. You have been on vacation and to the gym to spar. Even if the old Mel isn't back, a version of her is. And she is here to stay. Please go out with JR for me and see where it leads. And, Mel, you haven't slept with anyone in four years."

Kai jumped back and took her sparing stance. She knew I was going to be ticked. And I was.

"This conversation is over. I don't even want to think about sleeping with someone."

"*It's been four long years, Mel!*" Kai said loudly.

I gave Kai this I-am-totally-going-to-beat-your-butt-in-the-best-friend-way look.

"You want to bring it on?" Kai retorted.

"Oh, it's on," I said, trying to keep a straight face. "Seriously, what is wrong with you?"

"Girl, I just want you to live a little. You have four years to make up for," said Kai.

"Are you up for a drive?" I asked her.

"Sure. Where are we going?"

"Anne Arundel County to look up Lynette Marlowe Danville or whatever name she uses these days. I got a hit on her LPN license."

"Dang it, we will have to take your car. We can't do surveillance in the 'Vette. It hasn't been driven in weeks. I miss it," Kai said.

"Maybe you and Will can take it out. I wonder what kind of cars our finance guys drive," I said.

"I know. A man's car says a lot about him. And you know I don't let guys in the 'Vette until at least the fifth date. Let me shower, and we can go. And we are paying Seth a visit when we get back."

When we got into the Escape, I plugged the address for Lynette into the GPS. The GPS predicted it would take forty-nine minutes. With DC traffic, I was predicting at least an hour and a half. I don't even know why I owned a GPS. I was always arguing with it and making it reroute me because I refused to go its highlighted route.

Kai had the Danville dossier in her hand and was studying it. I knew Kai missed being an agent, but this was her favorite part of our work. She enjoyed the thrill of the hunt. The adrenaline rush of the unknown. She was always ready for anything. Kai had her knife strapped to her ankle.

"So what is your theory on the Danville case?" Kai asked me as she continued to stare at the dossier.

"Well, since John Danville hasn't seen his daughter in seventeen years, I am assuming Amelia has daddy issues. If she grew up without a male role model, she's probably seeking acceptance from men. Maybe she ran off with someone her mother didn't approve of. Maybe she does other activities to fill the void of being accepted by her father. But since I can't find a solid hit on her, my suspicions start with her. But I also think Lynette is up to something since I found more recent hits using the last name of Danville than Marlowe. I am expecting our visit to be interesting."

"I get the same feeling as I analyze the data. Most nineteen-year-olds are traceable unless they don't want to be. If this address turns out to be a dead end, I think we should take a trip to John Danville's house and see if he has a picture, letter, birth certificate, SSN, or something."

"I agree. If this turns up nothing, we will meet with John. I just felt bad for him since he has Huntington's. I wanted to see if this would be an easy find. I want to help a man who is dying."

"You've become such a softie since you retired. This isn't about making happy families. You can't fix people—you find them. You have to leave the fixing up to them," Kai said.

"I know, but when you learn that life is too short in the most heart-wrenching way, your outlook changes."

The GPS lady warned me that I needed to make a right turn to reach my destination in half a mile. I realized that we were closer than I thought. I began to slow down so I wouldn't miss it and so I could see where we were going. I pulled into an apartment complex. The buildings were red brick colonial houses that were perfectly cemented together all in a row. Every building looked the same, and they were all two stories. The windows had white-painted shutters, and there was a few of them missing every now and then. The lawns were professionally manicured, which made me wonder why shutters were missing. Every building had a little flower garden in the front with a few shrubs. This flower garden was enclosed in a little black iron fence and gate. I calculated it to be about two steps from the gate to the front door, so it made the fence seem useless, but it was probably for decorative purposes.

We drove around until we found the building that matched Lynette's address. We weren't sure how many apartments were in each building or if each "house" was its own unit. There were no garages on the property that we could see, so Kai wrote down the license plate numbers of the three cars parked near Lynette's building. These might come in useful later if we weren't able to find Lynette.

Kai and I sat in the car and observed the surroundings and waited to see who entered and exited the building. Even though we didn't know what Lynette looked like, we could see if the building had secure access or if the front door was unlocked. We didn't need to draw attention to ourselves and some nosy neighbor call the police on us for breaking and entering. But nosy neighbors could be a PI's best friend because you could find out a lot of information from them, if you could sweet talk them into telling you. Kai and I had sweet talked lots of neighbors and strangers, which was a necessary skill to have in our line of work. It is surprising what people will tell you when you are willing to listen and seem genuinely interested. One of our most memorable sweet talking stories occurred in our younger days at the agency. We were working a missing person case that involved a young mother and an infant who had been missing for two weeks. Kai and I had decided to reinterview the neighbors of this young woman since the information gathered from the first team of agents didn't really turn up anything useful. We knocked on the door of the neighbor who lived directly on the right of the missing person in her apartment building. The man was elderly and walked with a cane. He reluctantly invited us in and told us that he had already been interviewed. We explained that we were just trying to see if he had remembered anything else.

He quickly said no, but I sat down on the couch next to him and asked him about his family. I listened for hours about his children, grandchildren, and great-grandchildren. Kai had made us tea and did a few things around his apartment for him. We asked him again if he could think of anything else that might help us find the missing person. I asked if he ever heard her talk or saw people coming and going from her apartment. He told us that he could often hear her talking on the phone and wrote down what he heard her say. He reached over, opened the drawer of a wobbly end table, and pulled out a spiral notebook. He handed it to me. It was almost an entire notebook of conversations he had heard with our missing person. We asked him why he hadn't shown this to the previous detectives, and he said that he didn't think they were nice and that they didn't ask if he ever heard anything. They just asked if he knew anything.

After scouring the information in the notebook, we were able to piece together a few names, which led to our missing mother and baby. This is what Kai and I enjoyed about being PIs. We enjoyed forging relationships with strangers and listening to people's stories. You just never knew what you would find out.

"It has been forty-five minutes, and we haven't seen one person or car move," I said.

"It is the middle of the afternoon; most people are probably at work, Mel," Kai replied with a snicker.

There had to be at least four other buildings we could clearly see, and no one had come or gone in forty-five minutes."

I gave Kai my "whatever" look. "I say we get out and canvas the place," I said.

"Sounds good to me. Let's go. I need to stretch my legs," Kai answered.

We unlatched the gate on the Lynette's building and walked to the front door. Kai turned the handle on the front door. It was locked.

"Dang it," Kai said.

"Knock and see if anyone answers," I suggested.

Kai knocked hard on the door, and we waited. No one answered, so Kai knocked again, this time harder. There were blinds on the windows, so I tried to peek in as we waited, but I couldn't see anything. Kai knocked a third time. We heard some rustling behind the door, and we looked at each other with eyebrows raised.

"Who is there, and what do you want?" a fragile-sounding voice said. It was a woman's voice.

"We are looking for Lynette Marlowe," Kai answered.

"Who is looking for her?" the voice replied.

"My name is Kai Silva, and I would like to speak to her about her daughter, Amelia."

We heard the doorknob jingle and watched the door knob slowly turn. I was anxious with anticipation as who we would find behind the door.

A middle-aged woman, maybe fifty, opened the door. She was sitting in a wheelchair. She had an afghan draped over her legs. She looked frail, and she sat slightly hunched over.

Even though her face was youthful, her body seemed aged beyond its years.

"I'm Lynette Marlowe," she said. She looked like it was painful to speak her name.

"Have you found Amelia?" she asked.

"Actually, we are looking for Amelia. We are private investigators. I'm Kai, and this is Melanie Alexander."

"You aren't the police?" she asked.

Seriously, did we look like the police, lady? I thought to myself.

"No, ma'am," Kai continued.

"So you don't know where she is?" Lynette said.

"No, ma'am. We didn't even know she was missing. Maybe if you tell us what is going on, we can help," Kai said.

"All right, come in," she said in an annoyed voice.

"Thank you," Kai answered.

Lynette turned her wheelchair around, and we followed her into her first-floor apartment. I took a quick glance up the stairs, and it seemed like there were two apartments in each building. I only saw one door on the bottom floor and one at the top of the stairs.

Lynette's apartment was lightly furnished and had all hardwood floors, which I am sure made it easy for her wheelchair. Had she been in this wheelchair long? I was replaying my conversation with John Danville, and he never mentioned that Lynette was in a wheelchair or was ill. I was very curious to find out how Amelia's very mother classified her as missing.

Her living room had a small couch and love seat. Lynette rolled her chair next to the couch. Kai and I took this as our cue to sit down. We sat on the love seat facing Lynette. I was looking around her apartment without being too obvious. I was looking for pictures so I could see what Amelia looked like. Most mothers had pictures of their kids around, right? The only pictures on the wall were landscape paintings. They weren't by anyone famous or well-known as far as I could tell.

"How long has Amelia been missing?" Kai asked. She was getting right to the point today.

"First, you tell me who hired you and why you are looking for Amelia. Is she in trouble?"

"I can assure you that she isn't in any trouble that we are aware of. We have been hired to pass along some information to her," Kai answered.

Lynette's face turned a shade of pasty gray, and I could see the lump in her throat.

"Did that bastard John Danville hire you?" she asked.

"We are not allowed to divulge the name of our client," Kai said. She wouldn't let me get a word in.

"Can you please tell us how long she has been missing and any information that may help us locate her?" Kai pressed.

"John Danville," she said ever so slowly. It was as if she was speaking in slow motion. "What a nightmare I have created for my own daughter." Her voice was quivering and filled with sadness.

"Amelia has been missing since her stepfather, Buck Marlowe, passed away in December of last year. Buck died from a long battle with lung cancer, and on his deathbed, he told Amelia that he wasn't her biological father. I married Buck when Amelia was four. I had Buck adopt Amelia so we could give her the last name of *Marlowe* so she would fit in more easily and people wouldn't ask why she had a different last name. We also told Amelia that Buck was her father—she had no recollection of her actual father. I wanted her to have a perfect family life—something I didn't have and something I didn't want to mess up for my daughter. When Amelia heard Buck's deathbed confession, she asked me what he was talking about. I wanted to tell her later, outside of hospice, but she wouldn't have it. She couldn't believe that I had lied to her all these years and tried to pass another man off as her father. She demanded to know who her biological father was and where he lived. She stormed out of his room that day, and I haven't seen or heard from her since. She didn't come to Buck's funeral. She was still living at home when she left, and she took a few things with her—mainly clothes and personal items. She didn't take any large items with her. She had a car that was under Buck's name, so I am not sure if she is driving it or not since he is dead. A few months after Buck's death and Amelia's disappearance, I fell on some ice and broke a disc in my back. I've had four surgeries, and the doctors cannot fix it. It is too painful to walk, so hence the wheelchair. I used to work at a nursing home, but I am unable to work now. It has been a rough year."

I could see the pain in her eyes, and I could hear it in her words. It was as if the words burned her throat on the way up. So our missing person was herself a missing person who was possibly looking for our client.

As I sat in this stranger's apartment, I felt oddly connected to her. I related all too easily to her pain. Her story didn't even punch me in the gut—it was a story I was all too familiar with. The part of Lynette's story I couldn't relate to is how she lied to her own daughter for all those years. Lynette wasn't telling a white lie—she was telling a lie that would change someone's entire life. Amelia as probably trying to figure out how her entire life had been a lie and how her mother was the keeper of such life-altering information. The man she had called Dad was not her biological father. How does someone digest information of that caliber while watching the only father she had ever known and loved die? I thought that Lynette would have probably taken Amelia's biological father's identity to the grave—too bad Buck beat her to it. I was trying to quickly process all this information, but I wondered what Buck's motive was. Was it guilt? Was he tired of leading a life constructed out of a lie? Or did he love Amelia so much that he wanted her to know the truth, no matter how much pain it caused?

"We are so sorry for the loss of your husband, Mrs. Marlowe," I said.

She did not respond. She just nodded her head yes.

"Do you know if Amelia could be staying with any relatives or friends? Did she have a boyfriend?" I asked.

"She didn't have a boyfriend. I have called every relative on mine and Buck's side that I know of, and none of them have seen or heard from Amelia."

"Do you all get along, or could there be a relative that would welcome Amelia without telling you?" Kai jumped in.

"We get along well enough as any family does. Some of us better than others," Lynette answered.

"Would you mind giving us a list of relatives and their contact information? Maybe someone knows something that will help us lead to Amelia," Kai asked.

"Okay. Would you mind getting my address book from my desk?" Lynette asked.

Lynette directed Kai to where her address book was located.

For the next hour, Kai and Lynette went page by page through the address book, and Kai wrote down all the information about each relative that Lynette had.

We had a list of eight relatives in the Baltimore/DC metropolitan area and eleven out-of-town relatives. We would call them all and see if they would tell us anything they wouldn't tell Lynette. In our line of work, there was always someone who held a grudge against someone else who influenced their decisions. I was thinking of our last case and how AJ Ruggle didn't call his mother because he thought she would disapprove. Mrs. Ruggle had never once mentioned to us that she thought she had a strained relationship with her son. Sometimes you had to read between the lines.

Kai and Lynette were still talking about the family members, and I could see Kai taking notes on certain ones. Kai could write as fast as she could talk, so she was writing what Lynette was saying verbatim.

"Do you have a recent picture of Amelia that we could see? We would like to scan it so we know what she looks like," I asked her.

I would scan the picture with my BlackBerry and transfer to the Mac book when we got back to our office.

"Yes. I'll go get it." Lynette rolled herself down the hallway toward what I assumed were the bedrooms. In a few minutes, she returned to the living room and handed Kai a framed picture of her, Buck, and Amelia.

"This is a lovely picture," I said. "When was it taken?"

"March 2010. Buck got sick in April that year."

"Do you mind if we take it out of the frame to scan it?" I asked.

Again, she nodded instead of answering.

I carefully turned the picture frame over and removed the back. I scanned the picture into my phone and made another copy just in case. I returned the picture to its frame and handed it back to Lynette.

"Thank you," I said.

"Have you tried to find her?" Kai asked.

"Of course I have. I have called every relative, neighbor, and friend I can think of. I have driven around town for weeks visiting her favorite places. I have visited or called all the families Amelia babysat for. No one has seen or heard from her. No one. She just vanished." Lynette's eyes were welling up with tears.

"Did you contact the police and file a missing person's report?" I asked.

"No, I knew she left. She is using her bank card. I can tell from the monthly statements, but there hasn't been activity recently."

"Can you provide me with some information that may help us find her?" Kai asked.

"Sure. What do you want to know?"

"Amelia's social security number."

"It's 001-00-0000," Lynette stated clearly.

"Can you verify her birthday? We have it as March 4, 1992," Kai said.

"Her birthday is March 5, 1992," Lynette corrected.

"Thank you. Can you also provide any previous addresses and jobs that Amelia worked?" Kai went on.

Lynette and Kai continued to exchange information. I was sitting in silence looking around the apartment and analyzing the new data. I was trying to see if any of the data fit anything in the apartment.

"Do you mind if I use the restroom, Mrs. Marlowe?" I asked.

"Down the hall. Third door on the left."

"Thank you," I said.

Kai knew what I was up to. I was going to go snoop. Lynette could see down the hallway from where she was sitting, so I knew I couldn't pull anything too funny, but I could at least peek in the other rooms and check out the bathroom.

None of the bedrooms looked like they belonged to a nineteen-year-old female. I made the assumption that Lynette had recently moved here. All the bedrooms were very tidy and also had hardwood floors. I caught a glimpse of a picture of Lynette and Buck on a nightstand, but I didn't see any other pictures of Amelia. Even though my mother and I weren't on the best of terms, she still had pictures of me and my brother at all ages of our lives all over her house. The bathroom was handicapped accessible, so I wondered if this entire complex was handicapped accessible. I opened her medicine cabinet, and there was nothing out of the ordinary except for a prescription bottle of pain meds. I didn't see any cosmetics, perfumes, hair items, or even toothpaste. I bet this was the guest bath, and she had a master bath off her bedroom. She probably kept the pain meds in here so she wouldn't have to go so far to get them. All of this information would help us to learn who Lynette was so we could figure out where Amelia might be.

When I returned to the living room, Kai was still quickly writing every word Lynette spoke. I think they were talking about Amelia's friends and their contact information.

I checked my phone, and we had been here two hours. I was hopeful that we had captured enough information to locate Amelia and deliver the information to John Danville. If she was really looking for her father, I wondered why she hadn't found him. There is always one relative or family friend who knows everything—certainly she could have found John by now.

"Mel, is there anything else you would like to ask?" Kai asked me.

"Did you get Lynette's contact information?"

"I did and I gave her our card too," Kai replied.

"I can't think of anything else. Mrs. Marlowe, thank you so much for all your time," I said.

"Is there anything we can help you with before we leave?" Kai asked.

"No, thank you."

Kai and I showed ourselves to the door.

TANGLED

"Do you know that we have spent more time talking to our client's ex-wife than our actual client?" I said to Kai as we got into the Escape.

"At least we got Amelia's correct DOB. We should get some more hits now," Kai replied.

"I know. Hopefully all the information we got today will help us find some more pieces. My heart goes out to Lynette. Her spirit and her heart seem so broken. She lost her husband, then her daughter, and then she ends up in a wheelchair. That is a lot of heavy change in a year's time. After hearing Lynette's story, I feel guilty for the way I have acted and felt over the past four years. I only had one of the events that happened to Lynette happen to me. I feel so selfish for acting like my entire world had ended for *four* years. Kai, how did you ever put up with me for *four* years? I can't even imagine how I would have reacted if I would have lost my husband, child, and mobility. Is this the wake-up call I have been waiting for?"

"You know that different people mourn differently. I knew time would bring you out of the coma you've been in. You've tested my patience over the last four years, but tests like these build character. I often put myself in your place and instantly knew that you would do exactly the same for me. Maybe this is your wake-up call. Or at least your perspective call—Lynette's story makes our lives look like a fairy tale. Now you know it could be worse," Kai responded.

"I never thought it could be any worse, but it really could. All of a sudden my baggage seems a little lighter."

"Well, now you won't need to visit your shrink this week," Kai joked.

"I know. I am turning into my own shrink. At least I'll save some money."

The traffic heading toward DC was lighter than on the way out. I knew the route home, so I didn't even bother turning on the GPS. My brain was processing all the new information we had received today in an attempt to unlock some more pieces of the puzzle. My current thoughts centered on where Amelia was. I didn't get a warm and fuzzy feeling that Lynette had put forth everything she had to search for her daughter, which led me to think that she had a good idea of where she was. This most likely meant she was with a family member, since Lynette didn't seem to have put forth an exhaustive search effort. I just didn't get that vibe when she was answering our questions. Apparently there was some discord among the family that she tried to downplay. I didn't know what it was like to be a mother, but if I were in Lynette's shoes, I would search for my daughter until I took my last breath. If searching for her consumed my life, I would let it. I would let every ounce of my soul be consumed with determination and hope. I would never give up. Never.

This is why I always replayed conversations with clients and people we interviewed. Analyzing the words and the expressions on faces allowed me to read between the lines. I had a feeling deep down that Lynette knew where her daughter was, but it was easier to pretend that she didn't know and that she had given up hope. It was always easier to avoid confrontation than facing the truth. The truth hurts. If Lynette did know where Amelia was, she made the conscious decision not to face her. Facing Amelia and accepting blame for lying about who her real father was would be painful. Seeing Amelia's reaction would be heart wrenching. Having to apologize would be soul wrenching. It was easier to pretend that all hope was lost. I started to wonder if the wheelchair was a prop too. Did it help Lynette hide behind the truth that she was fighting so hard to avoid? People saw a fragile, woman in a wheelchair who was a widow and whose daughter was missing. I bet people didn't ask her a lot of questions about all of that—would you? I wouldn't. My sympathy would weigh too heavy on my conscience if I would pry into Lynette's life and upset her. Was all this why Lynette recently moved? Kai and I would find out, and I was looking forward to the unveiling the truth.

"I know your mind is working overtime. What are you thinking?" Kai asked me.

"I am just replaying our visit with Lynette word for word. I think she knows where Amelia is. I just get this feeling that she didn't search high and low for her. And if you had a missing child, wouldn't you do everything humanly possible to find her? And wouldn't you look for her until your dying breath?"

"I got the same feeling. I didn't want to press her too hard on it though. She looked so fragile and hopeless. Like she has given up on living," Kai said.

"I can't decide if playing the fragile, wheelchaired widow is her defense or if she really has lost the will to fight for her life and her daughter's."

"At least we have a long list of relatives and friends to call and investigate. We should turn up something. We should find Amelia," Kai replied.

"I agree. Someone in that family knows where Amelia is or at least is in communication with her. If our instincts are wrong about Lynette, we have enough personal information about Amelia and people to interview that we should get some very solid leads," I said.

"How does that saying go? 'What a tangled web we weave when we practice to deceive,'" I said.

"And a tangled web Lynette has spun," Kai replied.

"I really do love our line of work. I love knowing the intricate details of other people's lives. It makes me feel better that my family isn't the only one out there with issues," I said.

"You and me both. Maybe this is why we do what we do, Mel. We hope to heal broken families just like ours. Or at least provide all the puzzle pieces and let the family decide if they want to put them together," Kai said. "I don't think there are any families out there without secrets. But the game becomes how good the family is at keeping and hiding them."

"Speaking of secrets, where do you think JR is taking me tomorrow night? The suspense and unknown destination is seriously stressing me out. I need to know what to expect so I can be prepared."

"I told you to be surprised. Why can't you just look forward to a nice evening out with JR?" Kai said.

"Because I can't. I have to know what we are doing so I can mentally prepare for it. I need to plan any necessary reaction and figure out what in the world I should wear."

"Mel, what you should wear is easy. A pair of sexy jeans, cute little gym shoes, and a shirt. I can consult," Kai answered.

"You know I am rusty at all of this. I am the girl who never changed out of her pajamas for two years. So you really can't expect me to know what is fashionable still. The only new clothes I have bought in four years are the ones you have bought for me. I guess I just want to seem that I have it together on the outside since I am still a train wreck on the inside."

"You are not a train wreck, Mel. You need to give yourself more credit. You have made a ton of progress in the past few months," Kai reassured me.

"But I still feel like a train wreck. I guess I just need to get used to feeling somewhat normal. I am just not sure how *normal* is supposed to feel anymore. Do you think it is too soon to be sort of dating someone else?" I asked.

"Too soon? No, I don't. It's been four years! There is no time line, no rule book on how soon grieving widows can date. You need to listen to your soul and your heart. I think you are ready for this. You need to be ready for this."

"I am sorry if you are tired of talking about this with me. I know I have rambled on like this on and off since Costa Rica," I said apologetically to Kai.

"I am just glad you are talking in complete sentences that I can understand," Kai replied with a chuckle.

"I know. I don't know how you put up with me for the first few agonizing months. But thank you for feeding me and making sure I didn't drown myself in the bathtub. And thank you for listening to my incoherent sentences. My memory still isn't clear on what transpired those first few months. But will you promise that when I am ready to know, you will tell me?"

"I promise, Mel."

We were almost into the District of Columbia city limits, and I was relieved to be in the city that I loved. My heart and soul just felt at peace here more so than any place else in the world. I sure didn't miss Whitehall, Montana. But I think Kai is right. I have made some progress in the last months, and I was beginning to feel better about it. I just didn't want to get my hopes up that the fog was clearing to wake up one morning blinded by it again. I didn't want to disappoint myself. I really wanted to believe that my mind had made the conscious decision to start living again. I just didn't know what this meant since I never thought I would find another purpose to live. I knew that the purpose of living in such a crazy world had to be for me and only me, but I never felt or thought that my life would be worth living without Ryan. I still felt that way sometimes, but I knew Ryan would want me to go on. I just had to figure out a way to go on and keep him with me at all times. I promised my mind, heart, and soul years ago that I would never forget him. It was easy to remember him when the fog of his death occupied my soul every second of every day, but the more the fog dissipated, the more anxious I became that Ryan was leaving me all over again.

Before I realized it, we were sitting in the driveway. Kai was looking at me with her Mel-to-reality look.

"What do you say we hit the gym?" Kai asked me.

"Yeah, I think some kickboxing would do me some good."

"Seth will be happy to see you. You know he still thinks you are broken," Kai said.

"Broken?"

"I think the more you show your face in his gym, the more he will believe that you haven't suffered some severe mental damage," Kai said.

"Thanks for the vote of confidence, Kai. I still owe you a serious butt-kicking for the Mel-hasn't-slept-with-anyone-in-four-years comment. Please keep adding fuel to my fire. You won't be able to get out of bed tomorrow well enough go out with Will."

"Your trash-talking is so intimidating. I might have to lock myself in my room," Kai sassed back.

"Bring it on, girl. I may be broken, but I have still have balls bigger than all the men we know. That hasn't changed."

"So you are finally dusting off the old balls, are we, Mel?" Kai egged me on.

"Is this part of Kai's Therapy Program for Widows?" I asked her.

"It sure is. Is it working?"

"I think so. There is a burning desire raging through my body that wants to whoop up on you in the ring. Maybe you missed your calling as a shrink," I said.

"Mission accomplished. Mel can finally feel more than every adjective associated with death. Welcome back to the world of the living," Kai replied.

"I don't know if I should thank you or hit you right now," I said laughing.

"I'll take either one." Kai laughed. She knew she was getting under my skin and making me mad. But she was right; it was nice to feel something other than death. I was ready to kick her butt in the ring.

By this time we were already in the house and headed to our respective rooms to change. We would walk to the gym and probably pick up dinner on the way home. My hate for cooking was one of the few things that remained unchanged after Ryan. It felt good to know that something in my life was the same, that some little tiny piece of me was still the same person that Ryan loved. I felt so different these days. A part of me died with Ryan, and I hadn't figured out who I was quite yet. My personality wasn't even the same from my perspective. I felt very old and mature for my age. I expected to bury my husband at eighty or ninety, but not thirty. At least I had been in love and had been loved by a man who thought the sun rose and set at my command. I did have to admit to myself though that being out of the house did make me feel better. I had rarely traveled and only when absolutely necessary for work or to fly to Fiji so I could even be more secluded from the world. Kai and I had been to Alabama for a case, and that was my first "real-world" trip, as Kai had called it. She thought it would be good for me to get my head back in the game. We were searching for a man whose ex-wife was looking for back child-support payments. The case was referred to us from a local attorney Kai and I knew. Now if you have to go to the back country of Alabama searching for someone who is behind in child-support payments, he's probably running from something else as well. We had uncovered information that our missing person was camped out in an illegal campsite outside of Clovernook. Kai and I were walking in the woods, and we heard what we assumed to be hunters. We had stopped, and before we could shout at them to let them know we were there, they fired at me and grazed my arm. The bullet probably would have taken a bigger chunk of my arm off if I hadn't moved or it might have even killed me. I actually never felt like I would die from this gunshot; I somehow knew my time wasn't up yet. Since we were in the middle of nowhere, I was taken by a medical helicopter to the nearest hospital due to the loss of blood. It took twenty-four stitches to close it. I cussed out Kai the entire way there and for the duration of my ER visit. We talked to the local police, and they took over the search and located our missing person. I was furious that they found him. As usual, our instincts were spot on. He was running from a felony warrant that was listed under an alias he was using. He sits in jail today, and I doubt he has paid back the back child support he owes. Sometimes certain missing people are meant to be missing. Our poor client didn't need to know that the father of her child was hiding out in the deep woods and wanted on a felony warrant. If our client would have left the whereabouts of her ex-husband alone, she could have concocted some story in her imagination that would have made her feel better than the truth. Kai thought that this experience would further traumatize me and was very worried that I would have a meltdown. I told her that I couldn't be any more traumatized and that it was too bad I wasn't standing more to the right. After I made that comment, she called my shrink, even though I assured her I was just kidding. Costa Rica was the next work-related out-of-town trip she let me go on. It was advantageous that most of our work was local.

I glanced over at my nightstand and saw the feng shui book I was reading. I was going to feng shui my bedroom to help generate positive energy and harmony in a room that caused me great pain. It probably didn't help that our wedding picture was poached atop my dresser and was viewable from every angle in the room. I hadn't changed a thing in four years. From my amateur feng shui understanding, a bedroom should lure you in and have simultaneous and continuous harmony and excitement.

My bedroom could use all of that. It apparently was all about the position of the bed, different types of lighting, lots of oxygen, soothing colors and art, and keeping the doors closed at night.

The book also said that all electronic and exercise equipment should be banned from the bedroom.

As I sat on the bed to tie my shoes, I decided that this would be feng-shui-my-bedroom weekend, and then I would feng shui the rest of the house. I was going to paint, buy new bedding and art, get an air purifier for the oxygen factor, and rearrange the furniture. The only feng shui principle I didn't agree with was the removal of the TV. But change was good for me. If I had to go down two flights of stairs to watch TV, maybe I would spend less time in my room. Hopefully running up and down all those stairs would tighten up my thigh jiggle.

"Mel, what are you doing? Getting ready for the prom? Let's go!" Kai yelled in her sassy voice.

I was so going to beat her to a pulp in that ring.

FOOTWORK

As I rolled over to escape the sunlight peeping through my bedroom curtains, I let out a gasp as my thigh made contact with the bed. My left side was stiff from sleeping on it all night because my right thigh had a bruise the size of Kai's heel. She threw a side kick that I wasn't able to successfully block, and she nailed me. I rolled over onto my back, relinquishing the fact that I would not be able to go back to sleep with the throbbing going on in my leg. In my pre-retirement days, I always had bruises, but I was younger then, and I enjoyed the pain that came with the satisfaction of beating Kai at a fight. It didn't happen often, but I had won a few. But the pain of this bruise didn't seem to justify losing to Kai. I turned on the lamp next to my bed to examine my bruise.

Holy crap! It was black. I don't mean a dark-shade-of-purple black; I mean midnight-pitch-can't-see-anything-in-front-of-your-face black. It hurt when I looked at it. I am declaring a rematch.

Oh crap! As my mind became fully awake, I realized that today was Friday! It was date night. I felt like throwing up. I don't think I had fully accepted the fact that I was going on a date tonight with a different man. I was secretly hoping that Friday wouldn't come. Would I know how to act on a date by myself without Kai around? I knew Kai couldn't be with me every second of the rest of my life, but I wasn't ready to be on my own yet. Was I confident enough about who I was now to talk about myself on a first date?

Would I break down and cry? Would JR even show up? I hadn't heard anything else from him, so maybe he would stand me up. That is what I would hope for. I currently had no problem running away from my fears. I needed coffee and some pain meds for my throbbing leg.

I put on my robe so the neighbors wouldn't see me in my braless tank top and boy shorts. My lovely Kai-inflicted bruise shot a sear of pain down my leg with every step I took—all two flights of them. I smelled the coffee brewing, and my body immediately craved the caffeine that would soon be entering its veins. I popped three extra-strength something and washed them down with a swig of my liquid candy. What a great way to start the day.

Even though the Danville case was actively at work in my head, I really didn't feel like working today, which was an odd feeling for me. I loved working. I always had. My personality demanded that I do something productive at all times. I flipped on the news network to see how more terrible and awful the world had become overnight. I gingerly sat down in the oversized leather chair in the hearth room and propped my battered leg up on the ottoman. I made myself justify sitting on the couch by thinking about the Danville case. I was eager to see what hits we would get now that we had the right DOB for Amelia and if any of her relatives had any additional information they were willing to tell us. Someone had to know where this girl was. But there was one theme that kept creeping into my mind: Everyone gets mad at their parents. It happens. But how do you skip your father's funeral? Just because Buck didn't provide Amelia's DNA, he loved her like a father and raised her as his own. That says a lot about the type of man that Buck was. I understand the not-speaking-to-your-mother part; I hadn't spoken to my parents in years, but if one of them died, I would be on the first plane to Montana. And if I couldn't get on the first plane, I would certainly be there in time for the funeral. Time is precious and non-renewable. There was something else going on. My first theory was that Amelia was hiding out with a relative. My bet was on the mother-in-law—Buck's mother. Mother-in-laws were their own breed and were known to be conniving, passive-aggressive, and crazy. I once sent Lilith a birthday card, and I spelled her name with two *l*s instead of one, and she edited the envelope and sent it back to me, unopened. My second theory was that Amelia had purposely run away from her life and her mother. Was she in school somewhere? Was she living with a friend? What was she doing for money? I hoped to find some answers and see which bet I would win against myself.

My whole body suddenly shuddered as I thought again about my date with JR tonight. "Crap," I said out loud. What would I wear, and where was he taking me? And did he really like me? I couldn't quite put my finger on why he would want a part of this mess. But I felt compelled to go out with him, drawn to him. I kept playing back how he told me he was drawn to me as soon as he spotted me at the Driftwood. My mind wanted to know what this meant. How could a complete stranger instantly know the moment he saw my face that he was drawn to me? My brain wouldn't let all this rest, so there was no way I could work today. I decided I was going to shop—shop for my new feng shui room and something to wear tonight. I hadn't shopped in years, and the only new things I owned had been purchased by Kai. I would make Kai go with me as my fashion consultant. She had impeccable taste in clothes and could through a runway-quality outfit together in minutes. She would buzz around the racks pulling pieces of clothing, and within minutes she had an armful of outfits that would fit perfectly and look amazing. It was a workout just watching her. She could probably make a better living being a personal stylist than a PI. We hadn't taken a day off in a few months, so we were due. I got up and winced as I moved my leg. Damn, did that bruise hurt. I had to get back in agent shape.

Before Kai returned from her morning run, I was dressed and ready to shop. Not like any stores were open yet, but I was ready. I had on some yoga pants that didn't rub against my bruise and an old army T-shirt of Ryan's. I tried on all the jeans I owned, and none of them fit right. Not one single pair. They were all a little too big; I had lost some weight and muscle tone after Ryan, so nothing fit right anymore. Why can't they make a pair of jeans that stretches and shrinks as your body does? Seriously how hard could it be?

Of course Kai was up for some shopping and decided that our destination would be Wisconsin Avenue in Georgetown where some of the best boutiques in DC were. Every time I stepped foot in Georgetown, I felt like I was a living part of colonial America. Georgetown was one of the oldest neighborhoods in DC, and you could feel it in the air there. My favorite things about Georgetown were the row houses and the waterfront. The row houses were on tree-lined streets, with black wrought-iron railings, and American flags flapping in the wind from above the front doors. My deep love for early America history was fed here; my soul was overflowing with patriotism and democracy. As I walked down the street, I could hear the words of the United States Constitution ringing in my ears; it was unavoidable.

> We the People of the United States, in Order to form a more perfect Union, establish Justice, insure domestic Tranquility, provide for the common defence, promote the general Welfare, and secure the Blessings of Liberty to ourselves and our Posterity, do ordain and establish this Constitution for the United States of America.

It was music to my ears.

After multiple hours of trying on fourteen pairs of jeans in numerous Georgetown boutiques and stores, number fourteen was the lucky winner. I felt like I had just run a marathon and won! Universities should offer a degree in the art and science of finding the perfect pair of jeans. I actually felt really cute in them and was glad to have found a new pair for tonight. This new pair of jeans made me feel like a new Mel who had a new outlook on life. Maybe there was something to retail therapy after all.

All this thinking about new stuff, triggered my mind to tell Kai about my feng shui idea.

"I've decided that I am going to feng shui my room this weekend," I told Kai.

"I think that is a wonderful idea. Your room could use a little remodel. So what does feng shuing your room entail?"

"I need to rearrange the furniture, get some more lighting, remove the TV, get more oxygen and some new bed linens and curtains. I think I might even paint the walls a nice soothing gray-blue and get some white curtains and bedding. I need to shop and see what is out there. I have been so disconnected from everything for so long."

"I am so up for shopping all weekend," Kai said smilingly.

"Good. Let's do coffee tomorrow morning, shop, and debrief our dates," I said.

"Just like the old days," Kai replied.

Coffee and shopping had been our Saturday ritual for years. All throughout our Stanford days and our twenties. We used to debrief our Friday-night dates; well, we always debriefed Kai's Friday night dates. I didn't always have a date, but when I did, I did my play-by-play debrief as well. Kai always had a line of guys waiting to ask her out. She was that stunning and approachable. She was the beautiful, smart, sexy girl next door, and every guy's dream. Kai was very selective about whom she dated, but she always had a date. Since I knew Kai's dating patterns so well, I knew she really liked Will, and it scared her to death. I was so looking forward to tomorrow's debrief session.

As we made our way back to our place, I was tired of hearing the thoughts in my head. I wanted to hear what was going in Kai's.

"So, how are you feeling about Will?"

"I cannot wait to go out with him tonight. He is the first date in a long time that I was looking forward to going out with. I plan to be absolutely stunning tonight and blow his mind. But I want everyone to know tonight that he is with me and only me. Mel, I really like him. We just have this chemistry and our personalities just mesh. We will see where it goes."

"So will he be here when I get up in the morning? Just so I know if I should get dressed before I come downstairs," I said, knowing I was playing with fire.

"Cute. Why don't you just invite JR to stay, and we will have a slumber party?" Kai sassed back.

"Why don't we just open a bed-and-breakfast?" I recanted.

Kai and I enjoyed friendly banter and sass. It was part of the secret to our friendship. We were never caddy or backstabbing—just brutally honest and sassy. We could both take the heat. That is why we became instant friends at Stanford; we had finally found our other half. We weren't like most girls. We hated drama. We were real.

By the time we arrived back home, it was time to get ready for our dates. My nerves were starting to get the best of me, so I decided a long soak in my claw-foot tub was just what I needed. It was either a hot bubble bath or a martini. I decided that it wouldn't be a great impression to have gin on my breath.

The doorbell rang at exactly 6:00 p.m. I thought that I was going to puke. Kai was in the kitchen so JR and I could have some privacy, but she would make her appearance in a few minutes.

I took a deep breath and opened the front door half-expecting some dementor to appear and suck out what was left of my soul.

But there stood JR. Handsome JR. I had to resist the urge to jump into his huge biceps and wrap my legs around his waist. What was wrong with me? At least the puking feeling burning in my throat was subsiding. JR was holding a huge bouquet of baby sunflowers.

"Hi, Mel. These reminded me of you." He gently kissed me on the cheek as he passed the flowers to me.

"Thank you. They are lovely. Do you mind if I put them in a vase before we leave?"

"Not at all," JR replied.

He followed me into the kitchen, and Kai was mysteriously gone.

"Glad to see you got my message about the shoes. Good choice. You look adorable tonight dressed down," he said to me.

"Thanks. Your text message was a little cryptic, so I wasn't sure exactly what the footwear requirements were. So where are we going anyway?"

"It is a surprise, but we will see how good your footwork is," he said.

My brain began to process the "footwork" information when I felt JR's hands on my face. My eyes refocused to the touch of his skin, and he was intently looking at me. His lips were an inch away from mine. My body was like cement. I couldn't move. I impulsively put my hands around his neck and my lips reacted to his—just like that. I was completely lost in his warmth and his scent. I felt intoxicated. My mind was unable to think of anything else.

JR whispered "You ready?" in my ear and I nodded.

"Bye, Kai," I yelled up the stairs.

"Bye," I heard her say from her room.

JR opened the passenger door for me, which is something that I thought every man should do. He drove a dark-silver Infiniti G35 coupe. I slid into the black, leather seats. My seat was warm. Did he have the seat warmer on all the way here to warm up my seat? I was impressed and enjoying the warmth on my back and legs. Too bad heat wouldn't make my Kai-inflicted bruise go away. I had taken more pain meds before JR arrived. I couldn't tolerate a throbbing leg tonight. I needed my mind to be clear and focused.

"So do you need me to help you navigate DC?" I asked smugly, hoping he would tell me where we were going.

"Nice try. I know my way around DC. Are you working on any new cases?" JR asked.

"We only have one right now, and it is going well. We met with a contact this week that provided us with some detailed information, so we should have some good leads next week after we interview some people. Our client is a father looking for his adult daughter. I hope we can find her for him. He hasn't seen her since she was very little. How was your week?"

"It is all confidential, but it was busy. I am usually unavailable during the week. I put in massive hours," he replied.

I could tell that both of us wanted to keep the conversation about our jobs to a minimum. It was all confidential and classified information. I used to get the same explanation from Ryan.

The route JR was taking was a familiar one, and I had a pretty good idea where we were going. We rounded the corner, and my hypothesis was correct—RFK Stadium. We must be going to a DC United game. More brownie points for JR. I hadn't been to a game in years, and all of a sudden, I was elated. And we must be going to a postseason playoff match since it was November.

"DC United tonight?" I asked quizzically.

"Very good. You're a soccer fan, right?" he asked.

"Absolutely," I answered.

He opened my door and helped me out. What a gentleman. However, he didn't let go of my hand, so we walked hand in hand to the stadium. We entered a specially marked entrance of the stadium that was at ground level. I could see a few players warming up on the field. One of the guys waved at JR and came over to us.

"JR, man. Hey, what's up? Nice to see you," the stranger said.

"Hey, Cade. This is Mel," JR replied.

As Cade shook my hand, he said, "It's nice to meet you."

"It's nice to meet you as well," I replied. I was trying to remain as calm as possible so Cade didn't think I was some starstruck celebrity gazer.

"You two ready to kick it around with us? I'll try not to embarrass you, JR, in front of Mel," Cade said jokingly as he hit JR on the back.

"Bring it on, bro," JR said back.

We walked onto the field, and JR put his hand in the small of my back to guide me, I guess. It wasn't like I could get lost walking to the big green field staring me in the face. The other players came over to us. JR still had his hand on my back.

"Mel, do you play?" Cade asked me.

"I played forward in high school, but I haven't played in years," I answered.

"How about three on three?" Cade suggested. "JR, Mel, and me against you three."

I unzipped my hoodie and set it on the bench near the field. I was silently praying that I wouldn't make a total fool of myself in front of JR and DC United. This is where the special agent in me kicked in. I was always very calm and cool under severe pressure and stress. I was getting into my agent zone.

Cade scored a goal, and then one of the other guys named Stu scored. The guys were trash talking each other and bantering me a little, but it was harmless. Heck, the guys at the agency were a hundred times worse than this. I was not phased by much. All of a sudden I saw this ball flying at my face. It was at eye level, so I couldn't head ball it. I went into agent mode without even thinking. I leaned backward to avoid the ball and threw myself into a backhand spring. I had learned to do a backhand spring and front and back flips during some fighting courses. I hadn't done one in years. I couldn't believe I landed it. The action stopped, and all the guys were looking at me.

"Impressive. Were you a cheerleader or something," Cade said to me.

"Actually I box—I was just trying to avoid a broken nose," I answered.

I could feel my cheeks start to blush a little.

JR patted me on my right thigh, I guess a celebratory gesture, and I let out a whimper.

"You all right?" JR quickly asked.

"Uh, yeah. I took a side kick from Kai in the gym yesterday and have a bruise the size of Alaska right where you touched me."

"I'm sorry," JR said apologetically.

"It's all right. I have a high pain tolerance. Just don't hit me there again," I said with a smile on my face.

We bid our farewells to the guys and headed off the field.

"Thanks for bringing me here," I said.

"Sure," JR said back, kissing me on the side of my head. We were still close enough for all the guys to see. JR was marking his territory.

"How do you know Cade?" I asked.

"We are old friends from Denver. We went played high school soccer together."

"Nice that you both are out on the East Coast."

"Yeah. He's a good guy," JR said. "We have club seats. I'll get you some water when we get up there. Are you hungry?"

"Water would be great, and I could use a bite to eat." I thought that maybe I should ask him for deodorant too—I was a little sweaty.

"You sure are something, Melanie Alexander," JR said as he kissed me on the side of the head for a second time in just a few minutes.

We watched the game from the box and ordered dinner. I had a grilled chicken breast and some fruit. This was a playoff game and was really exciting. JR and I just made small talk since we were both tuned into the game. I was really enjoying myself, and it felt good to be out. I appreciated JR's gentleman chivalry, and I felt like I was a princess. JR only looked at me, and I never saw his eyes check out any other girls. And there were plenty of beautiful girls there. I just found it interesting that I had to go all the way to Jaco, Costa Rica, to find him, but I was glad that I had. I hadn't thought about Ryan in a few hours, which was the first time in four years where he wasn't on my mind 24/7. A part of my mind was beginning to like JR. The feeling of hope had been restored to my heart tonight.

SECRETS

After a blood, sweat, and tears win by DC United, JR and I sat in our box and let the crowd thin out before we left the stadium.

"You up for a drink?" he asked.

"Sure, if you know of a bar where they allow sweaty, sneaker-wearing patrons."

"I know a few dives where they won't even notice—they will be too busy looking at the most beautiful girl that has ever walked into the bar. I will have to fight them off," JR said with that same adorable smile.

"I think I can take care of myself. I just like to be in a dress and heels when I go out."

"You are stunning dressed up or down," JR said.

I could feel the heat race to my cheeks. Dang it. Why did I blush all of a sudden?

"Thanks," I said in a whisper since I was almost too embarrassed to say it out loud.

"How is your leg feeling?" he asked.

"All right. It is throbbing, but I'll live."

"You want to go home?" JR asked.

"Not yet. I'll let you know when I want to go home," I replied with a sheepish smile. "Thanks for bringing me here tonight. I had an amazing time."

"You're welcome. You're an awesome sport. I like a girl who is up for anything."

Once again, JR opened the car door for me. My cell phone was ringing. It was Kai's salsa ringtone.

"Hey," I answered.

"Hey. How are things?" Kai asked with her giddy school girl voice.

"Great. What's up?" I asked her back. I wasn't going to tell her any details ask her how her evening was in front of JR. He didn't need to know.

"Will and I are on the way back from dinner and wanted to know if you and JR would be up for going back to our place and opening some wine?" Kai asked.

"Let me ask," I replied.

"Kai and Will want to know if we want to join them at our place for some wine," I asked JR.

"That sounds good to me. Is that all right with you?" JR asked me.

"Yeah, it sounds great."

"Kai, we'll meet you at the house in about twenty or so."

"See you, girl," Kai said.

"Bye."

"So tell me where you learned that martial arts move," JR asked.

"What martial arts move?"

"That was not a back hand spring you learned in gymnastics," JR said.

"Oh, that. At the gym. Kai and I have been sparring for a long time. The guy who owns the gym we go to is retired DC SWAT and is a black belt in judo. He has taught us many moves, and he works us very hard. I have been going back to the gym with Kai, so I guess it is all coming back to me," I said, hoping he would buy it.

"When was the last time you threw a backhand spring?" he asked. He so wasn't buying my story.

"Years I guess. I actually can't believe I landed it. It must have been my instincts. That move is just part of my defensive reflexes I guess."

"I have noticed that your reflexes are super quick and sharp," JR commented.

He was so fishing for me to confess something, and I wasn't ready to tell him about my agency days. I still didn't have a complete background check available on him yet.

"Thanks. I like to be able to take care of myself in a fight," I said.

"I'm pretty sure you could take care of yourself," JR said.

"Perhaps I could check out your gym sometime and maybe learn a few new moves," he said.

"Sure. Just let me know when," I responded.

We pulled up to the house. I wondered why Kai and Will were already back from dinner. If dinner hadn't gone well, she would have come home alone, but why didn't they go out dancing? Kai likes to stay out. For the first year after Ryan, Kai never left my side. She had lots of time to make up for, and she deserved to go out and kick it up.

I caught a glimpse of a Porsche Cayenne SUV in our driveway and assumed it was Will's. It was black, and it was sexy. I bet Kai was salivating at the mouth to drive it. I wonder if Will let her. I had never met a guy who told Kai no, and I bet Will wouldn't be the first.

"Look, before we go in, we need to talk in private. I need to tell you something, but not in front of Kai and Will."

My back was to the front door, and he was leaning over me. I thought he was going to kiss me, but instead he wants to talk in "private." I was too much for him. I am glad that he had finally come to his senses.

"Look, I'll make this easy for you. You can go. I told you when we first met that you didn't want to get mixed up with me and my baggage."

"No, that is not it at all. It is too cold to stand out here and talk because this might be a very long conversation."

"Okay. We can go upstairs to my room and Kai and Will can think we are up to no good or we can go somewhere else." I knew he was too good to be true. I wondered what his deep, dark secret was.

"I want to talk to you here. Let's go upstairs. I can take Will's flack if you can take Kai's."

"I can take it."

GHOSTS

Kai was going to give me so much crap for this, but I had to find out what JR's deep, dark secret was. She would never believe that we went upstairs to "talk." Luckily, the staircase was in the front of the house, so we snuck upstairs quietly. Depending on what was to come out of JR's mouth, he may not be staying long.

I led him to my room, and I closed the door behind us. I had a sitting area in my room with two armchairs and small table. I sat down in one of the chairs. I had spent many hours, days, weeks, and months sitting in this chair staring out the window after Ryan. This chair was perfectly conformed to my body, and the arms were worn from me sitting here so much. JR took my cue and sat down in the chair across from me.

He took both of my hands in his. I just wanted him to cut to the chase and get this over with.

"Mel, I don't know the best way to tell you what I need to tell you, but it may hurt. I've been waiting for a good time to talk to you about this, but such a time has yet to present itself. You're the first woman in a long time that I've been into, and I hope this won't change anything."

"I'm ready to hear it," I said. The anxiety was killing me. Just when I was thinking about getting used to the idea of maybe seeing someone, he has a huge bomb to drop. I sure knew how to pick them. Was he married? Did he have four baby mamas?

He let go of my hands and put them on my knees.

"Remember how you told me about Ryan on the beach? When you handed me your business card on the way to San Jose, my heart stopped beating when I read your last name. As we were in the Jeep, the night of November 11 flashed through my mind. Mel, I am not an accountant. I am a Navy SEAL, and we were doing a joint operation that night with the army. I was on a mission with Ryan the night that he died. When I saw you for the first time, I had absolutely no idea that Ryan was your husband. All I knew was that he was married to a special agent. I never even knew your first name. But when I saw your last name, I began to put the pieces together and knew that you were an agent. Mel, I am so sorry, but I had to tell you."

For the second time in my life, the excruciating, unmistakable pain of wretchedness flooded through my veins. My body shuddered as the paralyzing pain of despair reached my fingertips and toes. I closed my eyes and was engulfed by the black fog that had invaded my life four years ago and became my comfort. It settled in quickly, just like it had never left. And once again my body didn't know if it should cry, scream, or beat the crap out of something until it brought back Ryan. I decided to do all three.

The tears came first, which didn't surprise me. The tears had flowed easily for the last four years. I just sat there still frozen, paralyzed because my body was too heavy to move. The screaming came next. It wasn't full-blown Melanie-eruption screaming mode, but I was sure Kai could hear it downstairs. The days and weeks after Ryan's death I had screamed so loud and so much that I lost my voice for almost a month. I can still hear the sound of my weak, whispering voice in my head from the darkest time of my life.

"*What do you mean you were there the night Ryan died? Why did you get to see him before he died, and I did not? Who in the hell do you think you are knowing this and not telling me?*"

And this is where the hitting started. I involuntary started punching JR in the arm and chest. He didn't move as I was trying to beat the pain out of my body and into his. I was still crying, but not sobbing. I stopped hitting JR and sunk down to my knees. The tears were just flowing down my cheeks like a river, but no sobbing or words came. JR got on his knees too and wrapped his arms around me and pulled me into his chest. He just held me like this while I sobbed all over him. This is why I always wore waterproof mascara because I never knew when the tears would come, and I didn't need to weep mascara all over JR's shirt. I wanted to stop crying because I felt like an idiot crying in front of another man over Ryan, but I couldn't make myself stop. The wound in my heart and soul had been ripped wide open once again, and apparently it was filled with tears.

There was a knock at the door. I heard Kai's voice say, "Mel, you okay? What's going on? I heard you screaming."

I couldn't respond. I couldn't find my voice to speak. It was drowned in tears.

"Mel, I am coming in."

Kai opened the door, and I can only imagine what she saw: JR and me sitting on the floor and me quietly crying the Potomac.

"What did you do to her?" Kai asked JR.

Kai came over and sat down beside me. "Mel, you all right? What happened? Talk to me."

I still couldn't speak, but I felt comforted in JR's arms, and I didn't want to leave the only place of comfort I currently had.

"JR, tell me what happened," Kai demanded.

"I told her that I was with Ryan the night he was killed in action. The mission he was on was a joint mission with the navy. Will and I are SEALs. I had no idea Melanie was Ryan's wife until she handed me her business card and then I put the pieces together. I had to tell her. I also know that she is an agent. Ryan made a comment about her that night. I am sorry, but I thought it was the right thing to do."

"Damn you, JR," Kai reprimanded him.

"Mel, do you want JR to leave? I'll show him to the door myself," Kai said sternly. I was surprised by her tone.

I shook my head no.

"Do you want me to stay?" Kai asked me.

I shook my head no again.

"All right then. You let me know if you need me. I will be downstairs. Want me to bring you a martini?"

I shook my head yes.

I continued to be glued to JR, and the tears were starting to dry up. It was about freeing time. How much water can one person cry in a ten-minute time span? My mind was starting to work again, and I felt like I was coming to the surface for air.

Kai was back in a flash with my martini. She put in on the table. She rubbed my back and whispered in my ear, "You are stronger now. Reach into your core, Mel."

I heard the door close, and I came up for air. I was still sitting on my knees, and I pushed out of JR's hold. I had my eyes closed, and I felt JR's hands on my cheeks wiping off the wetness. I opened my eyes and reached for my martini and took a drink. The familiar smell and taste were calming to my nerves since gin had been my crutch for years. I looked at JR's shirt and pants, and they were soaked. There was even a small puddle on the floor next to us. I took another drink of the martini and set it back on the table. JR sat down on the floor with his back leaning against the chair. Why was he still here? Did he like being tortured by an emotional woman and her ghost? The martini was reaching my core, and the sting of despair was weakening its grip on my body. I had been here before, and this time it didn't sting as bad. I had to remember that no matter what I did or said or what anyone did or said, it would never bring Ryan back.

"Did I hurt you?"

"No. But you have one heck of a jab. If you want me to leave, I will."

I wasn't sure what I wanted or how long I could look into the face of a man with whom Ryan had spent his last breathing moments. I stood up and took off my hoodie since my crying rage had made me sweat. I was hoping that I didn't smell. I sat on my bed and took off my shoes and pulled my hair up into a ponytail. The cool air on the back of my neck was refreshing. I was sensing that this was going to be a long night, so I pulled a pair of yoga pants out of my dresser and decided I would change into them right in front of JR. He had already seen me in my bikini, so what was the difference. I was trying to remember what underwear I had on. Oh yeah, I was wearing boy shorts, so that was comforting. I didn't want to bare my rear in a skimpy thong. Some things were better left to the imagination.

"That bruise looks awful. No wonder it hurts like hell," JR said. I looked down at my bruise, and for the first time tonight, something hurt worse than my heart. The bruise had almost doubled in size and was still this horrendous shade of pitch-black.

"Apparently I need to practice my blocks."

"I'll practice with you," JR said.

"I might just take you up on that," I said.

I walked back over to JR and grabbed my martini. It was also refreshing.

"For now, I want you to stay and tell me everything about that night." I sat down on the floor next time to JR as close as I could get without being in his lap. Even though I had found my core, it was still filled with molten lava and bubbling. I was hot and he wasn't getting off easy.

"You know that information is classified, but I will tell you what I can," JR said.

I could tell he had other things on his mind, so my punishment was working.

"The navy and the army were conducting a joint mission to secure some intelligence targets in Kabul. Over a two-week period, we did two dry runs, and I was on Ryan's team, so I got to know him a little. He was always the lead and cared deeply for the guys on his team. The guys respected him and trusted him with their lives. He was one hell of a solider with balls of steel. He actually talked about you quite a bit. I thought, *I got to meet the woman who was on Ryan's mind 24/7*. Our dry runs went flawlessly, and on the night of November 11, we were called. The mission was going as planned until two rogue terrorists opened fire from a truck we had set on fire. To this day I don't know how they were still alive. Ryan pulled Casey behind him, and I was a few steps away heading over to provide cover. I started firing, and then I saw Ryan on the ground. Casey was with him, and I took both guys out. I knelt down next to him as Casey went to call our helicopter and get the medic. Ryan said to me, 'Tell my wife I love her and that she is the best agent I know.' Casey came back, and we loaded his body on the helicopter minutes later, but it was too late. Casey held his hand the entire flight and finally told us what Ryan had said to him when they were being fired upon. Casey cried that night too. The rest of the teams finished the mission."

My martini was gone, and I wanted another one. I was digesting and dissecting every word JR had said. JR's version was similar to the stories Casey and the general had told me, so it was comforting knowing that I hadn't believed and mourned over a totally different set of facts all these years. JR's story once again confirmed that Ryan didn't suffer horribly and that I consumed his thoughts during his final moments. JR did provide one piece of new information: there were insurgents in a truck that the team had set on fire. I never knew before where the shots came from that took Ryan's life. I could spend another four years analyzing and contemplating this, but it wouldn't change a single thing. However, hearing Casey's name and what Ryan said to him again brought up something that I had been trying to ignore for years. I had this thought that maybe Ryan's fate ended that night in the Kabul desert because Casey's daughter, Melanie Ryan, was meant for great things. A wave of comfort went through me, and I almost shivered in response to it. Perhaps if I put this thought—this sliver of hope in four years of total darkness—at the center of my core, it would bring me the inner strength I needed.

"Thanks for telling me. I just need some time. I also need a refill. Want anything?"

"Mind if I join you?" JR asked cautiously in case he would set off Mt. Melanie again.

"I would actually like for you to join me. I am sorry for tonight. I told you to walk away from me in Jaco. The wound was just reopened tonight, that's all."

"I am glad I didn't take your advice in Jaco," JR said with a smile on his face. "Mel, you are human. And you are still well worth the risk." He put his hand in the small of my back, and we headed downstairs.

As I came into the kitchen, Kai and Will were on the couch in front of the fire talking and drinking wine. They were quite close and whispering. Kai was practically sitting in his lap. I was certain that Kai was telling him about her crazy BFF. There were two empty wine bottles on the island. No wonder they were so snuggly in front of the fire.

"I can open up another bottle of wine or make you a drink. We don't have any beer."

"Can I have a water?" JR asked.

"Water, really? They're in the fridge. You make me feel like a lush. How could you not need a drink after spending the evening with me? I needed more than one drink to spend the evening with me."

"I don't know how much Will has had to drink, so I want to be clear to drive."

"Do you think Will *will* be going home?" I said as I raised my eyebrows toward the happy couple on the couch.

"Well, even if he stays, I still have to drive."

"You can always sleep on the couch," I said. "So if you want to have some drinks, the bar is open." I was waiting for his response to see how he felt about sleeping on the couch.

"The couch would be great, thanks. So, how about a Captain and Cola?" he said.

"Oh, a rum man. Nice. I think we have a bottle of Captain Morgan. Let me look."

I mixed JR a glass of Captain Morgan's rum and Coke. I was impressed with his choice of drink. A man who drinks a Captain and Cola is one who is always in control and exudes sophistication. It seemed fitting for JR.

I went over to the love seat in the hearth room and sat down. Kai and Will both looked up to see if I needed admitted or if I was back in the world of the living.

"May I?" JR asked. I am glad he still felt he was on probation with me. I still hadn't decided if he would be allowed permanent visitation privileges yet, but I think I liked having him around. Kai and I would so have to have some girl talk tomorrow.

We had no choice but to touch each other as we sat on the love seat; it simply wasn't big enough. His leg was putting pressure on my Kai-inflicted bruise, and I winced.

"Your leg?" JR whispered.

"Yeah. It will be okay."

"You should see the bruise you left on my leg," I said to Kai. "It is the size of a cantaloupe and black as a Montana midnight."

"I'm sorry. Maybe next time, you'll have a better block," Kai snickered at me.

I could tell that she had had some wine. She got sassier the more she drank.

"Thanks for the sympathy," I said back.

"So, girls, tell us some stories from your agent days," Will said. "Kai was filling me in on your previous careers."

"You guys know that information is classified," I said.

"At least fill me in on how you two became agents. I missed Kai's history lesson," JR said.

"We became agents after we graduated from Stanford because we thought we were bad asses," Kai said.

Oh, she was going to be lovely in the morning. I would have to mix her my special hangover smoothie. It looked like pureed grass, but it made you feel like you never had one drink.

We all laughed, and this encouraged Kai to continue.

"Mel's dad was a police officer, so she was always a great marksman. I loved to box and kickbox, so we just applied and were accepted. We graduated top in our class from the academy and fell in love with it. After we graduated, we were assigned more experienced agents as partners, but after a few years, we became partners. The rest is classified."

"Why missing persons?" JR asked.

"That was how we could be partners, so we were game," Kai said.

"Do you miss it?" Will asked. He and Kai had untangled themselves when we came into the room. Kai was now leaning up against Will's shoulder and had her knees in his lap. He had his arm around her knees. They looked like a couple who been together awhile and who knew how their bodies fit together just so. We would definitely be having some girl talk tomorrow. Kai usually played a little harder to get.

"Some days, I guess. It just isn't who I am anymore," I said before Kai could answer.

"I do and don't," Kai said. "I like running our own cases, but sometimes I miss the adrenaline and excitement that can come with agency work."

I looked over at JR. "Need a refill?" I asked.

"Sure."

"Anyone else?" I asked as I noticed Kai and Will's wineglasses were empty.

"I'll have another glass," Kai said.

"Are you the DD, man?" Will asked JR.

"Not tonight. Mel offered up her couch, so I will be drinking some Captain Morgan and Colas," JR replied as he pulled me closer to him.

Will turned to Kai, and she whispered something in his ear.

"Mel, I'll have the same, if you don't mind," Will said.

Well apparently Will would be staying over too.

I brought everyone's drinks and sat down, a little closer to JR this time. I was going to feel this martini because my cheeks were feeling hot, and I was getting that little lackadaisical feeling in my head.

JR and Will were talking about the DC United game, and Kai was either almost asleep or passed out on Will. I wondered how long they had been drinking. I hadn't seen her drink this much in a long time. And why would she pick drinking at home instead of out in the city? Kai loved the nightlife.

As I laid my head down on JR's shoulder and took another sip, I was thinking about the events that had transpired this evening. It had been a roller coaster of emotions in a few-hour period and I was emotionally drained. Hearing stories of Ryan still felt like I was being stabbed in the heart with a sword. However, my emotional roller coaster had a new passenger: JR. Part of me wanted him to stay, and part of me wanted to tell him off and kick him out. I was mad that he had lied to me and that he was with Ryan during his final moments. But for some strange reason, I felt comforted in his presence. I couldn't comprehend how I could want tell him off and be wrapped in his arms at the same time. Maybe I was starting to feel again, and I was just a little rusty. This was all too heavy for my brain, so I decided to get lost in my martini.

HANGOVERS

The smell of brewing coffee was in the air, and it awoke me from my sleep. I didn't immediately recall coming up to bed last night, and I was still in my clothes. The other side of my bed was still made, so I made the conclusion that JR had slept on the couch downstairs. I was a little worried that my memory was cloudy about going to bed—or any events that may have transpired. I winced at the reminder of my Kai bruise as I rolled over to get out of bed. I really wanted to shower, but I also wanted to find out what was going on downstairs. I washed my face, brushed my teeth, reapplied my black mascara, spritzed on some mango-pomegranate body spray and redid my ponytail before my curiosity got the best of me. If I could have shaved my legs, I would have felt like a new woman.

Before I rounded the corner to the kitchen, the aroma of eggs and pancakes floated past me. I knew it had to be JR and/or Will because Kai didn't cook, and based on how much she had to drink last night, there was no way she was up. And I was right on all accounts.

"Hey there," JR said. He poured me a cup of coffee before I could even ask for one. He had pancakes on one burner and omelets on two others. I didn't think that we had enough ingredients on hand for pancakes, but apparently our pantry was better stocked than I realized. I was glad the pantry and the kitchen were getting some use.

"Hi. Thanks for the coffee. Everything smells fantastic," I said. "Did I fall asleep on the couch last night? I don't remember walking upstairs to bed."

"Yes, you did, and no, you didn't walk upstairs—I carried you," JR said with a smile.

"Oh, sorry. Thanks. Was the couch okay?"

"I didn't mind carrying your beautifully and peacefully sleeping body upstairs," JR said as he stepped closer to me. "The couch was fine. Thanks for letting me stay."

"Thanks for wanting to stay after Mt. Melanie erupted. It wasn't one of my better moments."

He took the coffee cup out of my hand and placed it on the counter. He picked me up and sat me on the island. The granite was cold. My heartbeat started to do double time, and I was nervous with anticipation with what JR's next move was. He gently placed his hands on the side of my face and leaned in. He stopped an inch from my waiting, quivering lips and said, "I like the danger zone." He began to kiss me. I could smell the rum on his breath. The only thought currently running through my mind was if we had any spare toothbrushes in the house. After my brain switched back to the present action going on, it decided that the kiss was nice. It had been a long time since I had met a new day with a kiss. It was almost as nice as my cup of liquefied candy. The kiss didn't last long, and JR went to attend to his breakfast.

"Kai or Will been down yet?" I asked JR as he started another omelet.

"Will is out for a run. I haven't seen Kai yet."

I must not have had as much to drink as I thought because I instantly gave JR a quick and hopefully not obvious once-over. He was wearing the same clothes as last night. It was highly doubtful that Will was out running in dress slacks or his underwear. So did he have clothes in his car? I scanned the room for a backpack or bag, but didn't see one. I was suddenly and unexpectedly creeped out that Will possibly had a change of clothes in his car. Did JR have clothes in his car too? It was almost like they had planned to stay last night.

"Oh, please tell me he's not out running around our neighborhood in his boxers," I said with a slight hint of sarcasm. I didn't want to seem too obvious.

"He had clothes in his car. We are SEALs; we travel prepared for anything," JR replied with a wink.

I took that to mean that JR had clothes and who knows what else in his trunk.

"I am going to go check on Kai. I bet she needs my special I-didn't-think-I-drank-as-much-as-I-did smoothie."

I knocked on Kai's door, and I didn't hear any response.

"Kai, it's me. Are you up?"

I still didn't get a response, so I went into Kai's room. She was in bed, under all the covers, and I could just see the top of her head. I sat on the bed, which left me the impression that Will had not slept on the couch, and pinched the back of her arm.

"Ow. Let me sleep," Kai said groggily."

"Do you need me to make you a grass smoothie?"

"Can I wash down some Tylenol with that smoothie? You are the best. Where's Will?"

"He's out for a run, and JR is in the kitchen cooking up omelets and pancakes. These guys act like they live here."

"I shouldn't have mixed the rum with the wine. It hurts to open my eyes."

"So, did Will sleep on the couch?" I asked slyly.

"Ummm. No. But it hurts to think and talk at the same time. Can we have girl talk later please? I just need a few more minutes; then I will be down."

"I'll have your smoothie waiting. It's nice to take care of you for a change," I said with a hint of sass.

"Shut up," Kai said painfully.

My special smoothie was a miracle drink. It was pureed spinach, mangoes, bananas, protein powder, and rice milk. It looked like liquid grass, but it was drinkable. And you felt like you never drank one drop of anything in about one hour. It had something to do with the antioxidants and nutrients that helped to ward off the alcohol effects. We always had fresh fruit and veggies in the house—thanks to Kai—so it was never a problem to whip up. JR was watching me make my concoction and had a curious look on his face.

"I can't believe you girls drink that for a hangover," JR said.

"Don't tell me you are afraid to drink some concoction that looks like pureed grass," I teased.

He took the glass from my hand and took a cautious drink. After a brief second, he swallowed. "It looks worse than it tastes. Not bad. How's Kai?"

"She'll be fine. She'll be down soon."

JR and I sat down at the table to eat. The omelet was delicious, and it was nice to sit and have breakfast with JR. Again, I wasn't sure why he was still around this train wreck, but he was good company, and the man could cook. I did find it a bit odd that he and Will made themselves at home. I wasn't sure if that was a compliment or not. Will was out for a run, and JR was rummaging through our kitchen cooking up breakfast after their first night staying here. I never ran the morning-after scenario through my head last night or this morning. This thought suddenly sent racing surges of panic through my body. This had to mean something I wasn't ready for it to mean.

Just then the front door opened, and Will walked into the kitchen.

"Hey. Do you mind if I get some water?" he asked.

"Not at all, check the fridge. How was your run?" I asked back.

"I like the scenery down here. It makes it easy to run."

He grabbed a plate off the island and sat down with us. Shouldn't this be awkward? Shouldn't this be awkward because the guy who had just *slept next to my best friend all night* was sitting at my table like we were old friends? Who were these guys?

Maybe I was still asleep, and I was dreaming that I was on a reality show. Was I being punked? There were no uncomfortable vibes in the air, or maybe he had slept on Kai's couch and didn't have anything to feel awkward about.

I heard Kai's feet shuffling down the hallway. I hadn't seen her like this in years. Her skin was pasty, but she had managed to pull her hair in a ponytail and change into some gym clothes.

"Hi," her froggy voice said. She reached for her miracle smoothie and drank it as if it tasted like candy.

"Can I get you a plate?" Will asked.

"Umm. No thanks. I'm vegan," Kai answered.

Will immediately got up and pulled out her chair. Kai was a little uneasy on her feet. I was beginning to think Will slipped something in her drink. And if he did take *advantage* of her in such a state, I was going to cut his balls off right here at the kitchen table. I knew he didn't and wouldn't because special agent Kai would have reminded Will of his manners, but I hadn't seen her like this since our college days. Perhaps it was the perfect combination of wine and rum that Kai's body did not appreciate.

"Mel, you up for the gym later? I would really like to get a good workout in today. We could practice some blocks. I'll take it easy on your leg," JR said with the cutest sly smile. He was really starting to grow on me. I almost wanted to go over and sit on his lap. But I refrained.

"Sure. I'll introduce you to Seth. He owns the gym and is former DC SWAT. It is about an eight-minute walk from here. You both are welcome to join us," I said to Kai and Will.

"Sounds like just what I need this morning," Kai said.

"Are you sure you are up for it?" I asked her.

"There is nothing your miraculous blended grass potion can't fix," Kai replied.

"Count me in," Will said.

We all sat around the kitchen table, which hadn't been this crowded in a long time. We talked about random topics—soccer, the news, our families, and DC. It was like four old friends who are just able to pick up where they had left off even if they hadn't seen each other in years. I kept having to remind myself that I actually hadn't known JR all that long—well, really not long at all. My mind couldn't help but analyze what all this meant. And Ryan had been on my mind all morning since I couldn't get the image of JR being with Ryan during his final moments out of my head. It felt as if a living artifact from that night in Kabul had shown up four years later. I felt oddly connected to JR this morning since he had been with Ryan that night. JR would be forever connected to me because of where he was on November 11. But I wanted to be connected to JR for me, not for Ryan.

"Mel, I'm going to get my bag out of the trunk and then we can hit the gym," JR said.

"Okay. I'm going upstairs to change as well," I replied. *So he did have a bag in his car after all.*

Kai and I walked up the stairs together, and when we were finally out of earshot of Will, the girl talk began.

"Do you find it weird that JR and Will have a bag of clothes in their car and that they act like they live here?" I asked Kai.

"That is the first question you are asking me?" Kai replied. "They are SEALs. They probably always have a bag ready to go in their trunks."

"And how much did you have to drink? I haven't seen you hung over like this since our Stanford Vegas trip."

"It was that rum. I cannot stomach it. I wasn't drunk, but my body was not pleased with it," Kai said. "Back to you. Did JR sleep on the couch?"

"He sure did. What a gentleman," I replied. "Apparently Will didn't."

"No, he didn't," Kai replied with a sly smile.

"Are you going to give me details? Or at least the cliff-note version?" I had lowered my voice when I heard JR open the front door. Kai and I were at the top of the stairs in the hallway.

She smiled and raised her eyebrows at me. I knew what that look meant. I hadn't seen it in long time, but our signals never changed. Kai had had an enjoyable time last night. She *would* give me the details later.

"You go, girl," I whispered at her.

"And I can't believe JR is still here after you made him sleep on the couch," Kai said.

"Shut up. I don't start my relationships on sex," I said. As soon as the R-word rolled off my lips, I knew Kai would be all over me. I didn't mean an actual "relationship." But before I could come back with a rebuttal, Kai was on it.

"Relationship?" Kai said in the next octave. "Did you just say 'relationship'?

"*Shut up.* I didn't mean in it in the official 'relationship' context. My brain just selected the wrong word, Kai. Back it up, girl," I said a little shocked myself.

What the heck did that mean? I just stood there awestruck. I must have had this look of shock or the "Mel's-freaking out face" because Kai put her hands on my shoulders.

"Mel—it is okay. Don't freak out on me. It is okay to feel this way. Go get dressed for the gym. You can beat the daylights out of something or someone there," Kai said to me.

We both walked into our respective bedrooms and changed into our gym gear. As I sat on the bed putting on my warm-up pants, I winced at my bruise. It hadn't gotten any bigger, but it was still pitch-black. It no longer throbbed, but it hurt as my pants brushed it. I was really beginning to feel like a wimp about this whole bruise thing. I told myself to suck it up—I had bigger problems to focus on. Two of these problems were at the forefront of my brain—finding Amelia Marlowe and figuring out what to do about JR. I wish I could turn my brain off. And Kai was right—why had JR stayed? We all know guys have different "priorities" than women do. And one of those priorities was a physical one. Situations like this made me wish I had been closer to my brother so maybe I could have gained some insight into the male brain—if there was anything to see. I was done thinking.

I met Kai in the hallway.

"Aren't you cute?" she said when she saw me. "Oh, you so like him."

"What do you mean?" I asked as I smacked her arm.

"Your hair is in two, sexy low-side ponytails, and you have on a fitted tank top instead of some baggy T-shirt. And I can almost see your sports bra, the tank top is so low."

"Shut it. Is this pick-on-Mel day?"

"You are so sensitive. I'm glad to see you so inspired," Kai said as she winked at me.

I bounded down the stairs, ignoring Kai. So what if what Kai had said had a hint of truth to it. Was it my fault I could be cute in less than ten minutes? Man, I was sassy. What had gotten into me? I had to stop talking to myself in my head.

In a little less than an hour, we were all walking to Seth's gym. I wasn't quite ready to show JR off as—well—anything. What would Seth think? Well, it had to happen sometime, I guess.

As soon as the East Coast sun hit my face, it felt therapeutic. A little sunshine could go a long way to putting some zing in the step and some happiness in the soul. The Fiji sun had kept me from having to be admitted into an institution. Kai made me sit on the beach every day even on the days when I was so depressed, it was difficult to make myself breathe. The Fiji sun was my personal happy lamp. The warmth on my face reminded me of Fiji, and it was nice to be warmed while walking in the cool, fall air.

"You are adorable," JR whispered to me as we walked.

"Thanks. I still hope you think that after I embarrass you in my gym."

JR chuckled as he put his massive arm around my shoulders. "I am sure I will, but I guess a good fight will let me know."

"At least this time I am dressed for the occasion."

"I really prefer the bikini. I'm thinking about starting a beach boxing league," JR said.

I just rolled my eyes at him, and he pecked me on the cheek. I was hoping no one we knew was within viewing distance. I just wasn't ready to be labeled "Moved On." I could hear the neighbors now: "I saw Mel Alexander with a new guy today. That poor girl has finally moved on."

As soon as we walked into the gym, almost all the action came to a stop. All eyes were on us and our "guests." Seth came right on over.

"Kai, Mel, it is nice to see you. Who are your guests?" Seth asked. He got right to the point, didn't he? Well, of course he did. He was buddies with Ryan's dad, so he had to see who this was. At least I didn't have to worry about him ratting me out to Lilith. He couldn't stand her either.

"Seth, this is Jenner Romero and Will Greensburg. JR and Will, this is Seth Rodriguez. He owns the gym," I said.

All the guys shook hands as I stood there feeling awkward. Kai and I had never brought guys to the gym before with the exception of Ryan. If we were still with the agency, Seth may think that JR and Will were colleagues of ours, but I knew for a fact that wasn't what he was thinking. But guys think differently than women do anyway, so maybe Seth didn't think anything of it. Maybe he thought they were cousins who were in town visiting. Why do I analyze every single thing? I was really beginning to drive myself crazy with all this thinking. That is one thing I appreciated about men. They really didn't subject themselves to deep thinking often; they were more simpleminded. Most male minds can't multitask, which makes them unable to process or analyze multiple strands of information simultaneously. Men really did have it made in this life. And I was beginning to think about why some women choose to be with other women.

The guys were still talking with Seth, and I really wasn't listening to the conversation, so I had no idea what the topic was. I just realized that Kai was no longer next to me; she was warming up on a treadmill. Great, so I am standing here thinking to myself looking like an idiot. Well, at least most people thought I was still the "crazy widow," so perhaps my blank stare didn't seem that out of the ordinary. I walked over to some free floor space and began stretching. I soon joined Kai on the adjacent treadmill. Kai and I really don't talk about anything in depth in the presence of other people. We don't like people knowing our business. So we just ran in silence, which didn't bother me one bit.

"Mel, you warmed up? Seth says we are up first in the ring," JR said to me.

"I sure am. Let's go."

Now that I knew that JR was a SEAL, I secretly prayed that I wouldn't make a complete fool of myself as I stepped off the treadmill.

Since I now knew what kind of skills JR had, it was obvious he was taking it easy on me, and I was a little offended. So I decided to kick it up a notch. I still had the skills; they were just a little dusty, but my body knew what to do.

I fueled my determination with the bottled-up anger and sadness in my soul. Having two taxing emotions fighting for first place in your core and brain took amazing energy to properly channel. These two emotions had been feuding in my body for years and literally had driven me to the point of mental and physical exhaustion—to the point of not being able to remember who you are or how to get out of bed. But just in the past six months or so, I started to put the anger and sadness to good use. I channeled them when I needed an emotional or physical energy boost, and I decided to put them to good use right now. I began to recall a sequence of moves in my head, and I executed them flawlessly. My mind was chanting, *Jab-cross-jab-knee, jab-cross-hook-uppercut, jab-uppercut-hook-cross, hook-cross-hook-front kick, hook-uppercut-hook-front kick, jab-and-cross-and-hook-and-up, jab-and-cross-and -hook-and-up, double-up to jab-cross-hook-up; jab-cross-hook-up.*

MONUMENTAL

When I was finally alone and standing in a hot shower, I replayed the whirlwind events of the weekend so far, which was only half over. JR was still downstairs and was going to shower next. We had hit the gym pretty hard, and I was a sweaty, stinky mess. JR and I, if there was such a thing, were still fairly new, and I didn't appreciate him seeing and smelling me in my after-gym state. I wondered why he was still hanging around. Was he going to stay all weekend? As the hot water massaged my muscles, I wondered what is his intent was. He wanted to do lunch and tour DC after we were showered. So I guess date night had turned into date weekend, but JR didn't even ask if I minded if he stayed. I hope he didn't feel obligated to stay because of Ryan. But he had been a perfect gentleman. My mind was a flurry of thoughts. In one aspect, I really liked JR being around, but I didn't know even know anything about his family or his life. I decided that I would interrogate JR on our historical DC lunch tour.

I went to Kai's room to blow-dry and iron my hair and to squeeze in a little girl talk while JR showered.

"Will and I are going to Annapolis for the afternoon," Kai said.

"Oh, I love Annapolis. We haven't been in years. Are you going to his place, the base?" I asked.

"I think Will and JR live off base, but I am not sure. We are going to have lunch at a little place on Main Street that Will likes. I think you and me were there once. It is next to the really cute and cozy coffee and pastry place. I don't even know if that place is still there, but I remember a sandwich place next door. It should be an adventure, and it will give you and JR some alone time," Kai said with raised eyebrows.

"Annapolis is so charming. I love the old courthouse and sitting by the Chesapeake watching the boats. JR wants to do lunch in DC and sightsee, but I appreciate you be so considerate to think that JR and I need alone time," I said smugly.

"Are you going to make him sleep on the couch again tonight?" Kai asked.

"Who said he was staying?" I retorted.

"Well, he doesn't show any signs of wanting to go home, Mel" Kai said.

"I know. It kind of freaks me out that he is still around. What do you think is going on?"

"I just think he likes you, and he probably doesn't get much time off, so he is just soaking up the Mel."

"But we haven't even talked about it—he just stays," I said. "And aren't you funny with your 'Soaking up the Mel,'" comment.

"Just enjoy it. Stop thinking so much about it. He's into you. Just spend the afternoon and evening getting to know each other better. Enjoy the beauty of the city. And don't think. I know how that head of yours works. It hasn't worked right in years, and now it is making up for lost time. Please promise me you will stop over analyzing this. We can talk about it next week while we work if you want. Your heart and soul need to be happy and need to laugh. Now get out there and get laid," Kai said as she slapped me on the behind.

I bumped her hip with mine. "You know I am not ready for that. Why do you press my sanity? You know it teeters on the edge," I said with a glare in my eyes.

"I just want all of you to be happy," she said is an octave higher than her usual voice.

"So will you be waking up in Annapolis tomorrow?" I asked Kai, turning the tables.

"You'll never know what the moonlight and dawn will bring. I guess you'll know when you get up tomorrow," she said slyly.

I was happy for Kai. She deserved to be living up her single thirties without me to tend to at home. She was long overdue for some date nights and spoiling by guys who drooled at her feet.

I was dressed, my hair was straight, and my face was painted. A smile came automatically came across my face as I thought the word *painted*. My father had always said, "You paintin' the barn in there, Mel?" I think I was going to call home next week. It was time.

JR and Will were sitting in the hearth room watching ESPN. They were showered and dressed. JR had on jeans and a long-sleeve button-up shirt. He really was handsome, and I felt a few little butterflies in my stomach as my eyes met his. I had on Kai-approved jeans and a V-neck charcoal-gray cashmere sweater. Kai had made me take off the T-shirt I had on underneath my sweater. She said I wasn't old enough to hide the tatas yet. So I had put on a scarf before coming downstairs. I felt like a prostitute with such a low-cut shirt on and the tops of my cleavage showing, but the scarf helped, and it was winter after all.

I went and sat down next to JR.

"Hi. You ready for a DC-filled afternoon?" I asked.

"Yes, ma'am. You?" he replied.

I nodded my head yes.

"Later," he said to Will. I was certain that these two had already plotted who was staying where tonight, so not much communication was needed.

When we go to the front door, JR said, "You look beautiful."

"Thanks," I said as I felt my cheeks blush. I so wasn't used to hearing that.

"There are lots of lunch options," I said as we headed down the front steps.

"Delis, Asian, there is a Moroccan place, pizza. Your choice."

"Why don't you take me to your favorite place," JR said.

"There is this delightful little deli over by the Smithsonian that has the best sandwiches and one of the best views."

"I'm game," he said.

As we started to walk, he grabbed my hand and said, "Mel, I think I should have asked you this earlier. Do you mind that this has turned into a date weekend?"

So he was thinking about it. "No. It is actually nice. If you want the truth, I can't believe you are still around. Seriously. You saw Mt. Melanie erupt, my best friend hung over, and were interrogated by Seth at the gym. Why are you still here?" I said with a smirk.

"I like the excitement," he said with a smile. "It's nice to have a weekend off with a beautiful girl." He winked at me.

And then it happened. Out of the nowhere, I stopped, stood on my tiptoes, and kissed him right in the middle of the sidewalk on a Saturday afternoon in the nation's capital. I had no idea what came over me, but my body was no longer under the control of my brain; it was under the control of my heart. The kiss was passionate. We had no idea that we were in the middle of a city with over five million people. I was keenly aware of where JR's hands were, waiting to feel them be in violation of my moral code, but they never moved. He had his hands on my sides, my face, and back, but he kept it PG. My mind had stopped thinking, and I just soaked up the moment. I felt my blood heat up as it raced through my veins. I heard a few catcalls and whistles, so I decided it was time to stop entertaining the people of DC. As I pulled away, JR kissed me ever so gently on my forehead, and I almost melted into the sidewalk. The chemistry had been ignited.

I leaned into his shoulder while we walked.

"Do I want to know what Seth was interrogating you about?" I asked him.

"He is just protective of you. He asked how we knew each other and what I did for a living and what my intentions were with you."

"He *what?*" I asked surprised.

"He asked if I knew that you were a widow and that if I hurt you in any capacity, he would spill my blood in his ring."

"Are you kidding me? I feel like this unstable, mental case. I am sorry he spoke to you in that manner."

"No worries, Mel. It just means that people care about you, so you must be one special lady. Why does Seth care so much anyway?"

"Seth and Ryan's father were good friends. I think Seth thinks of me like a daughter."

"Has Ryan's father passed too?" JR asked.

"Yeah. He died one year after Ryan. I think he died of a broken heart from Ryan's death and mental anguish from being married to Lilith, Ryan's mother. Lilith is one crazy lady."

"I'm sorry for your losses, Mel," JR said in the most sincere voice. His eyes were even sincere.

"Thank you. So, what did you tell Seth your intentions were with me anyway?" I asked with a sly smirk on my face.

JR chuckled and said, "I told him that I had nothing but good intentions for you."

I smiled sweetly at him and a surge of an unnamed feeling rushed through my body. I startled myself because I didn't expect to feel, and now I couldn't put a label on how I felt. I decided to change the subject so I could buy myself some time to figure out what I was feeling. Was I so damaged that I couldn't even define how I was feeling? But at least I was feeling again about someone else. "Enough about my traumatic life. Tell me about your family and where you grew up," I said.

"Well, I grew up in Denver, and I am the third child of seven. I have six sisters. My mother is a preschool teacher and my father is a real-estate agent. I had a pretty typical childhood. I played baseball, soccer, and snow skied and snowboarded. With six sisters, you pretty much get left alone since they cause so much drama."

"Wow, six sisters? Tell me about them."

"It goes Lucy, Lainey, me, April, Alice, Marleigh, and Marisol. Lucy is thirty-four and is married with two daughters and lives in Dallas. Her husband, Nick, owns a few restaurants, and Lucy stays at home with my nieces. Lainey is thirty-one and is a nun. I will tell you about that later. April is twenty-six and lives in Denver. She is married to Keith and just had a son, Gavin. She teaches first grade where we all went to elementary school. Alice is twenty-four and is in the Peace Corps in the Ukraine. Marleigh is twenty-three and is currently in rehab and has a BFA in sculpture. She is an amazing painter and sculptor. Marisol is twenty-one and goes to the University of Denver and is studying biology."

"Do you get to visit often, or do they come and visit you?"

"They haven't visited me here yet, but I try to go home a few times a year, especially when Alice is in town."

"Alice is the one in the Peace Corps, right?"

"Yea. She went in right out of high school. She's always had a heart for service even when she was a little kid."

"And Lainey is a nun, right?" I asked, trying to remember everyone correctly.

"Two for two. She is a Roman Catholic nun at a convent in St. Louis, Missouri. She dropped out of college her junior year and became a nun. She just came home one weekend and told our parents and left. She never mentioned going into ministry or becoming a nun before. It was quite a shock to my folks."

"I can imagine," I replied as I tried to take in all the information.

Suddenly, I looked to my right and realized that we were standing in front of the Washington Monument. I stood there facing the beautiful symbol of America. I was always awed by the rich history of DC. Even though I walked by the Washington Monument often, it still took my breath away.

I felt JR's hand around my waist. "This monument was built in honor of the first president of the United States. It stands over

555 feet tall, and you can see for over thirty miles from the top. It was finished on December 6, 1884."

"You are quite the tour guide," JR said as he kissed my head.

"I just feel so lucky to live here and embrace my nation's history. I love being surrounded by landmarks that have a rich, meaningful past, and no matter how ugly the world gets, living in DC reminds me what it means to be an American. Don't you feel your patriotism tugging at your heart as you stand here?"

"This nation is why I am in the navy. This city is an instant reminder of why I do what I do."

We stood there in silence for a few minutes soaking in the ambiance of this country's founding fathers and the sacrifices we as a country have made for freedom and all the lives lost in exchange for it, including Ryan. If I would have been alone, I would have sat down on a nearby bench and cried, which I had done before. Just being in DC reminded me of Ryan, but my deep, personal ties to serving my country also made me cry. Compared to some parts of the world, I absolutely had nothing to cry about, except a broken heart, which people on every continent understood. There would be no tears today. I was going to channel my patriotic sentiments into the present and enjoy the freedom Ryan lived and died protecting.

A few minutes later we arrived at one of my favorite DC eateries. It hadn't changed much in four years. I scanned a paper menu, and that hadn't changed much either. As usual, the place was packed, and there wasn't a seat available in the place; there rarely was. When the weather was warm, people would sit outside anywhere they could and eat. There was a little square of grass adjacent to the cafe, and you would often see impromptu picnics on a warm and sunny day, which were treasured in DC. I loved this place for two reasons: the deliciously appetizing raspberry-mint mayonnaise they used on their sandwiches and their peach tea, which they served hot or cold.

"If you see any seats open up, grab them, and I will order," I said as I handed JR a menu.

"Any recommendations?" he asked.

"My favorite is the turkey BLT, but the American sub sandwich ranks number two." The turkey BLT had organic applewood-smoked turkey bacon, which was mouthwatering—well, at least that is what it had when I last ate it four years ago with Ryan.

I was scanning the tiny dining area to see if anyone was leaving, and I saw a couple sitting at the window bar gathering their belongings.

"I think that couple by the window is leaving. Can you snag their seats if they do? Do you know what you want?"

"Make it a BLT since it comes so highly recommended."

I ordered two turkey BLTs, two peach teas, and two orders of their famous national trail mix, which was sweet-and-salty nuts, popcorn, dried Pennsylvania apples, chocolate-covered gluten-free pretzels, and pieces of caramels. Well, at least that is what it had in it four years ago. Even though my life had drastically changed in four years, apparently my culinary memory had not.

JR had secured two chairs at the window bar, and we people watched as we waited for our food. DC, like any major metropolitan area, was a great place for people watching. I was off in my own world wondering what the stories of the people walking by were. I was suddenly snapped back into reality when JR put his hand on my thigh. I was so used to being alone that for a few seconds I forgot I was with JR.

"Tell me about your family," JR said.

"Well, you know I grew up in Whitehall, Montana. I have one brother, Mitch, who is three years older than me. My father is a police officer, and my mother was a secretary at the local elementary school. I played soccer since I was in kindergarten. Whitehall is a small farming town, so there isn't much else to tell. My brother Mitch lost an arm in a car accident when I was seventeen, and that really impacted my parents. My mother has never quite been the same since. I don't get home often—I just don't fit in there anymore."

"How's Mitch?" JR asked.

"I guess okay. He is married now and has two sons, last time I heard. It has been a few years since I talked to him."

"Why don't you talk to your family?" he asked.

"I have always thought it has to do with Mitch's accident. I was so grateful that he was alive, even though he only had one arm. I was the only one who felt that way. My parents and Mitch were very devastated and thought I was plain awful for not feeling sorry for Mitch. But I wasn't sorry for him—I thought he should be grateful that he was still alive. You can live without one arm. I became the outcast in the family at that point while all their attention was on Mitch and helping him cope. I have always been the glass-is-half-full kind of girl. When life throws me lemons, I make lemonade. I left for Stanford about sixteen months later and have only been home a few times since. My family didn't even come to Ryan's funeral. It actually has been on my conscience to call them. Life seems too short to let petty things keep you from your loved ones. But that is my exciting story."

"I can't believe they didn't come to Ryan's. Did they come to your wedding?"

"No, we eloped to Vegas. Kai was there though. Kai is like a sister to me. I can't function or live without her. Families are an interesting entity all right."

"They are. I see mine at least a few times a year. My parents don't travel as much as they used to, and they like to stay close to home, especially for Marleigh. April, Marisol, and my parents often visit Lainey. April has been trying to convince Lainey to leave the convent for a few years now. April thinks she can't possibly be happy being a nun. April and Lainey were really close growing up, and I think April really misses Lainey. I talked to my mom last week, and she said that Lucy wants to move back to Denver and is trying to convince her husband, Nick, to open a restaurant in Denver. Lucy is really close to Mom and wants her to know her granddaughters."

"Your family seems close. How do you keep it all straight?" I asked trying to get any advice that could help me get along better with mine.

"Well, when you grow up with six sisters, you kind of learn to keep up with it all. I am probably more in tune with women than most. They have made me a little girly I guess."

"So you became a SEAL to remind you of your machoism, right?"

JR laughed. "I became a SEAL to have an excuse to be 'unavailable.' As the only brother of six sisters, I am often called as the mediator."

"So why do you think Lainey became a nun? And why is Marleigh in rehab? Sorry, I don't mean to pry."

"No problem. My personal opinion of Lainey is that she is just going through a phase. We went to church every Sunday, but Lainey likes to take things to the extreme. But I don't see her being a nun forever. I guess time will tell. I have my theory about her. It is a long story that I will tell you later. As for Marleigh, she just got in with the wrong crowd, but she has been clean in rehab for a few months now. The rehab career placement program is trying to find her a job as an art teacher or art director at a gallery. I am hoping she stays clean. My parents are really supportive of her."

"Can we talk about something?" I asked. Suddenly my brain couldn't focus on anything else. I couldn't take the anxiety any longer. I would probably regret this later, but life was too short.

"Sure," JR replied smoothly. At this point he probably was not afraid of anything that came out of Mt. Melanie. I was going for it.

"What are we doing?" I asked.

"What do you mean?" JR replied.

"I mean you have stayed the entire weekend so far. Please don't take this the wrong way, but this is all so new for me. Why have you stayed? I just want it all laid out on the table."

JR put his sandwich down and turned toward me. He leaned into me and stared at me intensely. My body tensed up with anxiety of what he was going to say and do. My lips were silently chanting for a kiss, and they got one.

I put my hands on his knees and raised myself out of my chair just enough until my lips met his. I kissed him with all the passion I had in my soul. I felt the tears starting, and I was trying to fight them. A part of me was mourning Ryan as another part rejoiced for the life I had left to live.

JR whispered in my ear, "Mel, people are looking."

When I opened my eyes and came back to reality, I suddenly realized that we were still at the restaurant and the entire place and a few onlookers outside were staring. I felt my cheeks blush a little, but dang it, life was too short. It was just a kiss, people.

"Sorry," I whispered as I bit my bottom lip. "I'm not sure what came over me. But thanks. Your sisters sure did a helluva job preparing you for drama," I said. "Thanks for understanding me."

"I'll have to remember to thank them," JR said with a smile. You never have to thank me. I'm leaving on Tuesday for my next mission. As you know, everything is classified, but I will not have access to my phone. I just don't want you think I changed my mind about you because you haven't heard from me. I'll just be out of commission for a while, but I will be back."

"I want you to come back to me, but you know I have been down this road before, and it scares the daylights out of me. So I am apologizing in advance of any Mt. Mel eruptions that might occur."

JR kissed my hand and held it to his shoulder for a few seconds.

My nerves had taken over my stomach, and I suddenly couldn't eat any more. If the same thing happened to JR that had happened to Ryan, would I be strong enough to carry the pain once again? Why couldn't I pick a guy didn't have one of the most dangerous jobs on the planet? What in the world was wrong with me? Was my karma tainted?

"Is Will going with you? Can you tell me what type of mission it is or at least what part of the world it is in?"

"Yeah, Will's going with me. I can tell you that it is a reconnaissance mission in a dangerous part of the world. I'll be going by plane and boat, if that helps. I'm sorry I can't tell you more. But don't worry, I'll be back safe and sound in no time. This mission has a low risk for casualties."

Yeah right. Like not worrying was easy. I got so used to Ryan leaving that I was numb from the thought of JR leaving too. I knew that JR would never tell me anything more than he had. I had tried to make Ryan tell me using many methods over the years, but he never told me—not even when I wore my sexiest lingerie. I just had to let it go and let JR go. It was almost easier to let him go and assume that he wouldn't return, so if he did, I would be surprised. My heart was still closer to being broken then mended. But I still had a little hope laced with a little happiness run through my veins. This was better than any drug or therapy I had been prescribed. The sound of JR's voice brought me back into reality.

"So, where is my DC tour guide taking me this afternoon?" JR asked.

"Well, we have two tour options this afternoon: historic and patriotic or countryside estate. Your choice."

"A gentleman always entertains what the lady wants," he said with that warm, sexy smile that released the butterflies in my stomach.

"You may regret letting me chose," I flirted back. "Historic and patriotic it is for the navy man."

Maybe he was a gentleman, but he was indeed crazy for entertaining my ideas. But I was really beginning to like it.

I knew exactly where the historical and patriotic tour would start and end—with men. Two of my favorite men and many men in between.

"Our first stop on the afternoon historic and patriotic tour is one of the tallest phallic symbols in the world. It's made of granite, marble, and blue gneiss. As with most things in our beloved nation's capital, and the world, the building of the monument was interrupted due to war, the Civil War, for almost twenty years," I narrated. "This is why the White House needs a Mrs. President. We can multitask."

JR chuckled and said, "I didn't know that I requested the feminist tour guide. I want my money back."

"Oh, I'm sorry. There are no refunds, sir. Company policy," I replied.

As we admired the Washington Monument for the second time within a few hours, we made our way to the World War II Memorial, which was an easy walk from the monument.

"Here we are at the next stop on the historic and patriotic tour." I was really getting into this tour guide thing. "The WWII Memorial is one of the newest monuments to join the DC landscape even though WWII has been over for more than fifty years. The memorial is located at the Rainbow Pool, which is still a controversial topic. Many believe the location of the memorial at the Rainbow Pool has destroyed the historic and picturesque view between the Lincoln Memorial and the Washington Monument. With the Atlantic and Pacific Oceans anchored on each end, the fifty-six pillars representing all fifty states and US territories are cradled in between."

I was watching JR out of the corner of my eye, and he was a vision of a stoic solider. War memorials bring the severity of the price of war; it just stings your soul when you think about lives lost, families broken, and children orphaned. JR still hadn't spoken, but he was visibly moved. I knew what was going through his mind: he was looking at one possibility how his story could end. It was like looking into a mirror. I found it ironic that I had this thought since a large reflecting pool was behind us.

I took JR's hand and led him down to the Rainbow Pool and the fountains. We turned and faced the wall of stars. "There are four thousand gold stars on this wall, and each one represents one hundred Americans who died during World War II," I narrated once again. "Four hundred thousand."

"It's eye-opening to see the stars one after another laid out," JR said.

No solider likes to stare death in the face, so it was time to go to the next tour stop. I decided to lead JR out of the WWII Memorial, and we walked a windy and serene tree-lined path toward the Lincoln Memorial.

JR was still quiet as we promenaded toward Abe. I was going to ask JR if he was okay, but I started having a moment. Even though everything in my life had changed and been turned upside down, except for Kai, DC had remain my constant. Somehow the history had been my therapy. My release. My escape. The history that surrounded me made me realize I was part of something bigger, something hundreds of years deep. The soil underneath where I stood had meaning and it was something that I once risked my life for and would still risk it for.

"Mel, coffee?" I heard JR's voice say. It startled me. I didn't even realize that we had stopped walking.

"Yes, please. Five sugars and four creamers," I said.

JR smiled at me—the you're-funny smile. He better not question my coffee preferences. That would definitely hit a nerve.

"Thanks," I said as JR handed me my liquid candy.

We were almost at the Lincoln Memorial. "So, how are you enjoying the tour?" I asked.

"Educational and the scenery is breathtaking," he replied.

"I am so glad you are pleased. If you think the views have been breathtaking so far, wait to see the view from Abe."

"I forgot to inform you that this is an interactive tour," I said with a smirk. "And refunds are only granted if you beat the tour guide to the top."

I took off running as I spoke the last word. There were ninety-eight steps from the Reflecting Pool to the top. I hadn't run these steps lately—okay, years—but my adrenaline and cut-throat competitive streak would push me through. Plus I had been working out with Kai, so that had to help. Thankfully there were not many tourists here today, so dodging people wouldn't slow me down. I could hear JR's footsteps behind me, so at least he was running, and I wasn't looking like a fool tearing up these steps like a madwoman. I could hear JR's footsteps getting closer, but I knew I was still ahead. My legs burned, but I blocked out the pain. I erased it from my mind. As I came up the last ten steps, I thought I was going to collapse. My legs would not move unless I forced my mind to make them. I did a victory cheer in my head since my body could no longer move. I spun around to see where JR was. He was coming up the final three steps. He didn't look like he had even exerted himself, and instantly I was hot. I wanted a fair fight. This was the problem with chivalry—I wanted to win because I was better, not because I was a girl.

JR was breathing rather easily when he approached me.

"Did you let me win?" I quickly and sharply asked as I bumped his hip.

"Are you a sore winner?" JR retorted as he picked me up, spun me around, and kissed me.

"So is Abe here your main man?" JR asked as he put me back down, and we walked toward the nineteen-foot statue of Lincoln.

"Don't change the subject. We will discuss this later, but yes, Abe is my main man. Like Abe, I just want equality."

"My favorite spot is down here," I said as I tilted my head to the left.

I led JR down the front of the memorial until we arrived at the last two pillars.

I placed JR in the middle of the last two pillars. This was my favorite view in all of DC. It wasn't postcard perfect or unobstructed, but it was a powerful history lesson. The Rainbow Pool, the Washington Monument, WWII Memorial, the Capitol Building, the Potomac, and the reflection of the Washington Monument. I compared it to being at the top of the Eiffel Tower in Paris. You could stand in one spot and see the entire history of a country.

"I've never been up here before. Thanks for bringing me up here, Mel. I can see why you love this city and know your way around," JR said.

I looked down at my watch, and it was almost 5:00 p.m. I couldn't believe our three-site tour had taken all afternoon.

"I could use some food, Mel. How about it?" JR asked.

"Sounds good. You feel like eating in or out?" I asked softly, still in awe of the view.

"How about carryout in front of the fire?" JR proposed. "I'll take you out to dinner and dancing to celebrate my return. I need a nice, quiet evening around the fire with you before I leave. I want to soak up as much Mel as I can."

"You really do like crazy," I said with a giggle. "I like it. What kind of food are you in the mood for?"

"Lady's choice," JR said.

"Nice cop out. How about Italian? I know this great little place on the way home."

"Perfect."

I expected to see Will's Porsche in the driveway when we arrived home, but it was not there. I knew Kai could take care of herself, but it was so not like her to stay somewhere else for the night. She truly liked sleeping in her own bed. I checked my phone, and there were no messages from her. I texted her a quick message:

> We are home. Are you staying in Annapolis? You having a good time?

As I waited for Kai's return text, I got out plates and silverware and opened a bottle of Castello di Querceto Chianti Classico Riserva, one of my favorite Sangiovese Italian red wines. I preferred younger Sangioveses because they had a fresh strawberry flavor with a little spiciness. I heard my text message ringtone and it was Kai.

> I'm perfectly fine. I will be staying tonight so you can have the house to yourself. ;) I will see you sometime tomorrow. LMKIYNA.

I chuckled at the *LMKIYNA* because in my early widow days after Kai felt like she could leave me alone for an hour or so, she would text me every fifteen minutes with *LMKIYNA*—let me know if you need anything. I had to answer her within five minutes, or she would start to call to check on me.

JR had already started the fire by the time I put the food on the plates and poured the wine. I sat everything down on the coffee table and went back to the kitchen to get napkins and silverware and the wineglasses.

"I want to show you something. It will only take a minute," he said.

He led me out into the garden. I wondered what he was up to. The autumn evening air was chilly and gave me a case of the goose bumps when we stepped outside.

"Mel, I want you to look all around and tell me what you see."

"Um, okay. I see a starry night, the moonlight, hundred-year-old bricks, and tall, tall trees."

"What do you hear?"

"Um. Crickets chirping, traffic passing, leaves rustling, and the silence of the evening sky."

"Mel, if you miss me or are worried about me while I am gone, I want you to come out here and remember what you told me. These are the things I am out fighting for. You don't hear gunfire, explosions, and do not fear for your life by stepping outside. I want you to remember that I love this country more than anything, and I always come back home."

I was taken aback by JR's words, and I didn't know what to say for a few seconds. The memories of worrying over Ryan flooded back, and I began to realize that I would worry about JR too. I hated the feeling of not knowing where he was or what was happening. Back in the Ryan days, my work kept me distracted when he was gone. At least Kai and I had the Danville case to work, but it was only one case. I hoped it would be enough.

"That's sweet, JR. Thanks. And why do you think I will be missing you?" I said with a grin.

"Perhaps this will convince you," he said.

He took my face in his hands and kissed my lips with the most passion I had yet felt from JR. He moved his hands from my face to my hair and neck. He pulled me closer to him, and I thought I was going to melt. I began to feel flushed. Then he picked me up, and I instinctively wrapped my legs around his waist. He sat us down in a patio chair without losing any kissing time. My goose bumps were long gone.

We eventually made our way back inside. The warmth of the fire and the glasses of wine put a permanent rosy blush on my cheeks. After we finished our dinner, we were Kai-and-Will snuggly on the couch. We told stories about training missions, places in the world we had been, and college days. I learned that JR was an amateur snowboarder in his younger days. He said he would teach me since he couldn't believe that I had never skied before. And then JR started talking about Lainey.

"You aren't the only one with a ghost. My sister Lainey has one too. This is my theory about why she became a nun," JR began. "When Lainey was nineteen, she had a son and gave him up for adoption. The father, who was Lainey's first love, left her after she told him she was pregnant. He spread rumors that Lainey had cheated on him and was pregnant with another man's baby. It broke Lainey's heart. She started talking about adoption and how she didn't want to be a single mother whose son didn't have an involved father. My parents begged her to keep the child and offered to help her with the baby while she finished college. She gave the baby up anyway and has never seen him again. Lainey was really quiet after that and finished out her sophomore year. She talked to me a lot back then, and she told me that she wanted to become a nun. I told her to stay in school and give it some time. I thought it was just a phase. She came home one day during her junior year and told my parents that she was leaving college to become a nun to serve the God who she believed forgave her for her sin and granted her grace."

"Wow. My heart breaks for her. Are you two still close? Is she doing okay?" I asked as I tried to comprehend the pain and ghost of his sister.

"Not as close as we were. She is really quiet these days. I feel like she has lost herself and is serving a life of solitude as her punishment. I hate to see my sisters hurting, but I never imagined having a sister as a nun. I don't think it is her life calling.

"They are all lucky to have you as a brother," I said. No wonder he was good with crazy women—and that was only one of his sisters.

"You up for another story? Do you want to hear my theory about how Alice ended up in the Peace Corps?"

"Sure," I replied as I snuggled in closer to JR.

"Alice joined the Peace Crops after graduation, but I really think she followed a guy. Alice thinks nobody knows this, but I do. I was home from the Naval Academy one weekend, and I saw her get into this guy's car. So I followed them."

"You followed them?" I asked.

"Yes because I know what young guys want with beautiful girls," JR replied.

"I followed them to the Denver Peace Corps office. She left a few months later. And the rumor around town is that this guy left too for the Peace Corps."

"Does anyone else know about this guy? Are they still together?" I asked.

"I don't know. No one else in my family has ever mentioned him and according to my family, Alice doesn't have a boyfriend."

"If you want, Kai and I could do some PI work for you on the two of them. Free of charge of course," I said.

"That would be awesome. And if you find out anything or if he has put his hands on my sister, I am hunting him down."

"JR, she is grown woman. You can't hunt down her love interests."

"I just want to scare him," JR said.

My eyelids were heavy, and I was having difficulty focusing.

"Mel, you look tired. You ready for bed? Come on, I'll take you."

"Sorry, I am. I can put myself to bed. The couch is yours, or you can have Kai's bed. She isn't coming home." I hope JR didn't think he was going to get some since he was leaving Tuesday for who knows where for who knows how long. I was about to find out if JR was really the gentleman he portrayed himself to be.

"The couch is fine, and I *am* putting you to bed."

JR scooped me up and carried me upstairs. He sat on my bed while I washed my face, brushed my teeth, and put on my very unsexy pajamas—yoga pants and an old T-shirt. There was no reason to tease the poor guy. I pulled down the sheets and crawled into bed.

"Thanks for bringing me to bed before I turned into a pumpkin," I said.

JR chuckled. "Well, you could give Cinderella a run for her money in your pj's."

I smiled as I watched JR slide over my body very slowly until he was next to me. He had taken his time, and his hands carefully and gingerly had brushed the bottom of my bra. I wasn't comfortable enough to not have on a bra in front of JR. There was no need for him to see the tatas sag. My push-up bra was one of my wardrobe staples. It was just a weird quirk I had. I just felt more comfortable in a bra.

All of a sudden I had butterflies in my stomach, and I was nervous. Nervous about what JR's next move would be and what I wanted it to be. He kissed my forehead, and I had to decide if I was going to be a lady or not. The butterflies were stirring up all kinds of feelings in my body that I hadn't felt in years. I could totally find out if JR was a gentleman or if I could get him to be bad. I was very surprised at myself for how I felt. I hadn't had a guy in my bed in four years, and the first one that comes along and I am having an internal argument about if I am going to be a lady or not. JR started kissing my neck, and I was getting more nervous by the millisecond. JR was still calm and collected. He knew exactly where to put his hands and was taking it slow—like he wanted to make the moment last as long as possible. Maybe he secretly knew I wasn't going to put out. His hand made its way underneath my T-shirt and within a second he had my bra unstrapped, and I gasped.

"Sorry, Mel," JR said as he immediately retracted his hand.

"I just wasn't expecting that," I replied as I guided his hand back under my shirt. I couldn't control myself.

JR was absolutely in control as he become familiar with every curve of my body. I was mustering up the strength to stop before it got to the point of no return, and I made the decision to be a lady.

I broke my lips away from JR's.

"I can't do this tonight. I'm sorry," I said breathlessly.

"Come here," he said as he pulled me into him.

He kissed my forehead, and I snuggled up to him once more. I closed my eyes and forced the feelings away before I drifted off to sleep on JR.

EARTHQUAKE

I was shaken awake by a deep vibration and rumbling. A panic went over me when my brain filtered the possibility that this was an earthquake. I had been in Los Angeles once when an earthquake hit, and as the floor moves beneath your feet, it takes you a few minutes to understand that the ground *really* is moving. I immediately went into agent mode and did a surveillance of the room for further earthquake evidence. Nothing was swaying or moving, but the floor was still vibrating, and I could still hear the rumbling. I quickly looked to see if JR was still next to me, and he was. I wondered if he felt the vibrating and heard the rumbling. Suddenly, it was dead silent.

"JR," I whispered. Do you feel something?" I asked. "Is it an earthquake?"

He sat up and was instantly awake. "No, I don't feel anything. What's going on?" he asked me.

"I heard rumbling and felt the floor shake. I'm going to check it out," I said.

"Let's go," JR said as he got out of bed.

As soon as my foot hit the bottom step, the doorbell rang. I jumped back and almost fell off the last step. The last sound I expected to hear was the doorbell. I was trying to calculate how fast it would take for me to go back upstairs and get my gun and load it. Before I had made up my mind, JR peeped out the peephole.

"It is an older woman," he said to me. "Should I open the door?"

He moved out of the way so I could look out, and as soon as I saw the "older woman," I gasped.

"Mel, are you all right? Who is this woman?" JR inquired.

"Lilith Alexander. My ex-mother-in-law."

Before I could provide any further instructions, JR opened the door.

"Well, it's about time you opened this door. I was starting to think that you were going to ignore me out here," said the voice of the devil.

As I looked behind the leather-clad sixty-something lady standing on my porch, I saw it. I saw the source of my morning wake-up call. A pink Harley Davidson motorcycle. Lilith even had the gray spike haircut to go with it. I looked her up and down, and she had on a black leather jacket, fringed chaps, and black knee-high boots. A hot-pink helmet with skulls, crossbones, and hearts was in her hand. I saw painted on the side "RIP, Ryan."

I silently prayed, *Please let this all be a very bad nightmare. Please let me wake up.*

"It is nice to see you too, Lilith," I sarcastically said. I no longer had any connection to this woman, and I was going to give her the seven years of anger she had caused me. Paybacks were hell.

"My, my, my, Melanie Alexander, if that is still your last name these days. I now see why you haven't returned my calls. You've been out chasing some tail."

"So, are you the tail Melanie has been chasing?" Lilith said directly to JR.

"Ma'am. I'm Lieutenant Commander Jenner Romero. It is a pleasure to meet you."

"I see you are making your way through the military branches."

"When did you get a Harley? Did you ride it all the way from LA?" I asked her through gritted teeth.

"Well, darling, you never return my phone calls, so I just had to get out here and see what you were up to. I was deathly afraid that your alcohol problem had gotten worse. I have been worried sick." She put her hand up to her mouth and whispered to JR, "You know she has a drinking problem, right?"

As JR and I stood there in shock of what had just come out of her mouth, Lilith showed herself the way to the kitchen. I gave JR the crazy signal, and he smacked me on the behind as we went into the kitchen. He had a smile on his face. Yeah, like this was fun.

I decided to be as civil as possible since JR was present and thought coffee was the way to go. "Can I pour everyone some coffee?" I asked in my sweetest, most fake voice ever.

"There's probably not much else to drink except alcohol, so I guess I'll have some coffee," replied Lilith.

"I would like some too, Mel. Thanks," JR said. He decided to stand at the kitchen island.

"So, Lilith, how have you been? How's LA?" I asked her in a less sweet, fake voice, but it still came out sounding like I cared. Well, I thought it did anyway.

"LA's sunny. Mel, I know you've never been a big fan of me, but I really do love you. I came here to check on you and to visit Ryan. I hoped if I came all the way out here, since you haven't made your way to LA, we could spend a few days together. We are all each other has left of Ryan," Lilith said.

And that was it. Mt Melanie started to smoke as I heard these words. She was lying through her teeth. She was not a fan of me—now or ever. There was no way in hell I was going to spend time with her. And my memories of being *married* to Ryan reminded me of him—not *her*!

"It is nice to see you, but Kai and I have a case we are working and I really can't take any time off," I said through gritted teeth. "And for the record, you have never liked me and have said horrible things to me over the years and I don't visit you for a reason. My memories of being married to Ryan are what connects me to him *not you*!" I said in an escalated and not so nice voice.

Oh crap! I thought to myself. I had lost it, but I couldn't take this woman!

"Well, well. I should have come a long time ago because Kai has let you become a mean, crazy drunk."

"*A WHAT?*" I shouted.

"Ma'am, would like to step outside with me for some fresh air?" JR said to Lilith. I knew he was trying to mediate the situation, but I had this.

The five foot one Lilith got up out of her chair, pushed the chair over to where JR was standing, and stood on top of it. She stood nose to nose with JR and said, "I don't care what type of officer you are or if you are Melanie's current flavor of the week. You will not escort me out of my son's house."

She then turned to me and said, "It is such a shame. You are such a pretty girl, Melanie."

Mt. Melanie was shooting hot, burning lava into the air. I picked up her bag and her helmet and walked to the front door. I opened the door and threw them down on the stairs.

Lilith came into the entry and slapped me across the cheek. "It breaks my heart all over again to think that my precious Ryan spent the last years of his life with you. Since I am not wanted here, I am going to go talk to Ryan. Good day."

Lilith walked out of the door mumbling her crazy thoughts. I slammed the door and locked all the locks. I seriously needed a drink now.

"So, that was Lilith," I said to JR who was standing next to me speechless, with no expression on his face. He was examining my cheek.

"It doesn't hurt. It just stings, but if a slap was all it took to get her out of my house, I'll take it. I would have taken a gunshot."

JR was still silently examining my face.

"Remember, I have six sisters. I think I need to smolder Mt. Melanie," JR said.

He started kissing me, and all the tension in my body was released. Mt. Melanie was starting to recede. We stood there in the entry kissing for what seemed like minutes, and then the whole house shook as the sow started up her HOG.

I think I better take you back to bed so you can sober up," JR said jokingly.

"*Very funny*, flavor of the week," I replied back.

"Actually I think a brisk morning walk will sober you right up," JR said. "Go get dressed and I'll make breakfast to go."

"So where are you taking me this morning?"

"It is a surprise, but it will definitely be breakfast with a view."

I wondered what JR had up his sleeve and it put a smile on my face. I needed an escape after Lilith. I told myself I would analyze the Lilith visit with Kai and to focus on my time with JR. I put on a clean t-shirt, zip-up hoodie, brushed my teeth, pulled my hair into a pony tail, threw on some mascara, and went downstairs.

JR was wrapping up egg sandwiches as I entered the kitchen. "Those look yummy," I said.

"Breakfast to go," he said. "We'll get you coffee on the way. Give me five minutes and I'll be ready to go."

He kissed me on the cheek as he headed upstairs. I found a bag for the sandwiches and leaned against the island replaying the events of the morning. The sun wasn't even up yet and I had plenty to think about. I wondered why Lilith had come all the way from LA to visit. What did she really want? Before I had time to think about much else, JR grabbed my hand and we were out the front door.

"So tell me about Lilith. What was that all about this morning?" JR asked as we walked.

"Oh yes, the lovely Lilith. I honestly believe that she has two personalities. She always acted so sweet and perfect in front of Ryan, but as soon as he was out of sight and hearing range, she was the Lilith you saw this morning. Ryan never believed that his mother treated me this way, so I just tried to ignore her and not be available when it was time for a visit. Work was a really good excuse back then, but now apparently she just shows up. This is the first time she has shown up since Ryan passed. She constantly calls and leaves these ridiculous messages on my phone, but I never return them. As you heard, she thinks I have a drinking problem, which I don't. She stayed here with me and Kai for two weeks after Ryan died, and when I had a martini or two on a daily basis, she began to say I had a drinking problem and that is what killed Ryan. She said that I had had a drinking problem for years, and it drove Ryan to work too much, which led him to go on that mission. Kai made her leave after a few weeks, so Kai isn't on the Lilith-approved people list either. When Ryan's father passed away of a heart attack, Lilith really went over the deep end, and I can't blame her. She gets crazier and more obnoxious as the years pass."

"I'm sorry, Mel. That's a lot to handle," JR said.

"It's okay. Part of me feels sorry for her because I can relate to her grief. Another part of me wants to punch her face," I said. JR chuckled.

I heard my cell phone text message ringtone and knew it had to be Kai. Who else would it be?

> Morning. We are going for a run around Annapolis, and then I will be home. Will has to report to work soon. I hope you had a memorable evening :)

I texted her back with this:

> We had a memorable morning: Lilith stopped by for a visit, I threw her out, and she slapped me. The usual. JR is taking me out for breakfast. Don't know where.

Almost immediately, she responded:

> *Shut up!* Lilith was there? I can't believe I missed it. Happy breakfasting. Miss you. LMKIYNA.

"Kai and Will are running in Annapolis this morning before she heads back here," I said.

"I think Will has found a new running partner in Kai," JR said.

"You jealous?" I said with quite a bit of sass as I bumped into him.

"No. I'm thinking of taking up boxing," JR said with a smile.

"Oh, I thought maybe you were taking up boxing so you didn't lose to any more girls," I asked playfully.

JR put his arm around me and squeezed me tight. "I hate to burst your big, bad Mel bubble, but I let you win," he said. He started rubbing my jacket where the scar on my arm was.

"I am big, bad Mel. You saw how I threw out Lilith this morning. Heck, not even a rifle to the arm harms me," I said almost laughing.

"Your body tells a story, Mel. The ink, the scars, and the beauty."

"Not a story, a saga," I said.

"So where is our breakfast destination?" I asked him.

"My favorite place and your favorite place," he said, still ambiguous.

When the Lincoln Memorial came into view, which was my favorite DC landmark, I thought about JR's clue. This was *my* favorite place, but he has never said anything about it being his.

"So, is the Lincoln Memorial your favorite spot too?" I asked.

"Nope, but it's yours."

I apparently needed some coffee, which I was still a little ticked off that we hadn't stopped for some. We *would be* stopping on the way back; well, at least I would be stopping.

After staring at my good buddy Abe, it finally hit me as I turned my head, and my eyes followed the blue, glittering water with the white stripe to the other side. JR's favorite place must be the Washington Monument, which just happened to be at the other end of the water. I guess we were going to be dining alfresco–style this morning at the Rainbow Pool, which got its name because the Lincoln Memorial and Washington Monument are reflected in its water.

"Nice choice for breakfast," I said. "Actually, it is the perfect place for breakfast."

JR and I sat down on the steps of the Lincoln Memorial. The autumn air was a bit nippy, but the scenery and the company made the cold unnoticeable to me. JR wrapped his massive arm around me and nestled me in closer to him as we ate our sandwiches. As I looked at the beautiful, white obelisk in front me, I felt myself arrive at a place I hadn't visited in a long time: peace. My soul was a stranger to peace, and it was being cautious. I inhaled a deep breath of brisk autumn East Coast air, and it stung my nostrils on the way in.

DC was so peaceful at this hour. The perfectly still water of the Rainbow Pool was almost hypnotizing. My mind was off thinking about the early years of our country and how John Adams must have felt to be the first president to reside in the White House. And how a group of men wanted a better life for their families and all future generations. Why was I thinking of early American history? Maybe once you started drinking DC water, you became patriotic and it just ran through your veins. I got up and walked down to the edge of the pool. I leaned over just far enough so I could see my face, my reflection. Stress and sadness may have carved a few more wrinkles on my face, but I was recognizable to myself. I hadn't felt connected to myself in so long that mirrors were painful to look in and pass by. Over the past four years, they were constant reminders that I was Melanie the Widow, single again, and without Ryan. But for the first time, I saw me, and I didn't have any tears staring back at me. It was symbolic being here. My past was at one end of the Rainbow Pool and my future at the other. All of a sudden, an image joined mine; it was JR.

"You all right?" he asked.

"I am not thinking about jumping in if that is what you are asking," I replied back.

"Just so you know, I am a pretty good swimmer, so I would jump in and save you."

"I would never imagine that a navy man wouldn't know how to swim, but that is good to know."

"Attitude," JR said.

"You better believe it," I said.

JR gamely shook his head and put his arm around my waist, and we stood there in silence for a few seconds.

"Thanks for breakfast and for bringing me here. It is beautiful at this hour."

"It is an instant reminder of why I do what I do. It is images such as these that keep me focused when things get rough. I just pull up these images in my mind and remember why I joined the navy. I would risk my life every day in every locale in the world so my family and the most beautiful girl in the world could wake up free."

"You're a good man, Jenner Romero." I nestled my head under JR's chin and stared at the water for a few minutes.

We sat back down on the steps and ate. My sandwich was cold, but it didn't matter. I leaned into him and admired the view. Between the cold sandwich and the nippy wind, my hands were like blocks of ice. JR grabbed one and said, "You're freezing. Come on, let's head back."

As I took one last look at a view I have seen a million times, I felt different about it. My love for this country sometimes took the sting out of Ryan's passing because I truly knew what it mean to be an American. I was feeling hopeful. Hopeful that even after great personal tragedy, I still had the option to flourish. The option to freely be me. The option to mourn my Ryan while cherishing the breaths I had left to live in one of the greatest countries on the planet. Kai should win the Therapist of the Year Award. Maybe I had rejoined the world of the living.

We were approaching my preferred coffee spot, and I told JR we were stopping. I ordered spiced pecan, my seasonal favorite. It tasted like liquid pecan pie and reminded me of my mother's. I always looked forward to her pies every Thanksgiving and Christmas. She always made a pecan pumpkin cheesecake on New Year's Day. It was her way of blessing the New Year with sweetness. A streak of home sickness raced through me, and for the first time in years, I felt the inkling to go home.

As we approached the brownstone, I saw a black Porsche in the driveway and was relieved that Kai was finally back.

"Hey, girl," I said to Kai as we stepped into the kitchen.

"Hey. Hey, JR," she replied.

Will was right behind her. Kai looked incredibly happy to the point of being a giggly school girl.

"Hey, Mel," Will said.

"Hey."

"JR, man, you ready to hit the road?" Will suggested.

"Yeah, we should get moving. I just need to get my bag," JR replied as he headed upstairs. I followed him.

As soon as we were out of sight, JR scooped me up in his arms and madly kissed me all the way up the stairs. He sat down on my bed with me still in his arms.

"Please try to not get yourself shot while I am gone," he said slyly. "I promise I will be back. I'll probably miss Christmas, so 'Merry Christmas' early." He kissed my forehead this time.

"Merry Christmas in whatever language you'll be using at the time," I said.

"And Happy New Year if I miss that too," JR said as he kissed my cheek, then my neck, and then my lips.

"Good luck with your case. I hope you find your MP," he said.

MP was code for "missing person."

"Thanks, me too and thanks for the amazing weekend. I guess this is good-bye. I guess I should tell you to have a safe trip, but it feels like a bad omen."

"Mel, don't worry about me. I'll be back.

He sat me on the bed and got up and grabbed his bag. I didn't even remember him bringing it up, but apparently he had. He grabbed my hand, and we went downstairs.

The front door was open, and Kai and Will were standing by Will's Porsche talking. JR kissed me on the lips and said, "I hope you have a wonderful holiday season with Lilith." He could hardly get it out due to the laughing.

"Funny. Hopefully her HOG takes her back to the pig sty she came from," I said.

"Bye, Mel," JR said as he kissed my lips and got into his car.

HYDRATION

"We are staying up until I have heard every last detail about you and JR," Kai said to me.

"Same goes for you too, girl," I replied back.

"Fair enough," Kai said. "Should we start with coffee or gin?"

"Oh, I so missed you! Only you would suggest gin before noon and not think that I need rehab. Let's start with coffee, I could use another cup. But don't worry, we'll get the gin out. I'll need it when I tell you about Lilith's visit."

We settled into our usual seats in the hearth room with our cups of coffee and a warm, roaring fire. I loved having a fire going in the house in the late fall and winter months. It took the chill out of the air and was almost as peaceful as listening to the waves lap the shore. I found much comfort sitting with Kai after the whirlwind weekend.

"Spill it," Kai said. "And I am pissed that I missed Lilith. She always puts on a good show."

"It seems like the weekend was weeks long. So much happened that I don't even know where to start. Okay. After you left for Annapolis, I took JR to Mattie's for lunch, and he told me that Seth had interrogated him at the gym asking him what his intentions were with me. So embarrassing."

"So what did JR say?" Kai said.

"That he had nothing but the best intentions for me and then Seth told him that if he didn't, he would spill his blood in the ring."

"Awwww, I think it' sweet. You know Seth watches out for us like a father would."

"I know, but I hate having people in my business. I learned a little about JR's family. He has six sisters. His mother is a pre-school teacher and his father is a real estate agent. His sisters are an interesting bunch. One of them, Lainey, is a Roman Catholic nun. Another one, Alice, is in the Peace Corps in the Ukraine. His sister Marleigh is in rehab. I think he has two nieces and one nephew. I think his youngest sister, Marisol, is still in college."

"Interesting. What a hot mess of siblings," Kai commented.

"Well, if you think that is a hot mess, let me tell you what I did in the middle of Mattie's. I flat out asked JR what was going on—like why he had stayed the weekend." Kai gave me this no-you-didn't look.

"I know, I know, but I am so out of sorts that I couldn't stand the unknown. So I asked him."

"So, what did he say?" Kai asked.

"Well, he didn't respond with words; he responded with a kiss. I am a maniac, Kai." I just leaned over and totally kissed his face. Like full-out kissing in the middle of the cafe. I had totally forgotten where I was. JR pulled away and told me that people were looking. And they were! They were outside looking through the windows too! I have no idea where it all came from."

"Damn, girl. I am proud of you for going after it," Kai said.

"I feel crazy—like I can't predict or understand my emotions."

"I don't think you're crazy. Maybe JR isn't afraid to say how he feels. Maybe he knows how short life can be and doesn't waste any moments. He knows about Ryan, so maybe he just wants to lay it out on the table for you. Or maybe he is just trying to get you in bed. The main rule about guys hasn't changed: they still think with their little brain. So, trying to get you in bed is always a valid option us girls have to consider. Did he get you into bed?"

"No. I didn't sleep with him."

"*What!* I was so certain that you would," Kai said as she almost stood up out of her chair.

"I told you I wasn't going to. My head has been going in a million directions all weekend. You may be in for a long night."

"Mel, look. You have been on an emotional roller coaster for four years, due to no fault of your own. I expect you to feel confused, anxious, and uncertain about the JR situation. It is all new and tugs at the most vulnerable part of you—your heart. You can't expect yourself to know what you should feel and what you should say. Just enjoy the moment and take it one day at a time. I know you are worried about the occupational risks, but you need to be happy again."

"JR is very much the gentleman, which is another thing that freaks me out. He isn't fazed by how I feel or how I react. He wasn't shaken by my Mt. Melanie eruptions when he told me about Ryan or when Lilith rang the doorbell. Is he human?" I asked.

"I know I have told you this before, but maybe it is just your time to be happy once again," Kai said. "Karma does come around."

"Maybe I have forgotten what it is like to be happy. Maybe I should stop analyzing every word and every action and reaction. It wears me out. Tell me about Will and Annapolis. You seem happy as little schoolgirl in love."

"Funny. I wouldn't say that I am 'in love,' as you know how I am with the L-word. But I think I really do like him—like Carlos like him. He showed me around downtown Annapolis, and we ate dinner at this really charming restaurant near the water. After dinner he took me out on his friend's boat for an evening ride. It was so cold, but there is something about being on the water under the moonlight. It was romantic. We went back to his and JR's place, which is a total bachelor pad, had some wine, and talked," Kai said.

"You just *talked?*" I said it my most sassy voice. Kai knew exactly what I was asking. "But I don't need to know what else you did because I am stuck on the fact that you 'Carlos' like him. Keep talking."

"Well, I found out that he was raised by a single father and has never met his mother. A part of me is hoping he wants us to help him find her, but I am not going down that road until he wants to. But who says we can't snoop?" Kai said with her sneaky-eyebrow-raise look.

"We sure can snoop. What else are we going to do while they are away?" I said.

"*Oh my gosh*—I totally forgot about Lilith! Tell me! Tell me!" Kai almost shouted at me.

"Oh yeah, Lilith. I had forgotten for a few minutes that Lilith even existed," I said as I let out a huge sigh.

"Saturday night JR slept in bed with me; well, I think he did. I fell asleep on him, so I am not sure where he ended up. Anyway. I heard this horrible rumbling, and I thought it was an earthquake. JR was next to me in bed asleep and I woke him—he hadn't heard anything. We went downstairs and then the doorbell rang. He looks out the peephole and says it is an older woman, and I immediately knew it was the devil herself."

"Unbelievable," Kai chimed in.

"JR opens the door, and Lilith is decked out in motorcycle gear, leather chaps and all, and has a pink helmet in her hands. It had skulls and crossbones and said 'RIP Ryan' on it. I can see her HOG parked out front, and it is pink! She then proceeds to ask if Melanie Alexander is still my name these days, and when she looked at JR, she said that she knew why I hadn't returned her calls. She then gets in JR's face and asked him if he is the tail I have been out chasing."

"*Shut up.* She called JR 'tail'? She is either overmedicated or needs to be medicated. What did JR do?"

"He introduced himself as Lieutenant Commander Jenner Romero, and then Lilith says that I am making my way through the military branches." Kai's jaw dropped, but no words came out.

I continued. "I asked her if she rode her HOG all the way from LA, and she said that since I never return her calls, she just had to come out and check on me because she was afraid that my alcohol problem had gotten worse. She then turned to JR and put up her hand to her mouth, like I couldn't hear the crazy spewing out of her mouth, and told JR that I have a drinking problem."

"I am speechless. She's mental," Kai said.

"I really made the effort to be civil; it didn't last long, but I did try. I asked her if she wanted coffee and how LA was. Then she said that she knew I had never been a big fan of her and she loved me," I said.

"Oh what a liar she is. She's never liked you," Kai interjected.

"She said she wanted to come out and visit me since I've never made it to LA because we are all each other has left of Ryan," I continued. Kai was speechless and was shaking her head, so I went on. "I was starting to get hot, but was trying to keep my cool. I told her that you and me had a case we were working and I couldn't take any time off. Then I lost it. I told her she never liked me, had said horrible things to me over the years, and that my memories of Ryan connect me to him and not *her*!" I shouted.

"Unbelievable," Kai says under her breath.

"So JR trying to mediate things asks if Lilith wants to step outside with him and I guess she took that to mean she had to leave because guess what she did next?"

"What?" Kai cautiously asks.

"She gets on a kitchen chair and stands nose to nose with JR and says something to the effect that she doesn't care what type of officer he is or if he is my flavor of the week and that he will not be escorting her out of her son's house. Then she said that she should have come a long time ago because you let me become a mean, crazy drunk."

"*She said I did what?*" Kai screamed.

"She said you turned me into a mean, crazy drunk." I could hardly keep a straight face.

Kai got up and got the gin and poured some into our coffee cups.

"I am going to beat her face the next time I see her," Kai said.

"Hey, if you were to marry Will right now, you wouldn't get a mother-in-law," I said.

"Damn good point. That might just work out."

"Oh, there's more. She said something to me about how it was a shame that I was a drunk because I am such a pretty girl. I picked up her helmet and her purse and threw them down the front steps. I told her she was next if she didn't leave. And then she *slapped* my face. *Slapped it!*"

"She slapped your face? *Oh my sweet heaven!*"

"But it doesn't end there. She then said how it broke her heart to think that her precious Ryan spent the last years of his life with me."

"I'm pissed that I missed the Lilith freak show," Kai said.

"JR seemed to take it all with a good sense of humor. After she left he said he needed to smolder Mt. Melanie and then he kissed me. He said that I needed a brisk morning walk to sober up. He told me to get dressed while he made breakfast to go." I said.

"Oh yeah, you said he took you out to breakfast. Where did you go?" Kai asked.

"He took me to the Rainbow Pool, and we sat on the steps and ate egg sandwiches." I said with a smile.

"JR seems rather thoughtful since you love the Lincoln Memorial. Hmmmm—he is so into you," Kai said as she raised her eyebrows at me.

"Yea, it was very thoughtful of him to pack a breakfast and take me to my favorite spot to watch the sun rise. It was really sweet. I enjoyed myself," I said. Before Kai could question or comment on all of that I quickly asked, " How was your morning run?"

"Our morning run was nice. Annapolis is really pretty, and it is nice to have a running partner again since someone doesn't run with me anymore. And don't think for one second I don't know that you just tried to switch up the topics. We are not finished talking about JR," she said.

I shot Kai the shut-up look since she referenced me as the "running partner" and then she accused me of switching the topic. She wasn't fazed and went on, "We stopped for some breakfast at this place by their house. It was a little organic café. Based on what you told me about JR, I think Will is the more maverick of the two. After I got the Annapolis tour on Saturday, we went to the shooting range, and then he took me on a twenty-mile bike ride on a trail called the Annapolis Ramble. He just happened to have a spare bike, which I didn't ask about. The trail was scenic, and in the middle of it is this park, which we stopped at. It seems like you and JR had more intimate conversations this weekend and Will and me had more physical interactions. If I wasn't physically attracted to him, he would be a good buddy to hang with. But we have this chemistry. It is intense. He said he would call me when he got back, and that is how we left it. We will see where it goes. You know me, I don't really get all gaga crazy. There are plenty of men out there."

"We have always known that the quantity of men isn't the problem—it is the quality," I said.

Kai chuckled. "You got that right."

"I am actually looking forward to getting back to work on the Danville case tomorrow. I need a distraction from JR and the current state of my life. I need to find normalcy. My life has yet to be stable in four years. Am I a widow, or am I a girlfriend? I just need to find out who Mel is now. I need to work," I said.

"I hear you. I am thrilled that you want to find out who Mel is now. And we should have plenty of time to work over the next few weeks. What should we do for the rest of the day and dinner? I think we drank our lunch," Kai said.

"Hey, there is nothing wrong with a liquid lunch. I say we get some carryout and a can of paint. I want to feng shui my room. What do you say we eat, drink, and paint?" I asked.

"Sounds perfect."

ICING

I heard the ringtone on my BlackBerry and saw that it was nine thirty at night. Who was calling me? I didn't recognize the number.

"Good evening," I answered.

"Melanie?" I heard a strangely familiar voice ask as my mind began racing to associate the voice with a name and face. I was getting mad at myself the longer my brain processed the voice. There was also a strange background noise on the line—it sounded like an announcer over a loud speaker or bull horn.

"Yes, this is Melanie Alexander."

"Hey, it's Oliver Parrish." Kai gave me a "Who in the heck is on the phone" look when she saw my jaw drop. I mouthed the name "Oliver Parrish" to her and her jaw dropped as well. I immediately put the phone on speaker because this call was going to be entertaining because Oliver Parrish was quite the shady character. And where was he? I continued to hear the announcer, and I closed my eyes to see if I could isolate the words being announced.

"Oliver, this is quite a surprise. How are ya doing these days?" I said with a swagger. Kai and I trusted Oliver about as much as we trusted a hostage taker who had nothing to lose.

"Well, Melanie, it sounds like you have the spring back in your step. I'm doing just fine. I'm calling to see if you and Kai are still PIs," Oliver said with a patronizing tone I didn't appreciate. And then it hit me—*OMG*—Oliver was at bingo. Or at least that is what my brain determined from its analysis. Bingo? Was he scheming money off the top or was he really hard up for some cash? I scribbled the phrase "He's at Bingo?" on a piece of paper in my bedroom so Kai would know what I was thinking. She mouthed "Creepy" to me and I almost had to cover my mouth to keep from laughing.

"Well, I am glad so glad to hear that you are doing just fine," I said again with my swagger voice. And yes, Kai and I are still PIs. Can we be of assistance?" Even though the background noise was muffled, I swear I could pick out Bingo numbers being called.

"I have a case I am hoping you and Kai could take on for me. I am currently tied up with cases in my legal practice and do not have the time, so I thought I would throw this one over to y'all. I believe you like tracking down people," Oliver said. By the look on Kai's face, I thought she was going to cuss him out. She squinted her eyes and wrinkled up her nose, which were the precursors to Kai's temper and temperature rising. And this wouldn't be our first run in with Mr. Parrish either.

"Oh, I didn't know you were practicing law again. Are you moonlighting for the Agency or are you in private practice?" I asked, sounding a little bothered. My mind was still replaying the phrase "I would throw this one over to y'all." I almost wanted to pause and ask him to repeat himself to see if he was really stupid enough to say it twice. And my guess would be that he was. If my memory was right, Oliver was an attorney before coming to the agency, which is how we had the pleasure of knowing him.

"Private practice. I left the agency last year to pursue my practice," he said quickly. There was a story there and by the look on Kai's face, she thought the same.

"I have a probate client who recently had a stroke and I am unable to locate her son, who is the power of attorney. The son, Hal Mercer, is married to a Cammie Mercer also of Richmond. All of their contact information leads to a dead end and I cannot turn up any leads on them. You and your partner interested?" he asked abruptly.

Before I could respond, I glanced over at Kai and she was writing Bingo numbers on the piece of paper. I almost laughed out loud again.

"Let me talk to Kai and I'll get back to you. How soon do you need to know?" I asked. I already knew the answer would be "No." Kai and I would not get mixed up in any of Oliver's schemes, and this story had "scheme" written all over it.

"As soon as possible or I'm going to have to find someone else to take it," he said trying to pressure me.

"I'll try to call you tomorrow," I said. By the look of annoyance on my face Kai knew we would not be taking this case.

"Let me know ASAP," Oliver said.

"Will do and it was lovely to hear from you," I said in my fake swagger voice.

"As always, it is my pleasure. Give Kai my regards," Oliver replied. "Good night."

"Good night," I politely replied and then I hung up the phone.

"What a blast from the past—Oliver Parrish," Kai said with a smirk on her face and then we both just burst out laughing.

"What in the world is he up to?" I asked Kai in between my laughs. Maybe it was the gin, but I had tears in my eyes now from laughing so hard.

"I don't know, but you know it is probably illegal. And he didn't leave the agency to pursue his private practice. I bet he got *fired*," Kai said.

"You'll have to ask around to get the scoop. But he sure has some balls calling us up to throw us a bone," I said. "Apparently he forgot what Mel and Kai are made of."

"OMG! Are you thinking of the Sawyer case when we first encountered Oliver Parrish? Kai asked.

I hadn't thought of our first Oliver Parrish experience in years, but it was now at the forefront of my mind.

"How could I forget? You almost kicked his teeth in. Remember what he said to us?" I asked.

"Oh, Mel, please do the impression, please?" Kai begged as she laughed.

"I believe he said in his heavy twang, 'Dang, aren't you two a tall double drink of water? Whose calendars do you keep?'"

Kai and I started laughing as soon as my imitation of the Oliver Parrish twang rolled off my tongue. My Oliver Parrish imitation turned us into laughing hyenas—the kind of laughter that just keeps coming. Kai was laughing so hard that she couldn't talk, but I could vividly see and hear in my mind what Kai said to Oliver. So, I began in my best Kai impression, "Excuse me. I am not sure who you think we are, but we don't keep anyone's calendars. We are the agents you will be working the Sawyer case with, but you don't look like you'll be of much help."

Kai was now doubled over laughing on the floor of my room. I was laughing pretty hard myself, and we just couldn't stop. It felt really good to laugh this way. You can't possibly think of all the nonsense in your life when you are lying on the floor laughing like a drunken hyena. See, I didn't need a therapist—a little alcohol and Kai were all I needed.

We had finished painting my room this lovely butter cream. It literally reminded me of icing, and I had been craving a big piece of cake the entire time we were painting. We would shop for a new bedspread and curtains this week, but I felt like I was in a hotel room. We were able to stop laughing long enough to catch our breath and move the furniture around. We repositioned the bed so it wasn't in direct line with the door, and so we could easily walk around it. We put the bedside tables on each side; where else do you put those? We moved the TV to the guest room. I wasn't sure how long I could live without a TV in my room, but I was going to give it a shot. I guess I would have to find some books to read.

"We need to call John Danville in the morning and give him an update and then start making our rounds to the rest of the relatives in the area. Someone has to talk to us," I said.

"Sounds great. You can call John, and I will map out our route for the day," Kai replied.

"Perfect. Hopefully we can squeeze in some shopping too. I want to finish feng shuing my room," I said.

"I think JR is doing you some good. I can't believe you want to shop—like-shop-at-a-store shop. Your credit card company is going to be calling you to see if you are still alive or if your card has been stolen," Kai snickered.

"I think I have forgotten how funny you are. I will just be glad to get a room that looks like my room and not mine and Ryan's room. The energy feels really positive in here already. I think the room agrees with the new look," I said.

"I hope you have sweet dreams tonight," Kai said.

"I'll let you know in the morning. Sweet dreams, girl, I am off to bed."

"Night. I think am going to map out our route before I go to bed," Kai replied.

"Thanks."

As I lay in bed and admired my new feng shuied room, I felt like I was at a hotel—taking in the scents and scenes of an unfamiliar room that has the essential bedroom elements and no personal affects anywhere. I had taken down all the pictures to paint and hadn't put them back up yet. This was the first night I had slept without Ryan's picture on my dresser. I was a stranger in my own room.

OPPRESSED

I had gotten an entire night's rest in my new room and felt refreshed for the first time in a long time. I headed downstairs to get my morning java and get a head start on the day. I checked the clock, and it was almost 9:00 a.m. I decided to call John Danville.

The phone rang five times and I waited for it go to voice mail. I spun around in my office chair as I waited. Suddenly, the line clicked.

"Hello," a male voice said.

"Is this John Danville?" I asked cautiously.

"Yes it is."

"Hi. This is Melanie Alexander."

"Do you have a few minutes to speak with me? I wanted to update you on our search for Amelia."

"Yes, of course. Did you find her?" John asked.

"We have not located her yet, but we have been doing some research and interviewed Lynette. We have some solid leads on other relatives to speak to. We are going to do some research today and make our rounds with some visits to the family members. I know that it isn't much information, but we have lots of leads and will continue to provide you with updates. We just wanted to let you know our status," I said.

"Thank you both. If I can do anything to help, please let me know," John said.

"We are happy to help. I'll call you when I have new information for me. If you think of anything or receive any information that may help, please call us."

"I will," John replied.

"Thank you. It was nice speaking to you," I said.

"Thank you for the call," John said.

"Bye," I said.

"Bye," John replied and I heard the phone click.

I saw Kai's route paper on her desk and picked it up. She had mapped out three addresses to visit today, and they all were within an hour's drive from DC. I was always up for some sightseeing. Apparently we were going to visit Belinda Martin, Wesley Nash, and Vera Marlowe.

I heard the front door and knew Kai was back from her morning run.

"Morning," I said.

"Hey, girl. How did you sleep?"

"I slept all night and feel refreshed for the first time in a long time," I replied.

"So the feng shui does work after all," Kai said.

"Apparently it does. I called John Danville already and gave him an update."

"Oh good. Thanks. I see you found our route for today," Kai said.

"I did. I just saw it on your desk and had to look. It looks good. I guess we'll hit up Belinda Martin first."

"Yeah, I figured we would start with Belinda. I just need to shower and eat some breakfast," Kai said.

"I was thinking about making raspberry smoothies. Want one?" I asked.

"Sure. Thanks. I'll be down in a few," Kai replied.

We headed out to Belinda's around 10:00 a.m. Based on the address we got from Lynette, Belinda lived about twenty miles north. My adrenaline was starting to flow. Kai and I were listening to the radio and enjoying the ride out of the city. According to Kai's notes, Belinda Martin was one of Amelia's cousins on her stepfather's side whom she had been close with despite the age difference. Belinda was married with one child, a daughter, according to Lynette. When we turned into Belinda's neighborhood, it was the perfect picture of suburbia America. The subdivision was perfectly planned, and the houses were exactly the same distance apart. The lots were the same sizes, and the houses looked freakishly perfect—painted shutters and doors in classic colors, which I am sure is due to the credit of the homeowners' association, professionally manicured lawns, inviting front-porch rockers, paved sidewalks and bike trails, a community pool, and lots of play sets. It was the perfect kind of neighborhood to raise children and help shelter them from the world for as long as possible. I already knew what Belinda would be like, if she was at home. She would answer the door in designer jeans, T-shirt, and pony tail. She would probably be sitting at the table doing a craft with her daughter or making muffins in the kitchen. We winded our way around the subdivision and came to the Martin residence. The landscaping was perfect and pristine and looked like something out of a magazine. I was afraid that my shoes might dirty up the sidewalk. As we got closer to the front door, we heard rap music playing. Well, I could feel the rap music more than I could hear the lyrics, but the base was a-booming.

"Do you hear that?" I asked Kai.

"How can you not? Is that rap? Does she have a teenager? I don't remember reading in my notes about teenagers, but at least *someone* is home."

Kai rang the doorbell. We waited and waited and waited. Kai rang it again. We waited some more. I could tell Kai was getting irritated because she was tapping her foot.

"Let's go around back," Kai said.

As we got closer to the back of the house, the music got louder. The curtain on the sliding glass door was open, and we saw exactly why no one had answered the door. There was a woman in the family room. Kai and I exchanged quizzical looks. This woman had a huge blond up-do, a black suit with a lemonade-yellow collar shirt underneath, black heels, and tatas the size of a smart car. I saw a video camera on a tripod and silently pointed it out to Kai. We just stood and stared not sure who this woman was or what she was doing. There was never a dull moment in PI work. The woman stopped the camera with a remote and started it again. And this time we heard every word.

"Good morning, my loyal followers. You know what time it is? That's right, it is Belindee Martini My Boss Is a Weenie Time. As you all make your way into the office this morning, I hope today's weenie rap puts a smile on your face and keeps y'all from going nine to five on the weenie you work for:

> The alarm clock beeps; it must be another work day
> And I got to get to work so I can get some pay
> My mother flippin' job gives me the hives
> But at least I work from home and don't have to drive
> 'Cause I got road rage somethin' bad
> Those stupid talkin' textin' drivers make me mad
> I got to get logged on to IM
> So I can talk to my peeps in the AM
> My phone starts ringing off the hook
> It's my boss, who I can read like a book
> It's too damn early to be taking his calls
> But I know what he wants, he's lookin' for his balls
> All day long I hear people whine and cry
> If I don't solve their problem they're gonna die
> So solve your own problem, don't be asking me
> I don't freakin' care about your database tree
> And I sure don't care if your server's down
> Look up on my head, do you see a crown?
> No you don't, so I don't give a damn
> And I didn't get your e-mail cause it got flagged as spam
> As soon as the clock hits quittin' time

I'm adding some tequila to my water with a lime
And going next door to talk to my hoes
We'll gab about clothes and who's got a new nose
To all my fans out there, if your boss is a weenie
Send your stories to Belindee
Peace out, DC, and drink up those martinis

The woman, who I now assumed to be Belinda Martin, turned off the camera. She took off her six-inch, black, pole-dancing platform heels. She took off her suit jacket and then reached down her blouse and pulled out two huge yarn balls the size of volleyballs. Kai and I looked at each other with jaws wide open. I couldn't even make words come out of my mouth. Kai pointed to around to the front of the house, and we each went around our side of the house to the front, careful not to have our movements reflected in the windows. We met on the front porch with astounded looks on our faces; no words were needed. If Kai and I would have spoken, we would say, "What in the world was that hot mess?'" Kai rang the doorbell.

Belinda answered the door almost immediately. She was now a brunette. I guess the blond wig was part of the act too.

"Hi. May I help you?" she said.

Kai spoke. "Hi. Are you Belinda Martin?"

"Yes. Why?" Belinda replied.

"My name is Kia Silva, and this is my partner, Melanie Alexander. We are private investigators. Do you have a minute to speak to us about your cousin Amelia Marlowe?"

Belinda's face went snow-white. She gasped, "Did something happen to her?"

"We are hoping you can help us locate her. Do you know where she is?" Kai continued.

"I haven't seen or talked to her since her father passed away. I have heard through the family grapevine that she moved away," Belinda said.

"Do you know where she moved to or who in the family might know her whereabouts?" Kai pressed.

"Would you like to come in?" Belinda offered.

Kai and I curiously stepped into her home.

Her rap paraphernalia was spread out on the kitchen table. Belinda saw Kai and me looking at the blond wig, shoes, and yarn balls. Before we could say anything, Belinda quickly said with a laugh, "Oh, I bet you are wondering what that stuff is, huh?"

"It is an interesting collection of items," I said lightly. Since she didn't know we had been her audience for her latest rap, she probably thought the items were her bank-robbing disguise or her pole-dancing getup.

"Well, I have a blog where I post funny raps, and this is my disguise. Wanna hear my latest post?" she asked.

"Okay," I said.

"I need to edit it, but this is my first cut."

Belinda pressed a button on her laptop, and we heard the weenie rap again. I chuckled in a few places, and Belinda seemed to appreciate the feedback. Kai was bobbing her head ever so slightly to the beat. After this, I knew Belinda would tell us everything she knew about Amelia.

"That is really funny. And you wrote it?" I asked.

"Yes. After I was laid off a few years ago from my IT job, I started talking online with other people who had been laid off and naturally people talk about their bosses, so I just started to collect all these awful boss stories. I eventually decided to start a blog and post the stories and then one of my friends suggested I write raps about them and do podcasts and videos. It seems so silly to say it all out loud, but I've gotten a really great response to my blog and people are always sending me stories. Do either of you want some coffee or something?"

"I would like some water if it isn't too much trouble," I said. Normally when you have a drink with someone, the conversation lasts longer, and you have a reason to use their bathroom later.

You can learn lots about a person from the contents of their bathroom. You could google all the meds in their medicine cabinet. You could check the contents of their trash can and their laundry hamper. There was lots of information available in the bathroom. And I knew this glass of water would make me have to pee in a few minutes.

"Why are you looking for Amelia?" Belinda asked as soon as she brought out my water.

We didn't get the chance to explore the place when she retrieved the water since the family room and kitchen were wide open. I would have to use the bathroom later and scope out what I could.

"We are not allowed to disclose why we are looking for her or who hired us, but we have some information to deliver to her," Kai said.

"I have been worried about her. Amelia and I used to be really close. I was like an older sister to her. After her father died, she just kind of disappeared. The family would say that someone knew where she was, and she just needed to get away, but I haven't seen or heard from her since. Our family has some dark secrets, and I know that Vera Marlowe knows where she is, but she won't tell any of us. She just tells us that Amelia is fine, and we need to mind our own business," Belinda explained. "I didn't press the issue because no one hacks off Vera."

"Who is Vera?" Kai asked.

"Vera is Amelia's overprotective and a little bit crazy step-grandmother. She kinda runs the family."

"And you believe she knows where Amelia is?" Kai pressed on.

"That is what I hear. I don't particularly talk to Vera much, don't have a need to," Belinda answered.

"But why wouldn't Vera tell anyone where Amelia is?" I asked.

"Besides the facts that she is a nut ready to crack, Amelia is her golden child. She always has been. Vera treats her differently from the rest of us. She's always been real protective of her. I guess the family just got used to it. No one questions Vera, no one."

Well then, Vera was just the lady that Kai and I needed to talk to, and she *would* talk to us—by choice or by persuasion. I was anxious to get out of the rap zone and onto Vera's house. Difficult people were my specialty—the crankier and nastier, the better. My adrenaline was pumping. I loved tracking the trail of missing people and finding them. I know that this job saved me from being checked in to a mental institution or heavily medicated. Finding people gave me something to live for, and we were in the heat of finding Amelia.

Kai was jotting down some notes about some other family members since I apparently had zoned out for a few minutes. Kai would catch me up in the car.

"Thanks to you both for looking for Amelia. If you find her, please tell her to call me and that I miss her. And good luck talking to Vera," Belinda said with raised eyebrows.

"You're welcome. Thank you for your time and good luck with the rap career," Kai said.

"Thanks, I am hoping for a big break and a record deal," Belinda said with a chuckle.

I guess everyone wanted to be a rock star.

CHAINS

"That was interesting," I said to Kai as we got into the Escape. "I didn't even get to snoop in the bathroom."

"I know. The Marlowe family is an interesting bunch of folks. But seriously, who wears a getup, raps about bosses, and posts it online for the world to see?" Kai responded.

"Belindee Martini is hilarious. She could have dealt with being laid off in more destructive ways. I'm thinking right now that I could write a rap about Oliver Parrish and some other interesting characters we've met along the way" I said.

"I would love to see you rap, girl," Kai said with a smirk. "But I really do love what we do. People never cease to be ridiculous," Kai said.

We plugged Vera's address into the trusty GPS and followed the highlighted route.

We pulled on to a gravel driveway that led to a teeny, white house surrounded by overgrown, towering elm trees. The white vinyl siding was almost gray. The lawn needed mowed, and the weeds outnumbered the flowers.

We walked up to the front porch, which was surprisingly swept. There was a bright-blue plastic drum sitting in the corner. It appeared that it was being used as an ashtray. Kai knocked on the door, which had peeling paint. I could smell cigarette smoke oozing from the house.

"Who is it?" said a deep, raspy voice with a Southern drawl.

"Kai Silva and Melanie Alexander. We are looking to speak to Vera Marlowe regarding Amelia Marlowe."

The door slowly opened, but the woman with the voice didn't unfasten the chain, so the door was just cracked enough for a puff of cigarette smoke to slither through. Kai and I both turned our heads and tried not to cough.

"Who are you?" she said.

"We are private investigators, and we are looking for Vera Marlowe. Do you have a few minutes to speak with us?" Kai said.

"No, I'm busy," the raspy voice said as she closed the door. Well, slammed the door in our faces was more like it.

Kai knocked on the door several times.

"Ma'am, can we please have a few minutes?" Kai said with sense of urgency. "It is important that we speak to Amelia. We have important information for her."

"I said I'm busy," the voice said again.

Kai looked at me with her "how dare her" look.

Kai continued to knock on the door with a sense of urgency. She wasn't going to stop knocking. We might be here all afternoon. I was watching the time on my phone and after four minutes of solid knocking, Kai had hit a nerve.

"I'm so tired of this bullshit," the voice said.

As the door began to open, another puff of cigarette smoke came slithering through the door.

"You got some nerve pounding on my door like that," said the voice as she opened the door for us.

"I'm Vera Marlowe. You got three minutes to talk. And no, you ain't coming in."

I could see into her house and it had a smoky screen to it. I knew I would have to shower as soon as we got home from just standing in front of Vera Marlowe. Heck, I might strip down and drive home in my birthday suit so my car wouldn't stink. I was already beginning to smell like a chimney. This woman thought she could give Kai and me a run for our money. Too bad she was my senior and probably had brittle bones from all the smoking. I bet she would snap like a toothpick.

"Do you know where Amelia is? As I said, we have important information to deliver to her," Kai said in her coolest and sweetest voice.

"Who hired you two?" she said in stern voice.

"We are not allowed to divulge the name of our client without their permission," Kai responded.

"Is it crazy Lynette Marlowe?" Vera asked. "I told her I wasn't tellin' her where Amelia was. And that she better get herself to church and confess her sins to the priest."

"You told Lynette Marlowe that you knew where Amelia was?" Kai asked. I knew Kai was ticked that Lynette conveniently forgot to divulge this information to us. Why couldn't people just tell the truth?

"I told her that I knew 'about' where she was and that she was fine. That's all that liar needs to know."

Well, here is another fine example of a harmonious mother-in-law–daughter-in-law relationship. I knew we should have interviewed her first. The mother-in-law is always caught up in the drama because they cause it all. Why did every mother-in-law I know act this way? Did something happen to their DNA when their sons said "I do"?

"Do you happen to know where we can find Amelia?" I asked hoping that maybe Vera would respond to me better than she did Kai.

"And why should I help you?" Vera said.

"Because as Amelia's grandmother, I am sure that you have her best interests at heart and would want her to have the information we have for her," Kai said. I could tell Kai was so irritated, and the tone in her voice was starting to show it.

"What exactly do you have to tell her? You can tell me, and I will tell her," Vera said to us.

"Ma'am, we cannot divulge the information to you since Amelia is an adult," I responded. The tag team effort was on.

"I doubt any information you two have Amelia needs to know," Vera replied.

"Ma'am, regardless of your opinion, we would like to deliver the information to Amelia," I replied. The tone in my voice was even more irritated.

"Oh, come in," Vera said disgustedly. We slowly followed her in.

Kai gave me the let's-make-this-quick-and-get-out-of-here-before-we-get-lung-cancer look. I raised my eyebrows in agreement. We both just stood in front of the couch hoping that we wouldn't have to sit on it. It was probably fifty years old, or the cigarette smoke had yellowed it. The couch wasn't the only thing that was a shade of cigarette-smoke tar yellow. The walls were a nice shade of it, and the tile on the floor had a tint of tar on it as well. Mrs. Marlowe sat down in her easy chair that was well molded for her body. Kai and I sat down on the edge of the couch in unison. We weren't going to stay long enough to get comfortable.

She continued on, "After Buck's death and her mother's betrayal, Amelia came to me. Do you know of Lynette's betrayal?"

Before we could verbally respond, Vera continued.

"You see, Lynette Marlowe is a lyin' tramp. She convinced Buck that he should adopt Amelia and pretend that he was her biological father. And my gullible son fell for her trap. Lynette was never my first choice in daughter-in-laws. I always got a bad vibe from her, especially since she wanted Buck to lie to his family and friends and to Amelia. But he did. What a man does for a woman's loins. That tramp even tried to tell me that Amelia was Buck's, but I ain't stupid. But a son always tells his momma everything, and Buck told me early on that he was not Amelia's father, but that he was going to raise her like he was and that I was not to act like I knew the truth. I knew Lynette was trouble from the moment I met her. Just to think that my poor Buck suffered all those years living a lie. I think that is what killed him."

Vera lit a new cigarette with the one currently dangling from her mouth. No wonder her house smelled like a chimney.

Without missing a breath, Vera continued on. "I told Amelia to come live with me after Buck passed. She didn't need to be around anymore lies."

"We are sorry for the loss of your son," I said, hoping to make some type of connection with her. I wanted to get out of here before I became addicted to nicotine. "How long did Amelia stay with you?" I asked.

"She stayed a few months while she sorted herself out."

"Where is she now?" I asked trying to see if Vera would respond without thinking about what I was asking.

"You don't need to know where she is. Just tell me what she needs to know and I will relay it to her," Vera snickered back.

"Ma'am, I understand the need for you to protect Amelia especially considering all she's been through lately. But the information we need to tell her could have a major impact on her health. I know how difficult families can be. When my husband was killed in action in Afghanistan, my life was turned upside down. My own parents didn't even come to his funeral and I haven't really spoken to them in four years. This could happen to your family if you let it. Let us talk to Amelia and help her begin to heal," I said softly.

No one spoke for a few minutes and it was becoming uncomfortable staring at everyone in silence, but I was going to sit here as long as I had to in order to find Amelia. Since Vera hadn't responded yet, I took that as a sign she was pondering over what I had said. I decided to give her more to ponder about.

"Vera, I understand the severe pain and grief of losing a loved one and that is why we are private investigators. Sometimes people need a little help to put the missing pieces together in order to bring closure, make amends, or move on. You and Amelia need each other more than ever right now. She's your only connection to Buck. He sounds like an amazing man since he raised and loved Amelia as his own."

I saw Vera let her guard down a bit. I was praying she would come to her senses before I permanently smelled like a cigarette.

"Call the University of Pennsylvania and talk to the Psychology department. Since you two are private investigators, you can figure out the rest," Vera snapped at us.

Apparently I had hit a nerve.

"Do you have a contact at the university we should talk to?" I asked.

"No. Now get out," Vera instructed.

"Thank you for your time. Have a nice afternoon," Kai said.

Vera made no effort to show us out.

We got up and once again showed ourselves out. Apparently the Marlowe family was not versed in the proper manners of hosting guests.

Kai and I got in the car, and we stunk.

"I need a shower before I puke on myself because I smell so gross," Kai said.

"I think I have lung cancer now," I replied. "My eyes and nose are burning."

Even though it was November and chilly, we rolled down the windows and opened the sunroof. I had to fumigate the Escape.

"I'm looking up the University of Pennsylvania's phone number right now," Kai said. "Got it," she said as she dialed and put the phone on speaker.

"University of Pennsylvania, Psychology Department," a friendly female voice said.

"Hi. My name is Kai Silva and I have an urgent message for Amelia Marlowe and I was hoping you could help me deliver it to her."

"Is she a student here?" The voice asked.

"I believe so," Kai responded.

"I'm very sorry ma'am, but I'm not allowed to give out the contact information of students."

"It is very important information. Do you know Amelia?" Kai asked. She was trying to make it personal for the woman on the phone. Before the woman could respond, Kai continued. "Amelia's father recently passed away and her mother is in a wheel chair."

"You can try contacting Dr. Burge," the woman said and she hung up.

I was already looking up contact information for Dr. Burge on my phone.

"Kai, there is an article about a Dr. Burge doing a social human psychology experiment on a floating commune," I said slowly almost in disbelief. "It says the boat is called the *Floatin' Utopia*. If Amelia is on a ship, we can find her. All commercial vessels are trackable. That's the easy part. Finding out if she is on it and if she will talk to us, may be more difficult."

"So a floating commune? I think we have seen and heard it all now," Kai said.

"I'm calling the office of Dr. Burge according to the university website," I said.

The phone rang four times and then went to voice mail:

"You have reached the voice mail for Dr. Nathaniel Burge. Please leave a message and I will return your call as soon as possible."

"Hi Dr. Burge. This is Melanie Alexander and I am a private investigator. I have an urgent message for Amelia Marlowe. Can you please call me at 1-555-555-1234," I said.

"Let's head home and do some more research," Kai said.

"Agreed."

As we drove the cold, fall air was airing out the stench that was Kai and me. I wondered how long it would be until I felt like I was breathing fresh air. I seriously thought that my lungs were lined with nicotine and tar. I might have emphysema in the morning.

"Most large ships have computers, cell phone access, Wi-Fi, data ports, and even Internet cafés," Kai said. I'm sure Dr. Burge can get his voice mail. Maybe we can get JR and Will to sail us around the world to the *Floatin' Utopia*."

We both laughed.

"Mel, I am really proud of you for telling Vera what you did about Ryan. I know that must have been hard for you," Kai said.

"Thanks. I'm proud of myself for not crying, but I'm beginning to think that my story may be able to help others."

"I think it can," Kai said.

"Talking to Vera today has got me thinking about my family and Melanie Ryan. I think it's time to call my parents and Casey. Melanie Ryan will be four in a few months," I said.

"Wow, Mel. This is huge for you," Kai said. "I really think you should call them both."

"I have spent a lot of time lately thinking, and I guess Ryan's death has made me realize that you'll never know when you will breathe your last breath. So I want to clear my conscience and make sure I am in the right place. I can't make other people apologize, but I can apologize. I am hoping that seeing Melanie Ryan helps to heal the hole in my heart. Knowing that Ryan died so this little girl could grow up with her daddy makes Ryan's death a tiny bit less painful. I know that big things are in store for this little girl. I am comforted knowing that this little girl can fulfill the plans the world has for her. Maybe she is the next president. Maybe she will cure some deadly disease. And I am comforted knowing that my Ryan gave his life for Casey so he could raise his daughter. I've been doing a lot of thinking lately. I think spending time with JR makes me want to bring closure to the Ryan chapter of my life. I am not going to forget it, but just closing it. I can always open the chapter and read it whenever I want."

"I am so proud of you. I know how hard of this has been on you, and it takes a lot of courage to arrive where you are—to look beyond how Ryan's death impacted your entire life so you can see why he saved Casey and Melanie's life. He was a noble man, Mel," Kai said.

"Thanks. I feel better. I know you've been waiting patiently for these words for four long years. You are a saint. You will probably be knighted by the queen herself. But the veil of grief that has covered me for years doesn't feel as heavy anymore. I think I have finally accepted that it might be time to move on. I am just mesmerized by JR. I just can't believe how understanding and patient he has been with me. I just don't know if he is the real deal or not. And if he is the real deal, what did I do to deserve two good men? We know how hard a decent man is to find these days."

"Are you serious? I was actually going to give you five years before I committed you," Kai said with a chuckle.

"Funny," I said.

"In all seriousness though, you have been through hell and back, and you are asking why you deserve another good man? You deserve to have your pick of all the great men left on this planet. We just happened to have to go to Costa Rica to find ours," Kai said.

"So you feel the same way about Will? That he really is the real deal? I asked her.

"I do. Did you forget that we were once amazing special agents? We are highly trained to read people and understand their thoughts—their instincts. I never doubted Will. My instincts just told me that he was a good one. It takes one to know one. Know what I mean? And have you ever considered that maybe there are bigger plans left for you?" Kai said.

"I don't need any bigger plans than the mess I got right here. But I feel like the fog is lifting. I really am going to call home and call Casey. I don't know what I am going to say yet, but I need do this. My heart is just telling me to. I don't know if my broken heart can handle any additional emotional stress, but life is just too short to have regrets," I told Kai.

"If you want me to be with you when you make the calls, I will be," Kai replied.

"Thanks, girl. I may have you hold my hand like we are in junior high, but I am just grateful to be out of bed, dressed, feeding myself, and out of the house. I think this is the next stage in the healing process for me."

"So, does this all mean that you are going to make amends with Lilith?" Kai asked.

"Now you had to go and ruin a perfectly good conversation by bringing up the name of the she-devil. Heck no, I am not making amends with her. I don't think part of my healing process includes associating with crazy and emotionally unstable people. What is wrong with you?" I sarcastically said to Kai. Kai and I never argued—just friendly BFF banter.

Kai started to laugh. The more I laughed, the better it felt.

"We've never been on a commune—land or sea. I am hoping we get the chance to go aboard," I said.

"Me too. I am interested in the social experiment of a floating commune. Are the researchers interested in how people live in a commune that is contained by the ship's boundaries as compared to a land-based commune, or are they interested in the possibility of self-sustaining colonies of people at sea?" Kai replied.

"Do you think the future of the human race is sea cities?" I asked Kai.

"You never know. It is an interesting concept to consider though," Kai said. "Do you mind if we stop by the store on the way home? I need some fresh fruit—some berries, mangoes, and apples."

"Sure. The mangos remind me of Fiji. We need to figure out when we are going back." I said.

"We just got back from Costa Rica. How is it possible that you are itching to get on a plane again?" Kai asked me.

"I just miss the warmth of the sun and the peacefulness. I seriously could live there all year round."

"We are staying State-side for now. We have clients," Kai said.

"You're no fun. You just want to stay in DC for the boy." I knew that would set her off.

"When do I do anything for a boy? And have you already forgotten about JR? The only man who isn't frightened off by Lilith and Mt. Melanie," Kai bantered back.

"You better watch yourself. I'll make your pretty little face walk to the store," I said.

If you couldn't be a smart mouth with your best friend, then who could you be one with?

DEMONS

Of course I stopped at our neighborhood grocery store on the way home. Kai went to get her fruit, and I went to gather a salad. I loved our neighborhood store. It had been owned by Guy for as long as we have lived here, and he always had the best fruits and veggies in town. Even in the dead of winter, you could get mangos, berries, and peaches that were just lovely. Since I was thinking about calling home, I remembered how I always looked forward to summertime in Montana so we could get fresh fruits that weren't available all year round. I guess I was feeling a little nostalgic.

As soon as we walked in the house, I said, "I don't know about you, but I need a shower. I stink."

"Me too. I got to get this stench off before the house stinks," said Kai.

I immediately felt better after I washed the nicotine and tar off me. I literally had to scrub my skin numerous times to get the film off. When I got back downstairs, Kai was already in the kitchen.

"I am going to call Casey and Lucia and then check our messages. I'll be in the office."

"You want me to come with you?" Kai asked.

"Na. But I will need you when I call home. Why is it so difficult to talk to your own family?" I said.

"You know that families are complex, which is why we have jobs."

"True. Very true. Wish me luck and that I don't break down in tears on the phone," I said.

"You got it. Remember Detroit? You are one tough cookie," Kai said in her peppiest voice.

I had to think for a split second about Detroit. "I had almost forgotten about Detroit there for a millisecond. That seems like ages ago."

"How can you forget? We were rookies, and you fought off a crazy guy who had a knife while holding an infant in your arms."

"I had so much adrenaline and balls back then. I wonder how that baby is doing. The crazy dude's name was Garland, right?"

"Yep. And he kidnapped the baby and slit the mother's face, but she lived," Kai said.

"It sounds much crazier now. I should have been the one to die while on duty, not Ryan," I replied.

"Stop it. You can't change the past. Just remember who you are and what you are capable of, if needed." "You have handcuffed guys twice your size. Where is that, Mel? *Find her!*" Kai scolded.

"Thanks, girl. You should really be a shrink in your next life."

I sat down in my office chair and dialed Casey's number from my BlackBerry. My heart was racing and I breathed through my nose to maintain my composure.

"Hello," a woman's voice answered.

"Hi. Lucia? This is Melanie Alexander."

"Melanie! Hi! Casey, It's Mel!" I heard her yell away from the phone. "It is so good to hear your voice. How are you?"

"I'm good, thank you. I just wanted to call and say hello and see how you all were doing."

"We are doing great. As you probably heard me, Casey is home, which is always nice. Melanie Ryan is in preschool and loves it! She has a Christmas play coming up at the school if you are interested...."

"Wow, she's in preschool already? It doesn't seem possible. When is the Christmas play? Maybe I'll try to come," I said still wondering how Melanie was already in preschool.

"The play is December 19 at 6pm at Cherry Hill Preschool," Lucia said. I was writing it down. Maybe it would be good for me to go.

"And Mel, we have some exciting news. We are pregnant! I'm due in March."

"Congratulations! That's so exciting. How are you feeling?" I said, truly excited for them. I was thinking about the circle of life—Ryan, Melanie Ryan, the new baby. Life goes on.

"I feel great. We aren't finding out with this one, so it will be a surprise. There aren't too many big surprises in life, so we decided not to find out," Lucia said.

"Well, please let me know what you have. Is Melanie Ryan excited about being a big sister?" I asked.

"Yes, she is really excited. She already has toys of hers in the baby's room that she wants the baby to play with. We'll see if she is still excited when the baby arrives," Lucia said with a laugh. "Casey wants to talk to you."

"Okay, sure," I said. Talking to Casey was bittersweet for me, but I am a new Mel these days—one that believes in hope.

"Hey, Mel," I heard Casey's voice say.

"Hey. How are you? And congrats on the baby," I said. I was fighting back tears as I heard his voice, but I was determined not to cry. Determined.

""I'm doing good. How are you?" Casey asked. Everyone always asked me that question.

"I'm doing good. Really good. Kai and I have been busy working cases and I actually started going back to the gym."

"I'm glad to hear it. How's Seth," Casey asked.

"He's good—giving me a hard time as usual, but he's good."

"How's Kai?"

"She's good. Still running and hitting the gym hard," I said.

"Mel, it's really good to hear your voice. Do you need anything?" Casey asked.

"It's really good to hear yours and Lucia's. And I can't believe Melanie Ryan is in preschool. Lucia mentioned her Christmas play and I think I'm going to come. I would love to see who she looks like," I responded.

"That would be great, Mel. You know you are welcome here like family," Casey said.

"So, how are the other guys—Sam, Eric, Grant, Mark, Remy?" I asked.

"They are all good. Didn't you hear about Sam? He retired. I think the stress got to him. Maybe you should give him a call," Casey said.

"No, I didn't hear about Sam. Is he doing okay? When did he leave?" I asked. Kai was the one that heard information through the grapevine, but we hadn't heard about Sam.

"I haven't talked to him in a few months, but he's been out almost a year. I guess he's doing all right," Casey answered.

"Do you have his number?" I asked.

"Sure. 1-555-111-0999," Casey said.

"Thanks. I might call him," I said. And I just might. Ryan and Sam had been close friends.

"Mel, I really hope we see you at the Christmas play. And will you come over for dinner sometime?" Casey asked.

"Yes, I would like to come to dinner. Just let me know," I said.

"I'll talk to Lucia and I'll let you know," Casey replied.

"It was great talking to you all. And congrats again on baby #2," I said.

"Don't be a stranger, Mel," Casey said.

"I'll try not to be," I said. "Bye."

"Bye," Casey said.

I hung up and took a deep breath. Kai was at the doorway before I knew it.

"I am proud of you, girl," Kai said.

"Thanks. It was much harder than I imagined in my head. I kept thinking that I should be talking to Ryan, you know. But I didn't cry, and they want me to go to Melanie Ryan's Christmas play at preschool and have me over for dinner. I said I would go."

"Good! You should go! You need to go!" Kai said.

"Do you think I can hold it together when I see Melanie Ryan's face?" I asked Kai.

"Yes, I do. So give me the scoop," Kai asked.

"Well, Lucia is pregnant with baby number two, and she is due in March. Casey said that Sam Keller retired, which surprises me. Casey said that Sam was tired of the stress. Melanie Ryan is in preschool and loves it. Casey kept asking me if I needed anything and how I was doing. I told him that I had been going to the gym and that you and I had been working some cases. That was the extent of our conversation. What do we really have to talk about? Think about it."

"Now stop it. Give yourself credit for calling. Interesting about Sam, don't you think?" Kai asked.

"Yeah, I think so, but you know what they do. Maybe he cracked. Maybe he is undercover. Maybe he got tired of the life. Casey gave me Sam's number so maybe I'll call."

"Maybe you can get the scoop then," said Kai.

"Aren't you Ms. Nosey today?" I said sarcastically.

"I just want the facts. So put your agent hat on and get them for me," replied Kai with a sly grin.

"Girl, I don't know if you know this, but I ain't your bitch," I said, laughing.

"Mel, it's great to hear you laugh and throw my sass back at me."

My laptop dinged and Kai and I both looked at the screen.

"Oooh, there is an e-mail from our little boyfriend Oliver Parrish," I said.

"It must be blasts-from-the-past week—Oliver, Casey, Sam," Kai said.

"I know. Oliver wants to know if we want to take that Mercer case since we never called him back. In my best Oliver Parrish twang, I said, "I really don't want to see his face. I might just punch it, but then that might make me break a nail. So since I am a girl, maybe I should just keep my pretty little face at home."

Kai burst out laughing. "I don't know what has gotten into you lately, but between your impersonations and your interest in rapping, you may just make me pee my pants," Kai said.

"I think being a rapping PI is my next persona. Maybe all the gin has finally caught up to me. Maybe I got too much sun in Jaco. Maybe it is JR. Maybe Lilith is wearing off on me. Maybe Vera's nicotine has killed off my brain cells," I said. "So, what do you want to do about Oliver? You know I think he's shady."

"I know. I think he's shady too. I still don't know why he even contacted us. I'm going to ask Seth if he's heard anything through the grapevine when I'm at the gym next. I think we should turn it down. I just don't trust him and my gut is telling me I'm right," Kai said.

"I agree. I'll email him back. I don't want to get caught up in anything shady," I said. "I'm also going to track down the *Floatin' Utopia*. I should be able to quickly locate it online."

"I'll make some more calls to the University of Pennsylvania and see if I can get any more information," Kai said.

As I sat in front of the computer typing a response to Oliver trying to politely turn down his offer, I suddenly sat straight up in my chair. I realized that I would be in DC for Thanksgiving and Christmas this year. Since I was in a coma for the holidays after Ryan's death, and then I bought the house in Fiji, I hadn't celebrated Thanksgiving, Christmas, or New Year's in DC as a widow. Since Thanksgiving was quickly approaching, my mind was having a panic attack about the holidays. I really hadn't thought about the upcoming holidays until now; I guess I had been subconsciously repressing those thoughts. And then it hit me all at once. My chest tightened, the air seemed heavy and

difficult to breathe in, and my entire body froze. I couldn't celebrate the holidays in our house without Ryan. Every Christmas
decoration, the fresh evergreen scent of a real Christmas tree,
the lighting of the National Christmas Tree, and the Scottish
Walk all brought instant memories of Ryan. As we decorated our
fresh-cut Christmas tree, we would reminisce about the stories
the ornaments told. Each time we traveled somewhere, we would
try and find an ornament as a remembrance of our adventure. We
would visit the National Christmas Tree all lit up, which signaled
the official start of Christmastime for me. And how I loved the
Scottish Walk. Ryan had some Scottish blood in him, and he
thoroughly enjoyed going to Alexandria to listen to the Scottish
clansmen play their bagpipes and walk along the Potomac, which
was illuminated by lights from all the decorated boats. I suddenly felt claustrophobic about being in DC for Christmas.
Thanksgiving didn't even cross my mind since we never really
did anything special to celebrate. A few Thanksgivings we both
worked, and we usually got our Thanksgiving meal from a local
restaurant since I was an awful cook, and Kai was a vegan. We
had never had a traditional Thanksgiving meal in DC, and I
was okay with it. But I was not okay with Christmas. I loved
Christmas, and it was always such a beautiful and peaceful time
of year. I did not want to be here. I wanted to be in Fiji. I never
thought much about the holidays when we were in Fiji. The sun,
beach, and warm water really do chase the winter blues away. I
couldn't imagine celebrating Thanksgiving and Christmas on a
tropical island, so I never really gave the holiday season much
thought while secluded away at the beach house. The holidays
were going to hurt this year. They were really going to hurt. My
chest was tight, and I could feel sweat beads forming on my
brows. I wanted to run to Fiji. There were no Christmas trees,
no Thanksgiving turkeys, no snow, and no constant reminders
about spending Christmastime with loved ones. I was sweating
all over now, and I was gasping for air. I was having an anxiety

attack. I wanted to leave. I had to leave. I started to rub my neck, which was my anxiety tick. Kai said I used to sit in my room all day and rub my neck until the skin was raw. It was an uncontrollable reflex; I couldn't tell my hands to stop. I had to pack. I had to leave. I had to get halfway around the world to Fiji. I was just not in the happy-holidays mood. The more I thought about Christmas, the more rigid and anxious I became. I was outside of my body. I couldn't stop staring out the office window and rubbing my neck. The panic and irrational thoughts were taking over. I had to get to Fiji. I started making a mental packing list and figuring out how I would tell Kai. Hopefully she would come with me. We could work from Fiji. I didn't take one single thing from our brownstone to Fiji. Nothing. Fiji was neutral territory, and my body wanted to jump out of the chair and run to the airport. I had to fight the feeling to run up the stairs and pack. I had to fight the feeling to flee. I couldn't run away from life when it got rough. But I wasn't running. I was simply going to my other house. How could that be running? I was just vacationing, right? Why was I reacting this way? I wanted to run to the basement and throw away all the Christmas decorations. I didn't want one decoration up in the brownstone. Not one. I didn't want to leave the house until all the Christmas hoopla was over in DC. I didn't want to see anything related to Christmas. Nothing. I didn't want to hear one Christmas carol or open one Christmas card. I wanted to be the Grinch.

I closed my eyes and started saying "Fiji" under my breath while rubbing my neck. Everything went white.

"Mel. Mel. Snap out it! Snap out of it now! Mel!"

I heard Kai's voice and opened my eyes.

"What is wrong? Why are you chanting *Fiji* and rubbing your neck? It is so red; move your hand so I can see if it is bleeding. Talk to me, Mel. Talk to me now!"

"I can't do Christmas here. I want to go to Fiji," I said in a faint whisper.

"Why? What happened?"

"I can't celebrate the holidays here without Ryan. This house has too many holiday memories. I can't be here. Look, I have hives," I said as I pulled up my sleeve. For the first few years after Ryan, I was covered from head to toe in hives. Nothing made them go away except for relaxation. I never had hives in Fiji. And they itched like the devil.

"Oh, the darn stress hives! You are covered. Want some calamine lotion? Benadryl?" Kai asked.

"Just some gin," I replied. "I can't do this. I can't have Christmas here, Kai. I just can't. Can we throw the Christmas decorations away? I don't want to see any of them. There will be no tree. And I am not stepping foot out of this house until all the Christmas cheer and hoopla is long gone. I just don't have the strength. Can we go to Fiji? Please? Please? Please? I can't do this."

"You can do this. We can get new decorations and a fake tree. We can start our own Christmas traditions this year. We can do things differently. But you need to face it, Mel. You need to look your fear straight in the eyes and face it," Kai said.

Kai briefly left, and when she returned, she handed me a glass of gin.

"Thanks. I am a wreck. Look at me. I don't know what happened. I just started thinking about the holidays, and the anxiety just escalated. Then I went into a trance. All I saw was white. But I really can't be here for the holidays. I really want to be in Fiji."

"We haven't celebrated Christmas in three years, Mel. It is time to get back to the traditions of your life. You can't make the world not celebrate Christmas. Even if you travel to Fiji, Christmas still comes. You can't escape it. You might as well face it."

Kai looked at me, put her hands are my shoulders, and said in her most stern voice, "Melanie Audrey Alexander, it is time. It is time to face the demons. You look me in the eyes and tell me that you are strong enough to fight. And that you will fight. And that nothing gets in the way of Melanie Audrey Alexander."

Kai's grasp on my shoulders was beginning to hurt. She took one hand and stopped my hand from rubbing my neck. It was sore now.

"Mel, look me in the eyes and tell me you are going to fight the demons. I am not letting you go until you tell me. *Look at me!*" Kai screamed.

I shook my head no.

"*Melanie Audrey Alexander!*" Kai screamed in my face.

I dug way deep down into the pit of my stomach and found the words. "I, Melanie Audrey Alexander, am strong enough to fight the holiday demons and nothing gets in the way of Melanie Audrey Alexander," I said in a raspy voice. The words cut my throat as they came out. I wanted to puke.

"Louder, Mel. Say it like you mean it. Say it *now*. And nice try with the 'holiday demons.' Say 'all demons.'"

I dug deep down again, but this time it wasn't so painful to speak the words. My throat must have been numb now. I was numb. "I, Melanie Audrey Alexander, am strong enough to fight *all* demons, and nothing gets in the way of Melanie Audrey Alexander."

"Better. Now get up. We are going to the gym," Kai said.

"I am really not in the mood."

"That is precisely why you are going. Let's move," Kai said.

Bossy Kai always got her way, so apparently I was going to the gym.

PLUGGED

Kai had been making me go to the gym every day, and it seemed to be keeping most of the hives at bay. I still didn't want to celebrate Christmas in DC, but at least I hadn't had anymore anxiety attacks. I survived my first post-Ryan DC Thanksgiving. I had Chinese food. I threatened Kai's life if she tried to bring anything Thanksgiving related into the house. One holiday down and one to go.

Since it was Thanksgiving break, we had not had any luck speaking to anyone at the university regarding Amelia. However, I had successfully located the *Floatin' Utopia* via a ship tracking website and had been watching it daily. It was currently in the South Atlantic on the outskirts of the Bahamas. The United States Coast Guard could board any vessel they wanted for any reason, even a US vessel in non-US waters, but I was pretty sure they had better things to do then help us contact a cruise ship we thought someone, who may or may not be missing, to be on. We were very persistent PIs. We took turns calling all the university contacts we could find in regards to the psychology department. We even left messages for the dean. If no one called us back, we could always go for a road trip once school resumed. Sometimes people were more helpful to people standing in front of their face so eventually the person standing in front of their face would go away.

"Hey, Mel," I heard Kai say as she entered the office.

"Hi. I'm watching our ship," I said.

"The ship has been in the same spot for days. It is a cruise ship, Mel; not a speed boat. I promise that you won't miss it moving," Kai said sarcastically.

"Funny," I said. I know that the *Floatin' Utopia* isn't going anywhere fast. I am just stalling from calling home. I think it's time."

"Really? I am so proud of you. You should call home now," Kai ordered.

"Yeah, yeah, I know. I just haven't felt up to doing it, but I need to. I have to. I want to call before Christmas," I said. "I am anxious and nervous about what they are going to say to me. These people are my own parents, and I have anxiety about calling them. What is wrong with that picture? We probably need group therapy, but I just have so much anger still. It all stems around Mitch's accident and his stupid arm. But do you think I can ever forgive them for not coming to Ryan's funeral or for not visiting me afterward?"

"You can't change the past. You can't change people. Let it go, Mel. Even if they came for a visit now, it wouldn't change anything. I think you should call them and see what they say. Be the bigger person. Life is too short to hold grudges and exile people from your life. You know the fragility of life better than anyone else. They are your parents, and they just may surprise you," said Kai.

"I know. But I am not holding my breath for any surprises, but one would be nice. How do parents just not speak to their only daughter for years? But you are right. I need to be the bigger person. Funny how the child is the more responsible one now. Ryan's death taught me one thing: Life is too short and can change for better or worse at any second. Cherishing every happy moment is a necessity."

"Oh, we got another email from Oliver almost begging us to take that Mercer case, which means that something is definitely illegal about it," I said to Kai. "Knowing what we know about Oliver, we would probably end up in jail."

"For real. Who would bail us out? Seriously, we have no other friends," Kai said.

"Seth would bail us out, and I could always call Lilith," I said, unable to keep a straight face. Kai and both burst out laughing.

"Can you imagine the conversation between you and Lilith? I might just pee my pants thinking about it," Kai said.

"She would probably say that they had the wrong number or that I am a drunk and should be checked into rehab and the mental ward. You know she would tell them her big sob story about how me and my flavor of the week threw her out of her son's house," I said. "I am so writing a rap about her for therapy. I think it would do my soul some good."

"I can't wait to hear you rap," replied Kai.

"I just might be the next worldly sensation: special-agent-widow-turned-rapper. It would be an intriguing story. People like stories with dirt," I said laughingly.

"Okay, it is official. I am cutting you off from the gin. It is killing your brain cells or making them so drunk that you think you can rap."

"I'll just drink Jack or Johnny," I said.

"I think rehab might just be in your future, Melanie Audrey Alexander."

"As long as you commit me to a place at a tropical beach, I'll go," I said.

"Funny. Really funny. So, you've been thinking about JR?"

"A little. You've been thinking about Will?" I asked.

Yeah. I am trying to keep him out of my mind, but I can't. I got this tangled bunch of nerves in the pit of my stomach that just pulsates his name. It is almost making me crazy," explained Kai.

"You? Boy crazy? I don't believe it. Besides Carlos, you usually don't care if they stay or go. What's up, Kai?"

"I don't know. I just can't get him off my mind. I feel like I have a mini-Will sitting on my shoulder whispering in my ear. It drives me crazy. I can't stop thinking about him and the next time I will see him. And I have scared myself to death because I am Kai Silva. I do not chase boys nor do I need one to define my life and myself. But damn, is it nice to have Will around. I can't get him off my mind. I have been doing a self-psycho analysis to see what is wrong with me."

"I think for the first time, Kai Silva is head over heels in love. Wow. I never thought this day would come. We need to celebrate. Let's go out this weekend," I suggested.

"You want to go *out* out? Did you just suggest that we go out without me having to bribe, blackmail, or physically force you? What is up with you? I think I know. It is either the gin or a boy named JR," Kai replied.

"Shut up. But yeah, maybe it is JR."

"And I think you have to make a call," Kai said.

"I know, I know," I said as I let out a huge breath of air.

I could do this. I didn't even have to dial the number. My BlackBerry would dial it for me. I searched my contacts for "Ken and Irene," not "Mom and Dad," or "The Parents," or the "Fam" or "Home." Just "Ken and Irene." My mind was wondering what the subliminal message was behind how I had my parents filed in my BlackBerry. In this technology era, I would assume someone would have performed a study on electronic filing habits and ana-lyzed the results against personality traits. I wondered what my results would be. I had my parents filed under their first names; I had one friend whom I rarely called or texted since I lived with her. I bet my results would fall under "why does this girl even own a BlackBerry?"

All right, Mel, enough with the stalling. Hit the Call button. I had been thinking about this moment for months and probably subconsciously for years. I just wanted to call my mom and dad. I wanted to hear them say that they loved me and missed me. I just wanted to know that I had a family to go home to. My self-exam-ination of my soul revealed that I really was hurt by my parents and that I really want to reconcile the relationship. I thought a lot about them. How could they abandon me at the darkest time of my life? A girl always needs her mama and papa. I was ready to do this. I was ready to fix all that was broken between me and them. I needed to be able to fix something. I needed my family in my life. I wanted them in my life. I only had Kai. If I was ever going to heal, I needed to heal this. Losing my husband and my parents had been a double blow to my heart and soul. I often wondered if my parents would have been there for me if I would have come around sooner and not totally lost myself. I quit being an agent and bought a house halfway around the world. When I look back, I was running from life—from the pain of Ryan and my parents. Shutting myself off from people was my coping mechanism; if I didn't see people, I wouldn't have to talk to them. Yeah, it has taken me years to come to this realization, but at least I can now admit it to myself. I am still a train wreck, but I have to move forward. I have got to try to have a life without Ryan. I was no longer a wife or an agent, but I was still a daughter. Great, now tears were streaming down my face. *Get it together, Mel, and call home.*

The last thing I wanted was to call my parents crying. *Damn it, Mel.*

Kai handed me a tissue. "You can do this, Mel. I know you can."

I took a deep breath and dabbed the tears. Kai had witnessed enough of me sobbing over the years, but she still sat beside me. Kai reached out and grabbed my hand, and I pressed call and put the phone on speaker.

My heart was speed racing in my chest as the phone began to ring. Instantaneously this great tidal wave of anxiety washed over me. What in the world was I going to say? I began chanting under my breath, "Please go to voice mail. Please go to voice mail."

And then the ringing stopped.

"Hello," a familiar female voice answered.

"Mom? This is Melanie."

There was a moment of silence on the phone.

"Melanie, Hi! I can't believe it's you. How are you?" I couldn't determine if my mom was really excited to hear my voice or holding back tears.

"I'm good, Mom. It's really good to hear your voice. I just decided that it had been too long," I said. Kai was nodding in reassurance that I was saying the right things.

There was another long pause.

"It has been too long, Mel. I've missed you," my Mom said. I was surprised to hear her say that. She wasn't always open with her feelings.

"Me too, Mom. How's Dad and Mitch?" I asked hoping to offset the flying emotions. Even though I hadn't been home in years, I pictured Mom sitting at the kitchen table in her favorite oak chair. Growing up we all sat in the same chair at the table each and every meal. And somehow that just became *your* seat. Mom liked to look out the picture window opposite the table, and I bet she was staring at the neighbor's large field behind our house. I wonder if there were still cattle roaming it.

"Dad's doing good and Mitch and Becca are expecting baby number three."

"Oh my, that's great," I said. "How are you?"

"Real good. I'm retired now and on full-time grandma duty. I do a lot of babysitting for Mitch and Becca," she said. I could see the smile on her face because she always talked about being a grandma, so I knew she was really happy. I began to wonder if she looked the same or had aged any over the years.

Before I had the chance to respond, she asked, "Are you still working for the government?" My parents never knew that I as an agent—just that I worked for the government.

"No, I am no longer working for the government. It was too hard to go back after Ryan died. Kai and are private investigators now."

"Oh, private investigators. So what exactly do you do? Do you help the government?" she asked in a quizzical voice. Kai smiled when she heard this.

I got the impression my mother was not totally impressed with my current line of work. "Well, Kai and I own our company and we help look for missing people. So we mainly help people find lost loved ones," I said. I was trying to keep it as simple as possible.

"Oh I see. So how's Kai?" Again, Kai smiled when my mom said "Oh, I see," which meant she did not understand how we made a living looking for people.

"Kai's doing great. She's my roommate these days," I said.

"Oh, she's not married yet? I thought some guy would have snatched her up by now."

I saw Kai roll her eyes, and I had to keep myself from laughing.

"No, not yet," I said ever so sweetly. I finally had the courage to tell my mom what I had wanted to tell her for years. If I wanted to move on to the next chapter of my life, I had to do this. "Umm, Mom. Can we talk about something?"

"Okay, sure," my mom said hesitantly. She knew I was about to get serious. She was my mother after all.

"Mom, I called to talk about us. You haven't called since Ryan died, and you never came to his funeral. I know I haven't called either, but you really hurt my feelings and my heart. I needed you at the darkest time of my life, and you weren't there. I know people process death differently, but, Mom, I needed you. I have missed having you in my life. Actually, I have missed having you in my life since Mitch's accident. I want to erase the past and start again."

There was silence on the line. I couldn't even detect breathing. Did she hang up on me? Should I wait for her to respond? How could she not respond to all of that? I just laid some heavy stuff out on the table. We weren't talking about who was bringing what to Christmas dinner.

"Mom? Are you still there? Mom? Mom?"

Nothing. No noise, but no dial tone either. My mind immediately raced to the worst possible conclusions: I caused her to have a heart attack or a brain aneurysm. I pictured her lying on the floor in the kitchen with the phone dangling above her. The kitchen phone was an old, corded model mounted to the wall.

"Hi Mel, it's Dad," I heard a familiar voice say and I was instantly comforted. Had he been sitting next to mom this entire time listening?

"Is Mom okay? Where is she?" I asked.

"She's fine. She just needs a moment. It's good to hear your voice," my dad said.

"Hi, Dad. It's really good to hear yours. How have you been?" I asked. The tears were starting to well up in the corners of my eyes. Kai handed me another tissue.

"I'm good, Mel. Just enjoying the land and the grandkids."

My father was such a simple man, which was something I deeply admired about him. He enjoyed the simple things in life and rarely sweated the small stuff.

"Dad, have you been next to Mom this whole time? I just wanted to tell her how I felt and that I wanted to start over. Life is too short, Dad. I want to make this right," I said. The tears were now flowing from my eyes, but I felt a sense of relief flow out of my body with them.

"Mel, you know I am not the type that usually pours out the secrets in my soul, but until your Mother gets back on the phone, I should tell you something," Kai squeezed my hand a little harder.

"Okay, Dad. I'm listening."

"After Mitch's accident, your mother fell into some dark days of despair and anger. She put on an act for you and Mitch, but inside she was barely alive. She felt so guilty as a mother and blamed herself for Mitch's accident. Her guilt almost killed her, Mel. When you left for Stanford, she felt that she had failed you since she couldn't be the mother you needed your last few years in high school. She would sit in her room endlessly, sometimes without eating or sleeping for days. And then when you called to say that Ryan had passed, that opened up the I-am-a-horrible-mother wound all over. She fell into an even deeper darkness and blamed herself for your pain. She thought that if she would have been able to be a better mother to you, you wouldn't have left home, which meant you wouldn't have met Ryan."

I pictured my dad's face in front of me as I heard these words. I saw the deep creases on his forehead and between his eyebrows moving and reacting to his words. I had the same creases, so I knew how they worked. He was always very stoic; no matter what type of news he was delivering. I imagined him with perfect posture sitting in the kitchen chair. I bet one hand was holding the phone and the other was jingling the change in his pocket. When we had "family talks" at the kitchen table growing up, he jingled his change when the topic was serious or important. For some reason I imagined my dad's beard and hair to have some gray in them these days. I bet he looked a lot like grandpa—salt and pepper hair with a little more salt for all the stress his life had seen—stress as a police officer, a son who had a tragic accident, and a daughter who was a widow. I saw this entire imagine in front of as he spoke. This was the first time I had ever heard my father speak of such emotions and feelings; my mother was the one who talked about these things. I was surprised and hurt that she hadn't talked to me about how she felt over the years. I wondered why she couldn't tell me what she was feeling. I began to feel remorse—like I had failed her as a daughter. I should have been there to support her and help her. She had been in a fog just like me and I never even knew it.

I looked over at Kai and she had tears in her eyes. I was shocked. She never cried. My tears were still flowing, but I didn't feel myself moving to the sobbing stage. I was still feeling strong.

"Dad, I had no idea. I'm really sorry. Why didn't you or mom tell me all this?"

"I don't know if I can answer that. I guess the timing just never seemed right," he said.

Kai had let go of my hand to dry her tears. My shirt was wet down the front and the tears were still flowing, but I felt that I was making peace with this. My heart and my soul felt lighter. Suddenly, I heard a click on the line.

"Dad, are you still there?" I asked with a hint of panic in my voice.

"Yes," he said.

"Mel, it's Mom. I picked up the phone in the bedroom." As soon as I heard my mother's soothing voice, the voice of my early childhood, her face instantly appeared before my eyes. I pictured her sitting on her side of the bed, the right side, propped up on the pillows with her feet tucked underneath her. This is how she sat when she talked on the phone. I remember laying my head in her lap sometimes while she talked. I bet she still had the same wedding quilt on the bed too. I saw her dark-blond hair pulled up in her classic bun, which she wore almost everyday. I saw the laugh lines around her mouth and imagined them to be a little deeper. She had high cheek bones and wore rose blush on them. In my mind her face looked the same—just a little older. I bet she had the pearl stud earrings in her ears. They were her favorites. My mom's blue eyes anchored her face and drew people into her when she talked to them. I had really missed talking to her.

"Mom, I'm so sorry. Dad told me how you felt over the years and I had no idea. I'm sorry for the pain and that I wasn't there for you. I love you." Wow. I was completely surprised that I just said that. I was done being the old Mel who didn't speak to her family. Kai looked at me and smiled. She knew this was a milestone in my life.

"I'm sorry too, Mel," I heard the tears in my mother's voice. "A mother is supposed to be there for her daughter. I let you down. I let myself down."

"Mom, it's okay. I wasn't there for you either or even thought I needed to be there for you. We can forgive and start again. I'm ready for a new chapter. I've spent the last few years grieving and hiding from the world in Fiji. I bought a beach house there to escape the pain of my life. It took me a long time to realize life is too short. I miss you guys and Mitch too," I said with a strong voice. Kai was nodding again.

"Fiji? Isn't that halfway around the world, Mel?" My Dad asked. I think he was trying to break the tension.

"Yeah, it is off of Australia. The further away I could get the better," I said.

"I've really missed you Mel," my Mom said in a broken voice between the tears. "Can you forgive me for not being there when you needed me the most?" As soon as I heard my Mom crying, the sobbing started. But I wasn't sad this time.

"Yes, if you can forgive me too," I managed to get out between the sobs.

"Yes, Mel. We love you so much and have missed you so much that it hurts," my Mom said. "We've got a lot of family time to make up for."

"Yea, we do. I'm not exactly sure where to start," I said.

"We'd love to have you home for Christmas," said my Dad.

"I think I would like that. Let me talk to Kai and check out some flights," I said. Kai shot me her "what-the-hell-is-wrong-with-you-you-don't-need-to-ask-me look."

"Mel, it is so good to hear your voice," said my Mom through tears. "I love you darling," she said.

"I love you too Mom and Dad," I said back as the sobbing came harder and harder.

"I love you, Mel," I heard my Dad say.

"Let's talk in a few days, okay?" I said. I didn't know how much longer I could stay on the phone and sob, but huge progress had been made in one phone call than in years. The love that bonds a family together can be painful, fragile, difficult to navigate, but can also heal the deepest of wounds without one single stitch.

"Okay, Mel. We love you. Bye," said my Mom.

"I love you too. Bye." I pressed the end button. I processed all that had been said and was speechless.

"I'm so proud of you girl," Kai said as she stood up. She squeezed my shoulders and said, "I'll give you some time," and she walked out of the office.

It felt almost too good to believe—that after all these years of anger and grief, one phone call changed all that. I knew that my parents and me had a lot of talking to do, but at least we started talking again. I was happy and angry all at the same time. Happy that finally, after four years, I was making peace with my past. Angry that it had taken me four years to place that call. I dreamt about this moment for a long time—the moment where I was genuinely happy again and not consumed by gloom. I couldn't believe it had finally arrived.

"Mel!" I heard Kai yell from upstairs. The sense of urgency in Kai's voice startled me, and I looked around to see where I was. I was on the couch in the hearth room. I had no recollection of how long I had been sitting here. Was it possible that I had fallen asleep?

"You okay?" I yelled back.

"Yep."

Kai bounded into the room within seconds. "We just got a break. I just got a call from the dean's assistant. They have spoken to Amelia, and she agreed to have a video call with us on tomorrow at noon Eastern Time."

"That's fantastic! See, being persistent pays off," I said. "Or maybe being annoying pays off."

Kai let out a laugh. "I don't care if they called us back just so we would stop calling them; they called. If they would have helped us the first time we called, they wouldn't have had to listen to the hundred other calls we made," Kai said in her sassy voice.

"True. People's lives would be so much easier if they just did things our way the first time," I said in my sassy voice. "This is the stuff that makes me happy. Mr. Danville will be relieved that we were able to speak with Amelia and deliver his news. I'm not sure how Amelia will take it, but knowledge is power."

"I know. I feel bad for Amelia too especially after all she has been through," Kai said.

"If she takes the news really hard, she can't go anywhere. And as of a few hours ago, she was still in the Atlantic Ocean," I replied.

"You are obsessed with watching that ship. I hope she doesn't take the Melanie route," Kai said.

"And what is that supposed to mean?" I snapped.

"I hope she doesn't jump ship or request to be dropped off on some remote island," Kai answered with a laugh."

"You are such the comedian today. And just for the record, I never once thought about jumping off anything."

"But you did take the remote island route," Kai said with a smirk.

"Very funny," I replied a little bit mad. I was just mad that the truth hurt. "How long have I been in here?" I asked.

"A few hours. You were asleep for most of it. But you've had a long day and must be mentally exhausted. I really hope you know how proud of you I am and how much you inspire me. To be honest with you, I never knew if you would ever be the same Mel again. After the first few years, I was really worried about you. I know people take their own time to grieve, but I didn't see any signs of you moving on or wanting to. But these last six or so months, I have seen signs of life coming back. I began to see and feel that you had hope. Hope for life going on. I could tell that you were beginning to get some sunlight through your cloud of fog," Kai said.

I was speechless. I had no idea Kai felt this way. For some reason my mind went to Mother Theresa and thinking that Kai was a descendant of hers. How would I ever pay her back for all she had done for me?

"I had no idea you felt that way. I am so, so sorry for putting you through everything I have. Thank you for being there. I don't know what would have happened to me if you weren't my best friend. I'm so sorry I worried you for so long. Thanks for not giving up on me," I said as I felt tears pooling in the corners of my eyes. Kai and I didn't get sappy often, but just hearing how she felt all these years really made the core of my soul ache. Kai had sacrificed herself and her life for me. What great work had I done in my life to deserve her as my best friend and could I ever return the favor?

"Hey, we are not crying tonight," Kai said. "You have cried enough to supply a small town with a lifetime reservoir of water." If the situation had been reversed and I was the widow, I know you would have done the same for me. And knowing you would do that, is all that you owe me."

I was trying to hold back the tears because Kai was right; I had done enough crying, but I was damn good at it. I decided that some humor would be good right about now.

"So do you think people would think we were lovers if I got your name tattooed on my body?" I asked with a smirk. Kai knew that I was trying to lighten up things.

"If you ever have my name permanently fixed to your body, I'm calling Lilith and telling her it's time we checked you into rehab for your alcohol problem," Kai said.

I threw a couch pillow at her and we both broke out in laughter. Life was too short to cry and not laugh enough.

GURRRL

"Kai, the camera is ready. I'm logging on in five."

"I'll be right there," Kai replied. She was upstairs. I wanted to make sure she would be here in time to start the video conference.

"Hey," Kai said as she walked into the office and pulled her chair over to my PC.

"You ready? Who is going to do the talking? Me or you?" I asked her.

"I am feeling on my A game today. I can talk," Kai replied.

"Perfect. Here we go."

I logged on to the web conferencing website we were using. Amelia was already in the virtual meeting room when we connected and the video went live.

"Amelia Marlowe?" Kai asked.

"Yes, I am Amelia Marlowe," a mousy voice sweetly replied. I was glad Kai was doing the talking because that gave me the chance to study Amelia Marlowe. She was a beautiful young woman. After interviewing her mother, I wouldn't have expected her genes to produce such a beautiful, delicate being. Amelia had a perfectly rounded face, beautiful green eyes, and skin that was flawless with a set of freckles sprinkled across her cheeks. She had the perfect posture, which made her look tall and almost like a member of a royal family. She spoke with such precision and softness it seemed that she had been groomed from a young age to be a proper lady of society. Maybe she got it from her father's side of the family.

"Hi, Amelia. My name is Kai Silva and this is my partner, Melanie Alexander. Thank you for meeting with us today. I'm not sure what you know about us, but we are private investigators. We have some information for you."

"Yes, the dean of the university briefed me on the meeting today."

"Good. We were hired by your biological father, John Danville. He wanted us to locate you to deliver some information he has for you. He wants you to know that he was recently diagnosed with Huntington's disease. This disease may have genetic links, which is why your father wanted us to locate you so you could be tested and consult with a doctor for preventative measures," Kai explained.

Amelia's face was nonreactive. I couldn't tell if she was going to scream, cry, or sit there in absolute silence.

"What exactly is Huntington's?" she asked very quietly, without moving a single muscle in her face. She could do a Botox commercial without ever needing one shot of the stuff.

"Huntington's is a genetic disorder that causes degeneration of the nerves. We are not medical experts, so we encourage you to seek the advice of your doctor. As with everything else these days, you can do an online search for more information," Kai said. We had done a ton of research on Huntington's when we were first hired by Mr. Danville.

"So, you have talked with John Danville—my…my…father? How is he? Is he going to die?" Amelia asked, once again without moving a single muscle.

"Yes, we have spoken with him, and he is doing well. He gave us his contact information in case you wanted to contact him. Would you like us to e-mail it to you?" Kai said.

"Yes, please. I would like that very much," Amelia said in her sweet, doll-like voice, again without even moving a muscle or changing her facial expression in the slightest.

"We would be happy to send you the information."

"So can you die from Huntington's?" Amelia asked once again. Even talking about death didn't change her expressionless face.

"We are sorry, but we are not medical experts, so we would encourage you to conduct your own research or speak to your doctor. From our own research, Huntington's causes someone to slowly lose the ability to perform certain functions and has a cognitive and physical impact."

"Okay. I'm sorry for asking the same question again. It is just so much information to take in and comprehend. My life has been a whirlwind lately, and every time I turn around, there is a new piece of information about who I am. I apologize for all the questions. Thank you for finding me. I sincerely appreciate it very much. Would the both of you mind if I asked you just one more question?" Amelia said timidly.

"Of course," Kai answered. "And please don't apologize for asking questions. We will do whatever we can to help you."

My heart really felt for this girl and the hand she had been dealt in life. She had lived a lie told to her by her mother, someone every child should be able to trust. Her statuesque presence made me feel that she was broken inside, and floating in the middle of the ocean was easier than facing what was waiting for her on dry land. I chuckled under my breath because I could relate. I just preferred islands and Amelia preferred ships.

"If you were in my situation, what would you do? Since you spoke to my real father you must know a bit about my tangled background. What would you do with all of this information? Where would you start?" Amelia asked, still as a concrete statue.

I felt that this was a question I should field, so I did.

"Amelia, after my husband was killed in Afghanistan, I struggled with the meaning of life for quite a few years. I really struggled with simply living. But I have learned one thing: to treasure life and every second that you have of it. Follow your heart and don't have any regrets. I just recently called my parents for the first time in years. They never came to my husband's funeral, but for my own healing, I called them. I didn't want to live with the regret that I didn't make an effort to try and rekindle the relationship. My advice is to do what you need to do to bring healing and starting that healing process with family is a good place to start. After speaking to my parents, I felt a sense of relief and felt that finally something was right in my life. When I learned how my parents felt during the years we didn't speak, it opened my eyes to their side of the story. " Wow, I had gotten that out without one tear!

"Your husband was killed? Please accept my most sincere condolences for your loss. And thank you for your honesty. I just met you two, but you have been the most honest with me than most people in my life. Thank you for being so nice. It means a lot to me," Amelia said, but this time the muscles in her face were finally free from paralysis. I saw a small upturn of her lips, which indicated a smile—not an obvious one, but a slight one. Her stoic face and composure was how she dealt with the chaos in her life. She never let it show on the outside. It was her coping mechanism. I knew a few things about coping mechanisms too.

"Is there anything else we can help you with?" I asked.

"No. Thank you again for everything. My heart is telling me that I should get to know my father and the genetics that we share," Amelia replied sweetly. "And I need to call my mom too."

"I think those are both great places to start," I said reassuringly. "Can I ask you a question, if you don't mind?"

"Of course," Amelia replied.

"I'm curious about the *Floatin' Utopia* and why you are on a floating commune," I asked. I had to know. Kai kicked my foot under the desk, which was code for *Did you really just ask that?*

Amelia smiled and I could almost see her teeth. She said, "In exchange for a semester of tuition, I agreed to be part of a human psychological and sociological experiment. I'm planning on majoring in psychology, so I thought it would be a good opportunity to be a part of the first experiment of its kind. There are lots of researchers on board who take observations, conduct interviews, and have focus groups. Some of the main themes of this experiment are in regards to the commune lifestyle and philosophy and the differences between land based and floating based; the actual science of a commune on a ship—from growing food to purifying water; the psychological impacts of mental and emotional health from a floating commune life. I could go on and on with all the different research angles."

"If you think of anything else, please e-mail us. We will send you an email after this call with John Danville's contact information. You can just reply to that e-mail if you need anything else. Thank you again for talking with us today," Kai said. We had Amelia's e-mail from setting up the video conference. She had allowed the university to provide it to us.

"I will. Thank you again. I really appreciate you finding me on this ship. I hope you have a great afternoon," Amelia said with another upturn of her lips, which almost made a smile.

I logged off of the conferencing service.

"She is such a sweet girl," Kai said.

"I know. She is so formal too. Her vocabulary is so proper. My heart just goes out to her, but I think she will do the right thing, and I hope she can find some happiness," I said.

"I'm proud of you for what you told her. I know it isn't easy for you to talk about Ryan, but you answered her question so calmly. That's twice now that you've talked about Ryan with complete strangers and without breaking down. I'm impressed, girl. You should be proud of yourself. Maybe you can use your experience to help others. I think you really reached Amelia by sharing your story. I say we go out and celebrate tonight," Kai said.

"You will use any occasion to go out and celebrate. But let's not celebrate me. Let's celebrate closing a case and being able to help a young woman. This is why I like being a PI—we can have these types of conversations with the people we find. We can go a little deeper with people than we could with the agency."

"Yea, I know. It felt good to talk to her like big sisters. Poor girl. I'm glad I have you or I would be a lost Amelia floating around the world," Kai said.

"And if I didn't have you, I would probably be dead," I said as I winked at Kai.

"You got that right, gurl," Kai said with her slang *gurl* instead of *girl*.

"Do you want to call John Danville, or do you want me to?" I asked Kai.

"You can. I am glad to have another happy ending—well, as happy as you can get in the PI business," Kai said.

"I think this was a happy ending. Amelia is finally getting some answers about her past. I will call John here in a few. So, since you kept me alive, I'll pay for our night out. So where are you dragging me to this evening?" I asked just to annoy Kai.

"Damn right I am dragging your butt out of this house. I am thinking we should go check out the scene at Patters. And you don't even have to ask me to pick out your attire for our outing. I already know what to put you in," Kai said.

"You better make sure it is rated G because I still owe you for the bikini-switch-a-roo you pulled in Jaco."

Kai laughed and I did too.

I looked up John Danville's contact information on the computer and dialed the number. While I waited for Mr. Danville to answer, I typed an email to Amelia with his contact information.

"Hello," I heard a voice say.

"Hello. Is this Mr. Danville?" I asked.

"Yes it is," Mr. Danville answered.

"This is Melanie Alexander. How are you today?"

"Hi Ms. Alexander. I'm doing all right today. How are you?" he asked.

"I'm doing well thanks. I have some good news for you. We located Amelia and spoke with her this afternoon. We have provided her with your contact information. She is currently on a cruise ship, but she does have e-mail access."

There was a long pause on the phone. I wanted patiently for Mr. Danville to gather his thoughts.

"I can't believe you found her. I'm so relieved. You said you spoke to her? How is she? Did she sound okay?" he asked very excitedly.

"We actually had a video conference with her, so we got to see her as well. She looked and sounded well. She was very nice to talk to. My partner, Kai, and I had a very nice conversation with her. She is a very well-spoken and polite young woman."

"I can't believe you saw her. I haven't seen her since she was very little," said Mr. Danville as his voice started to fade.

"After we shared the information regarding Huntington's, she asked how you were doing. She had some questions about Huntington's and we recommended that she speak to a medical professional," I explained.

"She asked about me?" he said quietly.

"Yes, she asked how you were doing and we said well. We told her we would e-mail her your contact information and I sent that e-mail to her just before I called you. So she has your contact information."

"I can't thank you enough for finding her and giving her my contact information. I feel relieved that she knows about my Huntington's and can get tested herself," he said.

Before I could respond, he said, "So you said she's on a cruise ship?"

"Yes. She's on a cruise ship for an experiment sponsored by the university she attends. The ship is a floating commune and researchers are aboard collecting data and observations," I explained.

"Oh, wow. Ok," Mr. Danville said. I had to refrain from laughing because my explanation did sound a bit ridiculous.

"Do you know when she will be off?" he asked.

"I am not sure. Amelia didn't tell us," I replied.

"Okay. Can you tell me what university she is attending?" Mr. Danville asked.

"I'm sorry. Unfortunately I can't," I replied sympathetically.

"I understand. I'm just glad she is fine and you saw her with your own eyes. I feel so much better."

"I'm so glad to hear that," I said.

"If I don't hear from her, can I contact you again to deliver a message if my health starts to deteriorate?" Mr. Danville asked.

"Yes, of course you can. We are happy to help if we can."

"Thank you. And thank you for all you've done for me," he said.

"You are very welcome. If you need anything else, please let us know. It was a pleasure working with you," I said.

"Bye, Melanie."

"Bye, Mr. Danville."

I hung up the phone. My heart really did go out to Mr. Danville and Amelia. They missed too many years of each other's lives, but hopefully they would use the future time they have together wisely. I chuckled at myself after this last thought because I should take my own advice. I really hoped Amelia would contact Mr. Danville before it was too late. I didn't want to tell Amelia that when an adult is diagnosed with Huntington's that the average life span is ten to twenty years post diagnosis. I just hoped she would act sooner instead of later.

"Kai, I called John Danville, so we need to send him our final bill."

"Okay," Kai called from the kitchen. I heard the blender, so I wanted to see what she was making.

I got up from my desk and walked into the kitchen, and Kai was making some grass-green-colored concoction in the blender. It looked like slime.

"What is that?" I asked as my squinted-up face peered into the blender with disgust.

"This is my special we-can-party-all-night power shake. I made enough for two," Kai said with pure joy and excitement in her voice.

"I will not be drinking that. I can't decide if it looks like snot or slime," I said with the disgusted look still on my face.

"Oh, you will be drinking it. It will make you party all night, gurrrrrrl," Kai said in her sassy voice.

"You can't make me drink snot. What is in that nasty slime?" I asked her.

"Pears, endive, a little spinach, water, and splash of blue agave nectar. You make me drink that hangover concoction you make so I don't want to hear it."

She poured the slime into two hand-blown glass iced tea goblets. Like presentation was going to help.

"Cheers," she said as she clinked my glass, which was still sitting on the kitchen island. After she came up for air, she said, "That is so delicious."

I gave her this I-don't-know-who-you-are look and went to the refrigerator. I got out an opened bottle of Riesling and poured myself a glass. After I came up for air, I said, "This is so delicious." I was not drinking her slime.

"Drink up, gurrrrrrl. Maybe you'll be in a party mode when we go out tonight," Kai said.

"What is up with the *gurrrrrrl*?" I asked her.

"I just love saying it."

We went to the hearth room to drink and chat. I loved sitting in front of a crackling fire in the middle of the afternoon drinking wine and talking. For a brief second, I thought to myself how drinking wine in the afternoon would make someone think I had a drinking problem. If that was the only problem I had after the last four years, I'd take it.

BROKEN

Kai really missed her calling as a personal shopper/fashion designer/stylist. After a few hours at Spa Kai, I was a finished masterpiece. I felt amazing. Feeling beautiful and sexy was better therapy than gin and a shrink. I had on a pair of jeans that were probably a size too small, but Kai said they were the size I should wear. I had on a gray boyfriend cardigan with a little turquoise camisole underneath. Kai decorated me with me a long silver necklace and a huge oval-shaped turquoise ring. I had on black-heeled boots that my skinny jeans tucked into. Bless Kai for making a hot mess just hot. That girl had a gift.

It took Kai half the amount of time to be "beautified" than it did me. She had on dark jeans and a flowing, white silk shirt that hung just right on her. The cowl-lick neckline sat draped perfectly across her collarbone. She had on wedges that had a black-and-white swirled design with large lime-green waves of color weaved in. As always, she was stunning.

The air was quite chilly tonight, so we took the Metro to Patters and then would most likely take a cab home. I wasn't about to walk home with heels on. I hated to admit it to myself, but I was glad to be out. The DC night life was a very good distraction from the voices in my head. I was looking forward to having an evening free from my mind and the thoughts that flowed through it. I was still yearning to be in Fiji but didn't want to hear Kai's face-your-demons speech, so I kept the "F" word to myself. I asked Kai if I could hold her arm while we walked to the

Metro so I could close my eyes and not see anything Christmas-related. I told her that if I saw one Christmas decoration or heard any Christmas cheer, I was going home. I was going straight home and booking a flight to Fiji—with or without her approval. Kai shot me her "I dare you" look. Look or no look—I was a grown woman and could do whatever I wanted. And I couldn't get JR off my mind. My mind needed an off switch.

Kai had always referred to Patters as a quaint, little pub. She said it was a bit more sophisticated than some other establishments she frequented. It was in a restored storefront, and Kai had been a regular since the place opened. This was my first time at Patters, and I immediately observed that the crowd was a little older—maybe thirysomethings. I said *crap* really loud in my head when I realized that *we* were prime members of that thirty-something crowd. The crowd wasn't older—I had gotten older and was in denial. We made our way to the bar through the shoulder-to-shoulder crowd. I wondered if it was always this crowded or if something special was going on tonight. I looked around trying to figure it out, but didn't see anything out of the normal. Apparently people were just out and about tonight. Kai ordered our usuals—a greyhound and dirty martini. We found a high-top table to stand at. It was a bit too loud to talk, but that was okay. We were both crowd surfing when I heard the word *causalities* out of the flat-screen TV above the bar. I whipped my neck around so fast that I heard the popping of my vertebrae. I was horrified with what I saw on the screen. I robotically got up and walked close enough to the TV so I could see it and read the closed captions that were on. I was glued to the screen. I no longer heard the buzzing of the bar. I couldn't move. Every muscle in my body was rigid and frozen. My eyes stopped blinking. I was in a CNN-induced trance. I was forcing myself to breathe as the images flashed in front of me. I wanted to walk away, but my body wouldn't move. My eyes were unable to blink. And then everything went black.

"Mel. Mel. Can you hear me?"

I knew it was Kai's voice, but I couldn't answer her. I felt something cold on my forehead and on my temples, but I couldn't raise my arm to wipe it away. My mind was racing with thoughts. I was thankful that I could still think. If I could think, I must not be dead, but that didn't explain the paralysis. And then I knew what was happening. I was having a heart attack. I had seconds before I would be dead—lifeless. I knew that at any second, I would stop thinking, and my life would be over. I wondered what my final thought would be. And then I felt it. The fog. The pitch-black fog that had consumed my soul for the past four years. It had returned, and I knew the end had come.

"Ryan." Was I still alive? I think that my lips just mouthed the word *Ryan*. I wanted to try it again to see if I was alive.

"Jenner." My lips still worked! And I was still thinking, so there must be blood still flowing, which meant I was alive. But did I just say *Jenner*? The TV. I had to get back to that TV.

"Mel. Mel, honey. Let's get you up so I can look at your head."

I knew that voice. Oh, I could still hear too. Why would Kai want to get me up? And what happened to my head? I pushed my right hand down and felt a hard surface. Oh, I wasn't paralyzed anymore. I could move my right hand! I was definitely alive!

Suddenly I felt this wave of motion come over me, and I was instantly dizzy. I tried to open my eyes, but my eyelids were very heavy. I put my right hand on my forehead to feel the cold, wetness that was on my eye. As soon as my hand touched my skin, I knew I was bleeding. That would explain the dizziness. So maybe I wasn't having a heart attack after all.

"Mel, open your eyes," I heard Kai's voice say again.

Before I could answer, I heard some indistinct chatter. I heard Kai say something about an ambulance. I heard her talking about me to another voice. It sounded male. Was it Ryan? Did I have a heart attack? I had to open my eyes so I could see what was going on. I pushed with all my might, and my eyes opened.

"Mel. Mel. Say something. What hurts?" said Kai. I heard her, but the fog occupying my brain sucked the meaning of her words right out of my head; apparently my brain had a different agenda. I just stared and was trying to hear the TV. Where was it? Finding that TV was all I could think about. Where was the damn thing? I had to confirm the thoughts that were racing through my head. Did I really see American military casualties on the TV? And then I felt it—a throbbing pain in my left elbow. And then the pain took over and shook me awake. I focused in on Kai's face, especially since it was only a few inches from mine. And then I saw the face that went with the voice Kai was talking to. It looked like Carlos. I scanned his shirt for a badge, and I found it. I couldn't make out the name, but I think it was Carlos. Or was I hallucinating?

"My elbow," I whispered to Kai. It didn't even sound like my voice. If my head was bleeding, why did my elbow hurt?

"Mel, your elbow hurts? I think it might be broken. You hit the floor pretty hard. I am going to take you to the ER unless you want to go in the ambulance. Does your head hurt? You hit the corner of the table on the way to the floor. You may need a few stitches."

"No ambulance," I whispered again. "Where's my phone? What did you see on TV? Why is this happening again? Where's my phone, Kai? *Where is my phone?*" I whispered very loudly. I wasn't sure why I couldn't speak at a normal octave. I had to check my phone for the news or any text messages.

"You can check your phone on the way to the ER. Let's go," Kai said.

I felt her hand on my throbbing elbow, and then I felt another large hand around my waist helping me to get up. I followed the hand to the arm to the face, and it was Carlos.

"Kai, is that Carlos?" I asked wearily.

"Yes, he responded to the call."

"Mel, you're going to be all right," Carlos said. "The paramedics are on their way."

I hadn't heard that voice in a long time. My ferociously throbbing elbow was occupying my thoughts, making it difficult to think. Did he say *paramedics?* Damn it, I didn't need no bus ride to the hospital. And then I heard it—the familiar and entrancing sound of the news. My eyes were glued to the TV. There it was! There was fire and smoke in the background. It appeared that an entire city was engulfed in flames.

"Yesterday was another dismal day for American troops after eight members of a military envoy were killed when their vehicles exploded into flames. The military has yet to release the names of the servicemen and women or the possible party responsible. The troops were in an area that has been involved in heavy insurgent fighting over the past several months. It has been said that insurgents in this area are very well armed and equipped and the United States is trying to determine who is the arm supplier for this group," the newscaster said so coolly, so calmly, and with no emotion whatsoever.

Kai grabbed my right arm, but we didn't walk. Two paramedics were at my side now and helping me onto a stretcher. *Great. This is exactly what I needed.* I wrenched my neck around to see the TV on the way out. I was determined to catch every last pixel before it was out of range. And why was I going in the ambulance to the hospital?

Once my head was free from the hypnotism of the TV, the pain of my elbow and the pain in my gut telling me JR was dead hit me. My throbbing temple and my bloodstained shirt was of my last concern. Hell, I had almost had my arm shot off once, and I was a widow. A little cut that required a few stitches was a paper cut in my book.

"They're dead, aren't they?" I asked Kai in my new whispering voice.

Kai grabbed the shoulder of my good arm and looked me squarely in the face. "Mel, is that what this is about? Is that why you blacked out at the TV? Mel, you listen to me: You don't know anything. Stop thinking those thoughts. You are only going to make yourself crazy," Kai responded. "Don't do this to yourself, Mel. I need you to focus on your pain or on me. Stop thinking thoughts that lead down a dark road. We will face the facts when we know them, but right now we know *nothing*."

"Have you heard from Will?"

"No, but that doesn't mean anything."

"Hell it doesn't. If they are indeed alive, they would have heard of this incident and let one of us know something," I told Kai in my angry whispering voice.

"How hard did you hit your head? You know that when you are on assignment sometimes you just can't communicate. No news is good news."

"My elbow hurts so damn bad I can't even surf the web on my phone to see if I can find out who the American casualties are."

"I am going to throw that phone out the window. Do you realize that you had a panic attack and passed out? You need to stop spiraling your thoughts out of control. You are freaking out for no reason, Mel. Let's take some deep breaths. Breath in your nose and out your mouth." Kai was demonstrating the breathing technique for me like I didn't know how to do it. After a few minutes of resisting, I started breathing with her. After my mind began to focus again, I realized that the paramedic was monitoring me and had stabilized my elbow.

"Kai, this is Ryan all over again, but this time I found out from CNN instead of the military showing up at my door. And I am pissed at myself for reacting so strongly to a man I hardly know," I said. "Why are the men in my life cursed with death?"

"Come on, Mel. 'Cursed with death'?" Kai said.

"This entire time I kept telling myself that Jenner meant nothing to me, and I had to forget him, but I didn't want to. I didn't want to like him even though I do, but I was afraid to like him. It must be my defense mechanism, you know. But as soon as I heard the TV, the black fog of Ryan descended upon me, and I knew. I knew that Jenner was dead. My soul couldn't decide if I should cry or scream, and now I am pissed. I am filled with this anger that has me divided into two. I am angry that I will never get the chance to understand why Ryan was taken away from me and why JR was dropped in my lap in Costa Rica. Why does this keep happening to me? What is it about me? Am I jinxed? *My elbow hurts!*"

"The wound is just fresh from Ryan," said Kai. "You are freaking out for no reason. The guys are fine," Kai said trying to comfort me. You have no proof that they aren't. And your elbow hurts because you landed on it when you blacked out. You scared the living crap out of me. I had no idea if you had fainted, were having a heart attack, or a seizure. You faint more than anyone I have ever met. Your fainting spells have taken years off my life."

"I'm sorry, Kai," I whispered to her.

The pain in my elbow was making it more difficult to think clearly. The pain was all I could focus on, so I closed my eyes, hoping it would just go away. Hoping it would all just go away.

The door of the ambulance opened, and a smiling, soft-spoken, middle-aged woman was asking me questions.

"You are at the ER at George Washington Hospital. Can you tell me your name?" the nurse asked.

"Melanie Alexander," I whispered. Why was I still whispering? I needed the mental ward more than I needed the ER.

"Can you tell me what happened?" she asked.

"I think I fainted and hit my head on a table and must have landed on my elbow. My friend Kai can tell you exactly what happened. She was there," I replied.

"Kai is in the waiting room. She can come back in a bit. We are going to get your vitals and take some x-rays of that elbow," she explained. "Do you remember fainting or how you felt before you fainted?" she asked.

If I seriously told her that I fainted because I thought my new love interest was killed in combat because my husband was killed in action a few years ago and I felt the fog come over me, she would definitely have a psych evaluation called for me. And I really did not need that drama right now. I really needed to get out of here. I knew I was broken. I had been broken for four years. I didn't need some psych ward shrink to tell me that.

"I felt light-headed before I fainted. It was probably a combination of the martini and the temperature in the bar. It was hot in there. I feel fine now except for my elbow," I explained. I was so hoping the nurse would buy my story.

I was beginning to sweat from the pain, and I was watching my elbow swell. It was three times its normal size and had a nice bruise forming. The nurse gave me a shot for pain and for a few minutes I couldn't decide what hurt worse—the shot or the elbow.

After being x-rayed, stitched, and splinted, I was finally able to go. I apparently had a hairline radial fracture to my elbow, which would require a splint for eight weeks. Convenient. I also had five stitches to my temple and would have to have the stitches removed in about a week. Again, convenient. Kai had been sitting with me for about an hour now and we were both ready to go. I hated hospitals. I hated the germs and the thought of catching something I didn't have when I first came in. I hated the antiseptic and stale air smell. I hated the sickness and the sadness. I was ready to leave.

Kai and I took a cab home, and I couldn't wait to get in the house and sit down. The ride in the cab made me remember Carlos, so I had to get the skinny on him. Even though it was well into the wee hours of the morning, I couldn't sleep. I probably wouldn't sleep with this ridiculous contraption on my arm for the next eight weeks. I plopped down in my favorite chair. It felt good to be home.

"I saw Carlos, right? I just want to make sure I've recalled the evening's events correctly. I would hate to forget the details," I said to Kai. I had had five hours of waiting at the ER to process the evening's events.

"Mel, you make my life exciting, girl. I will tell you that," Kai said with a chuckle. "If you wouldn't have had one of your freak-out Mel moments, Carlos would never have responded to the emergency call. So maybe I should thank you for fainting."

"You're welcome. I am glad my fear of people in my life dying comes in handy for you," I replied with a wink. "Continue on! I am waiting!"

"Well, after Carlos finished his shift, he met me at the hospital, and we had some coffee in the cafeteria," Kai said.

"But we had a really good chat," Kai continued on. "As I was sitting there across the table from him, I had this feeling of déjà vu come over me. It was like time had stopped, and we hadn't missed a moment of each other's lives. He isn't seeing anyone, and he told me that he misses me. He wants to take me out to dinner."

I really should go to bed because it hurt my brain to think, but I processed the Carlos information. "Are you going to go?" I asked puzzlingly.

"I don't know. I have moments where I tell myself that I am going and then I have other moments where I tell myself I am not. I haven't thought about Carlos in a long time, but seeing him today really stirred up my feelings. It's just been a really long time," Kai said. I could see that her brain was deeply processing her thoughts and feelings about Carlos. She had really been in love with him. And maybe that never goes away. My head was pounding. I had to stop thinking.

"You need to rest, girl. You want me to help you get into your pj's?" Kai asked.

"Na, I am just going to sleep right here. Are you okay with the whole seeing Carlos thing? I asked.

"Yeah, I'm good. We can talk about it in the morning. It's been a long day and night."

"Okay, I'm sorry for all the trouble, " I said. Seriously, how much more drama could I partake in?

"No worries, girl. I would be bored without ya. Here are you pain pills," Kai said as she handed me the prescription bottle we had filled at the pharmacy. "Night."

"Thanks. Night." I closed my eyes. I knew what I had to do and I had to do it in the morning.

MARATHON

After a few hours of sleep, the pain in my elbow woke me. I popped another pain pill and climbed the stairs to my room. I got my suitcase out of the closet and packed. I hadn't traveled alone since Ryan, but I had to go. I had to get well. What sane person passes out at the news in a bar and requires a splint and stitches? I really was still a hot mess. I couldn't go on like this. I had to get back to normal or something close to it. Kai would be pissed at me, but I was praying she would understand. She was my crutch, and I had to stand on my own. I hoped Jenner would understand why I had to leave if by some miraculous event he was still alive. I guessed his true feelings for me would come out. Would he wait for me or would he say "cuckoo" and move on? For all I know, he may be dead.

I logged on to my laptop and bought my ticket. I pulled out a piece of paper from my desk drawer and wrote Kai a note:

K,

I had to leave. I have got to get well. I have to stand on my own two feet because apparently I can't go out in public without causing drama. Who passes out at the news and breaks her elbow and requires stitches? I hope you can forgive me for going. You know where I am. I had to go and find myself again. I am staying as long as it takes to search the depths of my soul for the old Melanie Audrey Alexander. The one you met at Stanford and dodged bullets with during our agency days. I'm still sorry you left

the agency on account of me. You should go back. I promise that I am going to come back *me*. The current hot-
mess Mel is being left behind. But I have to go so I can
throw her into the depths of the ocean. I left the keys to
the Escape on the kitchen island. Drive it if you want. If
you are still talking to me when I return, we can celebrate
Christmas. The New Year will bring a new me. I promise.

Love,

M

I had one stop to make before I headed for the airport. I could
only imagine what I looked like as I walked down the National
Mall wheeling a suitcase with a splint, bandage on my left temple, and hugely oversized Hollywood divalicious sunglasses, but
I didn't care. At this point, the people of DC should thank me
that I was walking down the National Mall fully clothed and not
hysterically sobbing. And I wasn't using up tax dollars occupying
space in the city mental ward, so again, the people of DC should
be thanking me instead of staring. I silently prayed that the DC
paparazzi wouldn't think I was some strung-out Hollywood
chicklet and start snapping pics. I really didn't want to have to
jam their cameras up their noses with my good hand.

My gloved hands were beginning to go numb from the nippy
winter air and the breeze blowing off the Potomac. I hadn't
decided yet if I would miss DC on my extended healing island
sabbatical. I knew what I had to do if I wanted to heal the bro-
kenness. I reached into the pocket of my coat and pulled out my
beloved connection to the world— my BlackBerry. In order to
mend the holes in my soul, I needed to disconnect and recharge
without distractions. I cocked my good arm back behind my ear
and hurled my BlackBerry into the Potomac. Now I was ready.

I enjoyed the peaceful metro ride to Reagan and checked my
bag, which I hated to do, but my elbow hurt too bad to handle it
solo. I walked to the gate and just sat. I sat in silence. *I was doing
this*, I told myself mentally over and over again. I boarded the

plane in a state of numbness. I had left my best friend at home to spend Christmas alone. Kai had never abandoned me in my darkest moments, but here I was selfishly running to Fiji. I should have made this trip years ago. I should never have let myself act like this for so long. What in the world was wrong with me? I put my iPod headphones in so no one would talk me. I didn't plan on talking to anyone until I got back to DC. I didn't need anyone's nonsense in my brain. I didn't want to hear about some stranger's drama. I had enough of my own. Luckily the seat next to me remained empty, and I took that as a sign.

I began planning my self-therapy sabbatical. I would sun, walk, and may even surf. Three easy steps for extracting the pollutants of my soul. The new and improved Mel would then emerge. I knew that I would never be the old Mel, but I knew a version of her existed somewhere. JR had brought out a bit of the old Mel that felt familiar to me, and I liked her. I would do some self-discovery and rid myself of the demons that sent me into panic mode. I closed my eyes, hoping that JR and Will were both okay and that I would sleep all the way to San Francisco.

Sleep seemed to escape me on the first leg of my soul-finding journey. I couldn't shut off my never-ending, idea-generating brain and throbbing elbow. I was thinking random thoughts that wouldn't rest so I could sleep. I was thinking about Kai and for all I had put her through. I was thinking that this is the farthest travel I had done solo. I wondered about JR and if I would ever see him again. I wondered about Amelia and her father. I wondered if my Fiji sabbatical would actually close the doors to my past and open a new chapter of my life. And I even thought if it would be possible for me to be ever normal again. Would I be able to shovel out the dirt of my soul and cleanse my spirit? I even had the thought of trying to go back to the agency cross my mind, but it came and went quickly. I was beginning to get annoyed at my brain and all its thoughts. I needed a brain remote so I could put it on sleep or turn it off. The more mad I got, the quicker the thoughts came: *Am I crazy for leaving in the middle of the night and not talking to Kai first? Will I ever get married again? How long will I stay in Fiji? What if Kai would get married and move out? Can I live alone? Will my mother call me? Why can't I shut off my own brain!*

I looked out the airplane window and let the thoughts run wild, hoping my brain would be out of them soon, and I could sleep.

When the plane touched down in San Francisco, I had only slept for a few hours, but I felt empowered. Empowered to face my demons and get back to living life. I spent much of the four-hour layover shopping and eating. I purchased a new pair of flip-flops, sunscreen, and a bagful of snacks, since there was no food at the house. I would have to go to the teeny-weeny grocery tomorrow, but at least I would have some things to munch on until then. The thought of the market in Nadi brought happiness to my senses. I could smell the coconut, papaya, and pineapple. I could taste my favorite dish, which was *kassava*. It was tapioca cooked in coconut cream with mashed bananas and pure cane sugar mixed in. It was the perfect blend of yogurt, oatmeal, and the sweetness of coconut ice cream all in one bowl. I could eat it morning, noon, and night, and I just might. You could sample anything before you bought it, and there was nothing deep fried or processed. I would buy enough groceries for a day or two, and then go out to get more. That was the lifestyle there. The refrigerator at the beach house was one of the small ones that college students put in dorm rooms. So you had to buy fresh and shop often, and that was one of the things I most adored about Fiji. I would gorge myself with fresh pineapple, papaya, kiwi, watermelon, yams, and cassava. Beans would also be a staple in my diet here, since I really hadn't grown accustomed to the fish and poultry they ate. There was one popular dish called *kakoda*, which was locally caught mahi-mahi steamed in coconut crème and limes. I found it too chewy every time I ate it, and just couldn't get myself used to eating it. My mouth began watering for the tomatoes at the Nadi market that I would eat like an apple. Coconut milk was a main staple used in Fijian cooking, and I had grown to love it—even crave it. For a brief moment, I had forgotten that I was in the airport, when I heard an announcement about my flight boarding.

The next leg of my trip would be to Auckland, New Zealand. After I arrived in Auckland, I would hop another flight to Nadi, Fiji. The weariness of leaving secretly was beginning to wear off as I got closer to my island sabbatical. The beach house was only seven hundred square feet, but it was the perfect seven hundred square feet in paradise. The house was situated on a hillside and was located just right so there was a constant ocean breeze blowing through the house. Kai and I loved to keep the windows open and let the ocean air encompass us. Even though the house was small, it had windows galore so you could catch the breeze and the amazing ocean view. It was about a half mile walk down to the beach, but the azure blue water could be seen from both decks—the one off the family room and one off the bedroom. I couldn't wait to nap in the hammock on the deck and hear nothing but the wind, the surf, and the wildlife. The beach house was two levels, with the only bedroom on the top level. The galley-style kitchen, family room, and bathroom were on the first floor. The windows were floor to ceiling and the walls were wood paneling. The house had solar panels and generated its own energy, which was wonderful. Fiji's climate is so steady and moderate that no heating or air-conditioning was necessary. All you needed was an ocean breeze on a hot day. If my personal sabbatical was a success, maybe I would rent out the beach house to other lost souls looking for themselves. If I couldn't overcome my past and my fears while living in paradise, there was literally no hope for me. And if kava, Fiji's ceremonial drink, which probably should be labeled as a narcotic, couldn't help you with your self-therapy, then you were hopeless. My first task in Fiji would be a trip to the market and a cup of kava. After a cup, you got that I-don't-have-a-care-in-the-world-and-everything-is-just-peachy feeling. Kava had sedating properties that relaxed your entire body. Your lips and tongue tingled, every muscle in your body relaxed, and you felt the weight of the world lifted. I looked at my watch as I stood on the jet way. This time tomorrow I would be in paradise.

The flight from San Francisco to Auckland was uneventful. I unfortunately had someone in the seat next to me, but I made it very clear from the beginning of the flight that I was not friendly. I pulled out my first-class amenity kit and located the sleep mask. Score! If putting on a sleep mask didn't say "Don't bother me," I don't know what did. The amenity kit was one of my favorite first-class perks. It was a little cosmetic bag filled with goodies— Chapstick, tissues, socks, toothpaste and toothbrush, earplugs, a pen, and hand cream.

My seat neighbor was a man in his fifties, who was dressed in a suit—a three-piece suit. I was not sure who wore a three-piece suit on a fourteen-hour flight. He could have at least taken off the vest. He tried to chat it up with me a few times, but I denied him my company. I answered him in German, and apparently he got the hint. Now that I thought about it, I think I said something like, "I only speak German, and I don't want hot coffee." But he got the hint. I had taken German, Spanish, and Mandarin Chinese at Stanford, and this was the first time my German had come in handy. I was quite proud of myself that the German rolled off my tongue so quickly and sounded fluent. Maybe this was another sign that I was crazy. When we boarded the plane, I saw that he had a United States passport, so I was betting on the fact he didn't know German, and I was right. I wasn't about to have fourteen hours of aimless and pointless chitchat with a complete stranger. I knew how I must look—an arm in a sling with a huge Band-Aid on my forehead headed solo to a remote part of the world. Mr. Suit probably thought I was running from an abusive husband; that is what I would think if I saw myself on an airplane. But in reality, I was just a crazy widow with a broken

heart and soul. But I was going to fix that. Instead of telling a
stranger about the hot mess that was my life, I would prefer to
listen to all the random thoughts flying about in my head. I once
again put in my earphones and pulled down my sleep mask.

After dozing off for a few hours, the metal clanging of the airline meal car awoke me. I looked at my watch, and it was way past
the DC dinner hour. I had requested vegetarian meals when I
booked my flight because I never trusted airline meat or its storage and heating methods. Mr. Suit next to me was wide awake
and looking in my direction since I was now awake. If he had
any sense at all about him, he wouldn't try and talk to me. Since
he was on a fourteen-hour flight in a three-piece suit, he must
not be a frequent flyer, which meant he didn't know the airline
etiquette. One such rule was that if someone has earphones on,
don't talk to them. Just because we are sitting next to each other
doesn't mean we are friends or that I want to make a new friend.

Just then one of the first-class flight attendants came to our
aisle. "Reverend?" Mr. Suit was a reverend? The flight attendant
asked him something about the kosher meal he ordered. *Nice one,
Mel*, I said to myself. I was going to hell for being rude and lying
to a man of God. Next time, I am buying two seats so I have
no chance of being rude to anyone, especially a reverend. I bet
the reverend had been praying for my lost, lying German soul.
When I was growing up, we went to church every Sunday and
every Wednesday. There was no argument about it. You had to
be really sick to stay home. And I mean like throwing-up-blood
sick. After I left for college, I only attended church on Easter and
Christmas. And after Ryan died, I hadn't set foot in a church, and
here I was sitting next to a reverend.

Another one of my favorite perks about first-class was that you
were served actual silverware, china, glassware, and a cloth napkin. I was convinced that the china and silverware made the airline food taste better. I ate my vegetarian meal of rice, beans, sadly
steamed veggies, rolls, and a side salad. I ordered a glass of white

wine and a piece of brownie for dessert. I would have opted for the cheesecake, but again I was leery of how the cheesecake was stored. The last thing I needed was to be ill from expired cheese. I sipped my wine and stared out the airplane window. I thought about getting out one of the books I had brought, but they were in English, so the Reverend would know that I was definitely some kind of crazy. Hell, I was some kind of crazy. Who was I kidding? Myself? I silently chuckled to myself as I thought how the books I brought would take up the entire desk at the beach house. There was little storage space at the beach house, so we kept the clutter to a minimum. We had just the required amount of furniture and nothing else. There was nowhere to put anything extra. I actually liked living a life of simplicity at the beach. The house was super easy to clean, and when you only wore bikinis, sarongs, and tank tops, there was little laundry to do, which was good since there was not a washer and dryer at the beach. Kai and I usually just washed stuff out in the sink and hung it out to dry on one of the decks. Island life was simple, refreshing, and relaxing. There was no hustle and bustle and keeping up with the Joneses. And that is exactly what I needed.

I looked at my watch, and it would be about six more hours or so until breakfast was served, so I had to occupy myself. I could feel the reverend looking at me and just knew he was itching to talk, so I pulled my sleep mask down once again.

However, this time I couldn't sleep. My elbow was beginning to throb, and I was getting anxious to get on the ground and let my healing sabbatical begin. Since I had nothing but time, I decided to begin unraveling the mess that was me. My mind had been spinning around the necessary steps that would need to take place for me to arrive at a happier place. I focused on those thoughts and began to formalize my plan. I wanted to cherish and engrave the happy times with Ryan in my heart and soul without them controlling my senses. I wanted to be able to remember the wonderful days with Ryan without crying. I wanted to think about things without having the thoughts of Ryan creep in. I did not want to forget Ryan, but I just wanted to be in control of when he appeared. I would always love him dearly and cry when I thought of us together, but I wanted to be able to control it. I was quite mad at myself for reacting at Patter's the way I did. Seriously, Mel? Seriously? I needed to get it together and hold it together. I wanted every single thought and feeling of Ryan to melt into my heart and only bring me happiness and joy. I wanted my eyes, face, lips, heart, and soul to smile when I thought of him. I needed to write the final Ryan chapter of my life and let the words scroll around my heart like a running billboard. I needed the words to be permanently inked on my heart so only the joyous and happy feelings could emerge because that would be all the heart would know. I had a permanent memory of Ryan and our life on my thigh, and now I had to ink my heart with all the happy memories I could. I began to make a mental list of all the times that I wanted to make sacred: our first kiss, our wedding, our first trip to Hawaii, our second anniversary spent in Paris, and our late-night fire-side chats at the brownstone. I wanted all of those soul-warming, happy, loving memories to fill my heart. I wanted to get rid of the sadness, and I was determined that Fiji was the perfect place to do it—Fiji was a Ryan-free zone. I made myself a promise right here on the plane: as soon as I was on Fijian soil, I would only allow those happy, sacred moments about Ryan. When I felt the sadness or tears coming on, I would focus on those sacred moments. I had to train my brain, and I would. There would only be happy Ryan thoughts at the beach house—in the Ryan-free zone. My husband lived as a hero and died as one, and that is how I wanted to always remember him. I had to extract the sadness and the anger that was inside me. I had to bury it at the bottom of the ocean. I had to make room in my heart to move on.

I felt a soft tapping on my right elbow that startled me from my sleep. I guess I had fallen asleep after all. I lifted the sleep mask off my eyes, and it was the reverend.

"Miss, I deeply apologize for waking you, but I didn't want you to miss breakfast. It is about to be served," he said in a slow, deep Southern accent.

I was having a difficult time waking up, but I managed to keep my cover and say, "Danke." (Thank you.)

I looked at my watch, and we were a few hours from landing in Auckland, which was a relief. I was beginning to believe that the clock did tick slower in this part of the world. Kai and I could entertain ourselves for hours and days when we traveled together, so the trip to Fiji never seemed to be this long.

Damn it, Mel! I shouted at myself in my head. Now the reverend knew I understood English, so he probably expected that I could speak it. Now I would have to come up with a broken German accent. *Think, Mel, think!*

Okay, I could do this. I could talk with a German accent. And the reverend had broken another flying rule: you didn't wake up sleeping passengers you do not know.

As I waited for breakfast, I dug through my purse to locate my pain pills for my elbow. It was still throbbing, and the pain was starting to radiate up my arm and down my back.

I set the prescription bottle on my tray, and that is when the reverend spoke. "Miss, I don't mean to pry, but are you okay? I noticed your arm and the bandage on your forehead."

"Yes, thank you. I am okay," I said in my best German accent.

"What happened to ya?" the reverend asked in his deep Southern voice.

"I fall," I said, trying to maintain my accent and illustrate the fact that my English wasn't that great.

I really was no mood to have this conversation with the reverend, so I began to fiddle with my iPod, hoping he would get the hint.

"Is Auckland your final stop?" the reverend asked.

"Yes, for sun and beach," I replied in my accent.

I craned my neck to look for the flight attendant, hoping my breakfast would come soon so I could stuff my face instead of talk to the reverend. Where was my breakfast?

"You?" I asked him back, hoping he would talk my ear off, and I could give my fake accent a rest.

"My destination is a small village in New Zealand where I am going to minister and provide some biblical training for a small church there," the reverend replied.

I was growing tired of the German accent, so I decided it was time to come clean with the reverend. He was in the business of forgiveness, right? And wasn't confronting my fears and the truth about my life what my tropical sabbatical was all about anyway? It was time to confess.

I dropped the phony accent and said, "Reverend, I have a confession to make. I am not German and speak perfect English. I wasn't in the mood to speak to anyone on the fourteen-hour flight. I apologize for being a rude and unfriendly seatmate."

"So is the bandaged head and sling a part of your act too?" the reverend quickly replied with a smile in his eye.

"Unfortunately, they are the real deal," I replied with a defeated tone in my voice.

"Are you running away from an abusive spouse?" he asked without even flinching.

I didn't know how to take his comment, so I chuckled and said, "The only abuse I am running from is self-inflicted." I thought about adding "mentally self-inflicted," but I didn't have to tell the reverend *everything*.

"Oh, I'm Melanie Alexander, by the way."

"It is nice to meet you, Melanie. I am Reverend Isaiah Brown. The line of work I am in makes me a good listener. Seeing that breakfast isn't quite ready, I have some time," the reverend said as he craned his neck to see what was taking the first-class meal service so long. And what was a reverend doing in first-class any-way? I took a deep breath, and with my exhale out came the truth.

"My husband was killed in Afghanistan four years ago, and I have been a tormented soul ever since. I thought that with time, my wounds would heal, and the black fog that consumed me would dissipate, but I feel far from healed. I quit a job that I loved and became a recluse. My best friend kept me alive, and then I met someone—a navy guy. I was out at a pub when I saw a news story about American military casualties in the Middle East, and I fainted. I broke my elbow and hit my head on a table. The guy I had recently met was on duty overseas. I felt the same panic and fear when I was informed about my husband's death. I am on a personal sabbatical to face the face I see in the mirror and to learn to love again. I have to get on with my life, but I want to convince myself that I will never lose the love and the memories of my husband. I am not going home until I feel that I have conquered my husband's death and engraved a piece of my heart with his love and our memories. I also am hoping that the sand and sun suck the fog out of me. I want to see and feel clearly once again."

And there it was. My unrehearsed, soul-bleeding version of why I was a hot mess. The words came out easier than I had imagined they would. I bet the reverend wished he hadn't spoken to me. He was sitting next to a plane stranger who just laid some heavy crap (I started to think of a four-letter word, but then remembered who I was sitting next to) out before breakfast and nothing else to do but talk as we hung above the ocean.

The reverend hadn't spoken yet, but nodded his head a few times. He turned to me and placed his hand on top of my good one. He looked me in the eyes and in a soft Southern voice he spoke. "The past should remind you of the road you have traveled, but it is not a map to your future. Your feet are free to travel down any road. You just have to tell them to do so."

The reverend paused and spoke again before I even had the chance to respond.

"The pain of losing a loved one is one of the worst events a person must face. Your soul aches with grief and anger begins to replace the blood in your veins. God didn't strike your husband dead, but someone controlled by the devil himself did. Don't let the devil win; fight him with the love you have for your husband. Fight him off. The devil wants you too, darlin', but don't let the grief and anger in your blood consume you. Fill your body, soul, and mind with God's love because God's love chases away the evil. Don't let the devil get you too, darlin'. God watched his only son be hung on a cross to die by men who falsely accused him so you and me could have eternal life with Him. Don't let your husband's or Jesus's death be in vain."

He lifted his hand off mine and turned back around, just in time for his breakfast tray. I watched as he gingerly placed his cloth napkin on his lap. Without turning his head, he once again placed his hand on top of mine. He bowed his head, and I did too.

"Father above, thank you for this meal. Let it nourish our bodies and let it fuel Melanie's body and soul with the energy it needs to fight off evil, Lord. In your way, Lord, show Melanie that her husband's death was not in vain and help her Lord to live for you. Bless this food. Amen," the reverend prayed with such vigor that my hand shook the entire time.

Thankfully the reverend didn't talk with his mouth full, so I was able to digest my food and my thoughts. I had never thought of the black fog in my life as evil. I had always labeled the insurgents who fired the shot that killed Ryan as evil, but I had never thought about how that evil had infiltrated my soul. Why had I let the evilness of the world in? I had been carrying around the evilness that took Ryan from me, and I had let it consume me for four years. All of a sudden I was angry. How could I have been so gullible? How could I give Ryan's killer exactly what he wanted for four long years? The evil fog inside me was a victory for the insurgents. They had gotten Ryan *and* me. And they had gotten me for four years! I left a job I loved for the evil. I almost made my best friend crazy for the evil. I had harbored anger and hate toward my family for evil. I had punished myself for evil. Why hadn't I come to this realization before now? I wanted to throw my tray table into its upright and locked position and scream and punch and stomp my feet so hard that the whole plane would shake. I thought for a moment and decided that I would no longer let insurgents be victorious over me. I would never again let them have the power and the satisfaction to control me. Ryan's body and my soul would no longer be their trophy. I smiled. I looked over at the reverend, and he was nodding off. His work had been done. He had saved my soul from the evil forces of the world. This was the hurdle that I had been tripping over for four long years. Why did it take me so long to realize that I was letting the very people that killed Ryan kill me? At least I had finally arrived at this point. Was this some type of divine intervention that seated the reverend next me? It was almost a surreal feeling to be here. To be at the place I never thought I would make it to—one of true peace and understanding. My Mel sabbatical was on the right track, and I wasn't even off the plane yet. I had already had a major breakthrough and it was about time.

SOLITUDE

I was sharply awakened by the thud of the airplane wheels touching down on the runway. It took me a second or two to realize that I was still on an airplane bound for Auckland. How long had I been asleep? I hadn't slept that well in years. When my peripheral vision came into focus, I saw that the reverend was awake and reading.

"Thank you for listening and for your advice. I hope you enjoy your time in New Zealand," I said considerately to the reverend.

"You are welcome. I hope you sustain no more injuries during your stay," he said with his deep Southern accent. Everything that the reverend said just seemed so comforting with that accent. I think I was going to miss that.

"I'm going to try," I said with a slight smile.

I had one more leg to travel, but it was a quick flight over to Nadi, Fiji. As I deplaned, it felt good to be halfway around the world and surrounded by beach, surf, and sunshine. I actually felt truly happy as I stepped into the airport. I would fight evil with every ounce of my being from now on.

After I went through customs and picked up my bag, which had miraculously made it to Auckland without being lost or confiscated, I purchased a bottle of water, Fiji brand, and sat down in a seat with a view of the stunning Manukau Harbor. The lapis-blue water and the kiwi-green grass was a picturesque scene. The sky was a lighter shade of blue than the water and had perfectly placed white cloud puffs. This was paradise to me. Living in one of the most powerful and influential cities in the world compared nothing to the South Pacific. I was entranced by the natural beauty surrounding me each time I arrived. Time seemed to tick by at a slower peace in paradise, and it was quite all right to me.

I heard an announcement for my next flight, which came quicker than I expected. I had been hypnotized by the therapeutic landscape outside the airport windows. I wondered how many people missed their flights out of here due to being totally consumed in the view and oblivious to the rest of the world.

I boarded the propeller plane and found my seat. There was no first-class section or any sections for that matter on this "I pray to every God and deity in the world that the propellers don't stop over the Pacific and I have to find my life vest and put it on as this scrap metal death trap sinks." I hated propeller planes. *Hated them.* I had just never believed the science behind how the propellers keep the plane flying. This is exactly the reason why I hadn't eaten in the airport. A mix of turbulence and nerves was the perfect catalyst for midair puking. If I lived to see Fiji, I would stop at the market on the way to the house. I closed my eyes and grasped my seat until my hand turned white. I spent the entire flight listening to the sound of the propellers to ensure they didn't stop. When the propellers stopped, the plane either landed or was falling from the sky and I knew how to inflate my life vest in seconds if necessary.

And before I knew it, we landed, and I was still alive. I opened my eyes and pried my hand off of the seat since it was now numb. My stomach was not pleased with the flight, but I would be on solid ground soon enough. I took my watch off because I was now officially on "island time" and would not plan my day by the clock. Instead, I would plan my day by the sun. As I waited to deplane, I searched my purse for my Fijian money so I could stop at the market. I had also remembered to pack my reusable shopping bag, so I got that unburied from the bottom of my purse, which I had nicknamed "the black hole."

Traveling around Fiji was simple and easy. I walked to a public bus stop from the airport and waited for an open-air bus, which were the public buses. They had a canvas flap that covered the windows on a rainy day. I enjoyed the open air windows so I could feel the ocean breeze in my hair, smell the saltwater, and hear all the sounds of the island. I waited for twenty minutes for a bus before one arrived. There were no empty benches, so I sat on the end of one occupied by a mother who had a small child on her lap. The little girl looked curiously out me and I smiled back and waved. She shied away and buried her head into her mother's arm. I enjoyed watching the people go about their daily business and the children playing in the streets as the bus drove through town. The sun shone warmly and brightly, and I was sweating. I had to get out of my DC-winter clothing and into my tank top, sarong, and flip-flops. I thought that I should have changed at the airport, but the thought never dawned on me until now. I guess the excitement of being island bound got the best of me. I had packed only a few beach outfits since the majority of my island wardrobe was at the beach house. I was at peace already, and my mind was filled with nothing but tropical thoughts. I took several deep breaths to inhale the saltwater-filled air and to exhale the evil inside me.

I got off at my stop and smiled at the market as I saw the rows of fresh fruit, veggies, and seafood under a bamboo-thatched roof. Some vendors had their produce set up on the floor, and others had a coveted wood stand. One of my favorite vendors was an elderly gentleman who had the gentlest smile. He was completely bald and wore little round glasses. His stand was painted a bright yellow, and he had an amazing array for fruits and vegetables. He always took mine and Kai's hands in his and said, "Enjoy the beauty of Fiji's harvest." I quickly found his stand, and he instantly recognized me. As soon as I made my way over to him, he instantly had my hands in his and said his trademark phrase to me. I smiled at him and said "Hello."

I filled my bag with tapioca, two coconuts, a bunch of bananas, two sweet potatoes, a small bag of dried papaya, four kiwis, and one small watermelon. I purchased a cup of kava to take home with me. Before I headed toward the beach house, I took off my long-sleeve shirt and tied it around my waist. It caused excruciating pain to take off a button down shirt with a broken elbow. I would have to take some more pain meds when I got to the house. It was heavenly to walk down the street without people hustling and bustling by you and bumping you with their bags and elbows. People here really appreciated life and the shortness of it. People just seemed happier.

When I unlocked the door of the beach house and *boom*—a whiff of stale air hit me in the face like one of Kai's jabs in the boxing ring. The house was just as we had left it earlier in the year. I set my things down on the couch and opened all the windows. I climbed the steps to the bedroom and opened the windows up there too. I stepped out onto the two-person, standing-room-only balcony and took in the view. I could see the turquoise water and the whitecapped waves. There were beautiful moss-covered mountains in the background. The house was surrounded by vines, grass, and trees. I closed my eyes and enjoyed the silence in the air. There were no cars, trains, or voices polluting the air. It was truly peaceful.

I opened my wardrobe drawer and changed into a tank top—which again hurt like hell—sarong, and slipped into some flip-flops. It was great to have on such comfortable clothing that smelled like Fiji. I tried to pull my hair up into a ponytail, but the pain didn't make it worthwhile, so I abandoned the effort. I made my way back downstairs. I put the food in the kitchen and checked the bottled-water supply, and I had enough for a few days. I could drink the recycled water from our rainwater collection system, but I just preferred the security of drinking bottled water. I stepped outside on our main balcony and swept off the leaves and insects with a little handmade broom we had bought at the market our first trip here. I got my cup of kava from inside and sat down in the hammock. My plan for the afternoon was not to get out of the hammock.

I was not sure what time it was or how long I had been asleep, but apparently my body was in severe jet lag mode because I was still in the same tank top and sarong. But I felt good. As I stared into the horizon, I thought of Ryan looking down on me from heaven instead of being a missing ghost by my side. I knew it would be easier here to not miss Ryan since this is not a Mel-and-Ryan place, but I felt differently. I felt that the anger I harbored in every cell of my body was putting itself to better use. I was no longer infuriated with Ryan's killer, but instead that anger was morphing itself into appreciation—appreciation for mine and Ryan's life together. Little Melanie Ryan flashed before my eyes. I had never seen her in person; I had received a birth announcement from her parents, so I still remembered her as a baby. The insurgents could never take away the birth of Melanie Ryan. They took away Ryan's life, but they saved a life of an unborn child and her father. I gave a quick smirk to myself to signal that I had one up on them. Ryan's death had saved two lives. *Ha!* Take that!

I decided it was time to shower—or at least make the attempt with one arm. I showered in the lukewarm water and changed into a bikini—a Mel-approved one. The shower water here never got hot, but somehow it didn't matter. I managed to get my arm out of the sling and shower one-handed. I almost cried trying to tie the bikini straps around my neck. Maybe I should have asked to have it amputated at the hospital. It was going to take forever for my elbow to heal. I decided to go to the beach today. I packed a lunch and a book to read. We had a portable beach chair and umbrella that I pulled out from under the bed. There was only one teeny-weeny closet, so we became experts in creative storage solutions. I put on a fresh sarong and threw some water and fruit in my bag. I applied my sunscreen and shades. If only life was really this simple. It was about a fifteen-minute walk to the beach, and my cheap flip-flops did nothing to protect my feet from the rocky terrain. It felt strange making this trek by myself since Kai had always been with me. I wondered how Kai was doing and if she had forgiven me yet for leaving.

I set up my chair and umbrella, sat down and dug my toes into the sand. The soles of my feet would be callus free after a few days of being in the sand. The sand and saltwater would also do a number on my pedicure, but I didn't have any polish remover, so I would have to live with it. The warm morning sun felt great on my skin. There was something therapeutic about the sun's rays on your skin. I wondered if the eighty-degree sun could zap the evilness right out me. It was amazing how the serenity of the beach cleared my head. I knew that I had to leave the old Mel here. I had to throw her into the surf. I had to wave good-bye to her as I watched her sink to the bottom of the Pacific. I had finally accepted that I would never be the Mel I was. I was tired of being trapped between two Mels—the Ryan Mel and post-Ryan Mel. I would go back to the States as the new post-Ryan Mel. I knew that I couldn't carry my hurt, heartache, and anger with me forever. I had to go on. I had to live for me. I had to be thankful for the lives that Ryan had saved. I kept remembering what the reverend told me: "Don't let the devil win, fight him with the love you have for your husband." The new Mel would be an evil fighter. I chuckled silently to myself as I pictured myself in an "Evil Fighter" superhero costume. Wow, maybe the sun had already fried my brain.

I ate a mango for lunch and then went for a walk along the water. I was about calf-deep in the warm, turquoise-tinted water. As I walked, I pushed the evil, the sadness, and the pain to the bottom of my feet and into the sand so it could be washed out to sea forever. I spent most of the afternoon walking. I gathered a few shells along the way that caught my eye, but mostly I walked. By the time I had made my way home, I felt lighter, happier. For the first time since Ryan, I was happy. I had forgotten what happiness felt like—I mean true happiness—the kind you don't have to work for. It is just there inside of you and automatically brings a smile to your face. I smiled for the first time today for Mel.

CIRCLE

I had spent the last few days just walking in the sun. I routinely got up every day and packed a lunch, a book, and went down to the beach. I spent most of the day there walking and thinking. I felt better than I had in four years. I felt relieved that I wouldn't spend the rest of my life walking around aimlessly, hopeless, and grief-stricken. I had spent the majority of the last four years believing I would never get over Ryan. But I was now feeling happy and hopeful, and it was about flipping time. Over the past two days, I had thought of my future for the first time. I thought I would go back to DC after New Year's. I hoped that our case-load would pick up. I wanted to work more. I wanted to have a purpose again. Suddenly, the intense itching of my stitches was making it difficult to think.

Over the past few days, the stiches in my forehead were itching more and more, and I could no longer stand it. They were becoming too much of an inconvenience. Since I arrived, I had used my hair, floppy hat, and sunglasses to hide them. I put sunscreen on them, and I would have to continue to do that even after they were out, but at least I wouldn't have thread sewn to my face. I had some medic training at the academy but had never removed stitches on myself or anyone else before. But they had to come out, or I would end up with a railroad scar on my face forever or would die from blood loss from scratching them. I had packed a variety of tweezers and a pair of little scissors from my bathroom drawer in DC in anticipation of this moment. I went into the bathroom, which was big enough for one person to turn around in at that was it. There was just a small sink attached to the wall with a mirror above it. And to complicate things, I had to use my right hand since my left arm was still incapacitated and hurt like hell to move. I had a difficult time getting just the right angle in the mirror. Damn it—this damn sling was really beginning to get in the way. There was a small three-drawer dresser with a mirror in the bedroom, so I went upstairs. I sat down on the dresser and moved my head around until I found an acceptable angle. I gently and carefully lifted up the knot, put the tweezers down, picked up my little Barbie-sized scissors, and snipped. Whew. It worked, and I didn't stab myself in the eye. I gently pulled the thread out with the tweezers and voila! My face was thread free! It stung for a few minutes, but I would take the stinging instead of the stitches. Hell, this stinging was nothing compared to my throbbing elbow. I tried to tune out the pain most days, but the thing hurt. I examined the scar closely in the mirror, and I was impressed. Kai had demanded a plastic surgeon at the ER stitch me up, and I was glad she did. This would heal quite nicely if I could keep the sun off it. I knew if I put sunscreen on this scar and headed out to the beach, it would sting like the devil, so I decided it was best not to spend the day sunning. I had this surge of adrenaline running through my veins and wanted to get out. Perhaps it was from performing surgery on myself that made me feel on top of the world. I decided to take a day trip to Mamanucas, which was a group of about twenty volcanic islands, which you could see from from Fiji. I knew from previous visits that there was a ferry boat transfer to the Mamanucas islands from the Nadi airport. I grabbed my already packed beach bag and sun hat and headed to the bus stop. As usual, the sun was shining and there was a light breeze. I didn't walk with the sense of urgency that I did when I was in DC. I walked in island time. The children were in school at this hour of the day, so the streets were a little quieter. There were three other people at the bus stop as I waited. The sun was hot on my head and was thankful to have on the big, floppy sun hat. My stitches were stinging from the sweat on my forehead, so maybe I should have just gone to the beach. As I was contemplating what to do, the bus pulled up, so I took it as a sign that I should get on. I had a bench to myself this time and enjoyed the scenes of the city. It was nice to hear traffic and people again since I had been alone with my thoughts for days now. I felt alive to be among the people and everyday life. It reminded me that life went on.

I took two buses to the airport and then after an hour's wait, I took a boat transfer out to the Mamanucas. As I waited for the ferry, I stood at the dock and felt simply exonerated. I wasn't Mel the widow standing there; I was just Mel. As I stared at the Mamanucas islands and the wind rippled my hair, I was happy. My old-self-Mel happy. I was taking the ferry to Plantation island and hoping to just walk and perhaps find some nice shade to sit and take in the scenery. As I boarded the ferry I felt the air conditioning, which was a welcomed surprise. Perhaps the mind-blowing beauty of the Mamanucas helped to clear my mind and put my life into perspective. The crystal-clear turquoise waters that jutted out into the blue ocean water was mesmerizing. The islands had small mountains of forests, and the green was a lovely contrast to the white beaches and turquoise water surrounding the islands. It really was a picture off a South Pacific postcard. This reminded me about the brevity of life and how much beauty in the world there was to see—and I wanted to see it.

When the ferry arrived on Plantation island and I set foot on the super fine, white sandy beaches, I was in awe. I had never felt sand so soft in all my life—not even in Nadi. It was like walking on velvet. I made my way along the beach and could see all types of fish swimming in the water. And then I knew exactly how I would spend the rest of my afternoon. I found a spot to put down my bag and slathered some more sunscreen on me. I noticed that my skin was becoming a beautiful bronze from the South Pacific sun. I also had noticed in the mirror this morning that my hair even had some very blond highlights again, courtesy of the sun. I wasn't sure if island life or the sun was to credit for my successful island sabbatical, but something sure cured me. Last but not least, I put sunscreen on my scar. I crinkled up my nose in anticipation of the sting, but it was much more bearable than I expected. With my beach hat and sunglasses on, I walked about 10 feet out from the beach and sat down in the water. I was only in water about midriff high. I stretched my legs out in front of me and just watched all the fish swim by. My sling was wet, but I didn't care. It could air-dry on the way home. It was like being in an aquarium since the water was so clear. I could see all the way to the bottom of the sea. *Hell, I was sitting on the bottom of the sea.* I chuckled silently to myself because here I was a widow, who had hit rock bottom, who was now sitting on the bottom of the sea. I think my life had just come full circle.

I sat in the water for hours just thinking and taking in the beautiful world around me. Since I didn't have a book to read, my mind was working on something to commemorate this moment—this moment of my life coming full circle. I chuckled again to myself as I thought of Belindee Martini. *Yes, that's it—I'll write a rap!* After a little bit, I had it written in my head. I would write it down as soon as I was home. I found myself rapping silently to myself, but mouthing the words. I was hoping nobody around could read my lips.

> Hang it up, hang it out
> Hang it up, hang it out
> Tossin' away all that defines me
> Watchin' it sink to the depths of the sea
> Weighin' me down no more
> Now I'm shoppin' at the dream store
> Crusin' the aisles to find a new me
> Tryin' on some styles and likin' what I see
> Posin' in the mirror like a runway star

Finally able to hide my scars
All I need is a cigar and a chauffeur
And to complete my new look; a great big fur
Walkin' around with a full shot glass
Takin' a shot and tellin' Lilith to kiss my ass

My rap put me in a very good mood and I decided to take the ferry back to the mainland. I wanted to stop at the market on the way home and get some more food. I was tired as I rode the ferry back and credited it to being in the sun too long today. My shades and my hat did an excellent job of keeping the sun off my scar, but I got more sun today than usual since I spent so much time in the water. There was something about sitting in the ocean that was therapeutic for the soul. I would never forget sitting on the bottom of the ocean and what it meant to me.

After I got off the second bus near my place, I walked to the market and I picked up some mangoes, kiwi, grapefruit, sweet potatoes, and freshly made sushi. There was a lady who made fresh sushi to order, and I picked up four rolls so I could eat off it for a few days. As I walked home, I was looking forward to having dinner and going to bed early. I was tired and feeling the exhaustion of the sun. I was still rapping my rap under my breath and would also write it down before I went to bed tonight. I would hate to forget it. As soon as I got close enough to see the front door of my house, I stopped. I removed my sunglasses and squinted. It looked like the door was ajar. Did I forget to close it? I was positive that I had, but I couldn't be one hundred percent sure I had. My bag of "agent goodies" was in the house, so I was unarmed as I slowly approached the front door. When I got up to the front door, I examined it closely, and it did seem to be ajar.

My head began to race with the protocol that I should take. I sat my bag down and looked around. I pulled a long, green blade of island grass off a tree. It almost sliced my hand as I pulled it down. I could use this to choke whoever was inside my house. The intruder would stand no chance against Melanie Alexander.

Any idiot dumb enough to burglarize, invade, carjack, kidnap, or rape me would be begging me to let them go after I got my hands on them. I was annoyed that I had to work in paradise. During our very first trip to Fiji, Kai had stashed a Baby Browning semiautomatic pistol under the kitchen sink. This gun fit into the palm of your hand, but packed a huge punch and was extremely accurate. It was actually the size of my BlackBerry that was somewhere in the bottom of the Potomac. There was a small ledge between the underneath of the sink and the counter, and it was taped there. Every time we left to return to DC, we unloaded the gun and hid it, and it was always the first thing we retrieved and loaded when we returned. You can never be too prepared. I was beginning to convince myself that I was being paranoid and ridiculous. *Mel, you have one good arm and you are in Fiji. You are being ridiculous.* I had just reclaimed my life and my future today, and I wouldn't let anyone take that away from me now. Melanie Audrey Alexander was a fighter. And if I was totally being insane and there was no intruder, no one would ever know this even happened. I thought of my plan and had it. The sink was about three steps once inside the front door, and I calculated in my head how long it would take me to get to the gun, untape it, and get off the safety. The Baby Browning had a manual thumb-operated safety, so it wouldn't take me long to get it ready to fire.

I was standing at the corner of the house so I couldn't be seen from the front door or the balcony. I was listening for noises inside but didn't hear anything. I decided it was time. I would go through the front door and go for the gun.

I took off my sun hat, shades, and flip-flops in an effort to reduce any noise and slowly opened the front door just enough to stand sideways and crouch around the right side of the door. I paused for a second to see if I could hear or see anyone, but I didn't. I got to the sink in two-and-a-half steps, I reached my hand around the sink skirt, felt the gun, untaped it, and took off the safety. Suddenly, I heard the familiar creak of the third stair and instantly knew someone else was in the house. My adrenaline was pumping, but I knew exactly what I had to do. I slowly walked to the staircase. I had approximately three seconds before my intruder would be at the bottom stair and would be able to see me. In order to have the advantage, I had to provide the element of surprise. There was a wall that enclosed the staircase, so I was concealed until the bottom step. My plan was to ambush the intruder at the bottom of the step and place my gun on their temple. My three seconds were up. It was time. I made a crescent-moon yoga pose stretch around to the bottom of the steps. I had no idea why yoga poses were going through my mind, but that is what I thought. I pivoted on my foot, which would put me face-to-face with the most unlucky intruder in Fiji—make that in the whole world.

"*Hands up now!*" I yelled as I popped from around the corner with my gun cocked and ready to shoot. Nobody breaks into my house. It was about to be on.

I was stunned as I stood eye to eye with my intruder.

I lowered my gun and wiped the sweat from my brow, which was making my scar sting. I stood there stunned and speechless, but I could feel a smile coming to my face.

"Hey, Hi, sorry about that," I said sweetly and then on an impulse I jumped into Jenner's arms and wrapped my good arm around his neck and my legs around his waist like I was a giddy high school girl in some girls-gone-wild spring-break video.

Before I had time to catch my breath, he kissed me. My body melted into his and had no resistance to fight or stop.

After a few passionate minutes, my defective arm was being crushed, and I couldn't take the pain any longer.

"Sorry, but my arm really hurts," I said as I untangled myself from JR. "It's really nice to see you."

"I am assuming Kai told you how to get here and what happened," I replied.

"Yeah, Kai sent this for you," JR replied as he reached into his backpack, which was still on his back, and pulled out an envelope.

I opened it up and laughed. There was a new cell phone and a note. The note said,

> M,
>
> I can't wait until this package gets personally delivered to you. I know you ditched your BB somewhere, so here is a new international one. Call me when you get a chance. I'm hoping JR keeps you busy. :) We got the sweetest email from Amelia Marlowe and I've enclosed it for you. It warmed my heart. Stay as long as you want. Merry Christmas, girl. I love you.
>
> K

I folded the note in half and stuck in back in the envelope with the phone. It was a touch screen model, and there was no keyboard. I was not sure I would like it, but I would play with it later. I pulled out the other note in the envelope, which I assumed to be Amelia's email. It said:

> Dear Kai and Mel,
>
> Thank you for finding me in the middle of the ocean. I did not know at the time we spoke that I wanted to be found, but time has a way. I have since reconciled with my mother and our relationship is getting better each day. I've also been talking with my grandmother and trying to get her to reconcile with my mom. This whole experience has taught me that life is valuable and short, so I have taken to heart that my mother did what she did out of love for me. I finally got up the nerve to call Buck. He apologized for not fighting harder to see me over the years, and he explained how his broken heart prevented him from fighting for me. He said it was easier to fight the pain by trying to go on with his life. I've forgiven him, and we are using the time we have now to get to know one another. We are

a lot alike. I have been tested for Huntington's and do not have it. I do not know how to say this, but I cannot begin to thank you both, two strangers, for looking for me. You have changed my life. I think I want to be a therapist for children and young adults. Please keep searching for the missing—you never know, but they may just be lost.

Merry Christmas,
Amelia Marlowe

At this very moment I knew exactly why I left the agency. Perhaps Amelia would have never found healing, forgiveness, or her father if I was still an agent. For a split second I began to know why I lost Ryan—perhaps the pain of loss and the brevity of life is what inspires me to search for the missing; to carry the torch of hope for loved ones and families. The hope for reuniting, the hope for closure, and the hope for persevering on the journey of life. Suddenly I had peace in my soul; a peace that felt permanent. I could feel a smile on my face.

"Good news?" JR asked. I handed him the letter. I watched his face as he read it. He also had a smile on his face.

"You have a talent, Mel," JR said as he kissed my forehead. "You've changed this woman's life. I hope you feel it in your soul."

"I do. I feel warmth and peace and a comfort that has been missing for a long time. It is almost like I saved a life."

"You have saved more than a life—you have saved a family," JR said. "I'm proud of you, girl."

"Thanks," I said blushing. It felt good to hear that from JR.

"How's Kai?" I asked JR.

"She's good. Will's going to keep her company while you are kicking it up on Fiji. You look amazing. Island life is good to you. He rubbed his thumb on the scar on my forehead. Kai told me about your bar fight," he said with a chuckle.

"You should've seen the guy. He was huge," I said with a smile. "But I took him down."

JR laughed and I knew he didn't believe the bar story for one second. "So, while I was saving a family, what were you doing in the desert?" I asked. I was so grateful that he was alive and had traveled halfway around the world to see me, but I had to know about his mission after I saw that news report in Patters. I had to satisfy my curiosity. But I knew what his answer was going to be: "It's classified."

"You know that it is classified, but I was saving people too," he said with a wink. "Will and I were part of a team that rescued some innocent civilians and US military personnel from a volatile area. We also dropped off some supplies and picked up a few things. We came under fire, but it was expected and we were well prepared. I told you not to worry," JR explained calmly.

"Were there casualties? I saw US military casualties on the news," I asked.

"Mel, you know I cannot comment on that, but there were no casualties on my mission," JR said. "Maybe you shouldn't watch the news," he said.

Before I time to respond, he scooped me off the floor. "I didn't come here to talk about work. I came here to have some R&R and surf," he said.

He kissed me again, and I decided to save the rest of my questions for the morning or for the morning after that.